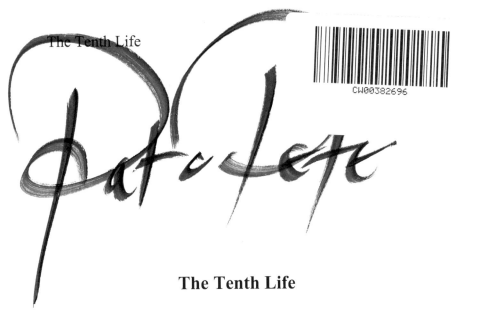

The Tenth Life

By

Michael J. Owen

The Author

Michael J. Owen was born in Weymouth but grew up in Pontypridd. He attended Pontypridd Grammar School for Boys and then Reading University, followed by Nottingham University.

A passion for radio was realised at BBC Radio Nottingham then commercial radio in Birmingham with BRMB. He has won major radio awards for his programming and has played a significant part in radio and music events across the UK.

He lives in Lichfield and is Chairman of the Television and Radio Industries Club of the Midlands and is a Freeman of the Worshipful Company of Smiths of Lichfield.

Over years he has been ruled by a variety of felines and fears for their future well-being.

Copyright

And still when mob or monarch lays

Too rude a hand on English ways

The whisper wakes, the shudder plays

Across the reeds at Runnymede

Rudyard Kipling

Dedication

My first cat was called Toby. He was always wiser and cleverer than I could ever be. He watched me and knew what I was thinking even though we were both seven years old.   Cats in this story have been inspired by our own cats – Tabatha had all the qualities of Craw; Misty was a grey manipulator like Piner, and Ruffy was a Nailz look-alike.

This book would not have got to this point without the close attention to detail of Peter Brown and Pat Owen who read the book so many times she could recite passages by heart.

My thanks go to them all.

Contents

Prologue

What is a hero? Someone brave, someone sporting, someone clever? Tom never saw himself as a hero. He was just an ordinary boy, living in an ordinary house with an ordinary family in an ordinary town with an extraordinary cat – a cat hero.

Some people had called Tom a hero after the battle of the Cathedral. Tom wasn't sure. His friend Victoria had been as brave as he had been and perhaps even more of a hero.

What he did know was that over a few days he had seen some awesome events and some real heroes – cats who were braver, stronger and cleverer than any man he knew.

Piner was his cat and had been one of the heroes of that violent fight. It was Piner who had forced Tom to meet the small band of brave cats who took on the might of the world.

It all started that evening in the bluebell wood.

Chapter One: The Pawmen

There was danger in the wood. Green eyes flashed open showing only two thin black lines in the sharp light. A head moved swiftly from side to side. The taut body was totally still. Then one ear tilted forward; the other, backward.

This was the time of the Pawmen. They came with stealth and brought death. They seized the unsuspecting, the timid, the ill, the old or those just starting with the *shudder*. Craw had to be especially alert.

Slowly and silently she stretched and reached out her back leg, pushing the stiffness from one limb and then the other. All the time she watched, listened and then sniffed the air for any scent, especially the scent of the Pawmen. A misty cloud full of wondrous odours always preceded their sudden appearances.

The first-time Craw had sensed the cloud she wanted to run straight into it and be enveloped by its wonderful smells. Even now she couldn't stop her tail rising into the air. Her fur stood on end as she remembered when she first sensed that mouth-watering cloud and heard the horrid cracking noise, the noise made by the Pawmen, the crack that meant the limpness; that meant death for a captured spirit.

The Pawmen were the scourge of Craw's world. Every free spirit had to understand the deadly intent behind the beautiful cloud. The odour of death—the end!

Craw held her head above the tall grass. Her eyes were alert, her ears pricked up and her mouth was open, breathing in the smells. She knew she would have to eat and drink before light before the Providers moved and before the Pawmen began their killer hunt for her and her kind.

Gently, she moved her paws, barely touching the tall grass. From a distance her progress would hardly be noticed. Craw kept low until she reached the thicker cover of the pine trees. There she would sit until she could catch her fill. This was good hunting ground, but she would have to move quickly; the Pawmen also knew this area well it was plentiful for their own prey: Craw and her kind.

Suddenly, she heard a rustle and the smooth rushing of another free spirit in the wood. Craw backed away from the water's edge, sliding into the shadows. Was this a friend? Or danger? She hunched down ready to leap and confront, or to flee. Craw blinked her eyes allowing her to absorb all the available light. She was prepared.

Then, Piner came into view. Piner was grey and his face was flat. Craw lifted her head. Piner was no fighter. He shrank back before seeing her and knowing her.

Slowly, the two spirits walked towards each other. Craw sniffed hard and caught the scent of pine that always betrayed Piner. Years ago, when only a kitten, he had set his second home among the pine trees and bedded on the dead needles. They would cling to his fur—small green specks among the grey, like a freckled overcoat.

Piner quickly scooted off with a trill of excitement as he saw a furry fill trembling near the water.

Craw saw Piner seize his chance. Leaping with a dramatic flourish, he hit the water instead of the little fur ball which disappeared beneath a tree root. His vision momentarily clouded, he wiped his face until the water dripped from his stubby little nose.

While Piner had been entertaining Craw with his little performance, the light had grown, and she knew it would be time to retreat to the safe place. This was the hidden space that Craw had found after her exile. She'd been joined there by other spirits who had also had to flee the homes they shared with their Providers. It had been a fearful time for spirits like Piner, who had been forced to desert comfort and safety. Craw watched him pathetically slash in the air at a feathered fill and then topple onto a pile of dry brown leaves.

There was a sharp bang in the distance. Craw drew back and listened as intently as she could. Then she sensed the smell—a wonderful smell that only the Providers could make. But this time Craw would not be fooled. She knew that behind the smell was the whine, the hum of the machine that blew the smells around their places. The beautiful cloud of smells would be wafted one way and then the other. This was something Craw had learned. At times, she felt she was learning so fast that she thought her head would burst. Now, she sensed that Piner had wandered off and feared the delightful odour might trap him. 'No! Not Piner,' she spoke aloud. He was so slow and such a poor hunter.

'Got ya!' The voice of the Pawman was followed by a laugh.

Craw heard a second voice. 'The man on the corner was right. He said he had seen one of them sneak in here. Doesn't seem as if he's got the disease but they'll tell back at the lab. Good job, lads. I'll check with the depot for any more sightings in the vicinity.'

'Come on pussy—we know you're out there!' the first voice called out. 'We know you're not that clever yet! Mark, it up lads. Paint another paw on the van. Let's make the point that we are the top team in town and that every job is done with care and consideration. Back to Paw HQ. It's starting to rain, they go to ground in the wet.' There was more laughter that stopped as an engine started up.

The Pawmen had struck again. Craw knew they'd come back. They always did. She might have to move on to a new refuge. But this time Piner was gone. Craw just stared through the dense undergrowth. She couldn't bear to move. Her mind was crowded with strange images. Perhaps she was going the way of the others, the ones with the *shudder*.

The first-time Craw saw the illness was in her enemy from next door—a sharp, snappy, whining Siamese. One day she saw him shiver when it wasn't cold, and he lost his way in his own garden in the bright moonlight. Craw saw the emptiness in him. Instead of fighting her for a few moments when he wandered into her territory, he would skulk away and whisper as if every squeak he uttered hurt his throat.

Then she saw the *shudder* for the first time. His little pointed face would swing violently as if he was trying to shake off an appalling pain. This shaking would become more intense, moving like waves from his neck to the tip of his tail, until he whined and fell to the ground. When Craw saw this, she ran to him and licked his ear, but his eyes told her everything.

Piner's clever words came into her mind. 'You and I had the whispering, painful throat, shivers and shakes but we didn't die,' he had told her. 'That means something. The *shudder* hasn't killed us and somehow, we see everything more clearly. We know the *shudder* didn't kill all of us. Do they think it will kill them and that is why they've sent the Pawmen after us?

He was always right. Craw feared that Piner wasn't a threat to anyone anymore and that in today's dawn light he had been taken from her and destroyed.
She was alone again in this battle against the world. Craw felt a tear drop on to her cheek, but it was just the rain. *Cats can't cry.*

Chapter Two: Catsaways

Craw sensed a powerful, natural smell. Her nostrils twitched and then almost skipped with delight—the pine, the silly, give-away smell of pine. Bedraggled, sopping wet, like a bag of bones, skinny Piner stood there completely still. In her relief, Craw nosed him.

'Get off!' he said. He shrugged, shaking the wetness from his fur. 'I couldn't help him.'

Craw was lost. 'Help who?'

'Skritt. He was always such a baby—so trusting even though you warned us all, Craw, over and over again. I wanted to cry out but daren't. What could I do?'

'What do you mean?'

'Skritt walked over to the Pawman. I saw him. His tail was up, his eyes open to the light. He wanted to lie down, to purr, to be stroked and be fed. I know because that was how I felt. I wanted to follow him.'

'Skritt isn't with us anymore?' Craw hoped that wasn't true.

Piner dropped his head as if he felt the guilt of Skritt's murder. 'Skritt, the best scratcher ever, has gone. Another lost to us and our cause.' Piner licked his paw. Craw understood that he had to show that in the midst of disaster, however the world had changed, the spirits would survive and behave the way that they always had. This ordinary, simple, everyday movement meant strength for Piner and Craw. Craw licked her paw and wiped her face as well and then touched Piner with her nose.

He rejected her approach and backed rapidly away. Craw saw Piner half rise on his haunches and pull to the left as if to run into the safe undergrowth. Craw drew up to her full height. She had always been a heavy cat; menacing, if needs be. She broadened her shoulders and stared into the darkness without making the slightest movement. Her tail was high and puffed wide. Something was there.

'What is the matter with you two?' a voice rasped out. 'Am I that ugly?'

Dreamer, Craw thought.

If he'd had a tail, he would have waved it, but Dreamer was tail-less. 'Have you seen a ghost, or did you never notice my little deformity?' He circled the two bemused yet relieved cats.

'Don't be silly,' Craw snapped, 'the Pawmen are about. Stop showing off. These are dangerous times.' She turned her tail to Dreamer. He was witty, clever, intelligent— *pompous, irritating, sarcastic*—but he was Dreamer.

'Okay, what's the big deal? Pawmen, strawmen—they are stupid! I've just sprayed their wheels for luck and to warn other spirits to keep away from their death wagon. Did they spot me? No chance! They were too excited and too busy talking into their little black box to their friends hiding at home.'

Piner turned on him. 'Skriit has gone!' he said. 'They've taken him, another of our dear friends. We are so few, and they are so strong, with their machines and black boxes!'

Dreamer dropped onto the ground. 'I didn't know. I loved Skriit, but he hated being away from his Providers. They never threw him out, you know. He walked because we persuaded him to leave. We talked him into it when we knew he was one of us. But he wasn't strong enough—he wanted the warmth, the care, and the cat flappery. They would have hidden him, and he knew it, but he chose to come. We've killed him, not the Pawmen—*we* did it.' He turned tail on his friends as if to walk away but slumped again to the ground. 'I loved Skriit and today I decided he was right.'

'What on earth do you mean?' demanded Craw.

13

'He was right. We were wrong. We were *so* clever. "Leave the Providers. Fight our own fight."'

'What do you mean?' Craw pushed Dreamer. 'We are being taken from our Providers. We are being hunted. The Pawmen have been given rights to hunt us. It has been decided that we are dangerous and could kill the Providers.

Dreamer's whiskers gently brushed the long grass. 'I'm sorry about Skriit, but his weakness was the right weakness. We must get the Providers on our side. We cannot win without them, however clever we become. We must be like Skriit—we must only trust the Providers who really love us and not those who pretend to.'

Craw looked up. 'Dreamer, no one was more trusting than me, but when I heard my Providers talk of giving me up to the Pawmen I knew I had to go. We can't trust *people.*'

'We have to trust them!' Dreamer shouted. 'And I will! We have no idea how many of us have survived the *shudder* and can think. It may be just the three of us. We can't take on the whole Providers' world!'

Craw sighed, knowing he might be right.

'In my dreams, I have visited my Providers,' said Dreamer.

Craw felt despair and fear and drew one paw slowly across her face. 'Dreamer, if you have seen something, dreamt something, felt something, you must tell.'

'The dream I had was of a time long ago,' began Dreamer, 'A time that was locked inside our cat memories—until now.'

Craw and Piner settled back and narrowed their eyes as they listened to his gentle tones.

'Close your eyes completely and listen to my dream. I am a cat in a dark room. There is a dreadful smell of decay and rotting flesh. My Provider is weeping over three small bodies in the room. His children are sick with a strange disease he calls the "Black Death." He cries and pleads for someone to tell him who has brought this plague into his house. Then his hand drops down and, as any cat would do, I offer sympathy. I rub his leg and look at his wet eyes. As he looks back at me, I see a change in his face his eyes narrow and he screams out, "It is you, damn cat! You are the killer. Only you could have brought this disease so close to us all!" He throws a heavy candle stick that hits my head and there is total darkness all around.'

'Is that it? That's the end?!' questioned Craw.

'No, listen to Dreamer,' sighed Piner. 'There is always more.'

Dreamer sniffed the air and twitched his ears as if he sensed Pawmen in the wind. 'Close your eyes again and see the past.' He checked that his audience had obeyed before continuing. 'My head was throbbing with pain and I felt the thick wetness of blood on my cheek. Slowly, I opened my eyes. The world was upside down. I was hanging from a pole, my paws tied above me. My carriers cried out the same sentences repeatedly: "These are the bringers of the Black Death. Seize your cats and take them to the fire!"

'A small black cat ran from an open door and attracted the attention of the growing crowd. I was put to the floor; I stared up and the son of my Provider was there. While the others were distracted, he had loosened my ties. His eyes betrayed him. He still loved me. He did not believe I was a killer bringing plague. He pushed my legs. "Go, beauty. Go. We don't think it was you, but father is so angry he would blame anything—even the rats!" I ran and ran as only a cat can. Then I awoke with the dream fresh in my mind.'

'What does it mean?' wondered Craw.

'It's a simple tale. We were all victims then, just like now. The Providers were dying of a disease they didn't understand, and they searched for a reason; for someone or something to blame. They thought I had given them the disease and so I must die, but I lived because the son of my Provider helped me.'

'So, I must talk to my trusted Provider?' Piner asked, tilting his head as if expecting a positive response.

'The lesson is that the Pawmen won't win if we have help. The Providers give and the Providers take away. They think their babies will get the *shudder* from us just like the man in my dream. I do not have the answers, but I shall dream and dream and dream again for the way to our salvation.'

At that moment, they all heard a sound, almost like a Provider's sneaking step. All three scattered to cover in the nearest spot that would hide them. Another sound followed and another—heavy, loud and threatening. Craw was brave enough to stop and turn. She saw a human figure slowly moving towards them. *This will be the end of it.* She felt her heart leap as she saw Piner waiting in open space. 'No, Piner!' she said. 'This is the end.'

Her mind was spinning so fast she wasn't sure whether to run or fight. Then she saw Twitcher—his tail fluffed in fury high in the air. Craw hadn't seen him for days. He was a street fighter; his ears were jagged liked chipped plates from his many battles. His nose was streaked with scars from his alley attacks. He had become Craw's enforcer. He wasn't just the mad tom cat she had once feared. Now he battled on her behalf. Twitcher was another cat who had become a thinker—the *shudder* had shaken his bones, but death had passed him by.

Twitcher was now standing his ground. He shouted out his warning. 'It's one of them—perhaps a crafty Pawman! I've overtaken him to warn you.'

'You always have to fight,' sighed Craw under her breath. She wished Twitcher had just warned them and they could have drifted into the trees. Craw tensed herself ready to leap at the intruder. She was too late. Piner was already in the air launching himself at the dark figure. Craw watched the others. Twitcher was on the right, Dreamer on the hard ground to the left, leaving Craw in the centre.

Without thinking, they opened their mouths together and the sound was ear splitting.

Only Piner was silent. He had leapt into the intruder's arms, not fighting for breath but stretching his neck seeking the Provider's touch. It was then that Craw realised she'd have to act before it was too late. She would have to lead the charge and inspire the others. Craw launched herself at this person who had discovered their hiding place and now could betray them.

Instead of hitting a pair of human legs, she found herself face to face with Piner who had leapt out of the enveloping arms. 'Stop, all of you! This is Tom, my Provider. He can do what Dreamer has said must happen. He can help us. I trust him just like the boy in Dreamer's dream.'

Tom had just had a noisy thirteenth birthday at home with cards and coloured boxes. His hair was almost white, and his bright blue eyes shone in the morning light.

'I brought him here,' Piner went on. 'He's been helping me. How do you think I got this fat when I can't catch a slow toad?'

'That's cheating,' said Twitcher.

'That's smart,' answered Piner with a flick of his tail. 'We have to learn to survive—and we *are* learning. Our thinking has changed. Those of us who have lived through the *shudder* are different.'

Craw saw total bemusement on the boy's face. Perhaps he realised they were arguing amongst themselves.

She heard Piner whisper, 'Don't give the game away. Play, kitty— otherwise he'll guess too much too soon.'

Dreamer fell onto his back and rolled overexposing his generous belly to the boy. He lifted his front paws, holding them apart inviting a tickle. Tom stooped down and stroked the white fur. Dreamer closed his eyes.

'He's got biscuits,' hissed the ever-alert Twitcher. 'Biscuits, biscuits, biscuits.'

The tickled Dreamer heard the word and licked his lips

in anticipation. 'Come on, little boy, open the box.' He sidled up to Tom and stared up at him.

'You know I've got something for you.' Tom spoke in a sing-song fashion. 'I'm going to get into such trouble. We aren't supposed to get anywhere near you, and we've got to report to the cat-catcher any time we see cats hiding.'

'This is it.' Craw felt that they would all be caught soon.

'No; listen and learn!' hissed Piner.

'And eat,' said Twitcher. 'Let's have some biscuits. Come on, boy!'

Craw's heart leapt as Tom stood up straight and took the biscuit box from under his coat. Just a handful of the small crunches would be a delicious delight. Craw decided that she needed to eat them so badly. She gave out a plaintive cry. It had always worked at home.

'Not so obvious, Craw,' nodded Twitcher. 'Keep it *kitty*.'

Piner sat staring upwards. 'Just look at the box. He'll get the idea. He's very sharp—for a Provider.'

'All right,' agreed Craw.

All of them sat staring at the inviting box.

Tom raised his eyebrows. 'I could swear you're ganging up on me to give you something to eat. I think you're all working together.'

'Come on,' said Craw, 'just open the box.' She gave out an appealing squeak.

'All right, come on.' The boy ripped the top of the biscuit box and sprinkled its contents on a flat stone. The spirits couldn't resist the temptation as they walked forward with their tails raised. Twitcher was the only one to pause and check around for danger. The others were busy licking up the special tastes.

'You're on guard are you, tough guy?' said the boy.

Twitcher nodded sagely.

Tom laughed. 'You nodded. You nodded!'

Dreamer glanced up from his meal. 'You know what the

Providers say—when the cat's away the mice will play.'

Craw swallowed her mouthful. 'The mice must be having fun. Catsaways we may be, but we'll be back.'

'Catsaways—is that a human word?'

'Sounds familiar.' Craw turned her head. 'That is what we are—catsaways, and we need more of catkind with us.'

Craw heard Tom speak. 'Are you talking?'

Piner gazed at his Provider. 'Of course, we're not,' he said, shaking his head.

'Of course, you're not,' said Tom tickling Piner under the chin.

But, of course, they were.

Chapter Three: The Atticats

Purrl stared hard and long through the tiny window. She would sit there for hours contemplating the outside world, watching the odd feathered fill shoot past her restricted view. If she stretched up, she could just see the tips of the trees in the garden reaching up to the sky. Sometimes, one of the fluffy grey tails would leap extravagantly from the tip of one tree to another, as if he was challenging Purrl to chase him even though she was locked in this room. They did the same when she had pursued these nasty creatures on the grass. They would turn and bark loudly like little dogs.

Purrl was a cat who sat. She'd always been a sitting cat, no matter where it was, for as long as she could remember. She sat anywhere and everywhere. She felt, on balance, that laps were the best, but it was vital to check out all competing possibilities. Chairs in most places were comforting especially if just vacated by a Provider. Squeezing in behind the sitting Provider gave you double the warmth but sometimes they'd go and sit somewhere else, which did spoil her fun.

'What are you doing?!' a voice questioned her dramatically.

'Thinking,' answered Purrl, screwing up her nose at her inquisitive brother Nailz.

'That's all you ever do—think, think, think! I remember when all you did was stare. I think I preferred that to all this thinking. You'd sit downstairs on the window ledge that faces the garden and stare—that was good. I definitely preferred that.' Nailz flopped onto the floor and refined the sharpness in his nails.

Purrl attempted to get her own back on the irritable

Nailz. 'It's a wonder you've got any nails left.'

'As if it mattered. There's nothing to hunt in here. There's no furry or feathery fills in this locked up house.' Nailz turned tail and stalked off into his corner. 'Tiggr would have found a way out of this prison.'

'Tiggr was good in the old way,' said Purrl, 'he was a great old cat.'

Nailz spoke from the dark of his far corner. 'He was our dad.'

'He was just the best.'

'The biggest and the best!' Nailz stretched as if to show he really took after his father, the much feared Tiggr.

Purrl sighed. The whole household had been upset by the decline of Tiggr. It seemed to happen quite suddenly. First, he lost a fight and sulked for days. Not even the Providers could get him to eat his favourite morsels. The ma Provider even offered him some of her own plate of juicy, creamy, chicken but he wouldn't eat.

'He wasn't only a bigger cat. Dad was marked like the biggest of cats. The ones that frighten even the Providers.'

'Tigers,' interrupted Purrl. 'They're called tigers, lions, panthers.' Purrl paused to think of more of her cat cousins.

'All of those, but I won't forget him. Everything I know about hunting I learned from him.'

'The old ways,' sniffed Purrl.

'I knew something was wrong when he stopped whacking me. If I was in his spot, he'd whack me. If I rushed a bit and surprised him, he'd whack me. He was a right whacker, our dad. I remember once he hit me with his right paw and I went right over the stairs. I think he frightened himself.'

'He never whacked me,' sniffed Purrl.

Nailz blinked. 'Well, you never did anything but stare, remember? You can't whack a spirit for staring.'

For a moment, they were both silent, and then Purrl saw Nailz prick up his ears. 'Do you remember when he whipped that steak off the table from next door?' he asked. 'There was such a shriek from the skinny one. She ran after him with a brush, but he didn't let go of that piece of meat. It was the biggest bit of meat I've ever seen in the whole of my life. He took it to the back of the glass shed and nearly ate it all. His belly was so big he could hardly stand up.'

Purrl purred at the memory.

'I would rush past him and stop and flick my tail in his nose,' Nailz carried on. That always used to really upset him. That would guarantee a whack. But he began to stare at the ground and not even see me. He forgot to get out of his basket in the morning. One day he forgot to go outside when it was time to go, you know?

Purrl knew.

'I tried to help him up that day when he slipped. He could hardly talk to me. His voice was a croak… a whisper. The Providers were unhappy too. So many times, they took him off in the little box and brought him back to give him the white bits in his food. He wouldn't eat them.'

'He wouldn't eat anything,' sniffed Purrl. She stood and fluffed the hair on her coat. 'Then he couldn't stand and began with the *shudder*.' This was the word the other spirits were using. They heard the Providers say the word. She thought back to the day Tiggr left them.

There was a loud knock at the door. A bright white light lit up the inside of the house. Purrl dashed under the long sofa in the main room. Nailz squeezed in beside her and gave her a worried glance.

The ma Provider's light footsteps could be heard on the tiled hallway. 'Here is the poor thing, wrapped in a blanket. There's nothing the vet could do. I presume he told you.'

'Yes, he did,' an unknown voice replied sharply. 'He reported the fact that you had a cat with the condition. You know that by law you have to inform the Inspectorate that you have an infected cat at home. We should have known when he showed the first signs.'

'We didn't know,' the ma Provider said quietly. 'We weren't sure. We thought he'd got cat flu or something.'

'I'm sorry, but that isn't the point. I have to tell you that the regulations are very strict. Fines are now imposed on those who knowingly harbour infected animals. I'm sure you're aware that people who are habitual offenders face imprisonment. The vet had a duty to inform us.'

Purrl's ears hurt as the ma Provider's voice grew louder. 'I don't know that such a thing is right! People are trying to protect their cats. I'm not sure the scientific evidence is conclusive. Some cats have been shown not to be infected, even after living with other infected animals. It hasn't been clearly shown as yet that this condition can be spread to us!'

There seemed to be a long pause. Then the strange voice spoke again, resigned yet forceful. 'I'm not here to argue the evidence, but to enforce the law. The Government imposed emergency powers and our department is authorised to organise all cat seizures. You *must* realise this is the only way we can contain the disease and protect people. Now, where are they?'

The pa Provider spoke up. 'What do you mean, "Where are they"?'

'Take him!' an agitated female voice shouted. 'He's dead. You're not taking any others.'

Purrl moved in closer to Nailz, who had started to chew his nails very quietly.

'It's all right, Lyn. Calm down. There are no others. This is it.'

'We have the authority under this legislation to enter your home and search,' the stranger said. 'Anyone found harbouring fugitive cats will be arrested and prosecuted. This is a serious matter. The vet has told us you have another two cats. We've confirmed sightings from an informant that they've been seen about in the recent past. So, would you like to bring the cats to us?'

'I've told you there aren't any here, and I know my rights as well as you,' the pa Provider replied. 'Even under the emergency laws, you have to have a search warrant before you can come in. The cats have gone. They were taken to be destroyed because we wanted to do it before this happened.'

'So, where are they?'

'As I said: destroyed.'

'*Where*? What vet?'

'Privately destroyed.'

At that the ma Provider let out a cat-like screech. 'Go! They've gone, and as far as I'm concerned *you* killed them!'

Purrl put her head between her paws. Was this to be their end? If they didn't go with the *shudder* like Tiggr they would be taken by these evil men; the ones the others were calling the Pawmen.

'We'll be back with a warrant. If they're here and you're harbouring them, we'll take them. The evidence is clear: *all* your cats have the disease in their brains. It shows in different ways and the carriers are the most dangerous, because while their brains are infected, they don't show it physically. They are the ones who must be hunted down and killed.' He dropped his voice and spoke calmly. 'This thing, this *condition*, has been contained in this area and we can't threaten the rest of the country or the world!'

The stranger's speech was stopped by the ma Provider. 'I know the law,' she said firmly. 'I know the emergency powers legislation. I'm a lawyer, for God's sake! We're not letting you in. Go and get your warrant, if you can find a magistrate who'll issue one. Then we'll let you in—but not before!' As she stopped, a slamming door indicated to Purrl that it had been firmly shut in the faces of the Pawmen.

The ma Provider called out to her house cats. At first, they didn't move but then Nailz could not resist the gentle voice of ma Provider. 'Come on, where's the other one?'

Purrl crawled out from her hiding place. She was picked

up, held very tightly and a kiss was planted on top of her head. 'It's all right, the nasty men have gone.' The ma Provider turned from Purrl. 'What are we going to do with them, Robin? We'll have to give them up.' She kissed Purrl again. 'But I can't! They're all right. There's nothing wrong with them, I know it! If anything, they're brighter, cleverer than before. This little one has stopped her constant staring.' She pointed at Nailz. 'And this one's stopped doing that repetitive scratching thing.'

That's a matter of opinion, thought Purrl.

'What scratching thing?' she heard Nailz say.

'That scratching thing you do when you're trying to attract their attention. It's usually when you're hungry. You know when you jump on their legs with your claws out.'

Nailz shrugged. 'But it works.'

'Sshh—they'll notice we're talking.' Purrl purred in the way that only she could. It was the loudest purr in the neighbourhood.

The ma Provider stroked her. 'I know it's crazy, but recently I think they're talking to each other.'

'Yes, of course,' said the pa Provider. 'But what's to be done? The kids will never forgive us if we give them up to those red-aproned enforcers.'

'The *kids* won't forgive you. What about *me*?'

'Okay, I won't forgive myself. But are we putting ourselves in danger? Will the condition spread to us? Are we putting the kids at risk? Don't tell me you'd rather lose them?'

'Don't be silly. But what can we do? If this thing spreads, we've got it already. It's too late for us. The number of people supposedly with the infection seems to be quite small and they've just got a nasty dose of flu.' She bent down and put the two cats on the floor. 'Quarantine them. Put them somewhere we can hide them and feed them, but not be in total contact with them.'

'Yes, but when the cat catchers come back, they'll have

all the investigative paraphernalia they need. Probably come with a sniffer dog as well.'

'If they were hidden—soundproofed, scent-proofed— that might be enough to protect them.'

Purrl and Nailz sat cleaning themselves intently while paying close attention to the plan.

'The attic—the rear end of the attic! It's almost like a false loft because it was built later than the original building. We didn't even find it ourselves until we'd been here for months—it was only when the builders knocked through that little wall.'

Purrl licked her favourite place deep in her tummy.

'There is the trapdoor. I could board it with a hidden flap for access for food and then... yes!'

The pa Provider went off muttering to himself as Ma turned to the licking cats. 'Don't worry babies! I'll protect you if it's the last thing I do—and it might be!'

***

Banging and crashing went on well into the night, and as much as Purrl tried to sleep she couldn't help going to observe the progress every so often.

'Checking up on us, are you?' said the pa Provider. Purrl rubbed against his leg and twirled her tail against the man. 'Nearly there, don't worry.'

At dawn the pa Provider slumped into bed and it was only then that Purrl felt she could sleep too. After all, she normally slept on the big bed. It was her place, her right even. All the spirits in the house knew that she slept at the bottom of the big bed. Purrl would never assume her place until the Providers had settled and put out the lights. Then it was her time. That was her signal. She would jump gently onto the bottom of the bed and get comfortable. This might require a certain sniffing and twisting and pushing up against the warm feet of ma and pa Provider. But they didn't mind because they were asleep.

Purrl remembered that Tiggr always had the best, most special spot. He would arrive in the darkest dark of night and jump practically into the face of the ma Provider. Quietly, he would breathe on her face and gently touch her cheek with his paw. Then he would burrow into the covers and lie against her warm body. Sometimes the ma Provider, even though she seemed asleep, would lift up the cover and let him under. Tiggr would purr so loudly that it was surprising the whole house didn't wake. But nothing would then stir until the Providers' ticking clock buzzed out loud in the morning.

At other times ma Provider would creep out of the bed as if not to disturb Tiggr, but as soon as he knew she was awake he would leap out of the bed as alert as if he'd never slept.

Purrl found herself dreaming that Tiggr was still there and when pa Provider woke, she almost expected to see him.

'Shh,' said the pa Provider. He leant over and began stroking Purrl. 'This will be the last time for a long while that you're going to be sleeping in that spot.' He repeatedly pressed her cheek in the way she loved. 'This will be the last time for both of us. Perhaps for a very long time and you won't be leaving here in the near future.' He looked towards the door and nodded to himself.

Purrl turned to Nailz.' Have you tried that flap in the door?' This was their way in and out of the home.

'Yes, of course,' replied Nailz.

'What do you think?'

'It might give us the chance to do a runner. We could have gone and tried to join the others—the free spirits. The ones on the run.'

'Yes, and we all know what's happening to them. They're being picked up one at a time by the Pawmen. They're fools. I'm telling you, if we're to win this we must work with the Providers.'

'No. I don't know!' wailed Nailz. 'Tiggr would have taken them head-on. He would have fought them all.' He went to the flap and tried again hitting it with his paw several times like a punch bag. Each time he knocked it the plastic door rattled back in his face.

Purrl was exasperated. She understood Nailz' desire to leave and join the others, but their Providers wanted them to stay and that had some definite advantages. 'We must trust our Providers. Think about it!'

Any choice was shortly taken away from them as ma Provider called them to eat. 'Come on you two. Time for the last breakfast!'

'Don't you mean the last supper?' the pa Provider laughed.

'If you like. If that's how you really see it. It means they'll live a little longer and even if we don't have their company, we know they're safe.'

'So, the time has come. I'll take Nailz; you hold Purrl.'

'What do we do?' squealed Nailz.

Purrl looked into his blue eyes. 'Nailz, we do nothing.'

'Robin, they're doing it again,' said the ma.

'What?'

'Talking,' she said.

'Don't be silly Lyn. Let's get them upstairs before they know anything's wrong.'

The ma Provider turned and picked up Purrl. 'There's a good girl. Come to mama.'

Purrl purred and stared hard at Nailz. 'Don't fight it. This is our best chance.'

The pa Provider reached down for Nailz who twisted and turned as he tried to get away. He ended up falling heavily to the ground.

'For goodness' sake Robin, hold him!'

'He twisted,' tutted pa Provider. He bent down to try and catch Nailz again.

'Keep still, for Tiggr's sake!' shouted Purl.

At that, Nailz seemed to heed her cry and stood still. As he stopped, the ma Provider spoke very quietly. 'There's a good boy and a good girl. Robin, I'm telling you they are talking.'

'All right,' said Purrl. 'Do something daft, we can't have them being too suspicious.'

Nailz, appreciating the situation and enjoying being naughty, turned on his tail and attempted to bite the end off, failed, and then ran to the rope scratching post. He did three twirls, tried to bite the white ball, and then ran extravagantly up the stairs. He skidded to a halt and waited underneath a newly painted ceiling.

'Yes, obviously very intelligent,' the pa Provider said. 'He has just happened to stop in the very spot we need him. My dear, I know we love these creatures, but they are not clever.'

'See,' smirked Nailz. 'Who says I can't fool them?'

'Now!' The pa Provider lifted Nailz high into the air and pushed him through a small hole that Nailz hadn't spotted. Purrl was bundled into the back of him. 'That hurt!' he squealed.

'Now you're in the attic, you're the attic cats!' The pa Provider just managed to push his head and shoulders into the hole and then disappeared.

Purrl peered at Nailz as her eyes rapidly adjusted to the small amount of light in the attic space.

'This is it?' Nailz said worriedly. He buried his head in his paws.

'It could be the Pawmen's van,' said Purrl as she sniffed and explored their new space. 'It's not bad. It's quite warm.' She nudged her ample frame against the chimney breast that ran through the roof. 'Actually, this is really warm. There's food here. There's crunches and stuff, lots of them. Time for a feast!'

Purrl set about the dish in front of her but Nailz jumped

back in surprise. He had bumped against a large plastic box. 'What on earth is this?' he asked.

'Don't be silly, you must remember. It's the box—the *thingy* box.'

'What thingy box?' Nailz questioned.

'Where you've got to go when you've got to go.'

'There is nowhere to go,' he protested to Purrl.

Purrl was exasperated. 'No, do your business; scratch the dirt, go outside—you know, what we all do when we have to!'

'What, in there? What about my special spot, my personal spot?'

'You can't use it because you can't get out! Anyway, we used to use one of these when we were kittens. You must remember?'

Nailz turned around and furrowed his brow. Purrl knew he couldn't forget that box full of little bits that were easy to dig and that scattered everywhere. 'Ergh. I don't want to use that with you watching!'

'My dear squeamish Nailz, you have no choice!' Purrl said smugly. She settled beside the warm chimney and allowed herself to relax. At least for now they were safe; safe from the world, safe from the evil Pawmen. They were the *Atticats*.

Chapter Four: The Catmen Call

Tom walked slowly along Borrowcop Lane towards his house. It was said that in Anglo-Saxon times there'd been a huge battle and thousands of warriors had been killed and buried there. The house opposite was called King's Barrow, which meant "King's Grave". Tom had often gazed at the hill out of his bedroom window and tried to think what it must have been like after the battle when they had to bury all those dead soldiers. Perhaps they had buried the treasure found in a field nearby – the largest hoard of Anglo-Saxon gold ever discovered. As he gazed up at the hill, Tom felt a hard blow to the back of his neck. He fell forward but managed to stand on his feet. In his heart he knew the hit wasn't friendly.

'Biggins, Boggins, Baggins,' a familiar voice echoed in Tom's ears. It was Billy Cairns, bully of the parish.

'Get off, Cairns! That hurt.'

'Did Billy hurt poor little Boggins? Diddums.'

Tom felt a disturbing anger rise inside himself. He wasn't in the mood for bullies. He had bigger things on his mind. He let out a great shout, without pausing to think of the consequences he turned, dropped his head, and charged.

It was the suddenness of the attack that took Cairns by surprise. Even though he was thirteen, like Tom, he was taller by a good head and shoulders. Tom's blundering head charge hit the bully boy right in the belly. Cairns uttered a horrid gasp and staggered backwards holding his stomach. Sense suddenly gripped Tom. He stopped and looked at the winded windbag.

'That's not fair,' puffed Billy.

'Not fair? How's belting somebody on the back of the

neck fair?'

'I'm telling,' moaned the bully. Tom realised that not only had he retaliated perfectly but that the bully was alone. He didn't have his usual gang of hangers-on with him. Billy Cairns was so rarely alone that this chance spurred Tom on to take revenge on all the occasions he'd seen him be a bully.

'Telling? Who are you going to tell? You can't tell your dad, can you?'

Billy seemed to shrink even more before Tom's eyes. 'I'll still tell.'

'Don't be silly, Cairns. This was just you and me. Let's forget it.'

Tom felt sorry that he'd beaten Billy by attacking a weak point. It wasn't just his soft belly—his father had left the family home last year. Everyone knew his reputation, Billy's mother often turned up at the Saint Cedd's Junior School with a black eye. He knew Billy still spent the weekends with his dad, who worked for the local authority on the vermin cleansing scheme and now the enforced cat gathering. Tom suddenly felt it wasn't wise to upset the enemy and put out his hand to help Billy stand up properly.

'What are you on, softy Buggins?' Billy gripped Tom's hand tightly and pulled him sharply towards him. 'I'll have you some other time when you're not cheating.' Billy was now standing tall and towering over Tom.

A voice came from the distance. 'Are you all right, Tom?'

Tom felt himself blush as Mrs Constance came to her garden wall. She was ninety something, very sharp and very lively. She lived in that massive house all on her own.

'Yes, I'm okay. Honest.'

'Wait till I spread the word that your beating was stopped by a cronky old dear.'

Tom was annoyed. 'Not my beating.'

'Come on, then,' Billy said.

'Tom are you sure?' repeated Mrs Constance.

'I'm going,' whined Billy. 'Kitty, kitty. I know you're a kitty lover, Boggins, and my dad will have you and your kitties.'

Tom couldn't stop himself from sniggering. 'Does that mean I'll have to fight him next?'

'Tom,' Mrs Constance called again, 'can you take Samson for a walk?' She waved a dog lead in the air.

'Tommee!' Billy was back to his normal irritating baiting. His voice was high pitched and baby-like. 'Tommee! Go and walk Samson and don't let me catch you out in the big world.'

'Cairns, you are just sick.'

'Go and walk the dog. At least you can't walk the cat.'

Tom turned quickly and dropped down again as if to repeat his charge.

'Tom!' Mrs Constance's voice was joined by the vigorous barking of Samson, who must have realised from the shaking lead that a walk was on offer. Tom turned away from Billy who appeared vaguely relieved. He thrust his hands into his pockets and slouched off back down the lane.

'Here's the lead, Tom.' Mrs Constance dropped the leather lead over the wall. Tom caught it and approached the gate, opened it just enough to squeeze in and hold the large black Labrador while slipping the lead over his neck. 'Don't be too long. I'll have a treat for both of you when you get back!'

Tom knew this meant a chocolate chip cookie for both of them. This was something not to be sniffed at; Mrs Constance baked them herself and each one was the size of a small plate.

Moments later he found himself being dragged along at some pace by Samson. The black beast zigzagged across the road dangerously. He even glared through the gates of Tom's own home, seemingly disappointed that his daily confrontation ritual with the Biggins family cat was no longer being observed. He had an intense rivalry with Piner, who would sit behind the gates quietly taunting the dog, looking superior and safe while being wildly barked at.

Samson had started sniffing him. The dog had picked up the smell of Piner. The pine scent must have penetrated his jacket when he held his runaway cat. Samson lurched off in another direction dragging Tom, the dog still obsessed with his poor pine-scented feline.

Tom thought back to the day Piner left, when his mother had said they'd have to give him up because of the danger cats presented to everyone. Billy Cairns' father had turned up in his official uniform with a red apron and his ID badge hanging round his fat neck. His van smelt like a mobile food shop.

Mr Cairns had spoken quietly to his mother for some time and then she called Tom over. He'd never forget her words to him.

'Mr Cairns says we'd better let the cat go,' she'd said. 'It's for the best. He'll be tested and then if there's nothing wrong they're gathering them in a quarantine yard at Dawkins, the cattery, and we'll get him back eventually. It's the strays that they're really worried about, and they'll have to be taken care of. It's too dangerous to let them live in the wild. The others will be safe in the yards. Catteries are really just like cat holiday camps.'

Tom had thought she sounded unsure. One glance at Mr Cairns' smug face told him that what he'd read on the *Save Our Lichfield Cats* website was right. The test was very expensive, dangerous and inconclusive. The website said the cats in the yard would all be killed eventually and looking at Cairns' smile he felt this was true.

'Tom,' said Mr Cairns, 'why don't you see if you can find our little grey chap and I'll take him to the...' He paused as if searching for the word. 'To the "rest camp".'

Tom sighed as his mother squeezed his shoulder and nodded her head. Reluctantly, Tom wandered off around the garden calling out Piner's name but with no great enthusiasm. Eventually, the cat appeared from under a bush, saw Tom and allowed himself to be picked up and gently held.

'Now listen,' Tom pursed his lips close to the little grey ear, 'they want to take you to this camp where you'll be fed and watered and if you're all right then they'll let you come back home to us.' The grey one stared straight into Tom's eyes. For a moment Tom was taken completely aback as the little grey head nodded. 'It will be all right,' said Tom without a great deal of confidence. 'If you become one of the runaways the men in the white van will track you down and that'll be it. Please believe me!' For some strange reason, Tom felt he had to explain himself to the small grey creature. 'If there was anything I could do, you know I would do it.'

The cat twisted gently enough to prise itself from Tom's grasp and land on the ground. He looked at Tom and slowly shook his head again. 'Don't do this!' said Tom. The grey one took five slow paces away from Tom, stopped and turned again.

'Don't go!' pleaded Tom.

Roused by the noise, Mr Cairns and Tom's mum had come around from the front of the house to see what Tom was up to. Mr Cairns spoke firmly but loudly. 'Stand still Tom. Don't move.' he turned, dropped his head and charged.

The grey one peeked at Mr Cairns quickly, then at Tom, and then ran to the busy corner of the garden covered with thick bushes and shrubs.

It was at that point Tom saw the gun. It was a long-barrelled pistol which Mr Cairns was holding with both hands. He was moving forward and pointing it towards the shrubbery.

'No!' his mother pleaded.

There was a loud crack. Instantly, Mr Cairns was joined by another cat-catcher with a large net and jointed pole. 'In there!' shouted Mr Cairns. 'Scare him out!'

The second man skirted the prickly bush and pushed into the undergrowth, brandishing the pole and holding the net high, like a gladiator about to strike an opponent. Tom saw a tiny movement at the base of large pine tree that was at the back of the shrubs.

Mr Cairns wasn't looking at his accomplice but at Tom, and as he saw Tom's eyes flicker towards the pine tree he shouted out, 'Over there! I can see it!'

A shot rang out and a grey shape fell from the branch of the tree. 'Yes...' hissed Mr Cairns. The two men ran forward, but Tom could hardly move. He saw his mother raise her hands to cover her eyes.

'What is this?' Mr Cairns kicked something with his black shin-length protective boot. As the man bent down to pick the creature up from the ground, Tom was aware someone or something was watching him. Near the apple tree was his grey cat looking straight at him. Was Tom dreaming? Was he going mad? He turned slowly to see Mr Cairns picking up the limp figure of a grey squirrel.

'Vermin, by any other name,' Mr Cairns said, shaking the large grey squirrel.

'I didn't know you were shooting the cats!' his mother said. Her voice had an edge to it.

'Stunning,' corrected Mr Cairns. 'It's a dart with a sedative. Shooting is out of the question.'

'For the moment,' muttered his smug companion.

'No. Public opinion would never let us carry proper guns.'

'For the moment,' mouthed the second man.

Tom watched as Cairns' assistant lifted up the lifeless squirrel. 'This isn't harmful. It renders them unconscious and stops them biting or spreading the infection.'

'It hasn't done much for this one,' said the stooge.

'No. Well, it isn't intended for squirrel use, is it, John?'

'No, Al. It is not.' The red-aproned hunter threw the

lifeless corpse into the net. 'Mrs Biggins, I know we haven't got your cat today and I can't answer for the consequences. The best thing is to surrender him to us if he should come back. You know the number. It's on the special leaflet delivered to all homes and it is being heavily advertised. Please ask for me personally if you want special treatment.' He raised his finger. 'And you, Tom Biggins... I hear you're a bit of a cat lover. Well, don't forget!' He spoke in a very deliberate way as if he was admonishing a small child. 'It's *real people* we're protecting.'

Minutes later, the van drew out of the drive and Tom watched as his mother closed the gates behind it. 'I wouldn't give our cat up now if they shot me with that thing,' she told him. 'But where is he?'

'Gone, definitely gone,' said Tom.

'How do you know?'

'He somehow got behind them when they were shooting and nodded to me that he was going.'

'What do you mean, Tom?'

Tom felt miserable. 'Well, he just stared at me and left. I don't think he'll come back. I think he knows they're after him.'

'Tom, sweetheart.' His mother put her arm on his shoulder. 'A cat can't know anything of the kind. But it is shocking! I'm going to complain to the council, to our Member of Parliament. Nobody said anything about guns. I'm going to ring the local radio station. Camps are one thing but shooting creatures even with a dart gun —it's not on. I'll call your dad. He's supposed to be an important man on committees for this and that.'

Tom could see his mum was upset and not just angry.

'What is the world coming to when innocent creatures can be gunned down in front of you or taken off to God knows what kind of place?! It all started when those people said cats were murderers and killing off wildlife and should be culled. That was the start of it—an anti-cat conspiracy, and just because they aren't sure what is causing this monstrous disease, they say "let's blame cats!" It's Mad Cow Disease all over again. That was supposed to make us go crazy and kill us all! Not to mention bird flu and swine flu and Coronavirus destined to kill us all.

Tom was beginning to wish his Dad was at home because his mother could get in a bit of a state when she felt things weren't right. He would never forget when she had an action group to stop them cutting down the great Lichfield oak. She had tears in her eyes that day. And when they threatened to move the statue of Captain Smith of the *Titanic* from Beacon Park back to Stoke-on-Trent, where he was born, Tom thought she was going to burst a blood vessel.

'I won't have it. I won't have it! What's the number of that useless councillor that hides when things go wrong? She's only bothered when her garden is threatened with a two-foot reduction for road widening. Well, I'm going around there now!'

Tom's grey cat appeared again. He came from behind Tom's mum and then disappeared, as if by magic.

Mrs Constance called from across the road. 'What was that awful Mr Cairns doing here?'

'Oh Esme—don't ask!'

Tom could see his mum was about to give Mrs Constance a blow-by-blow account of the gun fight on the Lane but then she said, 'Oh, I saw your little grey. When the van had gone, he popped up by Samson's bowl, had a drink and I will swear he winked. Cheeky cat!'

'They tried to shoot him!' shrieked Mrs Biggins. 'This is war.'

This moment marked the beginning of his mother's campaign to bring sense to the cat clearance programme. It turned out there were many other Mrs Bigginses all over the country, but the Government were holding firm. That night the whole family had listened intently to the Prime Minister on television talking about the limited outbreak of this disease in Lichfield. The man seemed confident— politicians always were—as he went on about previous crises involving animals and disease and mistakes that had been made by somebody else. But this time no mistakes would be permitted. 'The local quarantine regulations are excellent, Containment and testing are the key words that we've learned from Covid-9.' he said, 'but breaches of the regulations will not be tolerated. The police and military will back up the Cat Clearance Officers in all instances of law-breaking.'

The Prime Minister leant towards the camera. 'I am and always have been a cat lover. For millions of us our homes would not be the same without the nation's favourite pet.'

'Hypocrite!' His mum always shouted at politicians on television.

The Prime Minister didn't flinch at the interruption. 'There is absolutely no need for panic and the Chief Medical Officer has assured me that this cat "*shudder*", as it has been called, is being contained in the Lichfield area. I appreciate the upset but thank those in the containment area for being so understanding. The thoughts of the Government and the Nation are with you.'

'Switch him off. He knows nothing.' Mrs Biggins grabbed the remote and punched it with her finger.

Tom knew his dad would have to calm her down. 'Jenny, if they are responsible for spreading this disease to people, we have to exercise caution and go by the rules.'

'The rules are wrong! The rules are evil. This Government is pathetic!'

'Jen let's do this thing properly. You aren't the only person who feels like this. Let's join the action group—let's get involved and have a proper debate. The Government thinks it knows best and has imposed these rules to get the best result.'

'But they're out of control. The cat clearance people are

just doing what they want. Everyone is running scared and nobody cares about the cats.'

Tom's dad put on his 'be calm' voice. 'Jen, you know that isn't true.'

'It is! The Government has said these creatures are evil. They will have them tested and exterminated, and everything will be all right. I don't like it.' Jenny Biggins paused and stamped her feet. 'Even if they are carriers of the disease, nobody should be killed without a fair trial.'

The argument had raged into the night and Tom had gone to bed with every intention of trying to forget about the horrors of the day and read his new fantasy novel, which at least meant he didn't have to worry about the real world. It was a warm night and his window was open as usual. He couldn't put the book down but felt his eyes grow heavier and heavier.

Suddenly, the real world hit him on the head. His Aston Villa FC framed, and signed team photo smashed from his sideboard onto the floor via his forehead. He awoke with a jolt and, looking up, he saw the cause of the crash—there was the grey one, now stinking of fresh pine.

'Oh! Piner, come here.' Tom held out his hand and the pine-flavoured grey cat jumped onto Tom's bed, its tail in the air. Purring with delight, it let him stroke and stroke and stroke.

'What's the time?' Tom peered at his illuminated Wizard's clock. 'Four in the morning! Piner, what is this all about?' The cat purred and purred and then cried and jumped off the bed. 'I'm still tired! What do you want?'

The cat uttered a small squeak and jumped back on the bed. After the sixth time of this game Tom was exasperated. 'What do you want? I can't follow you. You must be so careful. That loony Mr Cairns will take a pot shot at you. The patrols are running twenty-four hours now, you know.'

With each set of squeaks and runs, Tom found himself gradually drawn onto the landing, then to the stairs until finally he stood at the front door. 'Am I supposed to be following you?' Piner stopped and did a cat nod. 'You do want me to follow you? Or am I going mad?!'

Piner answered by running back into the kitchen, jumping onto the work surface, and crying wildly. Tom knew this was the usual sign for his favourite packet of meaty morsels. 'You want this now?'

If a cat could say 'Does a dog like bones?' Tom swore Piner would have done. He ate like a cat that had been deprived of food for at least a whole day.

This was a clever and successful strategy. Night after night Tom was woken by Piner who would leap through the window and beg to be fed until bursting. Eventually Tom found himself waking up just before four and the arrival of Piner.

Inevitably, Tom's mother had noticed that the cat supplies seemed to be diminishing. 'How can these cat biscuits be disappearing?' she asked one day.

Tom bluffed. 'They asked us in school if we could donate biscuits and cat food to the Cats Protection League who are collecting for the cats interned at the camps.'

'Interned?' she said.

'Yes, interned. I don't know what it means, but it's like in prison!'

His mother had breathed deeply. 'All right, take all the food—we don't need it now he's gone.'

'No, it's all right,' protested Tom. 'The teacher said it was best done a bit at a time. They haven't got enough storage space.'

'I suppose she's right. Whenever you want some, just take them.'

***

That morning, Tom woke at the usual catting hour just before four. He sat up in bed feeling tired, fed up and worried about the future of Piner. He knew the grey cat would arrive through the window at some point.

That day had not been good. Billy Cairns had told the story of his father shooting at Piner to anyone who would listen. 'My dad went into the Biggins' garden and there was the deadly grey one. He said he'd never seen a bigger cat. It lashed out at him and his mate who'd already got the net and spike in his hands. Loony, it was, my dad said. It had got the shakes already. If you see a wild one on the run, you'll die if they get anywhere near you—within breathing distance my dad says. The Biggins' grey then launched himself at my dad straight in the air, I tell you, at his throat! They carry this specialist cat killing dart gun—last resort that is, only use the gun to defend yourself. It's a stunner but get them in the right place and they don't ever get up. He fired three times and then a straight hit right between the eyes. Ask Biggins.'

Victoria Passmore, from his class, had related the story to Tom. His reaction was one of vehement denial and a determination to put Billy Cairns straight if it killed him. It was only when Victoria spoke that he thought better of it.

'Nobody ever really believes Cairns about anything,' she said, 'so why should this be true? Anyway, wouldn't it be better if your cat got away?'

'He did,' said Tom. 'His dad killed a grey squirrel—a big one—but Piner isn't much bigger really. My Piner is still alive.'

'Shhh.' Victoria put her finger to her lips. 'Not now—better to live another day.'

Tom wanted to cry but felt he had in Victoria at least one supportive friend who knew the truth. 'Thanks, I appreciate it. The poor things do seem to have a massive cloud over them and Piner seems to get smarter and smarter.'

***

Right on cue Tom felt the 'smart' Piner pushing his face gently with his paw. Almost without waking, he got up, went downstairs, and went through the usual ritual. But just as he was about to open the box Piner uttered a sound that seemed to come from deep below his throat. Tom went to tear open the sachet again. The strange sound repeated itself and Tom was sure that Piner was making disapproving noises. He picked up several of the meaty packets in an attempt to identify Piner's favourite. Every time Tom went to tear open a sachet Piner would whine with disapproval. Tom found himself putting the packets in his pocket while offering Piner another flavoursome variety. By the time Tom's pockets were full, Piner was purring with obvious approval and displaying his now familiar 'follow-me' routine. Tail in the air, he would walk off a few paces and wait for Tom to catch up. The difference this time was that he didn't stop at the back door and instead kept up the routine onto the driveway.

'I can't go any further,' Tom said. 'I've got my pyjamas on.'

Piner would not accept the excuse. He ran to Tom and cried. He repeated himself, only ceasing crying if Tom walked behind him.

'This is silly. You want me to follow you?'

Piner purred and rubbed himself against Tom.

'I'll have to put some clothes on.' Tom thought all this hysteria was getting to him as well as to his mother, but still he dressed in his Nike tracksuit and old trainers and went back downstairs. Piner was still there, waiting at the front door.

'Tom, is that you?' It was his dad's voice. 'What are you doing?'

'Drink, Dad,' he whispered, desperate to keep the house quiet. He waited until he could hear his dad's heavy breathing that indicated he'd gone back to sleep.

He closed the door very slowly, checking he'd got the front door keys in his pocket. He set off, following Piner along the lane onto the Tamworth Road past Lichfield

Rugby Ground and into the darkness. He knew he was going towards the golf course but then he was in a woody clearing with a strong smell of pine in the air.

He had lost Piner. The grey cat had disappeared. In the half-light Tom could hardly see a thing but then an awful screech rent the air. He couldn't tell how many cats were screeching—it was intimidating, even frightening.

Suddenly, Piner was standing on his toes and he became aware of the other cats moving closer. Piner screeched out a complex set of sounds. At first, Tom thought they were going to attack him from all sides.

One of them rolled onto his back in a gesture of total submission; another licked its lips in anticipation. Tom knew they were harmless enough.

Tom took the biscuit box from under his coat. As they moved towards him in anticipation of food, he realised they were just ordinary cats—they were excited by the packets of hidden fishy, meaty delights and stared intently at them. These cats seemed so normal, not sick or diseased. If they were, he had probably caught the bug by now.

One of the cats paused as if sensing danger.

'You're on guard are you, tough guy?'

The cat nodded and turned around.

'You nodded. You nodded!' Tom laughed at himself. He looked at the cats that had stopped eating and were engaging each other with a variety of squeaks and squawks. 'Are you talking?'

Tom felt as if he'd broken into a cats' away-day. He was an intruder almost. He paused to tickle Piner under the chin who vigorously shook his head. This wasn't a cats' away-day; it was just a bunch of castaways—or just *catsaways*! Funny how the thought came to him—it was as if they'd given him the idea. *As if they were talking*, he thought.

Piner then performed his old trick and jumped straight into Tom's arms and yelled at the other cats as if he was talking to them

'Of course, you're not,' Tom said aloud.
But they were, of course.

Chapter Five: Catattack

Craw couldn't sleep the day after Piner's young Provider had visited. She would close her eyes, but her mind would spring to that give-away moment when Twitcher had nodded at Tom. That nod was a Provider thing—a *human* thing. A cat shouldn't have done it.

Eventually, she had fallen into a fitful sleep and dreamt of Tom leading the Pawmen into their hideaway. It forced her awake with a jolt. She began to prowl slowly around the hiding place. It seemed as if her friends didn't share her fears. As she passed them, they were all sleeping soundly, dead to the world, even. Perhaps they might be really dead to the world very soon.

Earlier that night everyone had behaved strangely. Twitcher decided he had to teach Piner to fight. 'Now listen, let's try facing up. If you can't face up, you'll never win a fight.'

'But I don't want to fight. I'm happy running.'

'You might have to,' Twitcher said. 'So, face me up and defend yourself. I won't whack you *that* hard.' He swung his left paw over his head and caught Piner with a glancing blow behind the ear.

'Ooh!' Piner said. 'I wasn't ready. That wasn't fair!'

'Fighting isn't fair. It requires skill, thought, and intelligence.'

Before Twitcher could continue, Piner leapt on his slowly swishing tail and bit it. Twitcher squealed very loudly and was about to jump at Piner.

Craw moved between them. 'This is supposed to be about *helping* Piner, not reducing him to a nervous wreck

46

who'll bite anything that moves! Including your tail! Twitch, I don't mind if you are going to teach Piner some skills but let's think *differently*. Let's think how we can fight together instead of the old cat way of one on one.'

'Always has been one on one, always will be,' Twitcher said adamantly.

'Maybe, maybe not. Let's think this out: when Tom, the boy, came in, we did something cats don't normally do or perhaps didn't do before the *shudder*. You remember? We instinctively went into a defensive mode *together*.'

'Not Piner,' Twitcher noted sarcastically.

'No—well, he had a different agenda. He knew what was happening. He'd invited Tom, he was hardly in attack mode. Listen, Twitch—the rest of us were ready to attack the enemy in a formation. We took on different sides. We were prepared to attack from all directions. It's using all our strengths. Yes, you came upfront and were the loudest of all, but we backed you from the sides. Think of that.'

The line of argument was not lost on Twitcher. 'I'm with you. I screeched with my tail hugely puffed up, but if there had been a scrap you two were there to add weight. When Tiggr was alive and I was learning hunting with him, he showed me the same thing. Hunting together was much easier.'

'So, perhaps it is natural to us,' Craw said. 'I need you to create our defence and attack plans. Use each of our strengths.'

'Whatever they are,' Piner said uncertainly.

'Let's find out,' Craw said. 'Twitcher, you're in charge of the fighting. You think how best to operate.'

Craw never thought Twitcher would take his new role so seriously. Twitcher made them line up, stand tall, then drop down to the ground and take paces in extra slow motion.

'Piner,' Twitcher said, 'you *are* good at this.'

'Am I?' Piner seemed amazed.

'I've never seen a cat get so low on its belly and move

so slowly. You're a natural. My lookout, my guard!'

Piner seemed enormously pleased, as Twitcher had done nothing previously but criticise his feeble physical attributes. 'Show me again. See, Craw? Magnificent!'

Piner got rather carried away by the praise and decided to leap at an unknown prey, glancing behind him to see if his tutor was watching him with admiration. As usual, he had not surveyed sufficiently far enough ahead and landed in a dark pile of something soft, soggy, and smelly. He spat some gritty pieces out of his mouth. 'That is stinking.'

'I'd bite the cow that left it there,' joked Dreamer.

Realising exactly what the dark material was, Piner began shaking his head vigorously to try and remove all the pieces adhering to his face and whiskers. This was followed by some serious paw licking and proper scrubbing.

'At least your mother showed you how to wash,' Dreamer said, mimicking Piner's frantic licking and wiping.

Twitcher seemed annoyed that this cow-dung had interrupted his serious training session. 'Come on! Craw is right, we need to work out tactics. Piner, you're still my lookout and spy. Dreamer, you may be dozy, but you can fight. I'll have you as back up. Craw, you stand to my right, watch and be ready.'

Craw nodded, feeling impressed and pleased with Twitcher's assumption of the role of military command.

'Marching,' Twitcher suddenly announced.

'What? What are you thinking of?'

'Marching! I know a wild spirit that lived up at the Whittington Barracks. The soldiers used to feed him. He got great food. Dry stuff in packets and some fantastically hard biscuits. He loved them. I wish he were here now. *Bootsie*, he called himself. He used to spend hours watching the soldiers practising—shooting and all. I used to say to him "How can you stand that frightful noise?" He showed me— he'd lie flat, cover his ears with his paws and his eyes would focus as if he was watching a gun go off and then see it hit the target. He'd be a great help on the military planning.'

Craw wanted Twitcher to work this idea right out of his system. 'But... no. You don't mean cat-marching.'

'Have you ever *seen* marching?' Twitcher sounded superior in his knowledge of this military art. 'Bootsie reckoned that marching up and down and up and down instilled discipline into the soldiers. It's all about discipline in the face of the enemy. That's when he decided to practice covering his ears at the shooting ranges. It's great for us to have fantastic hearing, but we all know how it hurts when you're right beside a massive bang!'

'Not marching but dreaming,' said a bored Dreamer who appeared to be dozing off. 'My dreaming shows me the way. Things we can do to help ourselves, solve problems, come up with great ideas.' He smiled. 'We're all different, but we need to sleep and perhaps dream.'

Craw huffed. 'And you dream more than most.'

Twitcher was in command mode again and wanted attention not chatter. 'Let us apply ourselves to the business of *Catattack*.'

'What's that?' Dreamer asked, impressed.

'Catattack.' Twitcher was equally proud with his own word creation. 'I have been thinking.'

Craw raised her tail in mock admiration.

'Yes, I have been thinking and I have invented the concept of Catattack. Well, when I say *invented*, I mean *adapted from previously acknowledged cat fighting techniques*. Yes, Catattack will revolutionise our approach to our enemies!'

Following this dramatic introduction, Twitcher began to outline his favoured method of approaching any enemy. 'Right—Piner, as you now know you're lookout.'

Now in total appreciation of his own role, Piner dropped to the ground, stomach flat to the floor, tail lowered, and eyes checking right and left.

'Dreamer—position please. If you are still awake.'

Dreamer apparently had little more than a dreamy idea of his role, and slowly shuffled into place. With him in line, only Craw was without a post. Twitcher looked sagely at her. 'Craw, you'll do the Catskill part.'

This was a new word for Craw, but most of them were these days. 'What part?'

'The Catskill part?' Piner chirped up without moving from his position.

Craw felt Twitcher's new Catattack concept was leaving her behind. 'The Catskill part?'

'Yes, the Catskill part—the top part. The *boss* job.' Twitcher twitched with a slight irritation. 'So, have you forgotten Catskill the Wise—probably the oldest cat in our world?'

'It sounds sort of familiar,' ventured Craw.

'Catskill?' followed up Dreamer. 'I didn't know he was called the Wise?'

'The Great, the Wise, different things to different cats!' Twitcher exuded confidence. 'Catskill was probably the greatest cat who ever lived. This spirit knew all about the cat past, the cat present, and the cat future. No one knows how old Catskill is. Catskill has always been here. It is said that Catskill has lived more than nine full cat lives—perhaps even the legendary tenth. Some say it was a tomcat, but others say it had kittens.'

'Can't be,' Craw scoffed.

'I've heard this spirit was a great fighting cat—a great whacker?' said Dreamer.

'A whacker sometimes—a thinker at others!' Twitcher replied. 'Catskill lived in all those clever houses in town even though nobody wanted him. You've been round there. The Johnson place, Darwin's House, and the greatest building in our world—the one with the three towers.'

Craw was catching up with all this information. 'So, Catskill the Wise knows everything?'

Twitcher nodded vigorously. 'All I know is that Catskill has been a thinker much longer than any of us. They say it was the Johnson house cat. They say he, she or it lives on the roof that dominates the town and has a way up and down that only it knows. They say no-one looks after it, but everyone does. Every Provider thinks it's their cat. Catskill has lived so long its offspring are scattered across town through a hundred generations. Some say it is the mother and father of us all.'

Craw turned, scuffed the ground behind her and gazed hard at her friends. 'Twitcher, thank you for the Catskill fairy tale but we need hard facts and direct action. I'm sorry, Piner. Tom may be on our side, but he is just a boy and he knows *exactly* where we are.'

'He won't betray us,' retorted Piner.

'Perhaps he won't,' Craw snapped, 'and perhaps we must go back to him, but we have to find a new home. Dreamer, we must find and talk to this Catskill the Great, the Wise, mother and father—as long as it isn't just idle Twitcher cat-chat.'

'Wait a minute I know a lot of that Lichfield cat crowd,' Twitcher said. 'They all say they know about Catskill or have seen him in their cat dreams.'

'But do they do know where this Catskill can be found? Will they help locate him?'

'If we can find them without getting trapped in the town, they'll help, I promise.'

Craw went up to him and nosed him gently. 'Twitcher, you're a star.'

'I'm on the case. I'll recruit them and all the smartest cats in town will be with us in our search for the Great Catskill.'

The problem with cats of all ages and of all generations was that the stomach, and the filling thereof, was a fundamental driving force. Craw realised that all this philosophising and battle planning led to a serious degree of hunger. She knew cat fighters could only do battle on a full stomach. Even this so-called Catskill would know that. 'Let's eat,' she said. 'We still have the crunches.' Twitcher knocked the box down and set about it, teeth bared, biting into the cardboard with indecent haste.

Craw smiled as she saw Piner push one of the small packets with his paw. He picked it up in his mouth and waved his head from side to side violently. This was just enough for a small tear to appear in the corner. Craw could smell the delightful treats that were inside, but however much Piner shook the packet the hole seemed to get no bigger. In the meantime, Twitcher had succeeded in shaking three tiny morsels out of the square box.

They were all so occupied with the aggravating business of trying to open those human containers that nobody noticed a dark shadow. It was small at first; a skinny shadow, hardly making an impression, but as the cloud passed across the moon the beam showed off the creature for what it was—a massive figure that stood tall in the moonlight. It screamed out loud and long.

Craw saw Twitcher react first. He dropped his box of treats and ran to the space that the intruder occupied, preparing to fight for the group's survival. There was a moment of silence that lasted only a cat's breath before Twitcher stood high, nails on both paws exposed ready for the fight to follow.

For the others it was like slow motion. They were still turning when they saw the first hit come. Twitcher hit out with right and left paws, slashing high onto the chest of his opponent. A horrifying cry followed the blows, but the creature fought back with great ferocity, lashing out several times in the dark. Fangs sparked in the white light and then bore down on Twitcher's exposed left ear. His cry rang out. He stepped back and crouched ready to leap hard into the underbelly of this vicious opponent.

'No!' Craw screeched. 'Stop, unknown intruder! We are

many and you are one!' Piner and Dreamer emerged from the dark, tails fluffed and high their bodies arched turning to one side to give them the appearance of huge cats. 'And there are even more of us.' Craw hoped her voice sounded firm and strong. 'Stop or be stopped!'

From the gloom appeared a huge black cat. Its four white paws shone in the moonlight. 'I can do for all of you,' the stranger's voice hissed in the dark.

'This is Twitcher,' Craw said, 'the legendary fighter. Take care before you take him on again.'

At her comment, Craw saw the cat drop down and assume the still position. This was the moment that a fight could begin again or end. All cats knew it. One cat might become the victor and the other backs off in slow-motion. It was the moment before the final flurry. 'Twitcher, pull off.'

He had not moved, his eyes pinning his opponent to the spot. 'I'll have it.'

'Not yet you haven't,' came the opponent's brief response.

'We are spirits fleeing the Pawmen. Fight if you will— and die you might. Talk to us and we can work together.' Craw gently touched Twitcher with her left paw. Even that caused him to raise his paws as if to strike. 'Shhh.' Craw sensed the newcomer didn't want a cat fight.

'Who are you?' said the dark spirit.

Craw stood guard. 'We are free spirits; we have beaten the *shudder* and we are seeking help.'

'And you are many?'

'We are many.' Craw answered with confidence and heard what sounded like a thousand mutters from her tiny band.

'Oh, I am tired—so tired,' said the voice.

'Come to us,' said Craw, and the massive cat heaved its frame into the hideaway.

'It's a female.' Twitcher seemed disappointed.

'Some of the most vicious fighters I've ever known have

been females,' interrupted Piner, 'especially when defending their young.'

Craw moved forward and gently nosed the huge creature.

'You really are friends?' said the black one.

Craw nosed her again. 'Have you had the *shudder*?'

The black cat sat dejectedly on her haunches. 'I don't know. I was ill, I could only whisper. I trembled when it wasn't cold. Now... I know I feel different.'

'You are with us. You are a thinker. Tell us how you came to be here.'

'I seem to have been walking for days. I lived at Dawkins—you know Dawkins?'

Craw raised her head up with a weary expression. Dreamer looked puzzled, whilst Twitcher seemed less concerned and more quizzical.

'The Dawkins,' the black cat continued. 'I came from the Dawkins.'

'Which means what?'

'Dawkins,' she repeated. 'They're breeders. Cat breeders. We are special. We were selected for our appearance, our pedigree—that's our background. The father of my babies was the purest of the pure. We've better looks than the standard moggie.'

Craw thought she'd heard the word and didn't like it. 'Moggie? What's a moggie?'

'Moggie is what the breeders call the common cat. The ones out there.'

'Does she mean us?' quizzed Dreamer.

'Please speak,' Craw said irritably.

'I come from Dawkins and I'm a breed, I'm not sure which. The Pawmen—you've heard of them?' There were nods. 'They would visit and visit. There would be angry shouting from the Dawkins people and the Pawmen would go away, but they always came back. One day they came with big digging machines and dug a huge trench around us.

The Dawkins stood in their path, but it made no difference. For us in the pens it didn't matter. We were still cared for by our Provider girls. They would clean us and fuss us and tell us not to worry but as the *shudder* took more of our friends, I saw our girls become more and more tense. Sometimes they cried as the bodies were taken away. But still they cared for me. I was having babies. It was my time. I had six beautiful kittens. We all know they'd leave us and move somewhere else. That's how it is. You can't keep your children forever. They have to grow up and live in homes of new Providers who will care for them.'

She paused and narrowed her eyes. 'Things got worse. More men came and put fencing all around us with tall shining lights. They kept them on all night. It was hard to sleep especially with my babies. They sleep all the time anyway but to get away from the light they would snuggle further and further under me. I didn't mind but it was hard for me to sleep for long. I think that's why on the night it happened I was awake.'

'The night *what* happened?' Piner asked, lost in the tale.

'The night of the darkness,' the black one said quietly.

'Go on,' said Craw. 'We must know!'

'I was dozing. All my babies were tucked underneath me except the thin one. He couldn't find space, he never could. All the lights went out; there was nothing but blackness. Try as I might I could see very little, but I saw the spots of light coming to our pens, heard voices I didn't know. They were new voices, high pitched and excited. I heard the ma Dawkins cry out. Then I knew we were in danger. At that second the Pawmen burst into my pen—my pen. They charged in with sticks and nets and they gathered up all my babies.'

Twitcher let out a cat growl.

'Yes, I fought just like you, fighter,' the black one said. 'But they were many and I was just one. They took my babies, picked them up and threw them in their nets. My thin one was cowering in the corner. I gripped him by the back of his neck and ran this way and that. In the darkness I saw one of my girl Providers lit up by their lights. I ran for her and she took the two of us in her arms. We were in her coat for a few minutes and then she dropped us gently on to some grass. She spoke quietly to me. "Go, Blackie, I can't help you," she said. I ran with my tiny baby in my mouth for the rest of the night and we hid by day. I tried to keep him warm and find food, but he wasn't strong.'

The black one stopped and dropped her head. 'I carried him for another night although he had stopped moving and crying and wouldn't take my milk. Sometimes the weakest of the litter lives and sometimes he dies. He's over there. I've covered him with pine needles.'

Craw went right up to her face and said, 'Show us.' The newcomer uttered a little cry and walked onto the open ground, head bowed. When they reached the spot, they sat in silence until Craw spoke. 'For the sake of this little one, and all the other spirits born and yet to be born, we will fight on. This is why we have to. And, Blackie, we want you on our side. Somehow your story must be told'

It seemed so long that they sat there. Finally, Twitcher turned and began to walk back to the hideaway. He stopped and faced Blackie. 'You are a good fighter—big, strong and frightening. We can use you.'

Dreamer follow Twitcher. 'Next thing to do is find Catskill.'

Piner walked slowly and deliberately behind them. As the three squeezed back in through the tiny rose bush entrance Blackie touched Craw. 'Did he say Catskill?'

'Yes,' Craw nodded. 'We have talked of Catskill and we need the wisdom of this great spirit. We hope it may have some of the answers that we seek. They may save our lives.'

'You don't know.' Blackie raised her face to the full moon. 'The Catskill is no more. That spirit is gone. Some say it was taken by the *shudder*. The town cats who were brought into Dawkins by the Pawmen had talked of the Great Catskill. They all hoped it would visit us in our need. No one has seen the Catskill, and no one has heard its night cry. It is no more.'

Craw felt her fur rise as a chill ran down her spine. Another hope was just lost to them. This great spirit who offered some hope had gone. She suddenly felt very alone in a complicated and frightening world. As she learned more, and her mind thought more, at the same time she realised that she still knew nothing of this world.

Chapter Six: A Leap in the Dark

The hailstones battered on the roof only inches above Nailz' head. The rain and hail had seemed to go on for days. The worst thing about it for Purrl was the ghastly crackle as the ice hit the slates. 'I cannot bear this racket!' she shuddered. 'It is so loud it makes my ears hurt!'

Nailz paused from his nail-biting activity. 'It's driving me daft as well. I can't bear it being cooped up here much longer. I'm going Provider spying.'

The thought of hearing some juicy conversation excited Nailz and his tail rose at the prospect. He had taken to wandering the length of the attic and finding gaps through which he could hear the conversations of the Providers. At one spot, a small hole enabled him to see into the office that the pa Provider used. It was right at the top of the house and almost built into the roof. This was a good spot, as the pa Provider would come up here to work and the ma Provider would bring him tea, slump on the seat and talk about the day or the children or her problems. Nailz felt he was the best-informed member of the household.

The most exciting thing to happen to them since they'd become atticats was when the pa Provider would slowly lift the secret flap after much puffing and panting.

As Nailz began his wander, he heard the muttering of voices and saw the tiny beam of light that meant the flap was open.

'Don't you dare!' hissed a voice in the half-light. Purrl was standing next to him. 'I've told you there is no point in trying to make a break for it. You'll get nowhere.'

The pa Provider was doing his kitty talk and reaching

for the bits tray with one hand. Nailz wasn't quite sure what had happened but as the box was picked up there was a terrific crash and a loud shout from the pa Provider. Nailz rushed to the now gaping hole and saw the pa Provider lying flat on his back covered in bits and pieces from the tray.

'Oh my God, I've got it in my hair!' he wailed. He was wiping his face and spitting as if he knew he'd swallowed something dreadfully unpleasant. Nailz eyes adjusted to the bright light and he saw his Providers and his best friend. *Samsy Provider*, that's what he called her.

The little girl was giggling at her flailing father who was beginning to stand up. Then she saw the two bright lights of Nailz' eyes. 'My baby's there!' she uttered with an excited cry.

Nailz suddenly felt warm and proud and needed to be beside his friend. In one graceful leap he went straight through the hole, hitting the pa Provider's chest, before he ended up twisting and landing almost gently beside his friend.

Samsy bent down and picked him up. She was the baby of the household, but she knew how to make Nailz go all gooey. He nuzzled up to her as she blew hot air on to his neck. It was the most delightful feeling and she was the only person who'd ever done this to him. It was such a delicious sensation.

'Put him down,' the pa Provider said. He stood up, brushing off the box bits from his front.

'No daddy. He's my baby.' Samsy cuddled Nailz to her chest, which he found almost unbearable; it had been so long since he'd been loved like this.

'Sam. Put him down.' Her father spoke in the singsong voice that worried Nailz. 'I know it's Nailz, and you know we're hiding him—but he might not be well, and he might infect you. So just put him down please no touching and then wash your hands like you've been told.'

'Oh, daddy!' Samsy protested.

'We've explained what's happening. You know from what they've said at school that we have to be careful. We shouldn't be hiding them in the house. Give him to me and let me put him back in the attic.'

'Oh, daddy, just a minute!'

Nailz realised he had been given a chance. Having been locked up for days he couldn't take any more. It was time to get fresh air, scratch the soil, wander about aimlessly, be free. Nailz did a quick twist and hit the ground running. Once down the steep flight of stairs from the top level, he did a sharp left onto the half-landing and then another left onto the final drop. He knew this run so well. He hit the flap at some speed, and everything went black.

There was a long pause until Samsy said, 'Daddy, he's dead.'

'I don't think so, darling.'

As Nailz felt the spinning hallway come into focus it was already too late. Jack, the eldest son, had picked him up and was trying to look into his eyes. 'His eyeballs are spinning round.' Jack lifted Nailz up to his chest.

'Oh no!' cried Samsy. 'What does that mean?'

The pa Provider attempted to bring calm to the scene. 'They are not spinning, Jack.'

'Well, they're pretty wild and crazy.'

'They are not!' Samsy shouted. 'Daddy, tell him they're not.'

'Jack, this isn't funny. Give him to me.'

At this Nailz took his chance and bolted again.

'The kitchen door!' Nailz heard the words and changed direction. He had been headed towards the French windows in the sitting room.

'He heard you, Dad!' shouted Jack.

Nailz aimed his whole frame at the kitchen back door. Once again, he felt this dreadful shock as his body hit the glass.

'He's trying to get out!' Jack shouted, running towards him.

Almost at the same time, Samsy, in total distress, ran into the room and shouted directly at Nailz, 'Somebody has opened the cat flap!' Everyone turned and stared at her. Her father bunched his eyebrows. 'Somebody,' she said very deliberately, 'has opened the cat flap.'

Nailz did not need another invitation. He did a double side-step underneath the pa Provider's legs, skidded past Jack and as he went through the door, he was sure that Samsy closed it behind him.

The shouting was loud and fierce, but this time Nailz had hit the flap and was in the open. *Freedom!* he thought. *I've done it!* He ran and ran and ran blindly, with no thought at all. Something just drove him on and on and on into the blackness of the night.

***

At the house chaos still reigned. 'Who opened that flap?' shouted the Pa Provider.

Purrl heard Samsy crying, Jack protesting his innocence and the ma Provider trying to comfort everyone. 'It doesn't matter how it happened,' she said. 'He's gone for the moment.' 'But what about...?' Purrl could hear nothing but the banging of several heels on several stairs and there was the ma Provider beneath the secret panel in the ceiling 'Stay there, baby.' She lifted a bowl up to the remaining atticat. Purrl sniffed the tasty dish of what seemed like very fresh meat and not cat's food. Even though she was desperately worried about what had happened to Nailz she couldn't resist the temptation of the meaty morsels. The ma Provider gently lowered the flap while still cooing comfortingly.

As the complete darkness enveloped Purrl she suddenly felt terribly alone. However, much she'd argued with Nailz she'd never wanted to be on her own. She needed some titbit of information she might just hear about the whereabouts of Nailz. She trailed around his listening spots and the points that he used to peer into the light from the rooms below. There was nothing to be heard except the inconsolable sobbing of Samsy.

'I'll find him,' the pa Provider announced. With that a door banged. This dramatic statement didn't seem to comfort Samsy very much who continued snuffling and Purrl felt even more miserable.

***

Meanwhile, Nailz was sitting in somewhere very dark and damp. He'd run like such a maniac that he'd taken sharp evasive turns and had run up one tree so high that he was completely giddy. Then, on his way down, he'd fallen from the branches and landed heavily on some leaves. He didn't stop to check if he was hurt but scattered off blindly in another direction, his final kick sending the pile of leaves spiralling into the air. As they drifted to the ground Nailz was gone again at full pelt towards a small hole underneath a fence.

It was then he found himself in a dark place. The hole hadn't been under the fence but led into a sort of building— a ruined building, definitely not a home like *his* home. At the thought, Nailz felt some harrowing pangs of regret. What had he done? He wanted to bury his head in his paws. He knew he wasn't like one of those cats he sometimes met on a dark night when he'd sneaked out. They were cats who lived by their wits, who found food from nowhere and survived in this harsh world. Nailz wanted to cry like he'd heard and seen Samsy cry, but he couldn't quite manage it.

'I'll go back,' he said out loud and frightened himself a little more. 'I'll go back this time and then it'll be all right.'

Feeling a little braver, he ventured out of the ruined structure and saw that it was at the bottom of a large garden. 'I know this,' he said with confidence. Talking out loud was making him seem quite courageous. 'Right. My road is behind this house, just round the front across the garden.'

Nailz set off at a cracking pace, pausing only to avoid a large garden gnome holding a fishing rod. 'Sorry!' He was brimming with confidence. He went around the house but stopped suddenly. There was no road. It was nowhere to be seen. There was a sort of a narrow lane. His confidence drained away in a second. Now he couldn't go home. He had no idea where he was. He was a stray, and someone would see him and give him up to the Pawmen!

There seemed no point in going on. At least he had a hiding place. So, he rushed back to the garden ruin in case anyone saw him.

It was just as he arrived that he saw the fox. He knew these ginger demons didn't like cats. They didn't seem to like anything very much and Nailz knew enough about self-defence to understand that a tree provided the best form of protection.

The fox stopped and eyed Nailz. Foxes were like dogs but were different. They had minds of their own and they lived in the wild. The fox tilted its head. Nailz feared the fox might be considering an attack. As he watched, it broke into a run and Nailz reacted by seeking out the nearest tree. 'Why is there never a good climbing tree at hand when you want one' he heard himself yelling.

He hit the first tree he saw and managed to dislodge several apples that were waiting to be picked. The apples cascaded to the ground and several bounced in the direction of the fox. It seemed distracted by the tumbling fruit but then ran to the tree where it could see Nailz cowering.

Nailz scuffed at another apple, which bounced on the head of the ginger beast. 'Catch that one!' he shouted. At the challenge the fox stood up on its front paws and craned its neck to see where Nailz was hiding. A sudden fear gripped him. While he had always understood that foxes couldn't climb trees, this apple tree had a ready route to the top—a leisurely climb in cat terms. The fox stood away from the tree and made an awful sound that frightened

Nailz. He moved higher into the branches, dislodging some more apples. He was so high up he'd lost sight of the fox and hoped that if he was hidden from view than the fox would think he'd been somehow spirited away.

From his lofty perch and through the leaves, he saw the fox wildly running towards the same hole in the fence Nailz had come through earlier. Surely the hunter was now the hunted. But by whom? He could see no one. Then another fear crossed Nailz' mind. 'A dog,' he heard himself say. He knew that foxes were frightened of dogs. Some cats said they hunted foxes in packs. Nailz wasn't sure but he could believe anything of dogs. This, however, did not serve to reassure him. If it was a dog his position was still precarious.

It was just as he was contemplating his next move that he heard a voice below him. 'Are you the scaredy-cat?'

Nailz didn't like the sound of this. 'What?'

'Are you the scaredy-cat? We've been watching one dash around like a headless chicken that a fox has failed to finish off.'

'I am just lost.' Nailz tried to see the source of the voice.

The voice moved in the darkness and seemed closer. 'I've never seen a cat dash around so fast and change directions so many times.'

Nailz prepared himself for a fight and as he tightly gripped the tree, he wished he had sharpened his nails for the forthcoming scrap.

'Are you frightened, spirit?' the voice asked. It still seemed threatening.

'I'm lost. I told you. Who are you? Where are you? What do you want?' Nailz hoped his questions sounded as if he was in control and that the stranger would not hear his heart as it beat furiously.

'Too many questions for a scaredy-cat, eh boys?' Through the gloom Nailz heard other voices agreeing with the ringleader. 'Come on, scaredy-cat, don't make us chase you off the tree.'

Nailz turned and saw the bright eyes that were owned by the menacing voice. The spirit had somehow managed to move above Nailz without making a sound. 'Have you had the *shudder*?' said the voice.

'I don't know.'

'Can you think? Have you learned? Do you hear or are you a mad cat in the first stages of the *shudder*?'

The questions came fast and furious and Nailz' head was spinning. He remembered he and Purrl had both been very ill a few weeks ago but nothing more than that. 'We were a bit poorly. My dad Tiggr was taken with the *shudder*. He died.'

Nailz heard one of them muttering. 'You're telling me your dad was the dreaded Tiggr? The best whacker on the road?'

'Yes,' said Nailz, almost timidly.

Another voice came from below. 'Let him down Tel, he's one of us.'

A paw tapped Nailz on the nose, almost gently. 'Go on, you're all right.'

Slowly, Nailz negotiated the gnarled twists and turns of the apple tree. He was always much better at going up than coming down. As he reached the final turn, he saw two faces beaming up at him but as Nailz prepared himself to fight he could see he didn't need to. They were welcoming him, tails raised.

From above Nailz' tormentor—*Tel*, the other one had called him—took one huge leap in the dark and landed beside him perfectly. He was a cat with great stripes that seemed to stretch across the whole of his body. He nosed Nailz, who tried to respond but was still feeling apprehensive. 'Do we seem familiar to you?'

Nailz peered hard in the dark but although he was sure that he'd never met this band before there was something oddly familiar about them.

'You don't get it, do you?'

This was all very confusing for Nailz. 'Get what?'

'Tiggr was our dad too.'

As he looked over them, Nailz realised that all three had Tiggr's tell-tale stripes. 'But how?'

'He wasn't always in your house,' Tel said. 'He was all over, was Tiggr. He'd been everywhere, whacked cats all over and then your Providers took him in, and he gave up the wandering. Our mother met Tiggr at the canal bridge. She was always a bit misty about it. What a reputation he had! We lived on the road by the old canal. Our mum says her Provider was totally shocked when she produced us three. The Provider thought she'd been cut.'

Nailz was confused again. 'Cut? You mean... hurt?'

'No, cut so you can't have babies. The Providers think we've got no self-restraint. Well, we have now. So, welcome, brother! We are the three musketeers.'

'The what? The musketeers?'

'Don't get into this,' said the smaller female. 'When Tel realised, he could think he decided the best way to learn was to watch the box—the big black box with the pictures. He'd watch everything. Our Provider got quite suspicious. We had to make him half-close his eyes when he lay on her lap to watch things. *Musketeers* is telly talk. He's learned everything he knows from that box, including the letters.'

The third musketeer cut in. 'Our Provider got really suspicious when he learned how to change the pictures.'

'Now that was smart,' came back Tel. 'I watched for days before I tried it. You just push the buttons on the button pusher. It's easy.'

'Easy, yes,' the female said, 'but she got really angry when she was watching something, and you'd go all stretchy and change to the ball game. Tel likes ball games!'

'Well, there's masses to watch,' Tel said testily.

'Yes, but you started to do it to wind her up. He'd go all gooey on her lap and then press the button with a nail.

She'd change it back and he'd do it again. She'd move the button pusher to another part of the room and then he'd get up and sit on it and roll over. The pictures would change every time he moved. Sometimes she'd give in and let him have what he wanted on. Then he'd stop messing about. She used to look at us and say, "He's doing this on purpose, isn't he, babies?" In the end we knew we would be handed over to the Pawmen, so we had to leave.'

'So,' Tel broke in, sounding bored with the story, 'the Three Musketeers is a story about three people working together for the good of everybody. And now we're the Four Musketeers, since you've joined us.'

'Have I?' said Nailz. 'Have I joined you?'

'Well, have you got a better idea? Don't forget we frightened off the fox!' Tel turned tail and stopped. 'Do you have a better idea?'

Nailz had to admit he didn't have any kind of idea. 'But don't you know my Provider's home? Can you take me there?'

Tel smirked. 'Course we can. Since we've been free spirits we've been all over, even to the big house with the three towers.'

'We can guide you,' the female said, 'but can you go back? Dare you go back?'

'Yes, I can. I can, and I do. Our Providers had made us the atticats. We were hidden in the attic—me and Purrl.'

'Who's Purrl?'

'Purrl is my sister.' Nailz stood up. 'Purrl is my sister and Tiggr's last baby and I've got to get her out.'

But isn't she safe in hiding?' The third striped spirit gazed quizzically at Nailz.

'I've got to get her out. Will you help me? All of you?'

'We can try,' Tel said as he moved into the middle of the group. 'These are my sisters and I wouldn't leave them behind when our time was up.'

'You called them boys.'

'He always calls us boys,' the third musketeer said. 'He wanted our mother to give him brothers. But she didn't. I'm Skoot and she's Toot.'

Tel turned towards Nailz. 'She runs, and she bellows,' he explained. 'It's a good combination. Come on; we'll share our eats and you can tell us more about what happened at your Providers home.'

At that Tel put his front leg right over Nailz's shoulder and winked at him. 'Good trick, that. Come on.' The four of them moved quickly to the right of the garden. Nailz followed them up on to a pile of garden rubbish and from there onto a small shelf that led to the back of a wooden hut.

***

Inside the house Samsy had not stopped sobbing.

'Now what's the matter with her?' Robin asked. 'Lyn, I've tried to explain. I've really tried to find Nailz, but it is difficult and it's so dark. I can't see a thing.'

'Come on, darling,' her mother said. 'Daddy has tried. He'll go out with a torch later and search for your little baby. Don't forget, we've still got one upstairs.' She brushed the hair out of her eyes. 'Robin, she's burning up. Feel her.'

Robin moved in close beside the snuffling little girl. He reached down and touched her cheek. He could instantly feel the heat of her skin. She was running a real temperature. 'Isn't that the first symptom of "you know what"?'

'You can't jump to conclusions.' Samsy's mother pointed to the other room. 'Get that symptoms list the man brought round.'

Within a minute he was back with the paper that described the dangerous condition. As he read through the list, he seemed more and more concerned. 'She has been very miserable and dejected in the last few days, hasn't she?'

'Yes, but that was because she missed being with the cats, wasn't it?'

Robin stood up and reached for the phone. 'I'm going to ring for the doctor. I want someone out here, *now*.'

'Oh, Robin—we haven't opened her up to the infection, have we?'

'Well, we don't know that. But we can't take the chance.'

***

Purrl was sitting in the dark, feeling sorry for herself and missing Nailz. She never thought she'd miss his incessant gnawing, but she did. After a time, she heard a voice that she didn't recognise speaking to the pa Provider. Quickly, Purrl moved through the roof to the small spy point near Samsy's room.

She could just make out the pa Provider and the newcomer. 'So, what do you think, Doctor?' Purrl could hear the tension in his voice.

'Difficult to say until we get the results of the tests. She's got a temperature and seems a little restless. I've never seen an example of the human form of the condition, yet these are early days, but we have to strike quickly. This fear of the infection jumping the species from cat to human has yet to be proven and is about to be tested We'll keep a close eye on her and I'll run the tests tomorrow. I presume it would be safer to ensure that she doesn't have any contact with cats, although I suppose it would be unlikely. With the collectors on the streets I imagine there'll be no cats on the loose.'

Purrl knew this was bad news but she did feel sorry for Samsy. Had she and Nailz given a sickness to the little girl? But as she sat in the dark staring at the pinprick of light, she feared that she might never see Nailz again if her Providers gave her over to the Pawmen.

Just then, she heard a resounding crash above her head,

69

followed by a loud scraping sound and then silence. Was this the Pawmen breaking their way in?

Purrl heard the pa Provider shout. 'What the hell was that? Sounded like a brick hitting the roof. I'd better check'. The front door closed, and all became quiet.

Purrl wondered if she should plan her break. However, all this rushing about had made her very sleepy, so instead she curled up on the nest the Providers had placed in the attic.

As she slept gruesome images came into her mind. She saw the Pawmen cutting a huge hole in the roof and then a great hand reaching in to pull her out of her hiding place. Then she saw a great metal pole knocking regularly and rhythmically above her head. In her dream she realised that this was the end. The second hole would enable the Pawmen to enter her hiding place and take her.

The silver moonlight made her look upwards. A voice spoke. 'Purrl, up here! Jump up.' She tried to shake away the image in her mind of a Pawmen. She saw Nailz, staring down at her together with the face of Tiggr, her dead father. 'It's me! Come on, I've ruined my nails trying to pull this slate back.'

Purrl wasn't sure how long it had taken for her to realise that Nailz really was above her, and that she was no longer asleep. But how was Tiggr there? She was sure he had died.

'This is Tel,' Nailz said. 'He's our brother—Tiggr was his dad and our dad. Come on, I've told them you're smart! Don't be so dumb.'

Purrl steadied herself and then launched towards at the hole in the roof. At first, she couldn't get a grip on the smooth, slippery tiles and fell backwards.

Nailz was his usual excited self. 'Come on Purrl, run at it!'

She backed along the spine of the attic and leapt into the air. It seemed as if she was airborne for ages. At last, she hit the hole with a force that projected her right through it. For the moment she thought she'd never stop but a cat stood in her way and stopped her tumbling off the roof.

She took a moment to compose herself and gazed at the new cat. 'This is all very well. You got up here, but how do we get down?'

Tel and Nailz peered over the edge of the roof. It seemed they had been clever enough somehow to get on the roof, but the way down was very precarious, and it was just starting to get light.

Tel turned to them. 'If we stay up here, we'll be like sitting ducks.'

'Don't you mean target-practice cats?' said Purrl. In the distance, she saw the Pawman's flashing white lights moving closer and closer, lighting up the roofs around them. Leaping in the dark from this great height would surely be the end!

Chapter Seven: The Glowing Sky

Tom woke suddenly and lay in his bed, listening intently with his eyes wide open. *If you listen hard enough and long enough until it almost hurts, you can always hear something.* He did. *Piner,* he thought. One glance at the clock told him that it was four in the morning. For two dark mornings Tom had woken at the visiting hour, but there had been no sign of his pine-perfumed favourite feline.

Slowly, he crept downstairs trying not to wake his parents. He hurried into the kitchen and then to the back door as he just caught sight of a fast-moving shadow. 'Here, Piney!' The shadow faded to nothing, as if it were a trick of the strange early morning half-light.

Tom went to the cellar and found his night-walking track suit. He kept it in the basement with some trainers ready for any night expeditions. His mind was working overtime as he feared the worst might have happened to Piner. The news last night was full of stories about how their area was one of the biggest 'clusters' of the condition in the city and an exclusion zone had been set up to prevent the spread of the infection. That was why the stray cats had to be hunted down.

Tom knew that meant Piner and his friends.

He gently unlocked the back door and wandered into the garden. Although their house backed onto the road, it was positioned quite high on the hill and from the rear of the house he could see far into the distance. Tom sometimes sat in the attic room at the top of the house and stared out at the surrounding landscape. It was a great view.

He wandered the garden, searching in every one of Piner's favourite spots, but the cat was nowhere to be found. Tom went back into the house. He couldn't sleep, so he sat in the darkness staring at a solitary tree and the lights in the distance.

Turning towards the glowing light from his computer screen he tried to log into the website that was supporting the anti-cat-clearance campaign, but it had been taken down again. His mother had joined the Cat's Protection League and went to their meetings—it seemed to mean they were now being targeted by the cat clearance people and the local authority.

Tom opened the window and hung out to look in the direction of Piner's hiding place, wondering if he should go there again and see if he had come back. On the horizon, he could just make out a glow—not artificial, but a golden glow, low in the sky. Tom was unsure about what it might be, but then he realised it was coming from Dawkins place, the cat breeders. A hideous thought ran through his mind and all he knew was that he had to get there.

He crept back out of the house and set off along the lane, and then down onto the Tamworth Road. He couldn't be sure how long the darkness would hold. It was a black morning and perhaps that was why he'd been able to see the glowing light in the sky.

As he moved down the Whittington Road with the golf course and the forces medical HQ to his right, he heard the low growl of a heavy vehicle coming from behind. Without thinking, Tom scurried off the road onto the small path that tracked around the golf course. Moments later, he was in the trees and not visible from the road.

It was a strange configuration of lights that lit up the road. *Not a car or a truck*, he thought. The vehicle sped up with a sudden surge. As it passed him, Tom saw that it was an armoured vehicle, a troop carrier like the ones you see on TV and in films. Its heavy-throated engine roared past but Tom didn't feel reassured. *You never see these vehicles on the road—why now?*

Tom waited in the trees to see if a second was its way. Once it was clear, he decided against following Whittington Road towards Dawkins. Instead, he cut across to the other lane that by passed the cattery. It would be better than following the same route as the soldiers.

There was only one house on the lane and that belonged to the Passmores. He'd been there several times. It stood a little way back from the road, so he didn't think they'd see him and there probably wouldn't be anyone up at this time anyway.

Once he was in front of the house, he saw a figure like Victoria Passmore in the window. *She must be awake,* he thought, *and might be able to help.* He knew Victoria was on his side and she was very sensible. He suddenly felt very lonely in the dark perhaps Victoria knew something about the glow in the sky coming from Dawkins. He reached down to the gravel immediately under Victoria's bedroom, picked up a hand full of small stones and threw them at her window.

In the gloom Tom stood back and found himself falling as he tripped on the low wall by the pond in the front garden. He fell flat behind the wall and hit his elbow on the stone. As he peered slowly over the wall, he saw Mr Passmore, Victoria's dad, peering through the curtains. If he hadn't fallen Tom would have been clearly visible from the bedroom. He ducked back, scraping his elbow again on the wall then lay still for some minutes before peeping up at the window. The curtains were drawn back, and he was safe. It had been a stupid idea and he would have to go on alone.

He felt a hand on his shoulder. He'd been caught!

'What on earth are you doing?' a voice came out of the darkness.

'Just walking,' Tom said as he was blinded by torchlight.

Victoria Passmore switched off her lamp. 'What do you mean just walking? You nearly gave me a heart attack.'

'I thought it was your dad.'

Victoria pulled Tom towards the small tree shading the kitchen. 'What about my dad?'

'Well, he appeared after I threw stones at your window.' Tom pointed up.

'My *parents'* bedroom window, you twit!'

Tom could see that Victoria was dressed. 'A mistake! I'm sorry. I shouldn't have done it. But I couldn't sleep and then I saw the glow in the sky, and I was nearly run down by the army and—'

'It was the army that woke me up!' Victoria interrupted. 'They've had things going up and down the road to Dawkins practically all night. I got dressed to go up to the field to see my horse. She'd hate all this racket.'

Tom gripped Victoria's arm. 'But what about the glow?'

Victoria looked away. 'I don't know. My dad wasn't happy last night, and he was talking to my mum—he said, "Don't let Victoria know, she'll be upset." But I still don't know.'

'I've got to find out,' Tom insisted. 'That's why I'm here. Piner hasn't visited me for three nights and I want to know what's happened to him. I thought we could go back to the hiding place but then I saw the glow and wanted to know what it was!'

'What's with the "we"?' said an unconvinced Victoria.

'You will come with me, won't you? Maybe something horrendous is going on. I need another witness in case no one will believe me!'

Victoria pulled Tom to the front of the drive. 'All right, but I must check out Maisie on the way back—I don't want her to be too spooked.'

At a slow jog they reached the lane that led to Dawkins. As they moved above the first rise Tom felt Victoria pull on his arm again. 'It's there,' she said. The red glow in the sky seemed to grow with each step they took towards the edge of the cattery.

Tom was hardly aware that their pace had increased until they were at the edge of the Dawkins premises. 'Where now?' he asked. He'd never been this close before. It was a good thing Victoria was here—she knew this area so well because she trekked all over on Maisie.

'This is the main gate,' she said, 'but there's a sign on it. What does it say?'

Tom peered at the sign. 'It says: '*This is a prohibited place under the Official Secrets Act, 1911-1989. Unauthorised persons entering this area may be arrested and prosecuted. Ministry of Defence.*' He backed away from the gate. 'That is frightening.'

Well, we won't go through it, then. If we back round through the old lane and in through the small kissing gate we can say we never saw a thing.'

'You seem very confident,' Tom replied. 'But they must know about the gate.'

'No chance—it's almost totally overgrown, but it is surprising what you can see from the back of a horse. Come on.' Victoria led him further along the lane, this time going down the gentle hill towards Whittington. When she stopped Tom could see nothing but a thick hedge. 'There you go.'

One minute Victoria was in front of him and the next she'd disappeared. 'Where are you?' Tom hissed. He couldn't tell where she'd gone.

'Here, silly.'

Tom could hear Victoria but couldn't see a thing. Then, rather like the Cheshire cat, her grinning face appeared like a floating ghost. 'That *is* frightening,' Tom repeated. He squeezed through the hedge between the rusty railings of the old kissing gate.

Something more frightening met his gaze as he pulled himself through the gate and watched the bright light in the sky. Victoria stared upwards, mouth wide open. 'No—no!'

Tom could see several soldiers outlined in the red light.

Their guns were clearly visible, held in front of their bodies, ready for action. In front of them was a bonfire. It stretched fifty yards at least and was three times the height of a man. Tom could feel the warmth on his face even at this distance.

One of the soldiers turned in their direction. 'Down!' Tom said. He grabbed Victoria they both dropped down to the ground.

'What does it mean?' she asked, shaking her head. She seemed in a state of shock.

'It's a pyre. They're burning something.' Tom slowly stood up and moved forward a few yards. Breathing deeply, he could smell burning hair, a sweet cooking scent in the air. Into the flames a man pushed a long metal pole as if he was stoking a fire.

It was then Tom saw the flaming bodies of cats— hundreds of cats.

He turned around unable to watch any longer. Shaking his head, he said, 'They're burning the cats. They're destroying them.'

Victoria squeezed his arm. 'Listen, listen!'

Tom heard a chorus of cat cries, regular and insistent. The breeding pens and rooms of the cattery were at the back of the yard, within sight of the fire. In the flickering flames Tom could see cats pacing around, crying separately and then in unison.

Victoria set off, walking briskly down the field below the brow of the small hill. It took him a moment to catch up with her. 'What are you doing?'

'I'm letting them out,' she said.

'How can we? There are soldiers there.'

Victoria ignored him and resumed her walk, and he had to follow her. She obviously knew the terrain and took advantage of the cover as she moved towards the cat pens.

'We can't get any closer. They'll spot us.'

'They're far too busy managing the fire and chatting,' Victoria retorted. They aren't expecting anyone here.

There's the cat killer.'

Tom could just make out the features of Mr Cairns, who thought he'd killed Piner. Suddenly, Tom felt angry and was no longer frightened at all. 'So, how can we get in and how can we get them out?' He crawled along the ground to within a few feet of the pens.

'There has to be a catch or a lock.'

Tom felt his heart skip a beat as he saw a torchlight shine on the pens. 'Oh no,' he said.

'It's mine, silly. But what about the locks?' Victoria's torch lit up the solid wooden back doors of the pens and the large locks positioned every several feet.

Tom picked up a stone as if to try and break one open.

'They'll hear us!' Victoria stood up straight. 'Let's check first. You work that end. I'll start here. They can't see us—we're behind the sheds and they're managing the fire.'

Tom ran to the end of the sheds and pulled the first lock. It was solid, as was the second and the third. He rattled the fourth far too vigorously and he saw Victoria duck down at the rattling sound. Tom ducked instinctively and dropped onto the damp grass.

Victoria sounded frustrated. 'This isn't any good—they're all solidly locked. We'll have to go back and tell people. I always carry my phone but not tonight.'

'But you said your dad already knows!'

'Well, I think he does,' Victoria countered.

'How can this be for the good of cats? Burning them! I can't believe that is right. Why didn't they announce it properly?' At that Tom kicked the grass and hit something hard. 'Ow! What is that?'

'It's a lock. Did you pull it off when you ducked down'?

Tom was mystified. 'Perhaps I did.'

They both heard a scraping sound, turned towards the sheds and could see the door pushing open. First one cat appeared. Then others followed: ten, fifteen, twenty—it became a rush as they followed the leader, tails in the air and without a glance behind. They gathered speed, hitting the hedge with such pace it created a whooshing sound as they went through the leaves and twigs.

They stood watching in astonishment at the mass break out. 'I can't count how many have gone through,' Tom said. He felt something sharp grip into his thigh. He winced but didn't make a sound.

Victoria pointed. 'You're being attacked!'

Tom immediately recognised Piner's snubby nose. 'Piner! I thought you'd been caught.'

Piner stood back and seemed to shrug his shoulders, as if to say, 'Of course I was caught. Where do you think I've been?'

Tom picked up Piner and gave him a huge hug.

'Tom.' Victoria was pulling at his sleeve. 'Time to go! They'll spot it's gone strangely silent.'

'Piner, are you coming home?'

Piner tilted his head as he often did. It was just a catty thing.

'Tom, he's got to go, and we must too!' There was a loud shout followed by a gunshot. 'They've spotted something. Come on, we've got to go!'

Tom followed Victoria, still clutching Piner who was trying to get onto the ground.

'Put him down and follow me,' Victoria ordered.

Reluctantly, Tom put Piner down and the cat turned towards him. It sat back on its haunches and looked right and left, almost theatrically.

'What on earth is it doing?' said Victoria. 'Come on, don't let him show you his silly tricks. We're out of here!'

'He wants help.'

'And so will we if we don't get a move on!'

In a flash Victoria had gone and so had Piner. Tom was alone. Several voices could be heard close at hand and he realised he was very vulnerable. A second later, Victoria did her bodiless head trick again over a low bush. 'This way!'

she shouted insistently.

They got through the gate and ran down the lane running as if their lives were at stake. Victoria headed down a ditch about fifty yards along the soggy floor and then over a gate into another field. They ran alongside a hedge for a hundred yards or so until they both collapsed into a heap.

'Where are we?' Tom panted.

'Maisie,' she said pointing at the stable that had been created out of some kind of upturned container from a lorry. 'Quick, in there.'

Tom squeezed through the big wooden door into the stable. It smelled of horse and straw. Tom wasn't a great horse fan but at this moment he could have kissed Maisie.

The two of them slumped into a bale of hay that helped form a stall for the horse. It seemed minutes before either of them could speak although Tom gradually realised it was almost completely light. 'It's nearly morning. I'll have to get home, or I'll be in dire trouble. What day is it tomorrow?'

'It *is* tomorrow, silly,' said Victoria. 'It's Saturday. Does your house get up at five o'clock on Saturday?'

Of course, not but what do we do? Do we tell people about the burning? Do we tell people about the killing?'

'And do we tell people that we let the other cats get away? What will happen about that? I've heard it's a five thousand pound fine and prison. We can't admit to it. Should we have done it?'

'Yes, Victoria, we had to. We couldn't let them kill the others. There's nothing wrong with them. Piner is smarter. He's really clever. Why did he stop? He spotted me, and he knew I'd got him out.'

'I don't know. It sounds a bit odd to me, Tom. More importantly, what if we've been responsible for letting diseased cats loose? I know it seems wrong to kill them and burn them, but what if they really are diseased?' Victoria sighed. 'I didn't tell you about little Samsy.'

'What about her?'

'Her family put their cats in the attic. She called them the "atticats". I suppose they invented the name. The cat killers came, but the cats were really well hidden, and her mum and dad wouldn't tell them where they were.' Victoria stood up. 'I went to see her, and she'd been taken to hospital. Her brother Jack says they think it's the cat thing.'

'You mean she's caught something from her cats?'

Victoria stared down at her shoes. 'I don't know, but that's what's being said. I think they'll lock us up if they find out what we did.'

Tom felt helpless. Had they done the wrong thing?

The silence was broken only by the horse shifting on its legs in the confined space. Suddenly, there was a massive light shining on them. Tom was blinded, and the horse was neighing and snorting loudly.

An aggressive voice shouted loudly, 'Down, down! Don't move!'

Tom felt himself almost lifted off the ground and then turned over in the hay. His hands were pulled behind his back. He was aware of a squeal as Victoria was forced on her face beside him.

The voice spoke firmly and calmly. 'It's just a couple of kids, Sarge.' Tom could hear a message coming through a radio, crackling and urgent in tone. The close voice spoke again. 'Right, you could be in serious trouble. Move!'

Tom and Victoria were hoisted into the air and bundled into the metal vehicle Tom had seen earlier. Three soldiers with blackened faces confronted them. No one spoke.

The vehicle shuddered into life, leaving the dark red sky behind them. It was then Tom glimpsed Piner by the roadside staring upwards with a little lost look.

Tom sat in the truck fearing he had lost Piner for good this time.

Chapter Eight: Cat Counterattack

Craw aimed her body towards the high shelf. She knew she had to escape, but a man with a huge pole was in her way and it was about to smash onto her head. Distracted for a moment, she missed the shelf by an inch and fell. Her body twitched, and she reached out with her paws but touched nothing.

The sudden jolt woke her up.

Each time she fell asleep she would dream a dream. This time the Great Catskill appeared to her as a huge spirit with its coat specked with blood. It was unlike any cat she'd ever seen. It pointed a paw at the three towers in the city and as it did, so Craw saw cats in their thousands sitting behind him gazing up at the tallest tower. She knew they were supporting her, and she felt overwhelmingly happy.

'You had a good day's dreaming,' Dreamer said. He was lying on his stomach at Craw's side and staring through the rose bush entrance.

'I'm awake?' Craw pushed out her paw to make sure.

'You certainly are. You were breathing like a noisy kettle. Then you'd do more of the dreamer stuff—twitching and moving. I could see you were dreaming. I am the expert after all.' Dreamer turned to Craw. 'Don't worry. Twitcher and Blackie, our new friend, took turns on watch. Twitcher organised a time for each of us to sleep and then act as guard. He left you out because you'd already gone to sleep. We know you haven't slept for days!'

'You should have woken me. I can stand my turn.'

'Craw, we need you alert. You may be our thinker, but everyone needs to dream. It's something cats have to do. It helps us relax, work things out, see how things really are and even how they aren't. Dreams repair us, so I hope you enjoyed yours.'

Craw stood up and stretched. 'Not altogether. I dreamed Catskill was still alive even though his hair was long and messy—not like a well-groomed spirit.' She lifted her rear paw from the ground and slowly pushed it as far away from her body as she could until it was practically parallel with her back. 'There is no Catskill. We have to rely on ourselves. As for the dreams—they're all over. We've got to move tonight and find a new hiding place. Somewhere safe and away from the Providers, but somewhere we can plan and think and get in touch with the other free spirits. Perhaps there are thousands out there waiting for a plan and we must come up with one.'

'Thousands.' Dreamer smiled. 'Thousands—what does thousands mean?'

Craw didn't know exactly. 'I'm not sure. I dreamt it. Thousands means many, many, many cats. It's a number, a big number—a word to describe a massive number. *Thousands.*'

'I like it,' responded Dreamer. 'Thousands, thousands and thousands.' He seemed to love just repeating the word. 'Thousands, thousands of free spirits all together. You couldn't ignore that, could you?'

'You couldn't,' agreed Craw.

'And you dreamed all that and the thousands bit?'

Craw was beginning to wish she hadn't told him now. 'Well, yes. Perhaps it's a Provider's word.'

'I'll be losing my position as dreamer-in-chief if you get going. Still, I'm glad you had the dream. Thousands of cats. Imagine it. That's really lifted my spirits.'

All this conversation had caused everyone else to wake up. As the ritual stretching and yawning was going on, the excited Dreamer related Craw's dream to everyone. 'Thousands of free spirits, cats as far as you can see!' he said. 'Thousands and thousands of them. You really couldn't ignore that, could you?'

Twitcher perked up as if something had just occurred to him. 'Yes, imagine thousands all marching together. What a sight that would be! Wouldn't that make people stop and think?'

Craw felt things were getting out of hand and she didn't want the reputation of being seen as the new Dreamer. 'Hold on! Think of today. We have to move and find another hiding spot. Food first, then we set off.'

A rustle and a crackling of dried leaves caused them all to freeze as if in a tableau. Craw sniffed the air and sensed the unmistakable odour of pine. 'Piner? Is that you?'

Piner rushed into the space puffing and wheezing. 'You won't believe it!' he said. 'This beastly machine has eaten my little Provider and his friend.' The words tumbled out of him but at least he was alive and back with them.

'Piner, what are you gabbling about?'

'My Provider and his friend, the one I've been visiting and trying to get him to understand. There was a breakout from the place where the spirits were locked up—many of them ran out as fast as they could.'

'Thousands?' said Dreamer.

'Well, lots and lots,' Piner explained. 'It was horrible, and some spirits were crushed by the moving machine.'

Craw sensed she might get the full story when Piner had relaxed and perhaps had something to eat. Things were moving so quickly. She gently pushed Piner with her paw. 'Something to eat, you lunatic adventurer?' She nodded at Twitcher who went back to the box which he held the box in his teeth and with one huge effort launched it into the air. As it spun in the darkness a shower of crunchy morsels hit them all over their bodies.

'It's raining biscuits!' yelled Piner. Twitcher attacked the box again like a cat possessed, swinging it wildly and then heaving it across their hideaway. The drizzle of biscuits became a positive storm and cats were jumping to catch some in the air or gobbling the debris on the ground. Twitcher became even more creative. He would lie flat on his stomach, stalk the box, grip the cardboard flap with his teeth, swing it into the air then sit back and watch the excited rushing round of his comrades.

Finally, Twitcher's efforts caused the box to split and the remaining contents of the container poured onto the floor. It was a veritable feast. There seemed more than enough for everyone as they took their fill.

'I'm as full as a stuffed cat,' Piner said. His stomach seemed to be dragging on the floor. For a moment they all felt happy and content. Dreamer closed his eyes as he always did after a good fill.

'Dreamer!' Craw snapped irritably. 'No time for sleeping. We're all fed but we must get on the move. We can't stay here any longer. Not after this breakout from the camp. The Pawmen will be after all of us.'

Craw forced them to realise they were going to have to go, leave the safety of this nest and take their chances in the dangerous open. The fun and the feast were over. Blackie was the first to move through the rose patch into the outside—she was the most restless.

Twitcher took up his role as head of tactics. 'Now, let's form up!'

Craw knew that whenever Twitcher assumed command Piner would run to right and left and in front of the gathered group. Then he would drop flat to the floor winking his eyes showing how alert he was.

'Scout in position!' yelled Twitcher.

Scout? thought Craw. *Where did that come from?* Words seemed to be falling on them faster than the crunchy biscuits from the air.

'Cover flanks!' was the second command. Dreamer stood behind Piner and drifted from right to left to show he understood.

'Back up!'

Craw slotted sedately into her given role at the rear of the column.

'Front up!' ordered Twitcher. Blackie took the lead position. Twitcher then took up his role to Blackie's right and nodded. Progress was essential. At the signal the column emerged out of the pine wood into the unknown.

Craw observed Twitcher constantly checking that they were all performing their roles. All ears were on alert, pricked and turning for the slightest sound. Even the activity of a small vole caused them all to stop. The vole was scrabbling in a hedge and then decided to cross the road. Suddenly the creature stopped in fear thinking its life was about to be cut short. However, these potential vole hunters were interested in other prey and they ignored the tiny trembling thing. Vole history would never be the same again as the small furry beast sauntered in front of its enemy and flicked its tail as if thinking that all cats must have taken leave of their senses.

'That furry crawler would have been a tasty morsel,' Dreamer said, licking his lips.

'No time!' muttered Craw.

The group moved on in formation with everyone following in their designated role.

'Look the terrible light?' Piner, in scouting mode, had kept moving his eyes across the sky. 'There—the awful light!' He held his head up to show to the others what he could see.

Above them was a dying amber light. Even as they watched, the golden colour sank further below the skyline.

'Where's that?' Dreamer asked.

'Always the questioner,' grunted Twitcher.

'I'm just keen to know,' Dreamer replied.

'It's in the Dawkins' direction.' Blackie turned around. 'It *is* Dawkins!'

Craw sensed the tension in Blackie's voice, and

everyone picked up their speed. Their paws, on the hard ground, rattled like a light shower on a tin roof.

They began walking and then followed the pace of Blackie who became more and more agitated as they reached the end of the lane. She looked up to the brow of the hill. 'It's there—Dawkins!'

On their way along the lane they kept their new formation. Anyone stepping out of line was given a sharp rebuke from Twitcher. Their progress was focused and swift.

Suddenly, a dreadful roar rang out. The sound was terrible, and they all felt it in their bones. Their formation was lost as they rushed across the road and found a ditch, a hedge or any hiding place. The noise grew louder and louder. Craw found it so unbearable she wanted to leave her hiding place and run away as fast as she could. Above the rumble, she heard Twitcher shout, 'Still!'

The growling sound hit them like a physical blow. The whole group was driven backwards. Everyone tried to hold their ground but the grass around them blew in their faces. Some backed off but again Twitcher cried, 'Still!'

The roar passed as a massive vehicle trundled alongside them. Craw felt a sense of despair. How could she talk to these people, with their destructive machines?

As she was thinking her miserable thoughts, Twitcher stood high in his ditch and shouted, 'Form up!' Craw was regretting that she'd given him this special control. 'We're going up to the strange glowing light to check it out and then find cover. Okay, Craw?'

Craw nodded, and the band set off, still in formation but with an extra degree of caution that hadn't been there before.

Blackie seemed to be driving the speed; it was as if she wanted to see again what was causing the sky to change colour. They hadn't gone far along the road when she cried out, 'I know it's Dawkins!' she said, desperation in her voice. 'It must still be burning!'

As the others stood their ground, Craw rubbed her cheek against Blackie. 'The worst has already happened there. You must put the horror behind you if you can.'

There was a concerned air amongst the rest of the group. Twitcher pranced up towards the rise of the hill and then rapidly ran back down again. 'I can see men, soldiers, I think. We've got to move away from here. We must find cover.'

Craw stepped aside from Blackie, blinked her eyes and nodded.

'Left and left!' shouted Twitcher. It was as if they'd practised this on the parade ground. They moved in unison in the agreed pattern and held the shape as they moved along the road and into the edge of the golf course.

Twitcher stopped and raised his head in the air. The rough sound of the vehicle was getting louder again. It must have turned and started back in their direction. 'Follow me,' he said.

The small band stepped on to a smooth, level patch of grass. It was finely cut, almost like a nice carpet, and Piner paused to roll over a small hole.

'Come on!' Twitcher hissed. 'Don't fool about! We've got to get through here.' He raised his tail and they went off the green, through some rougher ground and onto a patch of sand.

Craw had always loved this golden stuff. They'd had a whole pit of it in her old home and when she was young, she had loved scratching in it and then crouching down. She was roundly punished for it when she was caught, and her better instincts kept her away from it, but she'd never forgotten the delight of digging in that sand—so easy, so soft, so comfortable.

Craw paused to roll on the scratchy stuff, but then saw Twitcher on the edge of the pit, staring disapprovingly at her. 'We're going into army territory now,' he said. 'I've been here with Bootsie, but it is difficult territory. I'm going to take you through what they call the *trenches.*'

'Why?' Dreamer asked. 'Where are we going? Craw?'

'I think we need to get through the military place and perhaps find Bootsie,' Twitcher replied on her behalf. 'The other part of the place is quiet, there is nothing there. Nothing happens, Bootsie told me, and the local people keep out of the way because they used to make loud bangs there.'

'Well,' Craw said carefully, 'it sounds sensible to me. Any objections? Or better suggestions?'

The silence suggested that no-one had any of either.

'Come on then!' Twitcher was off again. They quickly moved across more greens and a large area of grass until Twitcher suddenly disappeared. Everyone stopped and stared at the nothingness.

'Hold up!' shouted Piner, low on the right. He had flattened himself to the ground and was advancing one paw movement at a time. 'Wait for me.' He crawled with almost imperceptible slowness towards the spot where Twitcher had disappeared. His tail was as flat as his belly and trailed on the ground. Craw couldn't believe that the awkward Piner had suddenly become a great cat stalker.

They all stood in silence and watched, hardly daring to breathe. Piner pointed his right paw, indicating that he wanted his right flank covering. Blackie took up the sign and moved to the right but then disappeared.

Craw's band was vanishing before her eyes. This was a disaster—only Dreamer and Piner were left! She turned sharply to catch Dreamer's eye only to see him leap to his left. Then he was gone as well!

Craw ran from left to right staring ahead all the time. She hurried to the point where Twitcher had first vanished then turned to Piner. Within a second he had gone like the others. Was this some atrocious trap that they'd unwittingly walked into?

Craw listened very carefully. She could hear nothing. There was silence. For a moment she wanted to cry out. She couldn't let her friends go so easily. What should she do? *What would the great Catskill do?*

Craw thought narrowed her eyes. She would wait in silence. Craw knew that was right and lifted her head up with her ears on alert.

At first, she heard a rough scratching from her right. Then more scratching came from her left. Somewhere in the centre there wasn't so much a scratching as a scuffling. A moment later, all this scrabbling sounded like a dirt symphony, a scratching harmony—a cat nails cacophony.

'They're all there—thank you, Catskill, for helping me again,' Craw whispered. 'But where are you all?'

There was no response.

'Where are you?' she repeated. She waited and waited but no one answered. 'In the name of the Great Catskill, where are you?'

'Here,' said a voice.

'Over here,' said another.

'In this dirt,' came Dreamer's voice.

'This is horrible!' said Blackie, somewhere in the dark. 'Where am I?'

'Stop this,' Twitcher said. 'It's the trenches! I told you I was taking you through the trenches.' He burst into a coughing fit.

'I don't want this dust in my lungs, trenches or not,' Dreamer grumbled, evidently not enjoying the experience. 'Were we supposed to fall into this hole?'

'Can we get out?' Piner asked, sounding sorry for himself.

'Can I get in?' Craw enquired desperately then the earth beneath her slipped away as she tumbled into the hole in the ground.

A different voice broke into the dark night. 'For goodness' sake, what a racket! Who is this bunch of moaning moggies?'

'Bootsie? Is that you?' Twitcher asked tentatively.

'Of course, it is, sunshine! This is my ground, as opposed to you and your bunch of amateurs.'

'Bootsie?'

'Yes?' he said tersely.

Twitcher was very precise. 'How do we get out of here?'

'You don't!'

This time it was Craw who was concerned. 'We don't?!'

'Twitcher,' Bootsie said, ignoring her, 'you didn't tell me you were bringing a battalion!'

'It isn't, Bootsie! We may be the only spirits left—we don't know. It's a battle and we need you on side! Now!' There was silence, and everyone was listening.

Craw had to take over. 'Bootsie, Twitcher has told us all about you. We need you with us or there'll be none of us left. They're trying to kill us. All of us.' She waited for a response. There was a long pause she could only hear the breathing of her own little band. 'Bootsie? Bootsie?'

There was no answer. Craw heard a running and scrabbling and then silence. 'Bootsie, are you there?' Still, there was no answer.

'Bootsie,' Twitcher said. 'Talk to Craw—she is the real thinker among us. I'm just the tough guy. Talk to her.' There was no sound. '*Please.*'

Craw could hear a spirit scratch the ground in a determined way. 'Bootsie, talk to me. I want to get my people out of your holes.' Everyone was listening in silence to this conversation. 'We know you've lived here with the army. We need you to help us. We've been through the *whisper* that leads to the *shudder* and we can think. You can think. You are one of us. You mustn't be a loner anymore. You have skills that we need. You know things that we don't. Help us learn. In the name of the great Catskill, please help!'

The silence was finally broken. 'You know the Catskill?'

'We know of the Catskill. Does it matter to you?'

'The Catskill was my father. My mother told me.'

'Bootsie...' Craw paused for breath. 'He was the greatest of all.'

'What do you mean, *was*?'

'We've been told he is no more. The Catskill is gone and that is why we must work together. We can't ask him for his great wisdom.' Craw stopped and waited for his response.

'All cats know they cannot stay with their parents,' he said. 'It is the way. We all must leave our home, but my mother and I lived together until she died. Then my Providers died, and I was alone until I found the soldiers. I don't need spirits to help me to survive.'

Craw felt her way along the uneven ground towards his voice. 'Bootsie, we need you. We need you *right now* to get us out of these holes!' She leaned into the darkness and was sure she could see a new set of bright eyes.

'You're not in holes,' he said dismissively. 'Where's that Twitcher? He thinks he's a tough guy. These are just passages. The soldiers call them trenches. It's just a walk out.' There was a moment of silence and then a set of four white booties appeared in the dark trench. 'I'm here—follow me. Watch my boots.'

'Boots?'

'My white boots!' Four little white feet danced into the trench. 'Follow me!'

'Come on!' Craw ordered them. 'All of you, after the boots. Come on, that way!'

Suddenly, the clouds cleared off the moon and there shining like luminous little socks were four white paws—not moving, but still high above the small group stuck in the depths of the trench.

'You can scrabble up here.' The voice came from above

the white boots, but everyone now knew the direction in which to focus their attention. 'One at a time!' shouted the disembodied voice above the dancing paws.

In seconds, everyone scampered towards the white signposts, one after another. The last to climb the slope was Craw, having watched everyone else make their way out of the hole.

'Follow me,' said Bootsie. 'We'll pass in front of the museum and follow my track beside the railings.

'Museum?' Dreamer questioned.

'The Regimental Museum. The soldiers keep all the things from their history in there, the things that have made them what they are today.' Bootsie sounded proud of the soldiers and their history.

'Like what?' Craw asked. She was growing frustrated with this talk of *soldiers* and *trenches* and *things*.

'Guns and stuff. Things that fire, things that explode, things that go bang. No more questions! It's getting lighter and the whole world will see us.'

Bootsie scooted off around the perimeter of the museum, passing a metal vehicle like the one they'd seen on the road. It was the colour of the sand they'd just left. At each road crossing, Bootsie would stop and survey the route ahead. Craw noticed that he was impressed with the teamwork of his new acquaintances. They had been well trained. Bootsie winked at Craw and nodded at Twitcher, 'You've taught them well Twitch. Military moves.'

Twitcher enjoyed the praise and athletically raced from side to side, checking the way ahead and then observing his following squad.

Bootsie had stopped in his tracks. 'Briefing, Craw,' he rasped. The squad quickly gathered round him. 'Okay, just to let you know about what you'll see—we've got to negotiate the main gate. The guard house is manned every minute of every day. Once we're past it, don't stop to stare at the barking bennies' playground.'

'What?' Piner asked.

'The army dogs—they learn tricks like going up and down steps and going through tiny tunnels.'

'I can do that without learning,' sniggered Piner.

'Yeah, well, they are dogs!' Everybody giggled at Bootsie's scorn. 'Right, follow me. We're going to cross the road and avoid the main gate.'

The cat squad moved in unison like she-lions on a hunt. They passed in front of a house that was opposite the camp and, as Bootsie stepped onto the drive, a light came on. Bootsie and Twitcher dropped to the ground and stared at the source of the light. It seemed an age before Bootsie's tail went up and then he set off like a bullet, crossing the road at an extraordinary pace.

Craw felt her tongue drop between her teeth as she could hardly keep up with the speed. Her legs felt as if they were getting heavier. The formation was lost, but the pace was maintained.

Without warning, Bootsie screeched to a halt, almost causing a collision as the following pack tried to break their speed. 'Stop here! I've no time for complainers. It's too dangerous in this area to fool about.' He surveyed them all to see if they were still breathing. 'Unfit, you lot! I don't know what the catworld is coming to. A little bit of sustained exercise and you're all totally smashed.' There was a certain amount of truth in his evaluation of the cosseted and cosy lives they had all led until recently. 'Listen up! There is shelter close by.'

A short distance away, Craw saw the outline of a house. 'It's got no roof,' she said.

'No roof, but shelter underground.' Bootsie paused and indicated that he wanted everyone gathered round. Then he spoke in a clipped, sharp fashion. 'There is open ground between here and there, but there are dips in the land that we can hide in on the way. So, let's go for it. Stop when I stop and hold your formation whatever happens. You know what I mean? *Whatever* happens!'

'Whatever happens?' Piner repeated the phrase and tilted his head.

'If someone doesn't make it...' Bootsie turned and stared at the large red board beside them. 'Those words mean danger to people and us. I know. I can read it. It says Military Firing Range, Access past this sign is forbidden at all times, if you ignore this notice your life is in danger.'

'That's a killer,' he said. 'If someone goes down, the rest must survive. Remember, they're taking no prisoners.'

Then he set off, signalling they should move in order. The ground wasn't difficult, and they moved easily over some mounds and ditches. They were not far from the house now and Bootsie indicated a rest stop underneath a board pock-marked with holes.

'Bootsie, what are these?' asked the inquisitive Piner.

'Targets—for target practice.'

Piner showed no indication that he understood.

'For shooting at!'

Piner pretended to duck.

'Always one comedian,' Bootsie grumbled. 'Unless you want to be the target we'd better move on.'

The thought of being shot at seemed to encourage another round of speed and in no time, they had reached the ruin. Bootsie stopped and indicated he was going inside first. They lay without moving on the ground. Bootsie was taking his time. Eventually, Twitcher went to the hole in the house where there'd once been a door. He peered through the ruins but could see nothing.

'I said wait,' Bootsie said as he appeared from behind them. 'Curiosity will kill the cat every time. Twitcher, I expected more of you. Before you make a move always double check.'

Twitcher looked crestfallen, and his tail drooped.

'Inside!' Bootsie ordered. He led the group into the house. There was no furniture, just bare walls and black charred floors as if fires had been burning within. 'We're going to explore,' he said. 'The usual cat thing—sniff everything out so you know if we're surprised, you'll be able to get out without any problem. You must know your way around in the dark. This basement is the only safe place when the firing starts.'

Craw flinched. 'Firing?'

'Of course. This is the perfect hiding place for you spirits. What lunatic cat would ever hide in a place that was fired at?' Bootsie slipped off down a set of steep steps. 'Come on, we'll organise a watch.'

As Craw was about to move onto the first step a horrifying shout shattered the silence. It was quickly followed by a massive clattering of boots on a pathway.

'Soldiers!' warned Bootsie from the darkness. The whole group ran and fell into the hole. The clattering was followed by a barked order. The cats in the darkness could now hear the crunching of boots on the rough ground.

Craw peered up through the hole at the top of the steps and there she could see the outline of a solder pointing a gun straight at her.

Chapter Nine: Cats Can Kill

A blinding, flashing white light circled in the dark sky every few seconds. It was so searing and powerful that Purrl almost cried out. Nailz and the living replica of her dead father were beside her. It still seemed like a dream and they were perched on this roof with no way of getting down.

Regardless of the steel in Nailz' voice he seemed very frightened and very unsure. 'Purrl, hold on! We've got to get down. The Pawmen are here to pick you up. Tel is a friend and we've got all the way up to the roof to help you out. His sisters are in the garden waiting for us to come down. We've got to go! Be brave. I've told them you are very brave and very clever. Don't be frightened.'

'We got up,' Tel said confidently, 'so of course we can get down.' This outwardly sure stance seemed in doubt as he rushed from one edge of the roof to the next seeking a way out of their predicament. 'Okay, I've got it. Jump!'

'Jump?' Purrl asked, scared.

'Yes, jump! We hit the glass roof, slip down to the edge of the gutter and jump onto the ground. It's what we do. We are cats, aren't we?'

'We are cats,' countered Nailz, 'but we are not acrobats or *acrocats*. I, for one, am not prepared to do a double somersault and land on my neck from this height.' Purrl noticed him drop his voice so he thought only Tel could hear. 'I am also not prepared to sacrifice my poor sister's life on a dodgy leap in the dark.'

Tel paused and stared hard at Nailz. 'Okay, what do you suggest?'

Purrl pointed. 'There in the sky—it's like the dawn and the horizon is on fire.'

Nailz and Tel turned and stared in the direction that she was indicating.

'It is a fire,' said Tel.

'A big fire,' agreed Nailz.

'A man's fire,' said Purrl. 'What are they burning at this time in the darkness? And anyway...' In her bemused state staring at the red sky Purrl had stepped three steps backwards. As it turned out, it was one step too far, for a second later she found herself tumbling down the hole that moments before had been her escape hatch. Her screech of shock was followed by silence.

She heard Nailz breathe in deeply. 'She isn't usually so clumsy. She keeps me in check.'

'That's women for you,' Tel said. 'Come on, let's find out if she's hurt. We're sitting ducks up here.'

'Sitting ducks?'

'Easy targets for the guns. Easy to shoot!' Tel moved to the hole that Purrl had dropped into. 'Are you all right?' he peered into the hole.

'Yes,' said Purrl as she licked her sore paw. It had hit one of the thick pieces of wood that ran across the attic.

'Can you jump back up?' Nailz asked with concern.

Purrl put her weight on her paw. It hurt so much she had to lick it several times. 'I don't think so.'

Nailz looked pained. He turned to Tel. 'She wouldn't say she was hurt if she wasn't.'

'We'll have to go in and think of another route,' Tel said. 'She can't get off this roof now.'

'But what about your sisters? Will they be safe?'

'They're cute. They'll have observed the Pawmen flashing their white light and realise we can't come down. They will take care of themselves. They're cool cats.'

Without another word Tel had dropped into the hole and Nailz leaped after him.

As they fell into the darkness one after the other Purrl thought the roof was falling in. 'What are you doing? You'll

be locked in here with me and none of us will ever get out.'
She began to wish they'd left her alone.

'We had to come in and check on you,' Tel said. 'We
couldn't leave you. We are thinking cats and we don't leave
our own. We never have.' He nuzzled up to her and sniffed
at her paw. 'I can't see blood or any serious damage.'

'Are you a vetman too?' Purrl asked, affronted that her
injury was given such short shrift.

'No, but I spent a long time with the vetmen when I was
terribly ill. I know their ways. Trust me—this isn't a break.'

Purrl was feeling aggrieved. 'So, does being locked in
their place make you an expert?'

'I know the difference between a hurt cat and a dying
one. I saw many *go* with the whisper, then the *shudder* and
worse. I had the *shudder* at the vet's house when I was there
for a bad leg. They watched me through it. They know it
doesn't kill all of us. We don't have time for this clever
chatter—we've got to get out of here fast, or the Pawmen
will be inside and that'll be the van for us!'

Purrl stood up and shook her paw vigorously. It was
painful, but she knew she'd just hit it on landing, and she'd
survive. She gingerly placed her paw on the wooden planks
beneath her. 'I'm okay, it's just sore.'

Tel glanced quizzically at both of them. 'How can we
tell what's happening in the house?'

Nailz nodded and then lead Tel to one of his best
listening spots. Through the tiny hole they could see little
but Purrl could hear voices she didn't recognise—the voices
of the Pawmen.

The leader sounded calm and calculating. 'We know
you're upset about the little girl,' he said. 'Let's hope it isn't
what we think it is and that she hasn't caught the cat's
condition. Maybe it's just a simple thing that can be sorted
with a few tablets. However, we still believe you've been
harbouring cats in your house somewhere.'

The ma Provider's voice was clear. 'Robin, we have to

tell them. We can't risk everybody else in the house. Here, this way.'

Purrl heard them move in the direction of the attic.

Nailz placed his paw on her shoulder. 'This is it, Purrl. We have to try and make a break for it. We both know the way. I'll lead you follow, and Tel will come behind you. Try to make sure you don't get too far ahead of him.'

Suddenly, the trap door opened to a thin beam of light. 'Come on pussy. Come to the nice man,' said a voice.

'Now,' Nailz rasped, and leapt through the gap hitting the Pawman full in the face using his claws to their full effect. The Pawman fell back off his small ladder, knocking his colleague flat onto the floor. Tel saw his opportunity, jumped out and hit the second man with all his force, catching the white neck with his grasping claws. Finally, it was Purrl's turn, and she jumped softly onto the carpet. She saw Nailz rush at top speed down the stairs and into the hall. The front door was wide open, and she couldn't believe his luck as he ran straight through the biggest escape hatch in the house.

She saw young Jack standing by the kitchen door, but she had no time to pause. Within seconds, she was in the open air standing on the drive. The door slammed shut behind her.

'Where is Tel?' Nailz asked.

'He was right behind me!' said Purrl. They both ran back to the front door but knew it would be no good.

'We can't leave him!' Nailz said frantically.

They saw Toot and Skoot underneath the large holly bush in the garden. Toot turned, raised her tail and went to the edge of the fence. As Purrl and Nailz arrived at the fence, Toot nodded to them to follow and Skoot stood back as they scrambled underneath. Toot hurtled across the lawn and into a small dense undergrowth where she stopped. 'We must wait for Skoot,' she said. 'She'll bring up the rear when Tel is out.'

They seemed to wait forever in absolute silence. Skoot dragged herself into the protected hideaway. She paused to catch her breath. 'He didn't make it,' she panted. 'I'm sure they've taken him. Once the door had closed there was nothing except shouting.'

'We have to go back,' pleaded Nailz. 'He only did it to help us!'

'That's how he is,' said Skoot. 'He's nearly been caught three times trying to help spirits escape. He calls himself the *tortoiseshell pimpernel.*'

'What does that mean?' asked Purrl.

'Some other telly thing. A man who helps people escape from evil. It's some character that rights wrongs and helps the oppressed like us. He's just weird.'

'We should all be that weird,' said Nailz. 'At least he's weird for good things.'

'But one day, when he was trying to help spirits escape from the Pawmen, he was caught,' nodded Toot.

'Yes, but he got away,' Skoot said. 'He pretended he was dead and when they lifted him out of their van, he did a runner. He is sharp. Now, though... this could be the time that Tel wasn't sharp enough.'

They sat in silence for what seemed like an age, until Skoot sat up and blinked several times. 'Right!' she said. 'We must eat! That's what he'd planned when we'd got you out. So that's what he'd expect us to do.'

Toot stood up. 'You're right. We'll be expected, and she'll worry if we don't show.'

Purrl was confused. 'Who is *she*?'

'Our lady,' Skoot answered. 'She's helped us since we've been totally free spirits. She's safe, and no-one thinks cats would want to go there because of the dog.'

'The dog?' Purrl hated dogs. Her fur curled and her back went cold.

'Don't worry,' said Skoot. 'He's a sweetie. Dogs are all right really, they just have to be handled the right way. Tel taught us that. He watched a dog training programme on that box and constantly wanted to try out the techniques. He used to say that dogs are like cats without the brains. Dogs want to be bossed around but cats hate it. Push a cat around and it'll leave you. Push a dog around and it'll love you. Show them who is boss and they're okay. Samson is a kitty.'

'Samson, yes,' Toot said smugly. 'He's a big black dog with a massive bark. Nobody would imagine that cats would get within a million miles of him. Tel tested him over and over again. He used to sit behind the gate and gaze straight at Samson. He'd bark and bark and bark, but Tel wouldn't move. Eventually, he stopped barking when Tel was there. That was the first stage.'

Skoot took up the story. 'He barked when Tel took the two of us to sit behind the gates but only for a while. The real success was getting Samson to come running when he was called. Tel really worked at it to get the sound right. In the end we'd go to the top of their garden and Tel would cry out like a baby. Eventually Samson would come running and then sit. When Tel managed to lick his big ears, we knew we'd cracked it.'

Toot laughed. 'That was when Tel got a taste for dog food. The lady would put Samson's food by the back door and Tel used to join in. Eventually the three of us would feed from the same dish. The old lady must have thought he was starving. He ate everything—or at least we did.'

'And you didn't get caught?' Purrl asked, impressed.

'Yes... and no.'

'How can it be "yes and no"?'

'Well,' continued Skoot, 'poor Samson could hardly get his snout in the bowl one day. We'd just shoved him out of the way. We were so hungry we weren't paying attention. We didn't hear the old lady sneak up on us. We all crouched on the floor ready to leave when she started talking kitty talk and in her hands she had two bowls of cat food—not doggie stuff. That was it! She's fed us ever since, and Tel really used to worship her.'

At that mention of Tel everyone stopped talking. There was still no sign of the television cat. He'd gone for good.

'Tel wouldn't want us to go hungry, and it is time to eat. Come on.' Skoot set off towards the hill at the end of the lane.

Purrl was very unsure. 'Wait a minute! Won't she give us up to the Pawmen?'

'No way! She's on our side; she hates the Pawmen. They tried to shoot a spirit in the garden across the road from her. She doesn't think the disease can kill her— whatever it is.'

'She told you?'

'She says it out loud and we just listen. Come on.'

Through the darkness the small band scurried along keeping out of sight for as long as possible. Every so often Toot would sniff in the air as if she was expecting a familiar scent. There was none. Tel was not in the vicinity.

Eventually, they came to a white metal gate; Toot and Skoot squeezed through the bars and slowly sneaked their way towards the front door of a large house.

'Listen,' Toot warned, 'when Samson comes, stand your ground. He'll bark a bit because you're new but glue your cat bottom to the floor.'

Toot moved slowly to the left of the front door. From the darkness came a huge black shape. Purrl was terror stricken. It bounded towards her and was several times bigger than any one of them. She could hardly believe it; she fought the natural temptation to flee and stood absolutely still against all her best instincts. She heard Nailz utter a low snarl. The black beast came right up to her and blew his monstrous breath right in her face. She had always thought a cat's tongue on fur was rasping and cleansing, but she was being licked by the biggest tongue she'd ever felt in her life and it seemed cold! It was a strange, but she heard

Toot speak above the licking and slavering the thing was doing. 'He likes you, don't move. Purr a bit! That really excites him.'

Purrl really didn't want to excite this big black brute anymore. His hot breath burst into her ear and her whole body went cold. The great tongue felt as if it was enveloping her tiny head and she could hardly breathe. When she did take a sharp breath all she could smell was something that reminded her of rotting food. It was disgusting. However, the loud lapping sound in her ear suddenly stopped as the black thing moved away from her and padded off into the distance.

Purrl felt the water from his mouth dribble down her chin. In the normal course of events she would have simply licked the excess fluid from her face, but instead she felt something smooth wipe her brow and heard a quiet voice above. 'I think Samson has found a girlfriend! Come here, you pretty little thing. Are you another of the new clever cats?'

Purrl opened her eyes and saw an old lady, who began caressing her ear and the back of her head.

'Purrl, keep focussed!' Nailz urged. 'I can hear you purring from here!'

'Oh, I think your friend is worried that I might hurt you. No, it's dinner time. Wait a moment, I think I've got what you want.'

As the white-haired lady turned towards the house Purrl ran to her group of friends.

The lady returned with a tray full of dishes that she put on the floor around them. The quartet failed to restrain themselves for more than a few seconds before running to the dishes—smelling, sniffing, half licking and then beginning to devour the delightful tastes. Samson sat in the distance and the old lady played with his ear.

The sky was just beginning to darken, and their spirits dropped as they realised they had probably lost Tel forever.

A sudden rustle of the bushes forced them all to scuttle for cover.

'Scaredy-cats,' said a voice in the gloom.

'Tel!' Skoot and Toot shouted in unison. 'You got away!'

'Am I not the *tortoiseshell pimpernel*?' He moved into a shaft of light and nodded his head. 'Yes, I've done it again. I shall be a cat of legend. Move over old Catskill! Tel's here.'

'What happened?'

'Well, when you all did a runner and the door closed, I was done for. I thought, "This is it! Curtains for the greatest escaper Catdom has ever known!" I didn't know where to go in the house, I was totally flummoxed. Then I saw a cat flap.'

'That was our way out, always,' confirmed Purrl.

'Well I hit it—hard!'

'Not as hard as I did,' muttered Nailz.

'Yes, I hit it hard,' repeated Tel, not wishing to be interrupted in his tale of bravado. I was stunned then as I staggered backwards, I was netted by the Pawman who smells of newly washed floors. He lifted me high into the air. I could see your Providers were shocked because the other Pawman shouted and punched his fist in the air. Then they tightened the rope on the net so I couldn't move at all.'

Tel scrunched his paws to his chest and wiggled his whole body as if he was trying to fight his way out of the all-encompassing net. The little group sat open-mouthed. The old lady and Samson watched transfixed, as if they knew that Tel was telling a tale of horror.

'I'm in the net so I thought *play dead*. That had got me out of trouble before. One of the children shouted that I was dead and to put me down, but the Pawmen were cute to my tricks. They said I'd done that before, and they wouldn't let me out of the net until they'd given me a shot.'

'Shot you?!' Skoot asked, petrified.

105

'A *shot, a jab*—the stuff in the needle that makes you go like jelly so you can't stand, and everything wobbles around you. That kind of shot.'

Terror had gripped his cat audience.

'So, I'm in the net. I can't move and then... and then I see the needle. It's massive and they're coming at me with it. There was no escape. The net was lifted off the ground and the one with the needle came from behind me. I was still pretending to be dead, but I was waiting for the sharpness of the needle behind my neck.'

'What happened then?'

Tel dropped his head and stopped his tale. 'Oh, I am hungry. My mouth is parched. Have we got some water?'

'Then... then what?' demanded Skoot.

'They jabbed me—straight through the back of my neck, in and out. Down I went like a stone. There was silence and they loosened the rope. I stuck my tongue out and rolled out of the net onto the floor, and then lay totally still. All I was aware of was the wet on my fur. It was the muck from the needle dribbling down my neck. I realised that the needle had gone into one part of my neck fur and come straight out. It hadn't gone into my body.'

Tel twisted his head so the gathered cats could see liquid on his fur. It was wet and raised and his neck was soaked. *Water is no good friend of cat fur*, Purrl thought. 'The Pawmen thought I was done for, but I was seeking out my chance through one eye. I saw the boy drop onto his knees and unlock the cat flap. He was my saviour. I didn't need an invitation! I was up and through his legs in seconds. The flap smashed right off as I pushed through so hard.'

Skoot and Toot raised their tails and nosed Tel. Purrl nodded to Nailz and they followed the gesture. This was truly a remarkable cat.

There was the sound of clapping in the air. The cat group stopped as the lady of the house stood to applaud Tel's performance. 'I don't know what you said but it was a good tale well told. Wasn't it, Samson?' The dog thumped its tail on the ground, and he panted his appreciation. 'I think they think you're just a dumb dog and they're probably right.'

Suddenly, she held both hands in the air and her eyes were wide open as if she'd seen something shocking. She gripped her throat and her chest, took one step backward then put out a hand as if to steady herself. She stumbled almost on top of Samson before dropping to the ground on her back. Samson barked and then put his face close to hers. For a few seconds he licked her face but then stood back as if asking for help.

'Oh dear,' said Purrl. 'I've seen this before. She is sick. Have we done this to her like with little Samsy?'

'Come on, Nailz.' Tel leapt onto the bench that the old lady had been sitting on a few minutes ago. 'You keep Samson barking.'

'How do I do that?'

'Just chew his tail. He'll think it's a game and bark and bark.'

'And bite my head off.'

'Just do it!'

'What are you going to do?'

'Use the phone and send a message.' Tel went up to the back door of the house. 'Okay, help me find the phone. I need one of those with the big buttons on and I will need help to knock off the speaker bit.'

They ran into a corridor that led into a small sitting room. Purrl saw the telephone first and jumped onto a wooden table beside a comfortable old chair.

'Well done, Purrl. Let's push the speaker bit off.'

'I need to get to the buttons.' Tel stopped again and listened intently. 'That dog outside has stopped barking. Toot, get out there and help Nailz excite the daft mutt. Come on you two, twelve paws must be better than one hand.' At Tel's instruction they pushed with all their might at the slippery, smooth piece of plastic. But however hard they pushed it wouldn't move. 'Everybody, push underneath!'

This did succeed in moving the awkward shaped thing a tiny way off the set but when they let go it settled back on the base again.

'Right, that's it,' Tel said. 'Stand back.'

Purrl and Skoot moved out of his way and he backed right up to the door.

'What on earth?' started Purrl but before she could finish her sentence Tel was flying through the air at a tremendous speed. He hit the telephone and it crashed to the ground with a splitting and cracking noise.

'That's done it,' said Toot.

'It started the dog barking at least,' responded Tel. Samson had obviously heard the crash and had come inside to investigate. 'Keep him out of my way,' said Tel. 'Purrl, he likes you - be nice to him.'

As if hearing her name, the huge dog looked at Purrl, stopped his racket and dropped on all fours.

'Right,' said Tel, 'I'm going to try to get help.'

'How?'

'By pressing the nine, the number on the bottom right button. Three times; nine, nine, nine. That's the magic number. These are really big buttons and that helps. I'm going to press them and then we do a runner. Hopefully there'll be somebody at the other end who will wonder what's up and come here. Here goes.'

Tel lifted one paw and produced one claw. He studied the phone intently. 'Right, I think I can do it. When I say go, I want the biggest, wickedest cat call you've ever done. Make it as long as you can. Then when it's over we run. Understand, everybody?'

Tel pressed the number nine button three times. They all listened closely until they heard a voice crackle out of the phone. Then, they started to make an evil noise. Everyone joined in and the cat shriek was such that it was almost unbearable to their own ears. Samson abruptly stood up and rushed outside to begin barking frantically.

'That's it, children!' Tel said. 'Time to make a quick exit.' He led the way and the whole group rushed down the path towards the front of the house and safety.

Purrl stopped at the gate and quizzed Nailz. 'But is it us? Have we hurt her? Are we really the killers? Cats can kill?'

'Or be killed!' Nailz screamed. 'Run now, or that will be sooner than you think!'

Purrl turned, skidded and ran.

Chapter Ten: The Glass House

Tom and Victoria sat on either side of a very large British Army sergeant. The harshness of the material on his uniform brushed against them. Victoria put her arm up to protect her cheek against the camouflage jacket.

'Sorry, darling,' the sergeant said. 'Is that irritating you? I have to sit here to ensure you don't attempt to escape.' He looked over at the driver. 'Dangerous pair we've got here, Corporal! Attempting to interfere with His Majesty's business!'

The driver nodded. 'Yes, Sarge. Frightening affair. Could be the glasshouse for them?'

'The glasshouse?' Tom interrupted. 'A conservatory?'

'Lock-up, gaol—it's an army prison,' said the driver.

'Now, now, Corporal,' the sergeant said, 'apply no frighteners to these young people. They *may* have committed no crime whatsoever! Anyway, the glasshouse is for offending soldiers only. We'll show you round if we've got some spare time. As for this cat matter... You know I'm a cat lover, Corporal. My dear lady wife has always had cats. And did I not help the young Bootsie, that stray cat that wandered onto the firing range?'

'You did Sarge. Star he was, Bootsie. He used to put his paws over his ears during target practice.'

'Certainly did. He was the most intelligent cat I've ever known.'

The driver pulled the vehicle up to the entrance to the military base. The soldier at the barrier barked something out. The sergeant responded in equally unintelligible fashion and the barrier lurched upwards.

There was a large sign by the entrance which said, 'Bikini Alert.' 'What's a bikini alert?' Tom asked. 'A bathing warning?'

The sergeant was unimpressed. 'Son, we're in difficult times and we're on emergency footing. Let's not be flippant.'

'I wasn't being flippant! What's so dangerous?'

The sergeant tapped the driver on the shoulder. 'Straight to the C.O., top priority.' He turned back to Tom. 'I don't know if you've been up to anything, but this cat problem is serious. We have a job to do as far as humanly possible, restrict this outbreak to this area. I have been given that job and I will do whatever is required to achieve that end. It's my job, it's *our* job and we are good at what we do. The Defence Medical Services for all the armed forces are here and we have everything we need to combat this disease and the power to do what is necessary.'

'What, you mean burning things?' Tom realised his mistake the moment he spoke; Victoria watched him, open-mouthed.

'Oh dear,' the sergeant commented, 'so we *weren't* just out to take care of our horse, were we? Now the C.O. *will* be interested in that.'

The vehicle pulled up in front of a grey building with another soldier on guard by the door. 'My advice to you is to tell us what you were doing,' the sergeant said as he pulled himself from the front seat and stood beside the driver's door. 'We'll get you home before your parents are even out of bed and it'll be all right. The C.O. is a good man; he's been on peacekeeping missions all over the world. He'll sort things. Be honest with him and he'll be honest with you.'

Tom sat upright as he saw the sergeant bristle with indignation. 'What the hell?' The soldier took a deep breath and glared at the drivers of a newly arrived vehicle. 'Corporal, tell those idiots that this is an army camp, not a funfair. Get them to switch those fairy lights off and tell me what the hell they're doing in there. Kindly inform the gate they do not have access to all areas of this military camp!'

'With great pleasure, sergeant.' He marched over to the van and loudly repeated the sergeant's request. 'Sergeant Wilkes has requested that you switch off your fairy lights and inform us of the nature of your visit. I also have to tell you that you do not have access to all areas of this camp.'

There was a shifting of figures in the van and some huddled conversation before Tom saw Mr Cairns and the other Pawman stepping out of their vehicle. They began walking towards Sergeant Wilkes.

Even though Tom held his head down Cairns spotted him. 'Hey, hey, hey! You've got a cat harbourer in there. I know it. Why's he here? Is it something to do with the breakout?'

Sergeant Wilkes drew himself to his full height—which was a good head and shoulders over Cairns—and spoke in hushed tones. 'Cairns, I don't like you. I don't like what you do, and I don't like how you do it. These young people are helping us with an army matter. They were tending to a sick horse in a nearby field and may have, *may have*, I say, witnessed something that could give a small clue to the matter of the cat breakout of some of the animals from Dawkins. This is an army matter and will be dealt with by the C.O.'

'No, no,' spluttered Cairns. 'Not according to the new regulations. Aiding and abetting the escape of felines from the authorities is a criminal offence.'

'Mr Cairns, I am sure that His Majesty the King, to whom we all answer, will have a view on that matter. Let's hope the alleged condition doesn't spread to the Royal beasts.' The final comment was more of an aside as he turned to Tom and Victoria and winked before turning to Cairns again. 'The C.O. is waiting, and far be it for me or you to waste his time. Why don't you go back to your cat pound and see if you can get any confessions from dumb animals?'

'That's where you're wrong!' Cairns shouted. 'They aren't dumb, not anymore. I *know* it. I'll be back, and I'll have the law with me. Tell your General that!' He turned back to the white vehicle and immediately turned on the flashing white lights. Tom saw his lips twitching, violently spitting out venom aimed at the sergeant.

'What a shame I can't catch what he's saying,' Wilkes said. 'Perhaps one day he'll be brave enough to tell me to my face, but I doubt it. Still, we have a job to do and we have to manage this however much we dislike it. So, come on you two.'

The two followed the sergeant into the building, along corridors and finally to a soldier standing at attention in front of a door. Sergeant Wilkes spoke to him quietly, and he stood to the side indicating that they could enter. In a room lit only by a desk lamp sat an older man. He stood up and addressed Wilkes. 'Sergeant. What have we here?

'You'll have to ask them, sir, though I have taken the opportunity of some gentle interrogation.'

'No rough stuff, sergeant?'

'Certainly not, sir! Strictly proper rules of engagement and no torture, in due deference to the terms of the Geneva Convention.'

'Good. What have you managed to extricate from the suspects?'

'Sir, the young lady was concerned about her stabled horse. Apparently, it is of a nervous disposition. She engaged the services of her young friend to accompany her to the stable. They saw light in the sky but seemed completely unaware of what that may have been. Given the time scale, sir, it would seem unlikely that they could have walked to Dawkins and then returned to the stable. They had obviously been there for some time.'

'Good, sergeant. Well, have you two anything to say?'

'No, General,' Victoria spoke as Tom was composing his reply.

'General?' he mused. 'At last, the promotion has come through.' He laughed, and Tom saw the sergeant was fit to burst. 'My dear, I am a simple soldier.'

Tom felt brave enough to get involved. 'But the Pawman said you were a General?'

'Ah, did he now? You don't think, sergeant, there may have been a hint of sarcasm in the man's comment?'

'I don't think he has the brains for it, Colonel'

'I'm sure you're correct. It's just a shame they have men like him doing this dirty work and we have to mind them.'

'If I may add, sir—he described the young man as a cat lover, and by implication one who might wish to help cats in distress.'

'As we all would.' The Colonel sat down in his chair and examined the two of them. 'I have to do this. It is law under the emergency acts. It is an offence to aid fugitive animals. Can you two assure me that that was not your intention and that you did not release the cats from Dawkins?'

'No, we wouldn't do that!' Tom blurted out. Victoria nodded furiously in agreement.

'Fine. We'll take all your details and return you to your parents. Then *you'll* have all the explaining to do. However, if you should be caught again in similar circumstances, I'm sure the civil authorities will not take such a lenient view. Now, it has been a very tough night for all of us, so go home and take care. Thank you, sergeant.'

'Yes sir.' Wilkes stood to attention, saluted, turned and winked at them once again. 'Quick march, you two! Straight past the guard room.' He touched their shoulders and led the way out.

When they reached the army vehicle, Tom climbed into the back and helped Victoria inside. It set off towards Lichfield in a slow trundle, and Tom slumped next to the window, gazing out at the fields as the morning light grew brighter. After a few minutes, he saw a shape in the field by the Lichfield Rugby Club, and nudged Victoria in the ribs.

'Ow!' she said. 'That hurt.'

Tom nodded vigorously to the window. 'Look!' he said. 'It's the Pawmen's van!'

As the Land Rover passed by, they saw Cairns shining a huge torch onto the field. Startled rabbits seemed frozen temporarily in horror without realising that the men weren't in the least bit interested in them.

The corporal tooted his horn vigorously while Sergeant Wilkes waved out of the window with unnatural enthusiasm. 'Thank you, Corporal. That should frighten off anything he was hoping to find!'

Tom watched with amusement as Cairns raised his fist to the army vehicle. Wilkes was laughing too loudly to notice.

The camouflaged vehicle drove off along the Tamworth Road and then turned onto Borrowcop Lane. Even at this early hour of the morning there was all kinds of activity. Tom couldn't believe it. His mother was on one side of the road and his father was on the other, standing beside an ambulance. Its lights were flashing as they put someone on a stretcher into the rear of the vehicle. The Land Rover pulled to a halt and Sergeant Wilkes jumped out, opening the door for Tom to step down.

'Lively down here,' Wilkes said to his corporal. 'It's like a war zone.'

Tom's mother stared at the vehicle with her eyes ablaze. 'What on earth? Tom? You're supposed to be in bed!'

Wilkes helped him out of the vehicle and stood protectively in front of him. 'Mrs Biggins?' he asked. 'Sergeant Wilkes from the Whittington military base.' He saluted and held out his hand. Tom's mum was stopped in her tracks. She wasn't used to being saluted by anybody in uniform. 'Tom here has been assisting us with a rather sensitive matter and has been very co-operative. He was helping out young Victoria here who was worried about her horse.' He dropped his voice. 'Believe me, they've both been quite brave under these difficult circumstances and have been immensely helpful. I think they've both been worried about this business with the animals. Treat him gently.'

'Of course, of course. Come here, Tom, and tell me all about it.' His mother looked towards his father; he was still standing by the ambulance talking to a policeman.

'Victoria,' his mother asked, 'are you all right? We must tell your mum and dad?'

Wilkes pointed his finger towards the big old house. 'What's all this fuss about? Do you know?'

'Mrs Constance,' his mother replied. 'She's collapsed and is unconscious. We heard a tremendous racket. Cats were screeching, and Samson was barking. Within a minute or so the police had turned up.'

The sergeant looked bemused. 'Cats! You don't think they did anything, do you?'

'Oh, that's all nonsense. There's nothing wrong with cats—nothing that'll hurt us. They're very smart, you know. The Beamans—Robin and Lyn up the road—are convinced that their cat was rescued in a raid by other cats. Lyn says it was like a planned attack. All their cats escaped from those dreadful cat catchers.'

A familiar white light flashed at the turn onto the lane.

'Not him again.' Wilkes nodded at the Land Rover. 'Corporal, out you come. I think we may need to instil some military sense into this situation.'

The corporal stepped down from the driver's seat just as Cairns was making his way towards the ambulance. Cairns stumbled as the corporal stood in his way. 'Sorry mate! In a rush?'

'These cats have gone too far this time,' Cairns said. From what I hear on the police radio this is murder!' I'm sure that this is the gang that I've been after! It has all their trademarks. The organised raid, the planning… and now a death.'

Wilkes laughed. 'Mr Cairns, I think you're suffering from what we soldiers might call *battle fatigue*. Perhaps we should find out exactly what's been going on before we jump to silly conclusions.'

'Listen soldier, this is my territory. I have jurisdiction over the apprehending of these diseased beasts. They think they're so smart.'

'You've totally lost it, Cairns.' Wilkes turned to the corporal. 'Call HQ and tell them we're investigating an issue that may be cat-related.'

'Sarge.' The corporal jumped into his seat and started transmitting his message.

'Nothing to do with you,' Cairns muttered as the ambulance moved off slowly along the lane.

'It has a great deal to do with me, Cairns.' Wilkes began to set off after him but stopped and turned towards Tom and his mum. 'Could you please take Tom and Victoria into your house and ring her mum?' he asked her. 'I imagine they'll be up by now—just reassure them there's nothing wrong and try and put them in the picture.'

There was nothing that Tom's mother loved more than being the bearer of important news. 'Of course.' She gestured to Victoria and Tom to follow her. Tom really wanted to find out what was going on but realised he was potentially in some serious trouble however much Sergeant Wilkes had helped him.

As Mrs Biggins gently shepherded the two of them towards the house Tom managed to slow down and stop so he could gauge what was happening. Wilkes had overtaken Cairns and was speaking directly to the policeman. 'Hello, PC Standish,' he said.

The police officer looked pleased to see a friendly face. 'Well, if isn't the top soldier in Lichfield!'

'I wouldn't say that, John—but it is a compliment coming from the top copper. They tell us we *do* have to fraternise with the local constabulary.'

Tom was taken aback as Cairns stepped between them. 'Excuse me interrupting this back-slapping exercise, but something serious has gone on here and I shall be reporting this lack of zeal to the emergency commissioners.'

'I believe that includes the Chief Constable,' said Standish.

'And the Colonel of the regiment,' said Wilkes. 'So, John, I think you'd better tell us what happened before the pest exterminator has a heart attack!'

'I am not a pest exterminator!' Cairns grimaced. 'We are providing a vital role in protecting the community from this virus. There be no spread on my watch. Too many mistakes made last time!'

Wilkes put his right hand on Cairn's chest and gently pushed him backwards while placing his left hand on the policeman's soldier. 'Officer, can you run past us what has been going on?'

'Of course. Come on, let me show you inside. It's bizarre.'

They began to walk towards Mrs Constance's place. The gates of the house were wide open. Cairns followed behind them, still shaking his head. Tom watched the three of them enter the house and was desperate to hear their conversation. An open window seemed very inviting. With the open gate, he could see them walk into the kitchen and then into a small sitting room.

'This is the story as far as I can find out,' Tom heard the policeman say. 'Emergency services took a 999 call from this number. In fact, we have a recording of the whole proceedings because the phone wasn't replaced on the receiver. There was nothing to be heard apart from a wailing of cats and then the sounds of them running off. The emergency operator is convinced they were miaowing to each other—talking, she said! Anyway, the ambulance turned up first, followed by us and the neighbours across the way who heard the racket. It was strange—her big black dog was sitting beside the body of the old lady. It seems she'd probably had a heart attack. But what was really weird was the kitchen. Who had made the call? There are no marks on the floor apart from cat paws all over the shop and the dog's marks. The cat ones are on the phone and even on the dial pad—as if one of them pressed the pad and then had called the emergency services. I've never seen anything like it.'

Tom could just see that Cairns was on all fours examining the paw marks and heard him mutter. 'Murder. As good as murder.'

'Don't worry, he's totally lost it.' Wilkes glanced at Cairns but furrowed his brow as he stared at the paw marks on the phone.

'Here, get up.' Standish pulled Cairns to his feet. 'This may or may not be a crime scene. I can't have you messing about with anything.'

'That print—that big print. It's the one. I'm sure it's the one!'

Wilkes turned Cairns to face him. 'What one?'

'The *one*, the really clever one. The one who got away from us twice. He's a leader. He's dangerous! Mad and diseased. He killed that woman—frightened her to death probably. That's murder in my book. I've got to get onto Inspectorate HQ. They'll be on to this straight away. I think we'll be asking for an extension of the mass cull. All cats within the exclusion zone will be killed.'

Cairns reached for the mobile phone clipped to the top of his overalls, but Wilkes gripped his hand very tightly. The Pawman grimaced. 'What are you doing?'

'Could we calm down a moment?' Wilkes said calmly. 'I think the officer and I will have to decide the seriousness or otherwise of this matter. As he says, this may be a crime scene and we can't have amateurs stomping all over it. I shall contact *my* HQ and John here will speak to the police.' He glanced over at Standish. 'Until that has been done, I imagine you'll tape this area off until you get further orders.'

'Correct, sergeant.'

'So, Mr Cairns, off you go to cat clearance HQ and report back to them what the professionals are doing.'

'I'll get him! I'll get them all with or without your help!' Cairns pulled his reddened hand from the tight grasp of the sergeant.

Tom backed away from the window as he saw Cairns leave the house and rush back across the road. The conversation between Standish and Wilkes was not over and Tom slipped back into the shade to listen.

'That man is dangerous,' Sergeant Wilkes said. 'He's become so obsessed with killing cats that not only does he think they're diseased but that they're more intelligent than him—which, let's face it, isn't hard!'

PC Standish laughed. 'Still, we have to go by the book. He may be obsessed but now he possesses certain powers— powers that mean we have to play it straight.'

'You are correct—I'll go and speak to the parents of the kid and see if we need to run the girl home. I hate all this business. It wasn't why I joined the army.'

'And it wasn't why I joined the police force. I insisted we gave up our two cats—they were poorly. My wife and daughters are barely speaking to me. I wish they'd sort out the scientific issues. My cats are at Dawkins waiting to be cleared.'

'Dawkins?' The sergeant put his hands on the shoulder of the policeman and led him out of the house. 'Let me tell you about Dawkins,' he said.

Tom could see his mother on her mobile phone indulging in an intense conversation and feared that as a result of his mum's story telling he might be in real trouble with Victoria's parents. On balance he felt at least he should try and hear what frightful tales his mum was telling. Walking across the road he saw her spot Cairns standing alone and dejected having been ignored by the police and the army.

Tom walked up to her and heard her change of tone.

'I'll call you back. I can see a man who probably knows what this is all about. His mum cupped the phone in her hand. 'It's that horrible Cairns man. I'll get back to you. Don't worry, Victoria is fine and they'll both have some answering to do.'

Tom watched as his mum went straight up to Cairns and poked him in the chest. 'Mr Cairns, you seem to be the only person who knows everything that's going on around here. I'm sure you can help me make some sense of it all.'

Suddenly, Cairns was the centre of attention. He puffed up his chest, rested his hands on his large stomach and launched into his prepared explanation. 'As I've been telling anyone who is prepared to listen, we've seen these creatures in action, and they are in danger of breaking out of our cordon. There was a gang up there hidden by owners in their attic. Although we tried to stop them, they broke out of the house and now the little girl, Sam, has got the strange fever. It was the cats, I'm telling you. They've given her the disease—the *shaking* disease. Her parents hid them in the attic. They've harboured the disease, this virus in their own home, and they'll be prosecuted for this. You mark my words; this will change attitudes as the disease has to be stamped out.'

Tom peeked at his mother, who had gone quite pale, and then glanced at Victoria who bit her lip. What had they done? 'Have we let killers loose?' he asked her.

Victoria closed her eyes and squeezed his hand tightly.

Had they really let killers go on the run?

Chapter Eleven: I Spy A Cat

From the blackness of the cellar there was nothing to see but the stark outline of the soldier, his gun pointing towards the spot where the small group of free spirits had gathered.

Craw heard a crackle that seemed to come from nowhere.

'*Blue One? Target secured?'*

The soldier replied into the air. '*Blue One to Earth Mother—target clear.'*

What did it mean? No-one moved. There was a sudden cacophony of sounds as more soldiers arrived.

'*This is Earth Mother. Clear ground air attack in ninety—nine zero—seconds.'*

There was silence and Craw sensed the soldiers had disappeared.

'They've gone—we're all right!' Piner said with relief.

Bootsie put his paws to his head. 'Back into the dark! It's the best place we can find. Everyone under those stone stairs and do what I do!' He disappeared into the dark. The others followed his white socks under the shelter of the stairs.

'It is disgusting here,' moaned Piner as he skidded into the leaves and wet soil under the stairs.

'Total silence!' Bootsie ordered. 'There'll be plenty enough noise coming. Watch me.' He rolled over with two front paws grasped even tighter over his ears.

A loud sound pierced the air then there was a sudden, brilliant, searing white light. This happened four times then a loud boom almost blew out their paw-bound ears. After the last one, boot after boot hit the surface of their hideaway. Men's voices shouted and screamed at each other.

Dreamer was panting. Craw realised that she couldn't stop a tremble developing in her right paw which spread to the left paw. The screaming seemed intolerable and it was obvious that he wanted to run away from the frightening racket. He stood up and staggered towards the steps. Without warning, Craw lashed out her paw and clipped him on the left ear with such force it sent him spinning back under the stairs. The others watched the flurry of leaves as Dreamer landed. Then they dipped their heads down as another barrage of gunfire blasted their ears.

'Still,' commanded Bootsie.

No-one moved. Above them came crawling sounds, as if someone was dragging a bag of garbage across the floor. It lasted for a few moments and then the throbbing grew and grew until it was over their heads. Then slowly it began to fade away.

'It's over,' Bootsie said. 'Attack complete. Mission accomplished.'

No-one spoke.

'That's it—done and dusted.'

Still no-one spoke.

'Come on! It's *over*. It's just a war game, a practice in defending their base?' He peered into the darkness. Craw felt dazed, her sight was blurred, and her ears buzzed but she could just make out a pile of leaves.

A shaking to the left of the stairs revealed Blackie, with a fine thatch of yellowed leaves. To Craw's right, Dreamer coughed and scattered a small shower of tiny twigs. A figure rolled over in the dark to reveal Piner covered by a layer of moss. Twitcher suddenly stood upright and sneezed a green spray of mould onto Bootsie.

'Disgusting', Craw just made out Bootsie's voice, but her body ached so much. Then there was a flurry of activity which set leaves and debris flying around. It was like a miniature storm sending all the muck on the cellar floor into the air. No-one could see anything.

Twitcher threw his head to the left and right before dislodging a small snail from his nose. 'That is disgusting. I'd rather die than have another one of those up my nose.'

Craw was aware through the confusion in her head that everyone was pawing through the pile of leaves, moss and soil that covered the floor of the cellar.

'Here,' said a startled voice. Craw could hear Blackie, but her eyes wouldn't focus. The others moved slowly towards Blackie attempting to make out what she had uncovered from the muck. Her paw pulled at the still object in front of her.

'Quick, help!' screeched Piner. Everyone began to paw the uneven ground. Then a shape became clear—a still black figure with a silver streak.

'It's Craw!' cried Dreamer.

Craw sensed the digging becoming more frantic and they pulled away the leaves and debris as quickly as their paws allowed them. She heard Blackie's voice

'Craw's too still. That's it. She's dead.' They stood close together as Craw sensed that they feared the worst. Craw wiped her face and looked at her tail raised behind her then croaked out to them as loud as she could 'I'm not dead, at least, I don't think I am. I'm here, just a bit blind and deaf not dead.'

'But who's this?' Bootsie pawed the limp body they'd uncovered from the leaves. 'It is just like you – stripes and all'

'It may look like me, but it isn't me.'

The cats gazed again at the half-covered body.

Bootsie turned away. 'It's a badger. I've seen them here before. Sometimes they cough and die. We should keep away from it. These things spread disease.'

'You mean like us? Like the disease we've got that has changed us but might kill the providers?' Craw stared hard at Bootsie through the dark.

'Well, the soldiers were always careful when they

dragged them away. I've heard them say the badgers spread disease to cows. We should be careful. Cover it quickly.'

Craw shouted out above their scratching. 'Leave it in peace. I wish the Great Catskill could help us now!'

Piner dragged some leaves across the body of the dead badger. Slowly, one by one the others helped to cover the creature. Craw neither helped nor interrupted—she simply stared into the open sky into which the men with guns had disappeared.

Craw sat very still desperately trying to think. How could the cats—even thinking cats—beat these mighty machines and their ability to make such a gruesome clamour? She felt someone move close to her and recognised the white paw of Bootsie. 'What's wrong?' he asked.

'Everything, I think,' she replied. 'What can we do? We can think, but we're not big enough or strong enough to fight these people. They're after us. There are the Pawmen with their weapons and the soldiers with killing machines. What have we got?' Despair filled her as she saw everyone gathered around her. All of them had fallen in submission onto the wet ground. She had to find a way, an answer.

Craw looked at Bootsie. 'I'm going to talk to my soldiers', he said.

'That'll be the end of you,' Piner scuffed up some leaves with his paw in a dismissive gesture.

'I've got to try it. We've got to get the truth across that we can think, and that we aren't hurting anybody. Winning armies have the best intelligence.'

'We've got intelligence!' Dreamer shouted.

'Shut up and listen!' Bootsie snapped. 'By *intelligence* I mean *information*. We don't know what to do. You hoped to find the Great Catskill—yet now you say that spirit is dead. The Catskill never dies because the name and all that goes with it lives forever.'

Piner looked puzzled. 'What does that mean?'

'I don't know. It's just what my mother told me. She said we all have to believe it for the future of Catkind.'

'Bootsie,' Craw interrupted, 'you carry on. We must find a way, or it'll be the end of what you call Catkind. Go on, tell us more.'

'An army may succeed through strength and firepower but gets nowhere without intelligence. Intelligence is vital. Good intelligence means you know all about the enemy— what they're thinking, where their main force is and what they're going to do.'

'How can we do that?' Dreamer asked. By stopping Bootsie's flow he earned himself another cuff from Craw.

'I'm coming to it. We need a spy.'

Dreamer was desperate to get to the truth. 'What's a spy?'

'It's someone who goes into the enemy camp and finds out what's happening. They listen, observe and report back. That's what intelligence is. It means you can base your action on what the enemy's going to do. We can plan *our* campaign when we know what *theirs* is.'

There was a moment of silence after he finished, and Craw then realised it was only because everyone was looking at her, waiting for a decision. 'It's a good idea, Bootsie. The reason we don't know what to do is because we don't know what they're planning. If we know what they're going to do then we can outwit them, perhaps. Maybe it'll just help us decide what to do. But how do we spy? They're after us, aren't they?'

'There are two ways—have a spy in the camp or send someone in.'

Twitcher snorted. 'They aren't going to help us.'

'But they might,' Craw said. 'They *have*. Remember Tom? He kept us alive. Piner found a way to communicate with him.'

Dreamer turned his head in the air. 'I've said all along we have to use Providers to help us.'

Craw turned to Bootsie again. 'But how do we spy?'

Bootsie took a deep breath. 'I spy—you don't.' He stared at Craw. 'What happens is that I go back to the camp. I get inside. Get to the important places and listen. Listen to the orders. Listen to what the lads are saying. I'll find out everything. They don't think we can hear and understand.'

'Bootsie, it's dangerous. What if you get caught?'

'I won't get caught. I know that place better than they do. I can be in and out without them knowing as long as I get enough time to hear what they're up to.'

'We're coming with you,' Craw said decisively.

'No, you're not. The essence of spying is that you're alone. If I get caught they don't get the rest of us.'

Craw understood what Bootsie meant but she didn't want to lose any of the strength of the little group. 'Bootsie, you know how far we've all come. We have to support each other, and we gain from being a group—hopefully being a bigger group.'

'Right.' Bootsie nodded his head and drew his paw over his eyes. 'You can come, but only so far. I know a safe house—an empty place at the edge of the headquarters' offices. You must wait there for me to come back with whatever I can find out.'

Craw saw agreement in their willing eyes. 'Good, that'll do it. We're with you.'

Bootsie stood up and sniffed the air. 'Okay, this is it— follow me and remember your formation!'

The group set off in the threatening light of the day with Bootsie leading. Speed was of the essence. Blackie, who had been so quiet in the ruins, took up her position at the head of the following formation with Twitcher close beside. Piner assumed his role as scout while Dreamer moved to the rear. Craw watched her little army in position and felt quite proud and pleased that they seemed to have some purpose to their movement.

Craw had no real idea where she was going. Bootsie was

forging ahead through the undergrowth. As they moved forward in formation it was easy to follow the white booties. Craw became more worried as she could make out the sounds of vehicles on the nearby road.

Suddenly, Bootsie disappeared. Craw could see Twitcher's head stand up straight and twist quizzically left and right. Dreamer ran in from his position on the flanks and whispered. 'He's gone.'

Blackie, who was closest to the front line, seemed to run around in circles as she sought out the missing Bootsie. In his new scouting role, Piner had crouched down but was unable to add any light to Bootsie's disappearance.

'So much for the value of spying,' Craw said to herself.

As if to answer her, a voice came out of the ground. 'Where are you? Come on down here!'

Blackie was the first to respond to the sound. She ran through the undergrowth to be confronted by a massive fence. She pulled up in a sudden halt and was bumped in the back by Twitcher who was following closely behind and then they disappeared.

'Down here!' the voice rang out again. The next to vanish was Dreamer, who had been vigorously sniffing the ground. One moment his nose had been pressed to the soil and the next he was gone.

It seemed as if they were being lost one by one. Then, at the same spot Bootsie leapt into the air as if being thrown from below. 'Come on! This way it is the only way in without going through the main gate and showing your pass.'

As quickly as he'd leapt from under the ground he was lost from sight again. A very measured approach by Blackie revealed a small space covered by low growing shrubs. Craw felt herself slipping down the hole. As she hit the bottom she scrabbled frantically at a steep slope in front of her. This time, the fence was behind her.

'Come on, hit cover over there.' Bootsie tipped his nose

in the direction of some small bushes. Craw followed Twitcher, Blackie, Dreamer, and Piner as they were all unceremoniously bundled by Bootsie into the dense foliage.

'We're in!' Bootsie said triumphantly. He turned his back on the little crew and looked towards the buildings that were laid before them. 'If I'm to get a result here, I need you to maintain military discipline, protect each other, hold your ground and if necessary make a tactical retreat.' He turned to Craw. 'That means if I don't get out!' He faced the rest of the group. 'I'm going to the command and control building where I can get in, hide and spy. You'll need to protect the rear and do everything you've been taught. Keep to your roles and hopefully we'll be fine.'

Bootsie moved closely to Craw. 'I shall be in the building as long as it takes. You'll have to keep your little army together and if you don't hear from me by the time the next hunger sets in then leave the way you came. You understand?'

Craw nodded. 'You'll be fine, Bootsie. This is your home territory. Maybe we all have to do this sometime. Go back home.'

However, before Craw could say any more, Bootsie disappeared!

***

Bootsie marched forward with determination rather than speed. He knew where he was going. As he reached the first building he jumped up on to the low shed that leant against the wall. A second later he was through a small opening at the bottom of a tall window. Shaking his bottom, he easily squeezed through the gap and was in a darkened, empty office. His next move wouldn't be much fun. There was a fireplace that hadn't been used for years; it would make a good hiding place, and he could also move through the chimneys to get to other rooms in the complex and listen to whatever was being said. It would be uncomfortable, and he would end up covered with dark black dust, but he had decided it was his best listening spot. He discovered this little complex when a kitten; once, he had unwisely chased a mouse up there and then found he couldn't get out. It was only the patient coaxing of a young soldier that showed him the way. *Well, here I am again*, he thought. But this time it was by his own choosing.

It was warm and almost cosy in the safe and sooty place and he felt his eyes droop.

***

Sometime later, he woke with a start. He'd no idea how long he'd been asleep, but the sound of human voices had roused him.

The weary voice of the top soldier could be heard from the room. 'Sergeant Wilkes, what is going on?'

'It's this cat thing sir. It's out of control. The lads don't like it and that business at Dawkins has unnerved them. These cat clearance people, or whatever they call themselves—they're on a crusade. For them the only good cat is a dead one!'

'Wilkes, we are here to do our duty. The Government fears this outbreak could spread out of this area and we cannot endanger people's lives. If that happens and this becomes a national or international problem, it'll be our fault. The aim is complete lockdown, containment and testing in this area. Nothing gets out.'

'I know, sir, but the locals are saying wild things. We came back from taking the two kids home, that Tom and Victoria. There was an incident across the road where an old lady had a heart attack and they think cats were involved.'

'You mean they caused it?'

'No sir—they *helped* her. There's a view that somehow these cats have changed, that if they've had this disease they're somehow smarter.'

'Wilkes, you're sounding like my wife—she always says that cats are smarter than people. I'll say to you what I say to her: that's just emotional talk. I hear from the Ministry that there is a growing campaign to uncover more evidence that cats have a part in this epidemic. The animal lovers are campaigning in London, so we must be seen to be behaving properly. The answer lies with the scientists. There's a whole team arriving from the Government's main lab to examine dead cats and those humans who are believed to be infected.'

'Do they do intelligence tests, sir?'

'On whom, sergeant?'

'The cats, of course.'

'Sergeant, if you weren't a seasoned soldier I'd assume *you* needed tests. Let me outline the plans in hand: the animals are to be tested over the next forty-eight hours. Results are to be rushed to London. It's our job to ensure the scientists can do theirs without being bothered or attacked and that the residents feel reassured everything is under control. This is top priority. All movements of escaped cats are to be reported and we have a duty to help hunt them down, but the science is vital. The experts will be arriving later today and setting up their field centres in a tented area in the market square. It's not only central but very visible, if you see what I mean.'

'Yes sir—we're to give locals confidence that everything is being done to ensure people's safety.'

'Not just the locals, sergeant, but the whole country. If not the world. We hope we have a limited outbreak that can be contained. It's the Ebola scenario, Sars and Coronavirus. Learn the lesson - contain and destroy the disease.'

Bootsie heard the sergeant stand and stamp his boots on the floor. He had learned to do that himself and would amuse the sergeant by standing and stamping down his rear paws at the same time. However, it was also a sign that the sergeant was about to leave. The door closed, and footsteps disappeared down a corridor and a short flight of stairs into the room behind him. He listened hard but could only just hear the sergeant's muffled voice.

He had to try to get closer. This was the reason he'd come to spy. The chimney dropped down to the right and opened up into a grate in the room that the sergeant now occupied. Bootsie extended his nails and scraped slowly down the sloping chimney, his nails rasping over the stonework. It was a painful process, and Bootsie was breathing hard as the light come into view. He began to slide and tried to stop himself, but his normally assured grip was letting him down. His speed increased, and he found himself falling, uncontrolled, down towards the light.

'What the hell?' the sergeant's voice rapped out.

The black stuff tumbled around Bootsie's ears as he fell into the open space.

'What's up there?' said another voice.

Bootsie twisted upright and made ready to land, but he hit what seemed to be a small ledge. Although his back and legs ached, and his mouth was filled with the black stuff, he lay very still. He desperately wanted to cough and fought the tickle in his throat.

'Is that a bird again?' Bootsie heard the sergeant ask. 'Check the chimney.'

A head appeared in the space and a voice echoed around Bootsie's head. 'No, nothing I can see, perhaps it's flown out.'

'It's a shame old Bootsie's not here. He'd have sorted it out. Do you remember the time he went up this chimney in hot pursuit?' There was laughter in the room.

Bootsie stayed still but felt happy that his soldiers still remembered him.

'Lads!' the sergeant began. 'The boffins are in later today and we've got to protect them from danger. They're setting up their labs in marquees, down in the market square. They'll be running tests on cats. It'll be our job to see everything is sweet. The eyes of the world will be on this and everyone wants a good result. Let's hope that'll be the end of it. The unpleasant thing is we must take some live cats in for them. The official view is that these cat chasers aren't really up to it and they've been upsetting the locals—the burning incident was unwise, even unnecessary.'

Bootsie was wondering how this information could possibly help his friends outside when there was a sudden knocking at the door followed by a loud screech.

'What's going on now?' Bootsie could hear the sergeant walk to the door.

A strained voice greeted Bootsie's ears. 'Sergeant, we've caught this one inside the perimeter fence.' A cat's cry filled the room. 'I can't believe it. We were on routine patrol of the fence when this big black thing ran out from the undergrowth right in our path. Fortunately, it hit the netting on the armoured car and got tangled up. It was such a racket I don't know what it was trying to do. It was almost as if it wanted to be caught.'

'Get one of those cat cages. We'll have to take him to the scientists when they show up. He'll be a prime one for testing—especially after behaving so oddly.'

The door opened again and, almost without thinking, Bootsie leapt onto the hearth. He could just see the light through the partly opened door where Blackie was being tightly held by a soldier.

'Bootsie!' the sergeant's voice rang out.

'Keep going!' shouted Blackie to him. 'Tell them what you've heard!'

Bootsie hit the corridor at top speed. There were three other soldiers in front of him. He moved to the left and then to the right. Two soldiers fell to the floor as they tried to grab him. Bootsie kept going along the corridor and down the stairs, passing one of his favourite cleaners who stood open-mouthed at the sight of him covered in soot. Within seconds, he was well away from the building and heading back to the fence—and freedom.

With one bound he hit the undergrowth and was under the wire. When he reached the other side, he paused momentarily, feeling something touch his back. He spun around and saw Craw, her paw to her lips. She indicated that he should follow her. They both rushed through denser and denser undergrowth and only came to a halt when they could go no further. The two cats were completely breathless, and both crumpled into a heap. Neither could speak even if they'd wanted to.

Bootsie soon realised that they weren't alone. He took a deep breath and nodded to Craw that someone was close at hand. He hissed quietly and prepared himself to attack.

A small bush was pushed back to reveal several other cats. He and Craw were outnumbered. He held his head. He had escaped the men but was now confronted by a new enemy.

He slumped in submission only to hear Craw draw her breath and then speak. 'We lost Blackie, but she saved all of us from captivity. Her madcap dash drew the soldiers just after we'd met our new friends.'

Bootsie saw Twitcher and those he'd led to the camp but did not recognise the small group of others.

'This is Tel,' Craw said, 'Nailz, Purrl, Skoot and Toot. They were running from the city and picked up the scent of our trail. They're joining us.'

Bootsie was glad he was still with friends even new ones. Blackie had saved him, and he was sorry to have lost her.'

'Blackie did everything to help me,' Bootsie said. 'That was brave.'

Craw gazed at her growing band. 'She saved you for us—all of us.'

'And her lost babies?'

Craw nodded her head. Her eyes were wet.

Chapter Twelve: Cats in A Trap

Craw was deeply troubled by a great problem. How could she ever take on the might of the Provider's world? Tel and his team had been a great find, however. She listened as he explained to Bootsie how they'd stumbled across each other.

'It was strange,' he said. 'We were rushing to get away from the old lady's house and running for our lives. We headed for the country and then picked up a trail with a scent of many spirits. Someone had sprayed the way for us.'

Twitcher raised his nose to the air. 'I was leaving a marker,' he said with pride.

Craw nodded. 'We must not forget we are still spirits and must follow our natural instincts.'

'But are we natural killers as well?' squirmed Nails. 'You know the *shudder* thing. The old lady fell over in a heap very suddenly.'

'We can't worry about that now,' jumped in Craw. '*We* are not dead, and we must survive.' She contemplated her expanded group. There were the originals—Twitcher, Dreamer, Piner and herself. Then there was Bootsie and now Nailz, Purrl, Tel and his sisters Toot and Skoot. Ten in total. Still a small group but one that was now easier to spot. 'So, Bootsie,' she asked, 'what did we find from the spying?'

'That the soldiers hate the Pawmen but have to go along with whatever they do. But I know the soldiers still like me—I heard them talk about me. Anyway, the important thing is that some medical scientists are coming in.'

'Some what?' Nailz asked in confusion. 'What are *they*

for?'

Bootsie laughed. 'They're coming to cut us up.'

There was silence for a moment before Craw said, 'Are you sure?'

'Sure as cats is cats. I heard them—they're setting up some science labs in the Market Square and they're going to cut us up until they find out why we've changed and if we can kill people with the *shudder*.'

'Cut us up?'

'And cut people up as well.' Bootsie said.

'Isn't that what they call *murder*?' said Tel.

'They do it all the time. Cut things out. Find things out. They're going to do it in tents in the middle of the city.'

'Well done, Bootsie,' Craw said, 'but I still don't know what we do with the information. How can this help us?' She moved off the mound and sniffed suspiciously. 'Can I smell something?' Noses twitched and heads turned. No-one could smell a thing.

Piner raised his tail. 'If these tests work, then they'll know we are smarter and can think. But we want to keep that to ourselves, don't we?'

'Maybe it'll show that we aren't killing humans,' said Purrl.

'And maybe it will show that we are killing them—we think, and they die.'

Craw was listening but distracted. She jumped back on the mound and sniffed again. 'You sure you can't smell anything?'

'No!' rang out several voices.

Piner spoke again. 'Somehow we've got to get the information from those experiments and hope we aren't killers.'

'What if we *are* killers?' Dreamer wondered.

'You must believe we haven't killed anyone yet.' Craw said. She sniffed again. 'Spying seems to be the answer. If we don't get caught, we may be able to spread the word.'

'Exactly, Craw,' said Bootsie, 'and that's why we have to find friends among the Providers—like my soldiers. But we must get the true story to all the spirits who think like us.'

Craw was tired and thought she couldn't be the only one. 'Before we bed down for the day, let's do some hunting and get some fill. Then we can think about sending the warning to anyone who can help us. We need to be close to the scientists, to hear what is happening, pass on the warnings.'

As she finished, Craw felt her fur rise. The smell—that wonderful cooking, meaty, tasty smell—was floating in the air.

A bang and a flash exploded, swiftly followed by several more. As she crouched to run Craw saw a cloud filling their meeting space. It was like smoke but didn't smell of burning. Twitcher had moved to protect her and he was looking for an escape route but within seconds had fallen at her feet.

'This way! This way, here!' Bootsie bellowed from somewhere in the cloud but Craw couldn't see him.

Toot ran past her immediate field of vision followed by Skoot who was making a monstrous din. She jumped into the air but seemed suspended there as if by magic. Then she disappeared into the cloud held by something that Craw couldn't see. Craw's legs wobbled—she couldn't stand, her eyesight was blurred. Her chest was pounding, and smoke filled her lungs and burned her throat. She couldn't move. She couldn't cry out no matter how she tried. Then, something touched her, a large black thing, thick and coarse. It poked at her, but she could do nothing. She felt as if she was burning on the inside.

A monstrous face with huge thick eyes and a large gaping mouth with many holes in it pushed up against her. It was a hideous, ugly thing. In slow motion, she slumped to the ground. Her paws were reaching out for help, but they trembled before her eyes.

'Got the fat one,' a metallic voice rang out in the mist.

'Three here,' said another ghost.

'I've got two, I think.'

'Nice one! Let the gas clear and let's see how many we've got.'

***

Slowly, the mist receded and there, lying on the ground, were the bodies of the cats, still and motionless. The Pawmen and the soldiers were wearing gas masks that protected them from the evil smell.

Sergeant Wilkes waved away the noxious fumes as he heard Cairns addressing the group. 'I told you we should have used some of the gas stuff before, sorted the lot of them and as for that big one—got you at last. You'll never get away again.' A black boot kicked out at the prone body of one of the cats. The lifeless creature rose in the air a couple of inches but slumped again on to the soil, legs awkwardly and unnaturally squashed under his body. The boot raised again this time aimed at the unprotected head.

Wilkes couldn't bare this. 'Don't you dare!' barked the sergeant. 'We've done your dirty work, and you're not killing or burning these cats. They're to go to the scientists in town.'

The steel toe-capped boot missed the face by a whisker. Cairns sneered, disappointed that he had missed his target. 'We're taking these back, but luckily this one isn't making it!' He raised his boot, once again, into the air over Tel's unprotected skull.

'See this, Cairns?' Sergeant Wilkes moved close to the Pawman, who felt something against his temple. 'It's a gun.'

'You can't use that.'

'I've been trained to use this in combat situations, and things get very confusing when you're using this gas.'

Wilkes saw the tracker dog straining at his handler's

leash.

'I said they'd leave a scent,' the dog handler said, rubbing the Alsatian's head. 'Good boy.'

Wilkes pressed the gun against Cairn's temple. When he spoke, his voice was cracked. 'There are witnesses.'

'They still can't see us properly,' Sergeant Wilkes countered, 'and this smoke plays tricks with the eyes. Now, I can count; one, two, three, four, five, six, seven, eight, nine, ten cats. I want ten delivered to the research lab.'

Wilkes observed sweat gathering on Cairn's brow. 'I've been hunting this particular gang. It was my idea to use the dog and get London to force you to start getting tough and use gas. These creatures have got something. I *know* it! They've outsmarted me for the last time. These are the only ones loose in town and now their time has come. Don't worry, they'll all get to the test centre, but they aren't coming out of there. I know what's planned for them.'

As the sergeant took his gun from Cairns' forehead, he took the gas mask off. Coughing slightly from the acrid air he wiped his eyes on his sleeve. The shock was almost too much for him as he saw Bootsie, the soldiers' cat, lying on his back in the most unnatural pose, his throat and neck exposed to all. 'Bootsie!'

As he called out the name one of the soldiers had already stooped down to pick up the limp figure of Bootsie. 'Is he dead?'

'No,' said Wilkes. He turned to Cairns. 'That, Mr Cairns, is the Barracks' cat. The Colonel loves that cat and if anything *unnecessary* happens to him when it's in your care I shall personally...' Wilkes lowered his voice and placed his lips close to Cairns' ear. 'I shall personally...' He repeated himself so quietly so no-one could hear.

Cairns went pale and began to cough uncontrollably. Tears poured down his face as the final mist of the stinging chemical penetrated his eyes. Cairns held his chest as he struggled to catch his breath.

Wilkes gripped Cairns' arm to prevent him falling to the ground, and then turned to the small group of spectators. 'I think Mr Cairns has taken in too much gas. I should have warned him that we soldiers are trained to cope with this stuff—it is very nasty. Now can we get these cats out of here and over to the test labs? Radio the Colonel and tell him we've found Bootsie. I'll take care of him.'

***

Blackie lay very still on a cage floor. She remembered how she'd managed to distract the soldiers and hopefully the others had escaped. The future of Catkind was in their paws and they had to be free. She twisted rapidly in a way only cats can, first one way and then the other. If she bent forward she could easily reach the strings that bound her.

She managed to chew on her bindings. They tasted vile, like worms covered in slime. She wanted to be sick; she coughed and coughed but there was only a black fur ball to show for her efforts.

As she was retching, a white light shone straight into her eyes and everything else disappeared into it. A voice spoke from behind. 'We've got a cat here, and we hear on the walkie-talkie that we've gassed the rest of this little adventurous crew. Funny really, they were ever so clever. It was as if this one was acting as a decoy to help the rest get away. Great military tactics. Perhaps Bootsie taught them?' He laughed but there was a slight hesitation in his voice.

'We'll take it from here,' said another voice from the middle of the shining brightness. 'I can assure you there's no thinking going on here. Cats are simple creatures only concerned with themselves and their stomachs. We'll get to the bottom of this disease thing very quickly.'

Blackie felt the cage being raised into the air. She rolled onto her left leg and felt a sharp pain. She cried out, unable to stop herself making a pathetic little sound.

'Careful,' said a voice.

'Don't worry,' said another. 'The black cat is going to

get sharper pains than this in the next little while. Open the cage and we'll take it with the rest.'

Blackie heard the cage open but was in the complete dark for a moment while her eyes adjusted to the strange glow in the room. People wearing white masks across their mouths were all around her. Bodies were scattered everywhere. Blackie couldn't count them all. Spirits of all types and colours—grey ones, ginger ones, tabby ones, pure white ones—all lying still and not moving. They must have been brought here by the soldiers. Blackie was the only one in the little cage and the only one moving. She looked around for anyone she might recognise, even one of her own like little Peeps. Then, she saw Bootsie lying close to her cage and although he was on his back with his white paws in the air she was sure he winked at her. What was he going to do now?

'These need to be put into the wicker cages,' one of the masked men said. 'Then we'll get them to our experimental laboratory in the Market Square. The little Beaman girl with the condition has been taken to the special clinic. That's created a real panic. If other children are in danger we need to get all cats away from them immediately,'

'We're scientists and this is a matter of life and death, not a war game.' Blackie saw the man place the first wicker basket on the floor. 'Right, put them in.' He bent down and picked up two of the grey spirits by the fur on the back of their necks. He dropped them into the basket just as the soldier picked up Bootsie. 'The lads aren't going to like this—he was practically our regimental mascot.' Instead of dropping Bootsie in the basket he laid him gently on the mat at the door entrance. Blackie could hardly believe her eyes as Bootsie rolled over and began to drag himself backwards very slowly.

'That one moved!' said the second masked man. 'Quickly! Grab him!' The soldier moved very, very slowly as the two white masked men jumped towards Bootsie. He was now on all fours and rolling around in an exaggerated fashion. 'Get out! Now!' Bootsie screeched at Blackie.

Blackie tried to stand but ended up tripping on the slimy wire. She couldn't do it! She couldn't get out. Some of the spirits seemed to wake up because of the racket. It was then that Blackie saw Peeps—her eldest baby with the black fur and the white circled eyes.

Bootsie began staggering as the men tried to grab him. 'Get out now! It isn't locked!'

Blackie had to escape to try and help her little one. With a massive effort she leapt at the wicker door which swung open. She launched herself off the table and with one swoop grabbed Peeps by the scruff of his neck just as he squealed, 'Mama.'

Blackie ran as fast as she could with Peeps between her teeth. He kept saying, 'That hurts,' but Blackie continued to run around seeking a way out. She could see no exit but turned towards Bootsie for guidance. 'That way!' he shouted, pointing his front bootie to the right.

Blackie ran in that direction and there was a small hatch about four feet up on the wall. She could make it easily, but not with Peeps in her mouth. She put him down. 'Watch this,' she said. She took a moment to gauge the distance, and then jumped onto the small platform the men used to serve food from the kitchen.

'Hurry up!' shouted Bootsie and waved his paw to the baby to jump up. Peeps swayed back on his heels. With a huge effort managed to catch his claws on the shelf but couldn't hold on. Slowly he slid down the wall, his claws screeching like the sound of nails on a black slate.

'What are you doing, Bootsie? Get off my neck!' The soldier shouted angrily at the white masks. 'What the hell is going on—I thought you'd put these to sleep!'

'Don't you worry about those two!' one of the white coats shouted back. 'Help us shut the door and get that one!'

The soldier put his hand up to grab Bootsie, who chose then to leap to the ground. 'Push off, Bootsie! You're going to get me into trouble!'

'Shoot that one, it's his fault!' screamed the other man in the white mask.

'Go, you two! Now!' Bootsie ran over to Peeps who was about to leap in the air for a second time. He held him in his teeth at the back of the neck. With a dramatic shake of his head, Bootsie threw the little kitten out of harm's way. Peeps went over the shelf through the hatch, crashing into something on the floor.

Peeps shook his head but was otherwise unharmed. 'He's fine,' Blackie said to Bootsie. 'You come up!'

'Coming!' Bootsie launched himself into the air. As he did so, everyone in the room heard a gun being fired. All the spirits and the men in the white masks stood still. Bootsie was still flying through space as his body twisted and turned. He hit the shelf and fell through the hole in the wall leaving a blood-red pawprint on the white shelf.

Blackie left Peeps, who was trembling with shock, and rushed up to Bootsie. 'Bootsie, are you all right?'

'No! You go. My leg is smashed, it's the end for me. But you must get the order out to carry on the fight. We must win or we'll all die. Never forget, Blackie—we haven't killed anybody!' He rolled and squealed in pain. 'Go now—you're the only hope!'

Blackie picked up Peeps, pausing for a second beside the now still figure of Bootsie. His voice was trembling. 'Don't forget me or my message,' he said. Then his eyes closed, and he was still.

Chapter Thirteen: A Cat Saviour?

Tom was in real trouble. His dad had sent him to his room and was threatening to go to school to tell his teacher about the shocking things he'd been up to. The thought of what Billy Cairns would say was too awful to think about. He could hear his whining voice in his ears. 'Biggins, the cat boy!'

Worse were the problems he'd caused for poor Victoria. Her parents had looked daggers at him when they picked her up.

Tom turned off his computer and tried to think of something that he could do or say. He closed his eyes and imagined what would be the craziest thing he might do. It came to him immediately and within seconds he was calling Victoria. The mobile rang out for what seemed to be ages before the call was answered. 'Victoria—it's me!'

'What do you want?' she asked. 'Don't you realise we are in dreadful trouble? I'm not allowed to speak to you. They don't know you've got my mobile number and my mum and dad will be so mad!'

'Listen, I've got an idea.'

'I don't want to know! Whatever it is, it is too risky.'

'But I haven't told you what it is yet.'

Victoria was silent.

'Victoria?'

'Yes?'

'Do you want to know?'

'Oh, all right!' she said impatiently. 'Tell me!'

This time Tom took a deep breath. 'I can't,' he said.

'What do you mean, you *can't*?'

Thinking very quickly, he said, 'Not on the mobile. I think we might be being bugged by the Secret Service. This is a big national thing!'

'You are losing it!'

'You know I'm not—please let's talk about it!'

'I'm grounded, Tom, and I can't talk to you.'

'Exactly—let's meet. The usual place, this side of the golf course.'

'I *can't*.'

'You must—otherwise all the cats will die. There's only you and me.'

'That is why it won't work! We need to find help.'

'You are terrific—brilliant idea! So, you will see me then?'

'I must be stupid. When?'

'In an hour.'

'Do you know what time it is?'

'Midnight. I'll see you by the first bunker on the Whittington Heath golf course by the soldiers' base.'

'I'll never be awake.'

'Don't worry, I'll call your mobile—bye!'

Tom knew she'd come. It was easier not to wait for an answer.

***

A tiny kitten eye peeped out from the low bush. 'Mama?'

'Yes Peeps,' Blackie said. 'It's Mama.'

'Mama, I'm hungry.'

'Yes, Peeps, and so is Mama. I'll find you some fills.'

'Mama, not the ones that move and wriggle when you swallow them.'

'Peeps, you'll have to eat whatever I get you!'

'Oh, mean!'

'At least you're here and alive. Don't you dare forget that.'

'Yes, Mama.'

145

Blackie felt afraid. As far as she knew there was no-one else free apart from her and her baby, but she had to face up to her responsibilities as a mother and find food. 'Stay here. Don't move, even if a Provider comes and you smell the wonderful smells. Don't move!'

'Yes mama,' said Peeps. He slunk back into the bush.

***

Victoria was wet, miserable, and uncomfortable. She had lodged herself behind a large tree just off the first sand-packed bunker at the golf course. She checked the time on her mobile phone. It was gone one o'clock and no sign of Tom.

Her hair was soaking. She was sniffing every few seconds and she didn't have a hankie. As she searched through her pockets on the chance there may be a tissue there she heard a rustle. She stood very still. There it was again—a little rustling in the undergrowth.

'Tom, is that you?' She spoke as loud as she dared. There was no response. Victoria searched again in her pockets for a tissue and could only find some cat biscuits that she'd stored because Tom had said they might come in useful. As she rummaged in her pockets the biscuits fell on the ground, she stooped but there was no point in picking them up.

She moved towards the road slowly, just in case Tom finally showed up.

Then she heard the rustle again. This time it didn't stop and into the space by the sand appeared a tiny little face that peeped at her and then rushed at the biscuits as if its life depended on it.

After he'd consumed the little pile, the kitten tilted its head and blinked up again at Victoria and she said, 'That's it. I think.' But, lo and behold, she found another handful of slightly soggy cat biscuits and proffered them to the peeping kitten.

This time he came right up to her with his tail in the air and began to lick the biscuits in her hand. The purring was almost deafening.

'Sshhh. I think you might wake someone up.' Victoria smoothed the little head and the purr became even louder.

Suddenly into the space launched a figure from the blackness, yowling and screeching at a level that made Victoria hold her ears. The kitten shrieked and cowered in terror only to see a cat in full flight launching herself at the girl who had offered some tasty morsels. Victoria felt Blackie hit just below her neck; her claws sank into the heavy jumper that she was wearing. Victoria cried out in pain and fell backwards as she was aware that Blackie had kept her claws fixed into her skin.

Victoria saw Blackie being pulled up into the air even though the cat was still gripping her skin with her sharp claws. Blackie seemed to be reaching out for the little one and on failing to hold her began to whimper.

'Quiet, quiet, you're all right. You're both all right.' Victoria was irritated by Tom's calm control.

'She's all right but I'm not!' gasped Victoria as she gripped the little puss with both her hands. 'My neck is bleeding and if these are diseased I might as well forget it!'

'You put the little one down and I'll put the black one down. I think they'll know we don't want to harm them.'

Victoria heard the black cat speak to the little one.

'She's talking to the kitten,' said Tom.

Victoria was irritated. 'Yeah, yeah, yeah, well, I wish you'd talk to me. Where the hell have you been?'

'I got held up. I couldn't leave because my mum had a meeting of her "catsy" people and they were talking about the medical lab that's been set up in the Market Square. They're thinking of holding a demonstration or something. That's what my mum's like when she's got the bit between her teeth. After several glasses of wine, they were getting louder, livelier and later and later but I just couldn't get out.'

'So, what do we do now, Mr Clever Clogs?'

'Put antiseptic on your neck, feed these two and try to hide them somehow. I think the black one may know something that will help us.'

'So, Tom, will you discuss this with her or will I? After all she has got my blood all over her claws. Shouldn't I go to the doctors?'

'Yes, that is so clever. You go and say, "I've been scratched by one of the infected cats. Am I dying?"'

'Well, am I?' Victoria asked.

'No of course not,' he said. 'Well, I don't really know.'

'That is not very reassuring. You're frightening me, Tom.'

'Yes, and that would fascinate the scientists, wouldn't it?'

'What? Am I now an experiment? I'm scared.' Victoria was aware she was glowering at Tom.

'You'll be fine. I just know it. But if you go to the lab in the Market Square and explain exactly what happened—that you were suddenly attacked by crazy cats and scratched and bitten—they must examine you. Then you'll be on the inside and you can find out what's going on.'

'Great, that's so *easy*. I get the shakes and die.' Victoria dropped her head. 'Tom, I'm bleeding. I've been attacked by a cat that may be infected and might have passed this disease on to me.'

Victoria became aware that Tom was holding her hand. 'Victoria, you may be the key, 'he said. 'The black one here has scratched you. If there is anything in this then you'll be ill like little Sammy and all the cats will have to die. It may be the end of cats as we know them today.' Tom pointed at the black cat. 'She seems to know what I'm saying, or at least knows we are trying to help.'

Victoria felt something wet on her cheek. She wiped away the tear, but not before Tom spotted it.

'I'll do something about these two and I'll look after you,' he said. 'I promise.'

Victoria was frightened but didn't want to show Tom how much. 'So, what was your great idea?'

'Well,' he said sheepishly, 'that we make a couple of scratches and say we'd been clawed or bitten by the cats we tried to help. Then they'd have to rush us into the medical place, wouldn't they? But now it's happened anyway.'

'You make me so angry sometimes!' Victoria turned away from Tom, but her jumper rubbed the cat scratches and they stung really badly. 'Ow, that is hurting.'

'So,' said Tom very slowly, 'we'll have to get help, won't we?'

'Oh, really, at this time?'

'If you'd woken up in the middle of the night and went to your parents and cried and told them, they'd have to do something wouldn't they?'

'I suppose so.'

'It's the only way. You get to see the scientists, and with some luck we can get into the lab. My mum was told at her meeting that anyone bitten or even dribbled on by a cat had to seek urgent advice and to go to the Market Square which was the emergency centre.'

Victoria narrowed her eyes. 'Is that where you got your brilliant idea from, listening to your mum and her barmy mates? Why didn't you just scratch yourself, clever clogs?'

'I wanted you in on the plan!'

'I've no choice now have I?' Victoria huffed. 'Okay, let's get on with it.' She paused. 'What about the little peeper and his mum? I assume that's what she is. Is she, little one?' Victoria stretched out her hand.

***

Blackie spoke quietly and gently. 'Don't blink, Peeps, they are going to take care of us.'

'I know mama. I heard what they said.'

149

Blackie screwed up her face. 'You mean you can understand the Providers too?'

'Yes. Remember I wasn't very well and had to hide in the corner and I could hardly make a sound as I was shivering?'

'Shuddering more like,' said Blackie putting her paw gently on Peeps' head.

'The next time I saw a Provider I understood everything they said. But Mama, you always said we knew exactly what the Providers wanted. That cats could get what they wanted any time just by being catty.'

'That was just a general cat thing. Now you're much cleverer than the old-style cats.'

'Victoria, they are having a conversation. I *told* you. The black one even patted the peeper on his head.'

'Tom, you're daft. But we don't want all cats killed off, so what are we going to do with these two?'

Tom put his head in his hands and stroked his forehead. Victoria jumped as he raised his voice and then stamped on a pile of loose leaves. 'Right, you two. I've decided this is what we'll do!'

Blackie and Peeps lifted their heads up at the same time.

'Yes. Just listen. We must hide these two somewhere safe, then you'll do the weepy bit early this morning. You text me, let me know when you're going to the medical centre and then we'll try to find out exactly what is happening.'

'Don't you mean *I'll* have to find out? And how exactly am I supposed to do that?'

'Go walkabout in the centre! Get away from the examination room, try and find out what's going on.'

'Then what do I do? Scream!' Victoria felt frustrated. 'I just don't believe you!'

'It's our only chance to find out what's going on and tell everybody!'

Victoria felt this was hopeless but did want to help.

'Okay, I'll do it!'

The two cats jumped in the air at the same time.

'I told you, they know—they both practically cheered.'

'Don't be silly! I'll see to these two and you do the pain in the neck routine for your mum and dad.'

'I resent that—pain in the neck.'

'Well that is where it hurts, isn't it? Now come on we mustn't fall out. I'll hide them in the roof of our Coach House. You know what it's like, it hasn't been touched for a hundred years but is dry and locked. All that's in there are boxes of my dad's files, old tables, several of my mother's Christmas trees and her jumble items, as well as my sister's rocking horse. My dad is always talking about doing it up and making it into a proper room, even installing my gran in there. It won't happen. There's not enough room for her gym kit! But there is a roof space that nobody ever goes into. I can climb up there and shut them in.'

Victoria was defeated. 'You have all the answers. How can we get them there?

'Easy—you're wearing your mum's best knitted jumper. Stick one in there and I'll stick the other in my running top.'

Victoria felt something hit her in the chest. It was the little baby clinging on to her.

'Well, it seems as if that's decided,' Victoria looked at Tom who put his arms out almost at the same time as the black one hit the target. The force of her leap almost set him backwards. She was a big cat.

'Okay, back to your place.' Victoria pulled the tiny puss up close to her nose. 'And you, little peeper: keep your nose hidden or the game's up for us! And don't fidget, 'cos it is a bit sore where your mama bit me!'

'So, you're not dying yet then?' Tom said with a smirk.

'Don't you dare! But I had better develop some symptoms, otherwise my dad will just dab on some antiseptic and that'll be it. Come on, let's work the idea out. It's nearly half past three and we've got to try and get some sleep.'

Tom outlined the thoughts he'd had and talked about the disease and its symptoms—the dry mouth, sore throat and then the sweats followed by this spinning head and shuddering walk. Victoria started to stagger, and the baby stuck his head out of her jumper and issued a kitty squeal of delight. This was such fun for a playful little kitten.

'Stop it, this isn't a game.' Tom nagged Victoria.

Victoria and the kitten were having too much fun to stop as she rushed along the dark road stopping and staggering around every so often. The little one would squeal and then purr loudly as Victoria set off on another wobbling run.

She was enjoying herself so much that it wasn't until she ducked behind a tree that she realised she didn't know where she was. In the excitement of the game she'd lost her bearings. But it was all right—Tom would be there in a second. She stroked the peeping kitten who was staring up at her waiting for the next roller coaster ride. 'I'll call you Peeps, but I think I'm lost. Let's be quiet and wait for Tom and big Blackie, your mum.'

She waited and waited. There was no sign of Tom. Victoria started to panic. Here she was, lost in the dark, in the middle of the night protecting an illegal animal. She might get sent to prison just like the authorities were threatening.

'Don't turn around!' Victoria felt a firm hand on her shoulder and heard a very unfamiliar voice. Was it a soldier? Or even worse—one of the Pawmen? 'What are you doing here? Have you been watching me?'

'No,' said Victoria. 'I don't even know who you are.'

'Why are you out at this time?' The voice sounded unpleasant and edgy. At the worst possible moment, the kitten let out a little pained sound that he usually uttered when he was feeling hungry or tired.

'What's that—a cat? You mustn't have cats. They all have to be given up. You shouldn't have this. Show me the cat. Is this a trick? They'll use anybody to get what they want.'

Victoria felt the grip on her shoulder loosen and she half turned. In the dim light she couldn't see a face and the clothes were dark.

'It's a kitten. Why have you got it? What are you doing? Is this a trick?'

'Why do you keep saying that?' Victoria said in annoyance. 'Do you think anybody would be using a young girl to trick you? Why should anybody want to do that?'

Gradually, a small shaft of moonlight shone into the space and Victoria saw a scruffy man with something over his shoulder—a cat!

'A cat—a dead cat!' she gasped out loud as her little bundle ducked back into her jumper.

Don't be silly! They're rabbits, dead *rabbits*, and they're for my cat! Well me, anyway.' He pulled a pair of wild rabbits tied by their feet from his shoulder. Victoria stepped back suddenly as she saw the shotgun on his other shoulder.

From behind them a deep booming voice rang out. 'Put the gun down. We have you surrounded.' There was scrambling in the undergrowth and Victoria could hear someone or something rushing round them. *It must be a group of soldiers.*

'Just put the gun down and you'll be safe,' said the mystery voice in a commanding way.

The man stooped down and placed the gun on the ground, looking around the whole time. Suddenly, a dark figure rushed out from behind a tree. It happened so quickly Victoria could barely make out what was going on.

'I've got the gun. Now just stand still.' Victoria nearly giggled as she saw Tom. He'd run past them and stood behind the tree with the gun pointed towards the man.

'Put your hands in the air—you are completely surrounded!' shouted Tom.

Victoria moved towards him as the scruffy man put his

hands in the air.

'There aren't any cartridges in the gun. I've got them here on my cartridge belt. Who are you? You're not army. Are you two together?' The man moved towards Tom and then there was a massive flash from the place where Tom was standing. A large branch fell down onto the man who dropped under its weight.

Victoria stared at Tom. 'What the hell happened?'

Tom was shaking like a leaf and the gun lay on the ground. 'He said the gun was empty, so I pointed it into the air and pulled the trigger. I've never fired a gun in my life!'

'You could have killed me, you fool! Or Peeps, the kitten!' Victoria looked down at the man under the branch. 'And you might have killed him!'

Tom ran over to the man on the ground and pulled the branch away from him. The man was very still. 'Is he dead?'

'He isn't dead, but he could have been.'

Victoria heard a muffled voice, only to realise it was coming from the man.

'Are you all right?' Tom asked as he held his hand out to the man.

'No thanks to you!'

'But you said there was no cartridge in the gun,' said Tom apologetically.

'They always say that. Haven't you ever seen a James Bond film? My head hurts, you silly boy!'

Victoria gently put the kitten on the floor. It promptly skidded away and hid under the fallen branch and Tom helped the man to his feet. 'You should go to the Sam Johnson accident hospital with a knock like that,' Victoria said. She dabbed the man's head with the end of her sleeve, desperately trying to wipe off the blood.

Tom stepped in to help her. 'We're sorry, but Victoria had a bit of an accident. We're not supposed to be out, and we've got to get her back to hospital and then hide the cats!'

Tom realised immediately what he'd said.

The man held his head with both hands. 'Look, I don't know what you two are up to but just give me my gun back and push off. I'll forget about the fact that you nearly killed me, and I won't go to the police.'

He was taken aback when Victoria retorted, 'Thank you and we won't go to the police either. Are you supposed to be waving a gun around at night? Whose rabbits are they and what's in that bag round your waist?'

'Oh, where's the little peeper gone now?' Victoria ran to the pellet ridden branch and began scrambling underneath. From another direction, the black mother cat appeared frantically running along the branch crying out loud for her baby.

'Two black cats,' said the man just as a little frightened kitten stuck his head through a branch and peered at the three people. Blackie rushed up to him, gripped her teeth around the back of her baby's neck and with one twist prised her baby from his trap.

'Two black cats,' the man repeated. 'I've got five of those.'

Victoria stood back in amazement. 'But you threatened us!'

'I found this little tribe of cats after the mess at the Dawkins place. I live in a cottage near the golf course. I've got a little smallholding and do a little private game keeping.' He reached to his waist and pulled off a small sack. 'You've got to if you want to feed that hungry bunch of kittens.' He held out the bag. 'I just stumbled across these rabbits. That's not poaching. It's conservation.'

Tom passed over the shotgun. 'We don't know what's going on, but it isn't right and we're just trying to protect the cats.'

'What do you think I'm doing? I've one of my own, my tabby who's now playing mother to this new brood, although they are a funny crew. They seem to talk to each other all the time. Come on, I'll show you—and anyway, I need a drink.'

Tom bent down to pick up Blackie. Peeps leapt into Victoria's arms as they followed the man on a short cross-country route to a small cottage that seemed hidden from the world.

As the man scrabbled under a plant pot Victoria stared at the front door and said. 'Is it made of gingerbread?'

'Don't be stupid,' he said. He pulled a key from beneath the pot and opened the door.

Victoria saw Blackie twist out of Tom's arms, her nose high in the air as if she scented something or someone really important. Through the nearest door, she went, and Victoria chased in only to see five kittens curled up contentedly. 'Blackie recognises them! She knows them. They are hers.' Then, she saw the man's Tabby, its tail raised and fluffed out, standing in the way and omitting a low warning growl.

Three people stood and watched, fearing a fight, when at that moment little Peeps squeezed out of Victoria's arms and fell to the ground.

She watched as he rushed at the dozy, sleepy kittens. He jumped into the middle of them, biting one, scratching another and nipping another's ear all in seconds. He was like a feline whirlwind. The big tabby sat back in astonishment.

Victoria yelped with pleasure as she saw the little band overwhelm the big black one.

'That's what I call a reunion. But I think you and I need to have a serious discussion!' The man sounded severe again.

Tom and Victoria followed him through a door to a small kitchen. She couldn't help herself turn around. She saw a contented mother lying on her back letting all her babies run around her and over her and lick her face with their tiny pink tongues.

Chapter Fourteen: The Cat Culling

'Put this one on here,' Watkins said, pointing to the tall table in the middle of the room.

Cairns nodded. Watkins was almost important, unlike the others. He had been appointed In Charge of Captured Cat Management, or 'Watkins IC/CCM' as it said on his door.

Cairns dropped the motionless figure of the cat, known to her kind as Craw, onto the tall table. It was positioned in the middle of the room with four long legs about a metre tall. The tabletop was like a small kitchen work surface, but it was just enough for a cat.

'Careful, Cairns,' Watkins said. 'This one is valuable. I've worked in this business long enough to know that you need to manage your specimens gently. Damage their bodies, or—worse—hurt them internally and the results might be invalid. Once we start the examination and the operations, we'll hope to have an idea of the cause of the disease and begin to evaluate the impact on people. There is only one question we are interested in: will this cat disease kill us all?'

Cairns poked the still figure of the cat called Craw with his rubber gloved hand. 'This one is really evil. Mind you, so are the rest of that little crowd.'

'Cairns, you talk about these animals as if they are thinking, living, breathing criminals!'

'Well, Mr Watkins, I think they are. You haven't seen what I've seen.'

Watkins pulled his white coat straight and sat beside the table. 'This is science, not silly stories told to frighten children.'

'There are children out there protecting this particular gang. I've got the evidence. These cat loving children aren't frightened!'

'This is a scientific investigation,' Watkins countered. 'We are here to get to the bottom of this and you'd better be careful what you say. As of today, there is a total news blackout about this story. The Government doesn't want any panic until we have some definite evidence. They've learned that from other pandemic scares. This could be the worst-hit bunch, but we seem to have it contained in this area.'

'All right,' Cairns said, 'I know. That prissy police sergeant has told me. He keeps on telling me that I have to be quiet. But the town is crawling with press. At the King's Head last night this journalist offered me cash for my story. Can you imagine that?'

'I can, but you'd be out of a job tomorrow if you said anything.' Watkins put the sad creature Craw on her side and pulled opened her eyes shining a small torch straight at her. The cat moved her paws in a slight twitch.

'Watch it—if she bites you anything could happen. You might be dead with the *shudder* by the morning.'

'Don't be stupid,' Watkins said. 'She is heavily sedated. The mask stops me breathing anything in and these gloves are thick enough to prevent her scratching me. The kit is better than the Personal Protective Equipment for the fight against the Coronavirus. This creature has to be prepared for the full examination.'

'We must have brought in a hundred of them—pretty much what you asked for. You've hardly got any more room in those cages.'

'That's true, and all newly caught cats will be taken to the second cattery building at Dawkins. There are facilities there to keep big numbers in relative security. Bonfires are on hold for the moment.'

'More's the pity,' interrupted Cairns. 'Provided you can stop them escaping again they should all have been sorted and finished off as soon as they got there.'

'Those cats that were destroyed were diseased and dying. There is no random cat-killing now—I hope that is clear. Now, leave me alone to prepare this animal for a surgical examination and you can get on with your work. We're working around the clock now and have got to have a quick solution.'

Cairns roughly pushed the limp cat to the centre of the table and walked out of the operating theatre into the holding bay. There were about ten cages on the floor. Inside them, Cairns saw the little band of cats that he so hated. 'My favourite cat friends,' he said soothingly. He reached over to a desk and picked up a ruler.

The objects of his affection were all sleeping on the floors of their individual prisons. Starting at one end he ran the ruler along each metal bar creating a sound like the rattle of machine gun. Each cat in turn jumped up, their eyes wide open. One ran to the back of its cage. Another raised its tail and hissed at Cairns. A third trembled with the shock and slipped to the floor. It was the cat that twitched who stood still and fixed Cairns with a stare.

'It's the tough guy! I remember you. Come on!' Cairns poked the ruler into the cage. Cairns pushed the ruler right up to him and poked the twitching one in the head.

'You!' said a voice. 'Stop that!'

Cairns turned and saw that a tall figure in a suit had walked into the room. 'I'm just keeping them in line,' he said in a subdued way.

The man in the suit was unimpressed. 'Who the hell are you?'

'I'm Cairns—I'm running this cat catching exercise.'

'Well, we're not running a torture chamber. At least I'm not. Listen to me, Mr Cairns.' The tall man moved within a few inches of Cairns' face. 'My name is Harrison. I'm the

Government's Chief Medical Officer in charge of researching this problem. I'm here to examine the adults that seem to have been infected or affected or whatever. But I will *not* have this type of intimidation in any institution that I'm involved with. So, leave now before I really lose my temper.'

Cairns looked back at Harrison. 'They're different, these cats. They're dangerous. They all need to be done for. Look that one is laughing.'

The doctor put his hand on Cairns' arm and spoke very quietly. 'Listen, I know this is causing massive stress all round. My medical opinion is that you need to have a few days off. I'll recommend it. Go on, go home. Have a good night's sleep. Things will seem different in the morning.'

'Not with this gang, they're dangerous.' Cairns walked towards the door. As he gripped the handle he turned to face the doctor. 'These few are different. One false move and they'll have you and make a real fool of all of you.' He threw the ruler across the room and it landed on the desk. 'You need to be careful, that's all!'

'Yes, thank you for the advice,' Harrison said quietly. 'Mr Cairns, I suggest that you should calm down and not make fun of these afflicted animals. Dangerous cats, my foot.' At that the cats gazed at the doctor's foot. 'If I wasn't feeling tired I'd swear they're making fun of me.'

'I told you—they *are* making fun of you. They've been making fun of me. Be careful.' Cairns didn't turn his back on the caged animals. Instead, he walked slowly in reverse, moving his eyes from cage to cage.

***

Nailz shouted out to the others. 'He's not as stupid as we think. He can walk backwards.' Tails hit the floor in appreciation of the wit. The doctor followed the startled looking Cairns while leaving the tent curtain wide open. Nailz saw a still figure of a large tabby illuminated by a large white light. Her pink tongue stuck out between her teeth. She was in total distress.

'Craw!' Twitcher shouted.

The body of the leader of the free spirits was lying on the table. The others turned to see that she had two metal clips that stretched her forehead unnaturally. Her face was in a frightening unreal grin that showed her sharp tiny teeth.

Twitcher started. 'They've put clips on her head! It's an experiment—it will happen to us all! We have to get out of these cages!'

'Not without Craw,' said Nailz. 'I shall drag her with my teeth if I have to. We will leave and get out of this place!'

'No,' a voice interrupted. 'No!'

'Who's that?' screamed Twitcher. The room went silent. There was no scratching and no movement.

'Listen to me,' the voice said. It was strained and echoed quietly through the dark, but it was Craw. 'We may be the captured cats, but we are the *knowing* cats. The men in the white coats are trying to find out our secrets. Since the *shudder* we are different. Dreamer, explain for me.'

The people have decided,' Dreamer said, 'that not only are cats going crazy but that this thing is being spread to the Providers. We know they're wrong because the *shudder* has changed us. It's made us different: better, brighter, sharper, even more able to manage these humans than we could in the old days.'

'Fantastic,' said Nailz, 'but we're all locked up!'

'Yes,' said Dreamer. 'And, as Craw says, they've brought the brightest, the best and the cleverest to the same place. We're all here. Locked up maybe, but we *are* here, and this has to be our opportunity—our *chance*—to change the cat world forever!'

'We can't rule the world, but we must find the answer,' said Craw, slowly and gently. Those who were able turned their heads towards the sound of her voice. She sat up even though the clips on her head were tight and pulled the hair from her face. As she strained, a strap pulled against her body. Her head reached up to the wide spotlight above. It covered her in a blinding white light that was the image of one of the great cats of the jungle.

From the caged cats there was a sigh—a sigh that filled the room, a sigh charged with hope.

'It is the Great Catskill!' shouted a caged voice.

'It *is* the Catskill!' said a second, and immediately many voices from many cages joined in.

'But it's only Craw,' answered Purrl.

'You have come to lead us and to save us!' said more of the caged voices.

'There —the sign!' a tiny Siamese screeched.

Craw turned her head and the clip fell away. She turned to the left and the second clip dropped off revealing a massive 'M' shape, part of her natural fur colouring that had not been shaved and was more clearly outlined on her forehead.

'It is the sign!' said a voice.

'It is the chosen one!' said another, a great longhair.

'Be quiet—the Great Catskill will speak again!'

Craw slowly turned her newly liberated head towards this caged multitude.

'That's Craw, not the Great Catskill,' said Twitcher as he sat back on his tail.

'It is the Great Catskill! She's here!' said one catty voice.

'It's a him,' said another.

'No! You never know—the Catskill can be a he or a she. It doesn't matter! The Catskill is amongst us. Here to save us, to make the great escape!'

Suddenly, every cage began to rattle and hum with an overwhelming purring.

Nailz watched as Craw pulled against the wires and the clips and strap. In the spotlight, she looked like the biggest cat in the world. As she turned to the wall Nailz saw her shadow in black—a cat that was the fastest, fittest, most frightening black cat ever—the jaguar.

The purring stopped. Craw began to speak.

'Listen I am not the chosen one. I am Craw. I am a simple cat. All Tabbies have the M sign. The Providers tell the story of one of Catkind—perhaps the Great Catskill who soothed the baby Jesus by its comforting purr. Mary, the mother of Jesus, bent down to write her initial on the forehead of this great cat and we still bear the sign. It is common to us all. Some of the Providers follow the writings of the prophet called Mohammed. His sleeping cat Muezza lay on his sleeve and rather than disturb him the Prophet cut off his own sleeve touching only the cat's brow, leaving for Muezza and all his descendants the sacred 'M' on his forehead.

'We are the inheritors of all the best of mankind. I do not wish to lead or direct you, but we must help ourselves. We have seen some great leaders in this crisis. Bootsie was one who shared with us his understanding of the soldier men. One day he will be a hero to Catdom just like the Great Catskill. My friends are here. We shall outshine every cat creature in the world. We shall bring honour and achievement to cats of all sizes, all types and all colours. Dreamer is here too. He is a cat of vision and he has had a dream that one day all cats will live together in peace and harmony with mankind. We are living through a terrible time. Many have died. Out of this we shall be stronger and better. We will come to understand how to live our lives with all other creatures of the world. We can have our dream.'

In the darkness Nailz spoke up. 'Even birds, mice, rats and the worst of all—dogs?'

'Nailz,' said Craw. 'Great change is with us, but we must survive this horror first!'

In the room there was a low noise that would have

troubled the ears of any human close at hand. It began as a slight hum, then developed into a throbbing sound and finally a great roar.

'Catdom!' Craw said loudly, 'I hear your noise! I hear your desire to survive. But we must be strong we must be clever, and we must live on! Most of all we must use the Providers.' There was a rumbling, snarling sound from the cages. 'We cannot survive without them and we must use them to our advantage. We *will* use them to our advantage!'

The rumbling turned into a chant as all the voices said, 'Catskill, Catskill, Catskill.'' Craw pulled herself up again, straining against the remaining binding. 'No.' The chant fell away. 'I am still Craw. But our strength is being together and acting together. Together we are great! In that way, the Great Catskill still lives!'

In the white tented room, not a cat stirred. They were humbled by the presence of Craw—the Great Catskill!

Chapter Fifteen: I Spy Cats

The shabby man went to the pot on top of the big black stove and turned the wooden spoon around and around. 'My name is Haskins,' he said. He kept stirring, mixing up the rabbit and pheasant that he'd thrown in the stew. He'd quickly de-feathered the birds and skinned the rabbits. 'It's only like taking their jackets off,' he'd said. 'No more than a peeling job really. I suppose they could eat this uncooked, but I feel I ought to prepare it a bit for them. You never know how delicate their baby tummies are.'

Victoria had found it ghastly and decided to think of something else instead. She turned to face him, wanting to thank him for his help and saving the kittens. 'Mr Haskins—' she started.

'Just Haskins!' he said. 'Everybody just calls me Haskins.'

'Well, Haskins... We've got a plan—Tom's got a plan, anyway—and... I guess you are going to help us?'

'No choice, I suppose. Roots wouldn't let me do anything else.'

'Roots?' Tom and Victoria asked at the same time.

'Roots, my cat. So-called because of his unfortunate kitten habit of digging up roots in the garden just as I was trying to plant things. The name stuck, and he's been my only companion of recent years. However, we seem to have a problem here. You've brought your cats and they've met with mine. That puts us all in dreadful trouble. I've had the soldiers over here letting me know of their preparations for the next *phase*.'

'You seem to know a lot about what's going on,' said Victoria.

Haskins fiddled with some papers on the table. 'Always pays to keep in with one's neighbours. They just like to let me know.' He put the paperwork down. 'We're being distracted. Now, this idea of yours—let me into the secret!'

Victoria felt slightly intimidated, as if a teacher was pushing her to give an answer to a difficult question. She half-glanced at Tom and nodded. 'His idea.'

'Well,' Tom started, '*we* felt we had to find out what was going on and I wanted to find my grey cat, Piner. Anyway, I don't believe these cats are dangerous—but I *do* think they're different.'

'If you say so,' nodded Haskins. 'So, what is this *master plan*?'

'We need to get inside the medical centre. We need to see what's happening. I want to find Piner. We know the old lady has been taken there and Samsy, the Beamans' little girl. They're saying anyone who has had contact with any cats since the cat sweep-up must go to the centre, especially if they've been scratched or bitten—and now Victoria has!'

Victoria felt she had to show the scratches as proof, but Haskins was staring at his papers. 'Why would you want to get inside?' he asked.

'If we could find out what's going on, I could let my mum and her cat committee know. We could tell the local papers, the radio station, put it on Facebook, on Twitter. The whole world must know what's going on because it's like a prison here and all the cats are being rounded up. It's an abhorrent story. Let's try and tell the truth!'

'And stop the killing,' added Victoria.

Haskins started to straighten the papers and square them up. 'Two youngsters visiting this high security clinic with a fantasy story isn't going to work. A major security blackout will stop all sources of information.'

Tom seemed crestfallen.

'However, there is some sense in your plan. The idea of

getting on the inside would certainly elicit some useful intelligence.' Haskins seemed to be almost talking to himself. 'You would be on the interior, showing up security deficiencies and the vulnerability of that temporary set-up as well as exposing the reality of the cat disease. I like it.'

Victoria felt as if they were being lectured to. The lesson went on and on. Haskins took off his rough poacher's jacket. 'The cover story needs to be very convincing. I like the scratch story. Show me, girl.'

Victoria pulled down the collar of her jumper and revealed the nasty scratches on her neck.

'That can't be pleasant,' Haskins commented. 'They'll certainly want to have a close examination of that. It is—obviously—real! From everything the chatter is saying, transmission of the disease could be from contact and certainly a blood injury.'

Victoria felt this Haskins man was too well informed. 'What's "chatter"?'

'Just gossip,' Haskins said. 'It's internet stuff and since coronavirus there are a thousand sites on Disease X and the next pandemic possibly another animal spread thing. I pick up things and people trust me. The plan makes sense to me, but what about your parents? It's practically dawn and presumably they'll be on the alert for you two when they discover you aren't fast asleep in bed.'

'And we're not supposed to be in touch with each other,' Tom said. 'I can't think how we can get around this.' He sat down and put his face in his hands. 'Not everyone is against us—it just feels like that. Our parents have just got our best interests at heart and at least one of the policemen is sympathetic. Some of the soldiers are quite kind. I don't think that sergeant likes what he's having to do—they're soldiers, not cat killers!'

Victoria was a little frustrated that Tom was just pouring everything out to this man they didn't know.

'And you think I've got good intelligence,' muttered

Haskins as he dropped down beside Tom. 'You are just going to have to go back home and try and get a bit of sleep. When your parents wake up they can't think anything unusual has happened. Then let us get together, and I'll take you to this medical place in the Square. We just need a good cover story.'

Victoria looked sheepish. 'A cover story?'

Haskins did not reply, and instead stared above both their heads. Victoria saw his cat, Roots, who seemed to be listening intently.

'Well I never,' laughed Haskins, suddenly lightening up, 'Roots likes the idea.' Blackie quickly leapt across the room and joined Roots near Haskins as if she wanted to show that she liked what they were saying.

Victoria was positive. 'I don't think they'll be a problem, Mr Haskins. I think they know you are proposing something and that we intend to help them.' Two tails rose in the air simultaneously.

This plan seemed to have received a vote of confidence from all parties, so Victoria and Tom set off from the cottage with the sky beginning to light up. They split up at the road leading to Victoria's. 'Tom I will see you in Lichfield as planned. Don't be late – text me if there is an issue although my phone signal seems to be very patchy.'

***

Victoria paced up and down outside the Garrick Theatre. She knew every show and drama that was on for the next six months. She thought she was on time but neither Haskins nor Tom had showed up. Had she made a mistake? There was no call or text.

From the corner of her eye she was aware of a man walking towards her—a man she didn't know. He walked right up to her and put his hand on her shoulder. This was an unwanted approach and she tensed.

'Victoria?'

She recognised the voice. 'Haskins? You're different.'

'I told you I'd polish up all right,' he said. 'Got my best suit and coat and given my hair a comb. Sorry I was late, but I had a hungry brood to feed and that takes time.'

'You are very smart, not rough at all.' Victoria thought she might have been rude but pushed on. 'Tom isn't here. Perhaps we should go without him.'

'Let's go for an Earl Grey tea in the Tudor Café and we can see if he arrives. We ought to give him a few minutes.' Haskins put his arm on Victoria's shoulder. 'It'll give us a chance to practice our story.'

They'd barely been in the café for a minute before Tom burst in, breathless as if he'd ran the whole way. 'Sorry!' he panted. 'I just couldn't get out of bed. I did text you, but it didn't go through. There's something wrong with the system!'

'That'll be them blocking the signals or something!' Victoria said. 'Mr Haskins says they'll do anything to intercept communications, but he has a plan. He is going to take me to the treatment centre and explain that I was scratched by a cat that he thinks might have been one of the ones that escaped from Dawkins. He's brought me, so I can be checked out.'

Tom pulled a funny face. 'That means you'll be alone. I wanted to be there as well.'

'That would be very strange. Why would you come with me? You can *visit* me—if they keep me in, which they might not.'

Haskins joined in. 'Victoria is right. I think it is for the best, Thomas. Let's find out the lie of the land. We may need help anyway. This whole situation is very scary—on my way here I met three army patrols and the cat pick up team. The city is surrounded. Everything and everybody is in lockdown again. Let's explore what is happening.'

Victoria could tell Tom was annoyed he had been overruled. 'Right then off you go. Perhaps I'll go back to bed! Contact me when you've been examined or when they tell you you've caught the cat disease.'

'Not necessary, Tom.' Haskins stood up. 'We're in this together and we'll need each other as things go on. Come on, Victoria—let's get you checked out by one of the doctors.'

Victoria was still a little shocked and upset at Tom's outburst. He'd always said that it wasn't possible to catch the disease from cats and now he was suggesting she might be infected.

'I'm sorry,' he said contritely. 'I didn't mean to say that. I'm tired. You go, and I'll hang around. They'll let you use your phone, won't they? I'll be here. Sorry.'

Victoria smiled weakly.

'That's settled that.' Haskins patted Tom on his back. 'We'll go, but we'll keep in touch with you as best we can.'

Victoria followed Haskins into the Market Square. It was covered with temporary structures of one type or another including a whole area covered by a giant tent. Even the statue of Dr Samuel Johnson, the great dictionary creator, was buried by white sheeting. Signs were pointing in a variety of directions with different instructions on each.

'This way,' said Haskins. He pushed Victoria towards a sign that was marked:

CAT INJURIES UNIT
For anyone who has received cat inflicted injuries or has been in contact with cats in the Lichfield City area.

A soldier was standing at the tent entrance with a gun clutched to his chest. Haskins went up to him. 'I think we've spoken before, haven't we? I'm Haskins, from the cottage by Dawkins' place.'

'Yes sir. I was at the planning session.'

Haskins jumped in quickly. 'My young relative...' He paused. 'My *granddaughter* here has been bitten by one of these loose cats, so I thought I should bring her over.'

'Yes sir.' the soldier pointed in the direction of another door marked *Examinations*. Haskins opened the door and gently pushed Victoria again, this time into a room with a desk and some chairs. Aside from being in a tent it was like any other doctor's waiting room.

A woman sitting at the desk looked up. She was wearing rubber gloves and a white mask. 'Sorry about the appearance,' she said, 'but we have to be careful. Right let me know why you're here and then we'll take it from there.'

Haskins explained their little cover story again and Victoria felt herself being led away behind a white curtain. She heard Haskins being fussed over by the woman in the mask.

'I'm sorry about this, Mr Haskins,' the woman said, 'but this has all been done in something of a rush and this is a makeshift field hospital. It's better we're away from all the conventional medical places in the area. We can't afford to let anything spread into the community. I must ask you to sign the Official Secrets Act before you leave. You'll appreciate the seriousness and the need for some degree of confidentiality at this moment.'

Haskins replied. 'Nurse, you will find that not only have I signed this kind of document previously, but that I still have to operate under its limitations. Haskins, Derek John. I am, albeit in reserve, still tied by the Act and other elements of secrecy.'

'Well,' the nurse stuttered, 'I suppose we can check that out, Mr Haskins. Nonetheless, will you sign, or should we contact higher authorities?'

'I'll sign—I'm sure my past is not relevant at this moment. However, if needs be, I can contact the Office and they will acknowledge my credentials. I'm simply a map man these days!'

'A map man?' said the nurse. *A map man?* thought

Victoria. *That was news.*

'A map man,' he repeated, 'no more, no less. It is now one of my hobbies, as well as a little hunting, fishing and shooting. I buy and sell old—*antique*—maps!'

The nurse passed over a form and Haskins signed without reading a word.

Victoria was thinking about Haskins when she felt an arm on her shoulder.

'Young lady, I'm Dr Jamieson. Now, tell me—have you had any other symptoms? Have you felt ill in any other way other than just soreness from the scratches?'

'No,' Victoria muttered.

Quickly and efficiently, the masked doctor exposed the site of the scratches on Victoria's neck. He examined them and gently dabbed some liquid on the red marks. Victoria was hopeful that her explanation was reasonably plausible. She desperately tried to remember the symptoms of the *shudder* as Tom had explained. All she could think about was staggering around with the peeping kitten in her arms, pretending to be sick and then getting lost.

Victoria scrunched up her nose and felt she should explain some more, 'Nothing really. Just a funny, woozy head— and I walked into a tree.'

'Did the cat jump at you? Did it seem unusually wild?' Dr Jamieson asked. He seemed concerned and Victoria nodded. He then rubbed again at the scratches with the liquid on cotton wool. 'You're going to have to stay here for observation and some more tests. We only have a few other patients here. When we've checked you out you'll either be sent home or to another special hospital. I'll have to speak to your parents. Who brought you in?'

'My—' Victoria paused. 'My grandad'

'That'll be fine, we've already got your details, so he can pass our advice on to your mum and dad. Unfortunately, you'll be allowed no visitors—at least while all the tests are going on. You're one of the few here that has had recent physical contact with a possibly infected cat. Not to worry! Nurse assures me that the scratches are very superficial. You're in the best place, in the best hands. I'll send your grandad in and he can say goodbye. If you have a mobile phone, we'll need to take it now.'

Victoria was offered some blue medical garments whilst Haskins was brought in. 'They've explained everything to me,' he said to her, 'and I'll tell your mum and dad.' In an awkward way he bent down and pecked her on the top of her head. Victoria wanted to laugh at his poor play-acting, but the nurse took her by the arm and led her away from Haskins.

'Don't lose those maps, grandad,' she said.

Haskins nodded slowly, smiled at the doctor, half-waved in a pale imitation of a real granddad and pushed his way out of the tented divider.

***

He had barely left the Market Square and the Medical Centre before Tom ran out from underneath the arches at the side of the old Corn Exchange.

'What's happened?' he asked excitedly. 'Where is she?'

'She's well,' Haskins said. 'She's inside and they're going to run tests on her.'

'But the tests won't show anything? It's just scare mongering.'

Haskins shrugged. 'We hope so, but we don't know so. They are obviously taking this very seriously- as am I. Let's hope she's okay. Tom, I do need to give you a little more detail on me if we're to carry on like this. I've given the medics a bit of an idea, but you should know as well.'

He walked off towards the Corn Exchange. 'Back to the cottage, Thomas. The next stage of the plan needs to be formulated, and I've got to sort your cover stories with the parents.'

***

Victoria was now sitting up in a bed waiting for some more tests. They had taken some blood, measured her blood pressure and done all sorts of other things. Now, they were going to wire her up to a machine. There was no way that she could talk to Tom and they'd said no-one could visit. She'd have to try and explore on her own when the moment was right.

She had no idea how long she sat on the bed. Eventually, the door opened and in walked Dr Jamieson. He was followed by the nurse who had also dealt with her earlier.

'I'd like to reassure you that there is nothing to fear,' he said. 'We are taking care of your best interests. As soon as we've finished all our tests, you'll be moved over to a regular hospital and then everyone will be allowed to see you. You're in very good hands and very safe. I'm going to get the nurse to give you one or two things that will help you get better much quicker. So, that's it. Relax, and I'll see you later.'

As he left he handed the nurse a set of medical instructions. She turned to the trolley and then came over to Victoria. 'There's nothing to worry about,' she said, 'it'll only be a little sharp sensation.'

Before Victoria knew what was happening, she felt a sharp prick in her arm and within a few moments she felt very tired and had to close her eyes. She could hear the nurse's voice, but it was as if she was disappearing down a long tunnel.

Victoria stepped into the tunnel and the ground felt squidgy beneath her feet, like jelly. She began to walk towards the light but as she moved it seemed to become more distant. She felt frightened but somehow, she knew she had to get to the light. It was then she heard a quiet, humming sound, growing and growing into a roar as if a thousand cats were purring as one. Victoria suddenly felt her whole-body jerk. She sat up in the high bed.

'This was a stupid master plan,' she said to herself. Her mouth was so dry, and her head hurt. *This must be how the shudder felt,* she thought. *Is this the end?* Her body twitched again but she was attached to something by the bed—it was a bottle on a stand. She rocked suddenly, pulling a needle out of her arm. She was free from the stand, the tube and the bottle.

Victoria lay quietly, watching a small trickle of blood run from her arm. All she wanted to do was leave, go home to her mum and dad and be safe. As she lay back on the pillow she expected someone to come, someone to have heard the rattle of the stand as she shuddered. 'Shuddered,' she repeated out loud. Did this mean that it was all true and she would die?

She had to find help. *Find the nurse, the doctor— anybody.* Victoria pulled herself from the bed and tried to stand up. Her feet felt unsteady and her hand was trembling. She grabbed the cover from the bed and felt terribly cold. She wondered why it seemed so dark everywhere. *Is it night-time? Have I slept all day?*

Shivering, she shuffled over to the tent curtain and it opened smoothly. 'Hello?' She heard her voice, but it sounded weak and distorted. 'Hello?' she repeated, more loudly. No one replied. Making her way through the tent, she padded towards a light at the end of the corridor—one just like the light in her dream. It was behind another curtain. 'Hello?' she said again. There was still no response.

Victoria pulled back the fabric. The room behind it was brightly lit, containing a single bed again surrounded by all sorts of machines. Victoria immediately recognised Mrs Constance, the old lady who lived opposite Tom.

She moved over to the bedside and Mrs Constance seemed to be breathing quite calmly. 'Hello!' It seemed to be the only word Victoria could say. There was no sound from the sleeping lady, but she did make a loud throaty snore. It was the nearest thing Victoria had heard to a human sounding like a purring cat.

Heavy footsteps on the stone flags drowned out the comforting snore. She felt frightened and exposed but she didn't know why. *I'm not supposed to be here, that's why.*

Instead of waiting for the steps to arrive at the room, she slipped to the floor and rolled under the bed. Amazingly, her head felt clearer and she wasn't shivering so badly.

Victoria heard some hurried shuffling footsteps followed by the voice of Dr Jamieson. 'Nurse, let me see Mrs Constance's charts.'

There was a silence and then a ruffling of papers.

'Good. This is all very steady. It simply seems as if she had a fainting fit combined with a bit of a heart flutter. I don't see any signs of anything else. Those cats around her don't seem to have marked or scratched her. Wake her up for me, nurse.'

The nurse fussed around the old lady and Victoria heard her speak. 'It's all right,' Mrs Constance said. 'I heard you say hello a moment ago—but I decided to keep my eyes shut.'

'No Esme,' the nurse said reassuringly, 'You didn't hear a thing.'

'Now, I'm not losing my mind whatever you think!' Mrs Constance replied. 'I definitely heard someone say hello. Anyway, what do you want? I've got to get back to my dog.'

'Mrs Constance, we need to make sure you are perfectly well.'

'I'm all right. What about Samson? He's a silly dog, not like the smart cats. He needs daily nursing.'

'Of course, he does,' the nurse said soothingly. 'I understand your son Hugh and the rest of the family are taking care of him. You've had quite a turn—probably a heart flutter which we've treated as best we can for the moment, and a fall. Currently, we think we can rule out any other infection from unusual sources, but we must be one hundred per cent sure.'

'Paff!' said Mrs Constance. Victoria stifled a laugh. 'One of you said hello. I definitely heard you.'

'Thank you, Mrs Constance,' Dr Jamieson said with a touch of impatience. 'We'll be off now. I'll see you later. Nurse let's check the others and the girl. She is still a worry for us, I think.'

Victoria listened as the footsteps left the room. *The 'girl' is still a worry...* Did they mean her? But she felt better as the woozy effects of the injection were wearing off.

She pulled herself slowly from under the bed and stood up. As quietly as she could she began to creep towards the door, but something snagged the back of her gown. She'd been caught! The nurse and doctor hadn't left.

'I knew it was you,' the old lady said. 'What are you doing here?'

Victoria froze.

'You're little Tommy's girlfriend,' Mrs Constance continued.

'I'm a *friend*,' Victoria said, 'but I am trying to help— trying to find out the truth about the cats.'

'There is nothing wrong with them. They're the smartest cats I've ever seen. That whole crew, they're brilliant. And they saved me. I know they used the phone. I've heard them talking about it in here. The policeman who followed up the call told me the cats screamed down the phone—at least, he *thought* that's what it was. I told him those cats are smart, smarter than those dumb cat catchers.'

Mrs Constance was sitting up in bed and one of the machines was starting to hum loudly. Victoria turned to the door remembering that the doctor was off to see the 'girl' and they might find out that she wasn't in the bed where she was supposed to be. 'I've got to get back to my bed. I'll try and come back later. I'm trying to find the cats.'

'Ho!' said the old lady, 'they're here all right. You mean

you didn't hear the noise before you came in? I've heard little bits and pieces of cat squealing when they were brought in, but this was different. I'm sure the walls shuddered. It started like a distant purring sound and was practically a rumble by the time it finished. It's a wonder the soldiers didn't hear it—although the nurse did tell me they are mostly at all the entrances to stop any protesters or journalists getting in. Why are you here?'

'I was scratched by a big black cat and the doctor seemed really worried.'

'Dearie, I listen to people and make my own mind up. I've seen some strange things with these cats. Don't you believe for a minute that they're killing you or killing the rest of us! I think they have caught something that's killed some of them. I've seen some of them—the old ones, the weak ones, the fancy ones—die. My friend Lilly nursed her Siamese for days when he couldn't even walk. But it hasn't hurt her, she's always been cranky, and she does fall over a bit but that's when she hits the Sherry bottle.' Mrs Constance giggled. 'Go on, get back to bed! Those cats may need your help. Don't forget I know more than I let on and I'll be listening even when I'm asleep.' She winked, giggled again and flopped on the pillow as if she were dead. 'Go on—you'll need more time in here to find out the truth.'

Victoria gave a little wave, rushed up to the door and peeked out. There was no one about. She turned and waved at Mrs Constance again before sidling out into the corridor. It took a moment to decide which way to go—there were lights at either end but no signs on the walls. *No time to hesitate*, she told herself. She rushed back to the light at the end of the corridor to her right.

Within seconds she was there. She turned to check that there was no one behind her and then pulled open the curtain to her room. It was then she got the shock of her life.

Instead of being near her bed, she was in another part of the tented structure and it was full of cages. She'd come the wrong way and walked into a prison! There was cage upon cage around the room and in each cage was a cat. Those that had not died were here, perhaps the brightest and best. With dread, she realised that these were the ones destined for the experiments.

There was an eerie silence in a space that contained so many creatures. Victoria saw that every cat had its eyes on her. She was the centre of their attention. She heard a cat speak—it was from another space in the tent, but she could see it because the cat was lit up by a light above it.

The cruelly trapped cat fixed its gaze on Victoria and fought against the straps. She spun and snarled as she tried to free herself. Then she stopped, stared at Victoria and let out a petrifying howl!

Victoria was desperately frightened in the dim tent with these caged animals. Was this the craziest cat of all? Would this creature attack her and kill her? Somehow, she couldn't stop herself rushing down between the cages to the strapped cat. 'This can't be right!'

She paused before entering the lit area. It was horrible. Should she let the creature go—could she set it free? Victoria wasn't aware how close she'd got to the cages until she felt claws gripping her flimsy hospital gown. They pulled her towards the cage, away from the cat in the light. She felt faint, as if the drugs were taking effect again. *Or is it the disease?*

'Look,' it was a voice in the dark.

'What?' she asked, bewildered.

'Look—me. Me?'

'Me?' Was it a cat voice? Victoria turned to see a small grey cat that seemed wet and miserable. She turned away but even with the sterile scent of the hospital in the air she could still smell a vague scent of pine. 'Piner? Tom's cat, is it you?'

'Me. Me-ow.' Piner drew his claws in.

'Miaow?' Victoria giggled. *This place is playing tricks*

on me. 'I thought you were talking, even calling me. But it is you. What's happening? I wish you could talk.' She felt frustrated. 'It's as if you want to talk but can't. Piner, I know you, you seem to be talking to this one, this poor one with the straps.' She saw Piner move gently towards the trapped cat and paw at the bonds.

'You want me to take off these horrible things?' Victoria paused. These cats were clever. She paused a moment and moved towards a pitiful creature known as Craw. Piner stood up on all fours and began a gentle purr. All the cats in all the cages stood up and purred.

This wasn't like the sound that Victoria had heard in her dream. This was a calmer and comforting sound. 'I'll do it,' she said. 'I'll untie you from these horrible straps if I can. I know that's what you want.' She walked slowly up to the trapped cat Craw on her high table. Somehow, she was still feeling uncertain. The scratches on her neck prickled. What if this cat became free and leapt at her? What if she was diseased and dying?

She put her hand out towards the shackled animal. The cat tipped her head, as if willing Victoria to stroke it.

Victoria's mind was spinning. 'Listen, I must trust you and you must trust me. Do you understand?' The captured cat looked towards the tabletop. 'Does that mean yes? I wish I could tell you that we have saved some cats, a black one and her babies, but you don't understand do you– any of you?'

Victoria saw the cats in their cages rubbing their cheeks against their imprisoning bars. It was the sound of contentment, a sense of peace.

They do understand, she thought. *Somehow, they know.* She touched the strapped cat. 'You do understand, don't you?'

She pulled clips from the trapped cat's head and then tried to find how the straps were tying her down. While some held her to the sides of the table, others seemed attached to her fur. Victoria scrabbled at the straps and loosened them. Some of the clips she couldn't remove. They were stitched into the cat's fur and there was no hope of taking them out.

The cats began scratching around in their little cages. They could hear something. Someone was coming, and Victoria was as trapped as they were.

Chapter Sixteen: The Origins of the Cat Plague

Victoria was only aware of her heart pumping and the eerie silence from the cat cages. She heard steps and voices. She recognised that of Sergeant Wilkes from the previous day. He paused at the entrance way to the medical centre. 'Shall we check on the cat cages before your briefing session with the staff, Dr Jamieson?'

'I hardly think that is necessary. Who is going to get in here? The place is better guarded than the average prison. The cats aren't going to try a mass breakout, are they?'

'I'll check—it *is* military training. I know the cages are inspected every 30 minutes, but you can never be too sure.' The sergeant took a step back and looked into the big tent. 'Why is the big cat on the table? I can see it in the spotlight.'

'It's drugged, or ready to be drugged before the tests begin. It's normal.'

Victoria felt her nausea return.

'I really had better check,' Wilkes replied as he stepped into the examination room. 'We don't want any more runaways getting into the general cat population. I don't want any cat getaways on my watch.'

'Sergeant, stop fussing,' Dr Jamieson said. 'We have a video link with the Government Minister in London after this briefing. The link-up is going to happen any minute. Everybody is getting very twitchy, sergeant. This has become political—they are really frightened of messing this up. The Coronavirus is very close in my memory and we know what happened there. That disease is still in everyone's mind but especially the politicians don't forget some important people died and the cause was initially linked to the consumption of infected animals and there was cross infection between people and animals.

You'll remember the disasters over mad cow disease? The foot and mouth outbreak? The killing of all those farm animals—most of it was totally unnecessary.'

Wilkes stepped back again. 'Remember? Don't you remember who had to do all the dirty work? The army— again! My boys didn't like having to slaughter thousands then, and they like it even less now. Cats are their pets, part of their family. This meeting had better come up with some good reasons for the experiments and then the killing or we'll have a riot on our hands—not my boys but ordinary people!'

'Sergeant Wilkes, this is a medical matter first and foremost! This briefing is to discuss those matters with your chiefs and mine. We won't be asked for an opinion on how cat owners feel—just what the medical and military options are.'

'Yes sir.' Wilkes saluted slowly. 'Sorry—you know where I stand.'

'Right, here we are. I've had the top people put in this tented area as well as the medical experts. I know it's next to the cat holding area but that is the only space big enough and it's where the big TV screen for the Government video conference is.'

Victoria knew this was her 'spying' moment and she felt even sicker. She could hear but needed to get into a position where she could see who was talking.

The first voice was deep and authoritative.

'Gentlemen,' he began, 'let me make the introductions— most of you know me by now, but to repeat: I'm Major-General Summers of the Royal Veterinary Corps, and I am the Gold Commander. Shortly, we shall be joined by the Home Secretary on a video link from the Home Office. The Prime Minister may join him but there is an emergency meeting of the cabinet—COBRA—taking place now to examine the issues that we'll be going through today. This is a potential national disaster. The Government desperately doesn't want to make a hash of this one because of the public sensitivity—not to mention the unfortunate mishaps with similar disasters: Covid-19, Sars, mad cow disease, foot and mouth, bird flu, swine flu, monkey pox. Don't forget, Ebola started through the eating of diseased bats.

Victoria had managed to get a small spy gap in the tenting and could just make out the scene.

The Major-General sat down and indicated for the assembled group to do the same. Everyone did so. Most had note-taking devices to hand, ranging from simple notebooks through to tablet computers and laptops.

'No notes are to be taken,' Summers said, eyeing his audience. 'Everything must be committed to memory. All phones should have been handed in.'

Tablets and notepads were placed down, laptops were switched off. There was silence in the room, as well as in the cat tent. Victoria could hear every word. All the caged cats sat totally still.

'First off, the medical scenario as we understand it. I'll be non-technical and make this as simple a story as I can. There are nine million cats in this country. Most are household pets, some are part wild or in the case of the feral cats, totally wild. They may be responsible for, at least, two hundred and seventy-five million deaths a year in the UK alone.'

The general paused for the full effect of this dramatic statement to hit those gathered in the room. There was total silence and shock on the faces of all those within.

'By that, I mean voles, mice, bats, frogs, birds and any other things cats take a fancy to.'

There was a burst of low-key laughter before he continued. 'Although we know that millions of people have cats at home, there are many who dislike or even hate them.

Twenty-five cats have been poisoned in Huddersfield in England. In San José, California, news of this possible epidemic seemed to have resulted in cats being disembowelled, skinned and dismembered. This was the repeat of something that happened as long ago as 1999. The US police suspect the same perpetrators. These incidents are occurring across this country and we have reports of some shootings of many wild cats in Rome, Italy. In Australia some are calling for a mass culling of all cats that are not indoors. It's a follow-on from the knowledge that Coronavirus began with infected animals in Wuhan at a wet market with the original host probably being bats.

Victoria heard the amplified voice echo around the tent. The cats seemed even more subdued—some were now lying on the floor of their cages and others seemed to have their paws over their ears as if they didn't want to hear.

'Ten thousand years ago a dreadful bug came into existence—something so small that only in modern times, with modern equipment, could we see it. This bug is called *toxoplasma gondii*. You won't need to remember the name. This thing spread to humans. When it infects us it can lead to brain inflammation, serious sight problems, even defects in babies. The bug was once thought to be harmless, but experts have since changed their minds. Scientists at Washington University, St Louis, the University of Georgia in the USA, and Cambridge University here in England were the ones to discover this. Now, Dr Fuller Torrey of the Stanley Medical Research Institute has found further links between people developing mental problems and keeping cats. CNRS Research Institute in France has linked the bug with brain cancer in its owners. Sporothrix brasiliensis, a mutant fungal threat, is feared to be rapidly increasing inside cats and can be transferred lethally to humans through bites and scratches. Professor Andrew Cunningham of the Zoological Society of London has said that these diseases that cause a zoonotic spill over and a novel pathogen can move from animals to people.

'Why tell you this story? Because T.Gondii can *only* reproduce in the bodies of cats! The cats even infect mice with the bug, and it makes the little grey creatures behave stupidly, recklessly and stagger around in circles so that cats can catch them more easily. This may be the cause of what is being called the "*shudder*" and may have been spread into the human population in this area where it seems there is the first known outbreak of this potential plague.'

Victoria heard a cat squeal and put her finger to her mouth.

The Major-General heard the cry. 'On cue. One of the captured cats must have heard me!'

The audience laughed again.

Victoria watched and listened in horror to the speech and put her finger to her mouth again. She hoped the cats would understand but, how could they? She'd have to get back to her room—perhaps she'd got this toxiwhatsit bug!

General Summers was speaking again. 'We've received the copy of the Long Island Cottage Hospital, New York study that shows black cats are really dangerous. They produce something called *Fel-d1* which creates appalling allergic reactions in humans. Said reaction can increase twenty times if you sleep with them, according to Dr Shahzad Hussain. So, whatever you do, don't sleep with a cat!'

The audience laughed again.

Victoria heard a cat call out.

It was Nailz again who called out. 'It's not us that are dangerous in bed. Don't sleep with a human—they roll over and flatten you!' This time the cats seemed to laugh.

The Major-General heard this louder mutter of cats. 'Perhaps we should turn the speakers down, or the cats will know our plans.' The audience snorted again. 'This isn't funny! I haven't finished with the dangers from cats. You'll know how unprepared we were for the SARS epidemic.

Scientists have traced the SARS virus to a cat eaten as a delicacy in China—the civet. Eminent Professor Yuen Kwok-Yung has stated that it is highly likely the virus jumped from cats to humans. So, if you think cats are warm and cuddly, be aware they can kill.

'That's the scientific summary. This may be something totally new, a killer virus that kills many cats but then breaks the species barrier like the Nipah virus. There is no doubt that all cats may be infected, some survive as carriers of the disease and then the virus crosses to their human owners. Governments across the world are awaiting the results of our research, but to avoid panic and maintain calm we must keep the details of what we've discovered secret until our Government is ready to act. Finally, Disease X has been identified by the World Health Organisation as a real killer and one that jumps from animals to humans. It's another zoonotic infection and this might be the one that could destroy humanity. You will appreciate our fears. Dr Jonathan Quick of the Harvard Medical School and Chair of the Global Health Council has called for urgent action on his fear of a global pandemic 'around the corner' which may originate and mutate in animals. This is a voice of the highest medical credibility and we may be the cutting edge of Disease X.'

'Horror of horrors - the Royal Society has just produced research that T.gondii, which started 10,000 years ago may have affected already 50% of the world's population linked to car accidents, neuroticism and suicide and stranger than all of that it actually drives risk taking in business and promotes entrepreneurial activity. You couldn't make it up.'

He paused and looked around the area. 'There is a total lockdown on all media especially social media. All phone signals, mobile and landlines within the designated area, are shut down. Secrecy is paramount.'

'Secrecy?' Victoria felt afraid and then jumped as a cat screeched.

'I don't suppose we can ask the cats to be quiet during the meeting?' Summers commented. 'Or are they really clever cats after all? They seem to be plague survivors!'

Another snort of agreement came from the gathering.

'I'll now hand you over to another of my military team,' the Major-General said.

Victoria was petrified. She was sitting in the middle of all these cats who might have some of these incurable diseases.

'Captain Cummings,' said a new voice. 'From the Royal Logistics Core. Our role, together with our colleagues from the Royal Engineers, will be to prepare for the final solution and the elimination of cats from this area to help demonstrate that we can kill them all, cleanse the locality and ensure that all humans are safe. Can we do it? We have previous experience during this country's animal scares. Our biggest pit was a grave for half a million animals. It can be done, and we've identified, together with the waste disposal industry, safe sites for burning and burial. We have men who have been involved in the Gulf Wars and Afghanistan. They don't relish this. But these are good soldiers. We're working with all our colleagues to bring their expertise to the logistical effort required to carry out the plan. I should add that the Australian Government is planning to unleash every weapon in its arsenal to wipe out 2 million feral cats and provide $5 million Australian dollars for ordinary people to serve as foot soldiers in what they describe as a battle. Let us remember the Coronavirus slogan *Catch it, Bin it, Kill it* might apply very well.'

He turned to a large map. 'This is our battleground—the sealed area. The red flags mark cat sightings, the green shows cat captures, once this map is all green, we'll have won the battle. It's a proper lockdown where we can contain the virus and stop it becoming international like Covid-19.'

The Major General cut in. 'At this point I should say that we are about to begin the medical testing on these cats, beginning with one particular group that has proved to be notoriously difficult to catch. Correct, Mr Cairns?'

Cat Catcher Cairns was in the room. He said 'Yes,' and nodded vigorously. A slow hissing could be heard from the cat prison.

Victoria felt the sense of hatred at that voice

'They don't like your voice, Mr Cairns,' said the Major-General.

'They know me, that's why.'

'Let's not get carried away. I'm sure they've nothing against you personally.'

'Yes, we have,' said Victoria.

'Oh, yes we have!' Victoria heard a cat mimic the sounds she made. This shout was approved by all the cats as they flapped their tails against the bars creating a strange rumbling sound.

Victoria feared they were copying her now.

'Perhaps they do resent you, Cairns.'

The audience laughed almost with relief as Cairns blushed.

'That's it,' Summers said. 'All Government ministers and senior advisers have been given the same information at the same time. The Home Secretary will address us now from the centre of national security at the Home Office.'

There was the face of a white-haired man and his voice boomed out from the big speakers. It was so loud that Victoria covered her ears.

'My thanks to the Major-General for giving you all the information that we have,' the Home Secretary intoned, 'as well as for emphasising the simple fact that cats could be instruments for the spread of this potential plague. I choose the words *could be* with some care, and also the word *plague* should perhaps be avoided in public. I am a patriot, but also a politician and we have to consider all the implications of the cat culling continuing. We will not be able to keep this as low key as we have for much longer,

189

although the media is—shall we say—*in our confidence* and will not release anything for the moment! Although there is pressure from Governments around the world to keep them closely informed and not let this get out of hand. The failure of the Chinese Government to isolate Covid-19 initially should be a lesson to us all.

The audience applauded quietly as the Home Secretary suddenly turned to his right. A cat had walked into the picture.

Victoria saw the caged cats raise their tails in recognition of the voice. 'I'm here for you all,' it said.

'I can't believe this,' the Home Secretary said. 'A cat has just appeared in this room! Let's hope she isn't crazy.' He spoke to someone off-camera. ''Can we get it out? We don't want her sending secret reports from the centre of Government.'

There was an uncomfortable laugh from those watching the screen as they saw a civil servant try to grip the slippery cat. She directed her comments to the screen and while no-one understood Victoria, somehow, felt it was an important message.

'It's Peta,' said the on-screen cat, 'I am here, trying to find out anything that will help you.' It twisted and turned violently, managing to land on all fours, before shouting out again. 'I know you're close to the screen there and I think you might be able to hear me. Before they drag me out—I am in and out of here and I will do whatever I can to save you and the whole of catkind. You are not the only ones who have had the shudder.'

The cat jumped onto the shoulder of the Home Secretary and curled around his neck whilst purring loudly. 'You've got to use your cat skills when the moment comes, ask the Great Catskill!'

The Home Secretary, quite a catty person really, thought it quite amusing that this intruder had casually wrapped itself around his neck. 'Pussy, down you go.'

Graciously, Peta walked across his shoulder onto the desk and as a security man opened the door she shot straight out.

'Extraordinary,' said the Home Secretary, looking totally unfazed. 'I should mention that we have had a long tradition of cats here at the Home Office—since 1929 when Peter the First was installed as the Home Office cat, followed by Peter the Second, then the Third and next Peta, she was a lady I'm told. So, perhaps I shouldn't be surprised to find a cat interrupting this cat conference. Now back to the business in hand: I have one thing to add to the medical briefing that you've just had. Most of you probably won't remember Major, he was a 12-year-old lion at Newquay Zoo. I used to take my grandchildren to see him every year. Well, the Chief Medical Officer has confirmed to me that he died of feline spongiform encephalopathy, mad cat disease, an exact replica of mad cow disease. This may be among us and in the cats—another theory.'

Victoria felt uncomfortable again and the scratches hurt. She hoped the cats would be quiet.

But they growled and snarled even more.

'What is that racket?' the Home Secretary stopped reading his script.

'Sorry, Home Secretary,' said Major-General Summers, 'we are next to the containment area where our cats that will be tested are housed. They just make sounds every so often.'

'I can understand why they are. They aren't likely to get out of there.'

Nailz shrieked again in what sounded like total defiance.

'I think that one sounds seriously annoyed,' joked the Home Secretary.

'He is, but he's clever with it!' shouted Cairns who couldn't keep quiet any longer.

Victoria realised everyone was against them in this tent.

Major-General Summers coughed. 'That's Mr Cairns,

sir, our chief cat catcher. He's convinced they're not mad, just clever.'

'My wife thinks the same, Mr Cairns.' The Home Secretary checked his papers. 'The job now is to complete the testing process. The cats will be examined by the Royal Veterinary Corps together with the help of specialists from the UK Defence Medical HQ fortunately close to us here in Whittington. The procedure will involve physical dissection of their bodies. We will cut into and examine the brains of these animals for any sign of the diseases we've been talking about. Like the coronavirus this started probably in one location and spread and today Lichfield has, as far as we can tell, the biggest concentration of affected cats in the world, a genuine major cluster of the disease. That is why we must act here, act decisively, aggressively and successfully.'

'Oh dear', Victoria feared the worst as another cat cried out in protest.

'Not a cat again,' said the Home Secretary. 'I'll start believing they can understand me in a minute.' He turned to his right and nodded. 'Colleagues, the Prime Minister and the President of the United States will be joining us for the end of this briefing. I hope this reinforces how seriously the world is taking this matter. The President's presence in London is top secret, however she may be joining you at your headquarters within the next day or so!' There was a rattling of tails on bars from the ranks of those imprisoned.

'Glad to see enthusiasm from the cats – if that's what it is,' said the Home Secretary as he stood up and shook hands with someone off screen.

'Please continue,' said a new female voice from the screen.

'Thank you, Madam President. It remains only for me to say to the medical staff that you will have to test them as thoroughly as you can to establish as quickly as possible if people will die from this disease—whichever one it is!

Time is not with us. You have hours rather than days. Gentlemen, this is an issue that will affect every community in this country—every community in the world. There must be no mistakes, but there may have to be painful decisions. We may have to destroy the nation's favourite pet—and kill every single cat in the country. It is my duty to protect the health of the nation.'

In unison, the cats howled their resentment.

'That's diabolical,' remarked the President.

'Madam President,' the Home Secretary said, 'it is the cats that are to be experimented on, they are next to the screening room and can hear us.'

'And we can certainly hear them—let's hope they co-operate. But may I speak to your people there?'

'Of course.'

Suddenly, a woman's face appeared on screen. 'I know this is going to be tough for you, but I want you to know that we appreciate what you are doing. We hope that this condition is not a human killer with the terrible impact of the coronavirus and that the relationship between humans and cats can continue for ever. We shall all lose if that is not the case. Cats were one of the earliest domesticated animals. They give so much pleasure to so many people. I want to go back to the White House and tell the house cat that she's still safe—and that we are too!'

Victoria turned to the cats and saw one swing its tail. It thumped his tail again on the bars and there was a slight ring in the air. Within seconds the ringing got louder and louder as all the cats began to bang the cages.

The President turned. 'A sound like bells? What is that?'

The Major General nodded at Sergeant Wilkes. 'Sort that out please, sergeant.'

'Sir! I think it's the cats, they're banging the bars on their cages.' The sergeant hurried out of the meeting area and said to himself, 'And what am I supposed to do?'

'Very musical cats you have there,' said the President.

The Home Secretary came back onto the screen. 'I think we can do without the musical interlude. I believe you all know what you have to do and how vital your work is. Thank you.'

The Home Secretary abruptly ended the transmission and the screen went blank.

'All right you horrible lot, just give it a rest.' Sergeant Wilkes shouted at the cat cages. He knew it would have no impact, but at least his lords and masters would know he was trying. There was silence. Not a cat tail was moving. The ringing had stopped. The sergeant was sure that all the cats were staring at him. 'You're weird,' he said as he turned to march back to the meeting. 'Really weird.'

Victoria was still holding her breath. She'd gulped in a mouthful of air when she'd heard the sergeant shout. Thankfully, Wilkes had stormed straight out but she was still trapped and had no idea how to get out and get back to her room without being seen. She slowly stood up and looked around her at all the caged cats. What on earth could she do?

She went towards Piner hoping he'd have an answer for her when she saw he was staring towards the door. Victoria turned and then heard a familiar voice. 'Why on earth are these poor cats locked up like this? It's inhuman.'

'Mrs Constance,' Victoria said. 'You should be in bed.'

Esme Constance entered the room, smiling and nodding. 'I should? Well, so should you. I knew you'd get up to something when you left me. I think we'd better pretend to be lost or we'll both be in trouble.'

Victoria rushed over to Mrs Constance and gave her a little hug. 'I've heard what they said at the meeting—these cats have got horrific things wrong with them and they're giving it to people all the time! They're going to experiment on them and us as well!'

'Now dear, my view has always been to trust your own instincts. I think these cats are smarter than the average cat.

Somehow, in some way, incredibly special.'

'What are you doing?' came another voice from behind them. Doctor Jamieson and two other people were standing in the doorway.

And we have just been caught, Victoria thought.

'Oh, where am I?' Mrs Constance said pathetically. 'What's happening? Oh, my dear—thank you for helping me. I don't know where I am!' She put her hand to her head and clutched at Victoria's shoulder.

Victoria was astonished at Mrs Constance's acting, it was totally convincing.

'Get her, one of you,' said the doctor. 'Gently, please, and get her back to her room.'

Mrs Constance smiled weakly at Victoria. 'Thank this little girl—she was trying to get someone to help me.'

'Okay, Mrs Constance,' Jamieson said patiently. 'Back to your room.' He turned his gaze to Victoria. 'You mustn't be here; these cats could kill.'

The doctor led her away from the cat prison and in the real direction of her room. 'Now, settle down and get some sleep,' he said. 'We have to get down to some real testing with you and we don't want you exhausted. You're very red faced. How do you feel?'

'I'm not really sure,' said Victoria as she walked into her room and was helped onto the bed. 'I think I have a headache.'

The doctor smiled and put the back of his hand on her forehead. 'I'm sure that's all it is.'

That's what Victoria really hoped too.

***

There was silence in the cat prison. After all the excitement, the cats were very tired. *Cats must sleep,* Craw thought. *In fact, normally we'll sleep most of the time, but these are not normal times.* She pulled at her bonds again. They were looser, but she was not yet close to being free.

'It says here in this paper on the floor of my cage...' Tel

started.

'Shut up, Tel!' a voice rang out. 'We all know you can read, and we don't need it now!'

'It says here that cats have been able to open cages,' Tel said as if he had not been interrupted. 'In this *Telegraph* newspaper, somebody called Celia says that cats in catteries have learned how to get out of cages by observing how the cages were opened.'

The floor of every cage was examined carefully. Every cat in every cage wanted to show off their reading ability.

'It says on the paper on my floor that the world is getting warmer,' said one cat. 'It says here that there are water shortages.'

'Too many storms!' shouted another.

'Not enough storms!' came a third.

'Listen!' Craw shouted over the top of the cat chatter. 'Stop reading! Tel has found out something useful. Somewhere, at some time, cats worked out how to open cages. If they can, we can. *You* can. I'm still tied and can't move properly, one of you could help me.'

'We've done it,' said two voices simultaneously. Skoot and Toot dashed into the open leaving their cages.

'Get back and close the doors,' warned Craw. 'You must show us how to do it and we can all get out of the cages. Remember: together we are strong. Skoot, what did you do?'

Skoot walked back to her cage with her tail in the air, evidently pleased to be the centre of attention. 'Like this,' she said. 'Toot was in his cage next to me and I reached out to touch him. When I did, I knocked a little piece of metal. It moved, but I didn't think anything about it until Tel said that cats learned how to open cages. I found I could put my paw through the front of my cage and push the metal bit. I pushed and pushed, and then Toot pushed the front of the cage and it came open. It worked because I was able to move the little bar and Toot finished it off.'

Suddenly, no one was interested in reading the papers. Cats were leaning across cages and pushing with their paws. Some opened very quickly but others were harder to push and needed greater patience.

Craw again pulled herself as high as she could. 'Think. Don't rush!'

The excitement in the room was so great that she couldn't be heard over the clanging of cage doors. Once freed, spirits rushed left and right, greeting old friends and meeting new ones. There were bodies running everywhere enjoying their new-found freedom.

'Stop!' Craw shouted. *This is all happening too fast. There's no plan, no order.* 'There must be a plan!' she yelled. 'Bright spirits, think. Please think!'

As she spoke, she heard a shuffling nearby that filled her full of fear. It was coming from the tent at her side. As she turned to it, the curtain separating the cats from the people was pulled back, and behind was a soldier with a gun in his hand.

There was no escape for her scuttling multitude.

Chapter Seventeen: Cats Can't Cry

Haskins was gently stroking the back of Blackie's neck as she rubbed hard against his leg. On his lap he had three kittens which in moments became four, five and six—all desperate for the biscuits he had cupped in his hand. 'There's plenty where these come from. Just slow down, you silly things! Tom, help me here. I can't cope.'

Tom went over to Haskins and picked up two of the kittens. They twisted and turned and purred at the same time.

Playtime was suddenly interrupted as the phone rang.

'Quiet.' Haskins turned sharply. 'Tom, put all the cats in the next room.'

It took Tom ages to round them up as they ran all over the place, but Blackie and Roots amazingly pushed or carried all the kittens into the next room.

'Clever,' said Haskins. The phone had stopped ringing. 'I'd better check because I don't get many calls these days.' He picked up the phone and played with the dial. 'Strange. It was the Office. Now they never ring me.'

'The Office?' questioned Tom. 'What office?'

'The Firm, the Service, Uncle, Auntie, the Suits— whatever name you happen to fancy.'

'You mean that Secret Service stuff is really true?'

'This is not the time to be suspicious!' Haskins said. 'Right, let's see what's up.' He went to a drawer and pulled out a small handheld computer. Tom was up on computers, but he'd never seen one quite like it. Haskins tapped on it for a few minutes and waited. He looked thoughtful but waited and then tapped on some more keys. Then the phone rang again.

'It's definitely the office,' he said, picking up the receiver. How did he know? 'Yes. I am...correct...I do...I can...now?'

To Tom the conversation sounded very one-sided and all the answers Haskins gave were so short.

'Okay.' Haskins put the phone down and put his finger to his lips. Tom realised he wanted silence. This time Haskins picked up a notebook and pencil then dialled and again the conversation was strange. 'It's H,' he said. 'D wants me.' There seemed to be a long wait. Tom could hear only the clock. The cats were noticeably quiet as if they knew this was an important call.

Haskins was on edge. 'D? You called? Yes, you know I'm in Lichfield.' He seemed more concerned as the conversation went on but scribbled nervously on the pad. 'I do have a cover—I'm the old nutter in the woods, you must have that on file; safe enough not to worry about and not a nuisance, undistinguished with an eccentric interest in maps. That suits me and keeps away nosey neighbours and any old foreign enemies who would like to see me depart this life drinking a dainty Novichok cocktail'

Tom sensed a hint of anger in Haskins' voice. 'Of course, I understand... Oh, do you? Well perhaps I can be of use.' He gave a showy wink to Tom. 'Yes. Ever helpful for the Service and the safety of the nation... Sarcasm? That wasn't sarcasm. Isn't this whole thing just a fuss over cats with flu? It's more, is it? Perhaps you should brief me a little more.' He stopped talking and started writing. Tom had never seen him so focused. He nodded, went to say something but then put his hand over his mouth.

Tom saw some movement out of the corner of his eye. A tiny paw was stretched under the door and scratched around. It quickly went out of sight but emerged again scratching frantically for something to grip on to. Tom wanted to burst out laughing or at least open the door. There was a bump, a squeak and then the little paw suddenly disappeared. Tom was convinced he heard a little whimper and imagined Blackie had gripped one of her naughty kittens by the back of the neck and pulled it from the door.

Haskins was totally absorbed and still scribbling. Sometimes he tapped onto the computer as if he was going to knock the keys right through the machine. Then suddenly he stopped. 'The Prime Minister, the President of the USA? Yes. I hear you.' For some minutes Haskins said nothing and just listened. Then, without warning, he put the phone down as if someone had annoyed him. He sat back in the chair and pursed his lips.

Tom was surprised. 'You put the phone down on the caller.'

'That was the end—it is the end!' Haskins glanced down at the notes and was very thoughtful.

Tom got up and opened the door not expecting the vision he was presented with. Blackie and Roots were sitting bolt upright and six little bodies were hunched in front of them. 'They look as if they've been told off.'

Tom turned around and Haskins stood up. 'This is trouble,' he said, '*big* trouble but then I suppose it always was bad news. Thomas, I'll be as brief as I can. If you don't understand anything just ask.'

Tom was sat by Haskins in the chair and all the cats and kittens gathered around as if they were going to be told some old cat tale. 'That person on the phone was an old friend Dorothy known as D. I once had her job, she is the most important person in the British Secret Service. As I'm here, they're bringing me back into play—out of retirement as it were. Even more dramatic is that the whole world is coming here. This is seen as a potential global disaster.'

'Here? To Lichfield?'

'Yes. Over the last few days they've kept this quiet from the world and the press has been issued with a level five Defence Advisory Notice preventing publication in the UK on all media. At the moment Lichfield is Wuhan in miniature. There may be a massive concentration of the virus in this area, so it perfect for the culling experiment.'

'What's a culling?'

'It means that all cats will be killed because they're dangerous to humans.'

Tom's mouth dropped open. 'All cats will be killed?' he said in disbelief.

'This is the final phase in their campaign. They are awaiting the tests on the people they've got and the hundred or so cats that are imprisoned in the Market Square. They've got plans—perhaps they will even find a vaccine if they have to, like the one they found to destroy the Ebola virus or Covid-19. This is the final solution to the cat plague and a lesson to the world. And I've been pulled in to help.'

'Why you?'

'Because this is now an international incident and I can get to work immediately and meet and brief the team when they come in tomorrow. I've joined the cat hunters and the search for the truth.'

'So, it's all over?' Tom asked. 'You've defeated us. You're not with us at all.'

'Thomas, it's not defeat. It's the truth that must be established. It's not over yet. I've never seen myself as a double agent. I'm not a scientist and I instinctively don't believe the cats are killing us. I'll do my job for King and Country and get to the truth. I'm sorry, but my interest is the interest of the country and *everyone* in it!' Haskins picked up Roots. 'Don't worry, my ginger monster, I include you in *everyone*—you and your new friends will be safe with me. Nobody will end your life.' He put Roots down onto the carpet and let him gently nudge Blackie.

Tom thought he saw the cats colluding.

Roots turned to Blackie who fell on her back and seemed to sigh with relief.

Haskins disappeared upstairs, leaving Tom to prepare

some food for the cats who were obviously desperately hungry. Moments later, Haskins reappeared. 'There's no doubt that we need to be in the lab in the square.'

'I know, but how?' He turned around towards Haskins, only to see that the old man was... different, somehow. He seemed taller; his hair was different, and he wore spectacles that made him appear important. 'What have you done?'

'Nothing,' Haskins said innocently, 'just a retouching here and there, and a special wardrobe. People, Thomas, are very unobservant.'

'Your voice—it's different.'

'No, young man—the same. Just a tweak, and more like it used to be.' Haskins stretched his neck and became even taller. 'So, time to get inside the cat prison and really learn something.' He picked up Roots again. 'Roots, you will be my Trojan Horse.'

Roots sat bolt upright and rolled his eyes as if he knew he wasn't a horse.

Tom and Haskins laughed. 'Why is he so offended?' Haskins smiled. 'I don't know about cats giving us a disease. I keep seeing evidence that they're smarter than ever.'

Roots nodded at the brood and at this instruction all the cats whirled and curled.

Tom watched this play behaviour, but it seemed as if Roots had ordered it.

'Maybe not smarter,' Haskins said. 'You know the Trojan Horse story?'

'Of course—the Greeks had surrounded and besieged Troy but couldn't get in, so they built a massive horse and gave it to the Trojans—and the Greeks just left!'

'But the Greeks were in the belly of the horse, hiding until the moment they could escape and attack the city from within,' added Haskins.

'So, we do it the Greek way? Build a massive ginger wooden cat and wheel him into the experimentation centre?'

'The *Secret Service way* is to have a friend on the inside.'

'On the inside?' questioned Tom as he saw Haskins smile.

'Yes, indeed. This is where my friend Dorothy comes in. She can help us, and I know she's disenchanted with the world of secret spookery.'

Haskins walked out of the room and Tom turned to Roots. 'Am I going mad, Roots?' he said to the cat. 'I still think you know more than I do.' He was feeling desperate as Roots pulled himself up and rubbed his head against his leg and then tilted it in a knowing way and Tom smoothed the cat's head.

A few minutes passed before Haskins was back in the room. 'I've spoken to my friend Dorothy, the new chief,' he said, 'and we're in agreement that I have badly let you down.'

Tom was taken aback. 'Really?'

'Yes, I must clear the ground for your parents and Victoria's. Explain your youthful commitment. I shall formally visit them, put their minds at rest and explain you're under observation for the duration of the crisis. *You* will keep out of sight until that's done!'

Tom felt obliged to silently agree.

***

Haskins double-checked that Tom was well-hidden behind the ledge at the front of Victoria's house before he knocked at the door. A woman he assumed to be her mother slowly opened the door and looked quizzically at him. 'Yes?'

'Mrs Passmore?'

'Yes?'

'My name is Haskins. I work for the Government— here's my ID card.' Mrs Passmore gave it a critical examination before waiting for him to continue. 'I don't want to alarm you, but Victoria is being cared for by our medical services for the moment.'

'Why—what's happened?'

'May I come in?'

'Yes, let me get my husband. John!' Her voice was sharp. 'Do come in, Mr...?'

'Haskins.' He followed Mrs Passmore into the house. She guided him towards the lounge, where he settled himself into a large sofa and leaned forward in a concerned pose.

Mr Passmore hurried into the room. 'What's this? What has she done now? It's that boy. I know.'

'Please don't worry,' Haskins said. 'I'm from the Government and my name is Haskins. I have had to intervene on this issue, as I think Victoria has been involved in a serious matter without realising what it means.'

'I told you,' Mr Passmore said to his wife. 'Keep her *away* from that boy.'

'Let me reassure you.' Haskins put his hand on Mr Passmore's shoulder. 'She is fine, and I assume you're talking about Thomas. I think he's a very well-meaning young man with the best of motives. Victoria has received some minor cat scratches and Thomas reported the matter to me. He has been very responsible.'

'But I told her not to see him after the last fuss.' Mr Passmore clenched his fist and hit the table. His wife frowned.

'Mr Passmore, Victoria is a very... *socially concerned* young woman and we are grateful to her for her efforts to rescue some cats and take them to the Government centre.'

'She did that? I thought she hated all this cat killing stuff. As, may I say, so do we.'

'Exactly, and I think you should be proud of how she tried to bring cats to the centre but was unfortunately scratched.'

'Oh no!' Mrs Passmore gripped her husband's hand. 'The medical staff assure me she is fine and showing no evidence of infection.'

'I must see her,' Mrs Passmore said insistently.

'Forgive me, but for the moment she can't see anyone. She is in quarantine and kept apart from everyone. This is purely a protective measure but, believe me, she is receiving excellent specialist care. You can't visit but I could arrange for her to call you.' Haskins smiled. 'Really, this is for the best. It will probably be for no longer than twenty-four hours or so. By then it'll all be resolved.'

'If you say so,' Mrs Passmore said.

Haskins noted the lack of confidence in her voice but smiled reassuringly, stood up and put his hand out to shake Mr Passmore's hand. 'It has been good to meet you. Trust me, Victoria is in the best possible hands and feeling fine!' He walked towards the door. 'Goodbye Mrs Passmore, and fear not!'

Mr Passmore followed him to the door and Haskins handed him a business card. 'Trust me—all is well, and Victoria is fine. Here is my mobile number. Don't speak to anyone about this before you talk to me. You must understand this is vital for national security—and as such you are now accountable to His Majesty's Government.'

'Like the taxman I suppose,' Mr Passmore said. He gazed at the card. It had a picture of Haskins on the front, and some paragraphs about protecting the community.

Haskins walked out of the door and it closed behind him. He knew Tom could hear him from his hiding place behind the hedge. 'Moving swiftly on, it is time to use my persuasive charm with your mum and dad.'

He was aware of Tom's insecurity. 'She won't have it,' the boy said. 'She'll shout!'

It was a short walk from one house to the next. Haskins opened the gate to Tom's house, walked up to the porch and pushed the bell. Tom ducked round the edge of their old

Coach House to wait.

Several long minutes later, Haskins walked into the road smiling broadly. 'Lovely woman, your mum,' he said. 'Understood perfectly what was happening when I explained I was there to open up the whole story to the world and expose the hypocrisy that was going on.'

'What?'

'Don't worry, Thomas—your mum thinks I'm a hero and that you're in safe hands. Being a spy makes lying easy. Let's help Victoria now—and I'd better tell you that your mum has signed me up for her cat's help group.'

As they approached the tented prison and medical HQ, Haskins saw a huge swing barrier had been installed with armed soldiers on guard. 'Stick by me and listen.' Haskins marched up to the first soldier. 'My ID'

The soldier turned to his friend. 'I haven't seen one of these since I was on guard at Camp Bastion.'

'Possibly not! But I'm here and I have been there. You were probably using my maps. I called that exercise. *Helmand and beyond.* Can you let us in? I have a young man here who is vital to my investigation of the cat issue.'

'Is there any chance of it being over quickly? It is not what we were trained for!'

'Trust me.' Haskins sounded so sincere. 'This is coming to an end.'

The soldier stood to attention and saluted. 'Yes sir, thank you sir. We are glad to have you with us, sir!'

Haskins leaned towards him, spoke quietly in his ear, turned and smiled strangely at Tom. The soldier smirked, nodded his head and shouted to his fellow guard. 'This is the man—do what he says, and you'll be okay! Come in, sir, and bring your young friend.'

'Tom, come on,' Haskins said, waving at him. 'Don't be afraid. We have to tell these good people what you know!'

As Tom walked forwards, the soldier patted him on the shoulder and winked at his colleague. They walked forward to hear another soldier shout out.

Haskins moved forward slowly, his hands lowered. He moved them upwards with his palms open. Again, he spoke to the soldier and turned to Tom. 'Come on, Thomas. Do the same as I did. Walk forward slowly. Extend your hands and then move them away from your body.' The tone of Haskin's voice was severe, and his speech was clipped.

This time the soldier was not friendly. He roughly turned Tom and dropped to his knees feeling every part of Tom's back, head and legs. He grabbed Tom's shoulders, turned him round, pushed out Tom's arms and kicked his legs apart. Then he ran his hands slowly and deliberately across Tom's body.

'Shoes off!' The soldier barked at him. Tom took off his trainers. They walked through the tent opening. Oddly, Tom saw the foot of Dr Johnson as part of the statue he knew so well covered by some white cloth.

'Move it—stop staring!'

The soldier pushed him forward quite roughly. Haskins held Tom by the collar and pulled him close. 'You must behave—and do as I say!' He saw the look in Tom's eyes that betrayed a new-found dislike for a man he had trusted and who had seemed to have tricked him. 'This is the real-world Thomas – you'll have to get used to it and sometimes it might not be nice.'

Haskins knew the layout of the tented village turning left, right and then stopping at a desk where another soldier was talking on the phone.

'We will make all arrangements as described for the President and Prime Minister, thank you,' the soldier paused.

'I'm H. Need I say more?'

'No sir! An interview area has been prepared for you as instructed by your department.'

Haskins turned to Tom. 'This is it young man. You know more than most. We need the truth.'

Tom was devastated.

'Just keep beside me.' Haskins turned sharply and pulled Tom with him.

***

Craw was very frightened as she saw the man with the gun. He examined the cages. No cage was unoccupied, the one hundred were in place. The soldier turned and walked away.

Nailz leapt out of his cage. 'Now is the time!' he shouted. 'We must take our cat freedom in our hands or we will all die. This is the end for us if we just sit here. Remember Catattack. Twitcher, you know how it works.'

Twitcher ran from his cage up to the trapped Craw. 'We all know how to kill—birds, mice and the rest. Just drop down on your bellies and follow the rules. We are many. We are the hundred. We can rule. We can't kill the people, but we can confuse and frighten them. We are the hundred, some of us will get free. You are the brightest and the best. You must break out. Some of you may not get out, but for Catkind do what you can.' Twitcher jumped up beside Craw. 'To the left I need twenty-five. To the right I need twenty-five. In the centre give me twenty-five and at the front I need the bravest twenty-five. This is our time. You are the saviours of Catkind. We are not trying to kill men, but some of you may need to attack them because they will be trying to kill us. I want the biggest and heaviest of you to face the flanks and attack the men—the hands and face are your targets.'

'A terrible time is coming,' shouted Craw. 'I cannot move, and I will be lost to you all, but my spirit is with you —as is the spirit of the great Catskill.'

***

The hundred moved out of their cages and dropped their heads. A slow murmur grew into a sound that filled the room and they moved to the exit of their prison. One hundred cats in unison. One hundred cats together in a phalanx. They moved as one into the corridor. The flanking groups split to their chosen place. The main body marched on. Apart from the deep breathing there was no sound.

'It is this way,' confirmed Twitcher. Like ants the group moved into the corridor. Most were on their bellies as they dragged themselves along the ground, slowly and surely moving towards freedom.

A black shadow stood in their way.

'This is the direction we must go,' said Twitcher. 'Stand together!'

'What the hell is going on?!' the shadow shouted. 'They're out! The cats are out!'

There was the sound of gunfire as the shadow aimed a gun at the hundred. Some fell, but the surge didn't stop.

'Stop them!' the shadow yelled. 'These are killers!'

Another shadow, another soldier brandishing a weapon. Shots rang out again and more fell but still the surge did not stop.

There were more shots, more shouting and more soldiers came running. The one hundred became fewer and fewer. Some of the strongest cats leapt high at the soldier's faces, clawing and hissing. There were screams from the men who couldn't fire their guns or pull away the tiny teeth that gripped the flesh of their cheeks.

'Stop!' a strong voice rang out. 'Cease fire. Let them go, I just need the ringleader. The top cat. These are irrelevant. Cease fire.'

Haskins stepped forward with his arms in the air. Soldiers had stopped shooting, and some were desperately trying to catch the fleeing cats or tear them from their faces. Tom stared in horror at the scene.

'Stop, I'm telling you! Leave them.' Haskins marched into the middle of the corridor and held up his hands. Cats were running around his feet.

'What's happening?' Sergeant Wilkes asked as he burst out of the headquarters section. 'You!' he said to Haskins.

'What the hell are you doing here with that lad as well?'

Haskins turned swiftly. 'Don't ask! Let the cats go, but make sure you have the leader. It's the same as any other war. Chop off the head and the rest will fall in line; these are the foot soldiers and dead ones at that.' With his shoe he pushed at the body of a cat on the stone floor.

'Yes sir.' Wilkes walked, vigorously shaking his head as he said to the soldiers. 'Everyone who has been bitten—and that is most of you—get to the medics now.'

Haskins took Tom by the shoulder, but Tom couldn't speak. He was staring at the bodies of the still cats.

***

Nailz backed away from the horrific scene in front of him. He'd been buried beneath a large tabby after the first shot from the guns. But he could see that a large number of cats had escaped. He knew he had to help Craw so in slow motion he retraced his steps to the area where Craw was still tethered.

'Craw?' Nailz lifted his eyes towards her. 'We went together and moved together but the men just used those loud banging things and some of us fell and never moved again. Someone shouted, and they stopped firing. Still many of our number have escaped.'

'So, it is down to the free ones now,' Craw said to him. 'Those who fell have given their lives to help the whole of Catkind—was it any of my friends?'

Nailz covered his head with his paws. 'I don't know. It should have been me.'

'We were one hundred imprisoned,' Craw reasoned, 'and now we are only two. You must get in a cage quickly, let's be trapped again.'

***

Haskins stared at the vile handiwork.

Two soldiers pulled back the tent flap. Cairns the cat

catcher accompanied them. 'This is a total shamble!' he shouted. 'You've just lost probably the smartest and most infected cats that took us so long to catch. These animals are dangerous! I should have killed them as I went along. The Dawkins fire should have been bigger.'

'I know it's hopeless,' one of the soldiers said. 'We don't know how they got free. Someone must have released the cages—someone on the inside. It's impossible that the cats could have done this themselves, but the top spy man said we should let them go!'

'What spy man?'

'The man—the "H" man. The man cleared from the top, from the office of the Prime Minister.'

'Another useless Government twit.'

Haskins stepped out from the shadows 'Excuse me—do you mean me?' He stood close to the tall Cairns, looking up at him with barely hidden aggression.

'I've spent too much time catching this lot—the smart ones, the hangers on, the gang members. I know which ones work together and now you've let them go! So, you *are* useless.'

'Mr. Cairns, you know nothing.'

'Neither, it seems, do you,' a third voice boomed out through the tent.

'Dorothy?' Haskins said. 'I didn't expect you to actually turn up!' I assumed you'd be up to your neck in it at HQ?

Of course, you wanted me in on this. Even better—I've brought Sheba herself.' She opened her huge handbag and a great black cat with green eyes dragged itself into the world. One soldier pointed his gun at the new arrival.

'Don't you dare!' Dorothy said. 'Your life won't be worth living!'

'D,' Haskins asked, was it wise to bring your own cat? There is disease on a mass scale here'.

'Haskins I wasn't leaving her alone in my London house. She is safer here with me than wandering the streets of Kensington. Now get me to those who think they're in charge. As for you, cat killer, hang on. I will want to speak to you!'

Haskins knew who was really in charge, but he seized his moment. 'All bodies are to be taken for examination! The scientists can experiment as much as they like, and we have in captivity what Cairns thinks is the boss cat.' Hearing the commanding tones, the soldiers began to collect the limp creatures.

A gasp came from the other end of the corridor. Haskins looked over and saw Victoria and an old lady standing there, their faces white with shock at the sight of the blood and the soldiers dragging away the bodies. Their dazed eyes followed the gruesome procession.

A sharp cry came from one of the cats. The trapped figure of the experimental cat straining against the ties that held her to the table. Haskins heard something coming from its mouth that sounded like spoken human words.

'She said "Stop them now,"' said Tom.

A soldier looked quizzically at the creature the cats know as Craw.

'That cat said, "stop them now," I'll swear!'

'Don't be stupid, boy!' Haskins said. He had to control the moment before everyone's emotions took over. 'That's just cat screeching!'

He turned to Dorothy. With her black coat and black cat sitting in her bag, she looked menacing, and there and then she assumed command. 'Now, clear this sorry mess up and let's find out what the hell is going on. H, what on earth have you been up to?'

'Just getting the major suspects together, D, no more and no less.'

'Clear the area. Get these patients back to their beds and this young man secured somewhere.'

Two soldiers led Mrs Constance, Victoria and Tom away. The black cat jumped out of the voluminous bag and stared sadly up at the captured cat called Craw.

***

Craw moaned. 'How many have gone to freedom?'

Nailz scratched his nails on the bars. 'I think most of them. I saw perhaps twenty go down.'

'That's eighty. Perhaps eighty who are free—free to roam and free to warn the others.' Craw's breathing grew heavy and she squeezed her eyes closed to shut out the horror. 'What have I done?'

'You have done what every cat would do.' A large black cat with big, green eyes raised her paw towards Craw. 'So far, all cats that have heard the story are waiting for your lead. We will all help. I shall assist in any way I can and listen and learn from my provider. I am Sheba, and I am with you.''

Craw simply stared as another small group of her friends were carried roughly away. 'But what can I do?'

'Trust us all,' Sheba said. 'Trust your friends, and together we can free everyone.' 'I told you, Craw, you have clever cats, clever friends—trust them and trust me.' Sheba flashed her green eyes, turned and leapt back into the bag of her surprised provider Dorothy. 'Believe me, cats everywhere are watching and waiting. Today, I've seen the result of a catmassacre. This is the beginning, not the end. I will do all I can, endure everything, watch and help if I get any chance.' She lifted her eyes towards Dorothy.

'Take Sheba. She must undergo the tests. I think she knows she must.'

The man's voice trembled. 'Roots... I must give them my cat as well. I must bring him and give him up.' He turned around and shouted at the soldiers. 'We have to put our cats under the knife because you let this gang escape from the cages!' He marched up to Craw's table and smashed his fist on the white top twice. The skin on the soft part of his fist split and began to bleed. He stared at Craw and she cowered. 'That mad cat catcher thinks this one is the secret to the disease. If there is an answer to the pandemic—this *shudder*, this flu, this plague—then she must have it in her pitiful body. Get the medics to take her apart. It might help the rest!'

Craw desperately looked for Sheba and saw her being put in a cage. 'Have faith,' Sheba said. 'You are the chosen one. Everything you have achieved so far is leading to the salvation of Catdom. I, Roots and all the others are ready to die to make sure you live!'

Craw lifted her head to the unseen sky. She felt wetness on her face; not rain but water dropping like human tears. *It's not possible,* she thought. *Cats can't cry… can they?*

Chapter Eighteen: The Cruellest Cuts

Craw's shackles hurt so much as they pulled at her flesh and fur. She had tried so hard to pull away from the metal claws that her skin was bleeding. Her instinct was to turn and lick the wounds, but she couldn't reach them. She pushed out her small tongue, desperate to touch them, but failed to reach the small patches of congealed blood. Every cat did this to keep wounds clean, to let them heal. Craw uttered a despairing cry.

Her sole remaining friend was Nailz. 'I'm still here to help,' he said.

Craw wished she had no more responsibility. Light flooded the room, momentarily blinding her.

'Here she is!' came the voice of Haskins. 'The supposed super cat!'

'You're the vet people!' a woman's voice barked out. 'Get this cat examined!'

Craw saw a woman wearing a green operating gown and a green mask over her face. 'I want a thorough investigation. I want to find out what's happening to her and if these creatures are dangerous. We also must justify the cat taking and the burnings. There are going to be some terribly upset people in this containment area if it turns out there's nothing in this. The ill people will have to wait— none of them seem to be dying yet, but that may take some time. It's like mad cow disease all over again. A massive overreaction, and then some sense after a million burnings.'

Craw wondered what she meant. The providers had lots of words. So many of them seemed like nonsense to her.

The woman muttered, as if she only wanted Haskins to

215

hear her and no one else. 'As always, it is the fear and frustration of our lords and masters, the politicians. Never able to comprehend the incomprehensible or act appropriately until the virus has run riot.'

The woman pulled herself to her full height—perhaps she just touched five foot tall. 'Let the testing commence. I want an answer, and I don't want to have to feel a fool in front of the Prime Minister or the President of the United States. This unit is now a Containment Level Four laboratory. There are just fifteen others like it in this country. They handle some of the deadliest organisms known to man; those most highly infectious, impossible to treat and, of course, ultimately fatal. This may be the next in a long line of such killers and we know our enemies and any number of terrorists would murder to obtain this kind of material. I can't stress how urgent it is that we know the whole story. I've brought my own cat to show that no-one is excused responsibility. She will also undergo the testing. We need to find out the truth!' She turned to Haskins. 'Why weren't we involved when this started? God knows how many cats killed and still no answers!'

Haskins looked embarrassed. 'They thought it might be just a localised outbreak—a limited thing like Foot and Mouth.'

'Well,' Dorothy huffed, 'someone will have to answer for this if they were wrong.'

Craw felt as if they were beating her to death with words.

Dorothy held up Sheba and handed her to one of the medics. The cat yelped and turned to Craw. 'Don't give up,' she said. 'There are free spirits on the outside and we are all working to get you free. I'm happy to do my bit on the inside—don't be frightened.'

She was whisked away from Craw. 'That's it, no talking to that one.' Dorothy laughed and winked at Haskins. 'This isn't going to be without pain for any of us!'

Haskins turned to walk away. 'Especially the cats.'

'Don't get sentimental on me, H. This is a job to be done.' She turned and addressed everyone sharply. All eyes were on her. 'The operation must begin *now*.'

No one seemed to have noticed Nailz. He was flat on his stomach and partly covered by a piece of newspaper from the floor of his cage, trying desperately to be ignored. 'Lie still, Nailz!' Craw hissed. 'I think they've missed you. Run when you get the chance.'

Nailz slunk even lower and stared out at the action in front of him.

Craw watched, shocked, as a massive, hulking figure entered the room. It surely couldn't be human, though she could make out two huge eyes and a large nose. The figure was covered in a green skin from head to foot. Its hands were pale, almost whiter-than-white. Three others, all the same, followed behind it.

Haskins surveyed the creatures and shook his head. 'Let's get out of here we're not wearing PPE.'

As the green creatures moved forward, their webbed feet stuck to the floor. With each step, there was a sucking sound as they lifted their feet off the plastic surface. One of them touched Craw's fur. It felt sticky and cold. Her hairs lifted at the disgusting sensation. She was helpless!

'Dorothy,' Haskins said, 'this is the medical team. They are prepared for any dangerous type of infection.'

'Strange,' Dorothy mused. 'Before we arrived there were a hundred cats to operate on and now you've just got a couple and a pile of corpses. How odd.' She stared at Haskins but turned as a terrible screech wrenched the air.

Craw's fur stood on end. Sheba, held in the medic's arms, had uttered a fearful shriek and was shaking uncontrollably. Her tongue hung out of her mouth and a bright yellow thick liquid dribbled onto her drooping black whiskers.

'Oh dear!' Dorothy plucked her from the medic and set

her on the floor. 'She's been having these little shaky fits.'

Sheba twirled and shuddered. 'Run now, spirit in the cage!' she shouted 'Run now! I've seen you, but they haven't!'

Nailz didn't need a second invitation—he was through the gate like a rocket, leaping into the air and skidding across the stone surface.

One of the soldiers reached for his gun. Haskins lifted his arm and pulled the gun into the air. 'Leave him! There are plenty of bodies to work on and no time to waste killing any more or chasing the escapees—least of all shooting one through the tent.'

On the floor, Sheba kept twisting and turning. However, Craw saw how she slyly watched Nailz disappear between two tent pegs. From the table, she couldn't tell whether he had truly escaped or not.

Two of the green monsters still held her. One moved slowly towards her with what seemed to her like a huge spike in his hand. Behind it was something bright blue. 'Hold her tight,' the monster said. A sharp pain erupted between her shoulder blades. After a brief pause, her whole body shook against her will. Her mouth was so dry. She could just about see the green figures in front her and their two eyes became one. There were no hands, just a strap that gripped round her neck like a snake. She had no strength.

Craw saw her still figure was on screen. Staring up at it were half of the Cabinet, a dozen medical experts, and an advisor of the American Government.

The Home Secretary spoke first. 'Gentlemen, there have been one or two problems, but we now have two of our top-Secret Service Operatives on the case. You will know D1 and H1. They are on top of the intelligence situation locally.'

'H1?' US General George Michaelides pursed his lips. 'He was killed in Afghanistan, wasn't he?'

'Almost,' said the Home Secretary. 'He's been brought

out of retirement to handle this, and just happened to be in the right place at the right time. We can use his expertise to bring this matter to a rapid conclusion.'

A sob was heard on the speakers in the Cabinet Office. This cat's body had been twisted into an unnatural position. The Home Secretary was concerned. 'I thought she was supposed to be unconscious? We've already been responsible for hundreds of cat deaths in that area. This one must count.'

He turned to his right and there was a short woman with a shock of red hair. 'We are pleased to have the Chief Medical Officer of Health for the UK to explain the aims of these operations: Jane.'

The woman addressed her remarks to the Home Secretary. 'While we have identified the spongy brain form causing cat madness and death, we have also found a prion protein—PRP—which paradoxically enhances memory, brain function, and general capacity. It creates a kind of supercat. That may sound as if we're in the realms of science fiction, but this is reality. The cat brains we've examined definitely have the disease and there is a possibility that it could be transmitted to humans.'

General Michaeledis stood up. 'We *must* have an answer on that. A yes or no. The President will be here tomorrow. We may have a massacre on our hands, and we must tell all those committed cat owners in the US, including my wife, that all cats must die. She already believes our cat is more intelligent than me. Get us the evidence, and fast!'

***

In the mayhem, Tom found himself in the charge of a solitary soldier whom he recognised. 'I remember you,' Tom said, staring at the soldier.

'You do?'

'You were one of the group that caught us in the first place. You had the army cat.'

The soldier dropped down onto his haunches. 'Yes, I was there. We don't like this much, kid, but if these animals are spreading some killer disease then you've probably got it for starters. You're on the list for the scans and other things.'

Tom leaned back against the wall. He could hear nothing but the hum of the fans as they blew cold air into the tented village. He suddenly realised he had nothing to lose now. It appeared as if the cats *were* deadly. If the disease didn't kill him, his parents would. Victoria's mum and dad would never let him speak to her again and the bully Cairns would never let this rest.

He was in the middle of a nightmare. He'd only wanted to help his cat and the little band that he met in the wood. They all seemed so clever. He was the stupid one.

The soldier, seemingly bored watching Tom, stood up and wandered to the tent flap. He rattled a message into the microphone on his jacket, letting the world know he'd still got Tom.

'I'm going nowhere,' Tom mumbled to himself, feeling useless.

Standing tall, the soldier turned away from Tom holding his ear as he received further communications. Tom noticed a tiny bright beam of light in the tent. He forced his eyes to focus and could see that it was daylight—and a way out! He winced at the thought of running once again but remembered the cats had been brave enough to try. Why couldn't he?

In one movement, he was past the generator and into the gap.

'Oh no, stupid!' The soldier's voice was angry. 'The kid's gone!

Tom stood in the gap and kept very still. He heard boots stomping around and shouting that seemed to go on for ages. He was hardly breathing. He felt something brush his foot but daren't look down.

Nailz lifted his paw to Tom's knee pushed himself off and vanished.

'Where are you?' Tom demanded. Nailz' head appeared from behind some tenting and then disappeared again. 'Where are you?' He moved towards the point where Nailz had disappeared and then the face of the cat appeared again, six feet higher up. 'Do you want me to follow you?'

He could hardly believe his eyes when he saw what Nailz had found. It was a kind of tunnel built into the tents with big pipes suspended on wires. As Tom gazed along it, Nailz appeared again at a lower level. He was jumping from level to level, showing how it was possible to move up and alongside the massive tubes. *He's showing me the way out,* Tom realised. He saw Nailz' tail flick and move along the air-conditioning pipes. 'Hold on! I'm coming.'

Underneath each tube was a sort of shelf supporting its weight. Tom inched slowly along one of them until he came to a junction. The pipes split left and right, with tenting hiding whatever was behind them. Every so often, Nailz would stop, wave his tail at Tom and hiss.

Tom found himself responding to the cat noise. 'I'm going as fast as I can. I'm not a cat.' Tom heard a voice right by his shoulder. 'This place is like a leaking sieve.' It was Haskins. Tom's heart stopped—he'd been caught again!

'Holes everywhere.' Haskins said. The man's voice was now at Tom's left. He didn't dare turn around.

'This tent is a joke,' Haskins said, 'and as for your soldiers? They can't even guard a boy. God knows what you'll do when the cat killing has to start for real?'

Only then did Tom realise that Haskins hadn't seen him, despite how close they were. The tunnel was his route around the tented square to freedom, but only so long as he was very, very quiet. He inched forward, slowly but surely.

Haskins sounded really annoyed. 'Go on—get back to your toy soldiers!'

'Haskins, this is hopeless.' Tom recognised the voice of the woman, Dorothy. 'I thought you'd got things under control,' she said.

'Don't they say, "Never work with animals and children"? I've done both. I brought the boy in and now I've had to give up poor old Roots as well.'

'Yes, and I've given up sickly Sheba. Remember, tents have ears, and this is thin material. It had to be done.'

Her voice became quieter and quieter until Tom couldn't hear what she was saying. Nailz rubbed against his leg. 'Have I got to go again?' Tom asked the cat in exasperation. Nailz zipped along the top pipe and pointed his nose forward. Tom nodded in silence and began to crawl on all fours.

The tunnel became narrower and narrower. He was quite slim, but even so it was difficult for him to get through the small channel. His head was at ground level and he saw webbed feet walking in front of his face.

'We're finished here,' someone said. 'There's nothing more that we can do with the animal. Most of the tests have been done and the scan results are quite conclusive. She's sedated and won't be going anywhere if she recovers but put her in a cage anyway.'

Tom could see the bottom of a cage. A green figure opened it and placed a limp cat onto the floor. It was Craw. The man held her in both his hands and her head hung down while her paws were together as if she was saying a little prayer. Tom felt sick. The voices faded into the distance and there was silence.

Tom could feel Nailz' breath on his face. The cat was staring at his friend who was in such a state. Nailz had only one thing to say. '*Rescue her.*'

'What did you say? It sounded like *rescue her*. Either I'm going mad or I can understand what you're saying. You just have a funny catty-like accent?'

Nailz nosed his way under the tenting and ran towards

the cage.

'Here I go again...' Tom crawled underneath the tent and saw there was no one about. Nailz was making sounds at the poor figure in the cage. She had something in her mouth keeping it open, probably so she could breathe. She was a sad sight. Nailz pawed at the catch. 'Anyone would think you knew how to undo this.'

Nailz stopped and stared again. 'Do it!' He lifted his paw and pointed at the catch.

'All right.' Tom reached at the catch, lifted it off and opened the door. As he did so, Nailz rushed into the cage and began to lick Craw's head. The first lick was so strong that it lifted her from the floor.

'What do I do?' Tom reached into the cage. Nailz stood back, letting him get to the still body. 'Come on, then.' Tom picked up the cat and she felt like a dead weight. She was so heavy for a small creature.

'This way,' said Nailz with his tail in the air.

'All right, I'm coming.' Tom held the poor creature tightly in his arms and squeezed back under the tent to their tunnel. He put her gently on the floor and wished he'd got a blanket or something.

Nailz stared at his jacket.

'Okay,' Tom said, 'the jacket comes off. Are you a mind reader as well?'

Nailz dashed off in the opposite direction as Tom scooped Craw up in his coat. Tom set off after him, but he'd gone again. Then, his tiny head appeared from under the tent. Tom reached him only to see Nailz disappear altogether.

As he turned Tom felt himself over-balance. Craw slipped from his arms and he heard a loud crack as his head hit the floor.

***

The lights in the tented medical centre were powerfully bright. The only sound was the deep hum of the air conditioning. There was a heavy weight on his chest, and it was hard to breathe. He couldn't tell if he was dead, or merely trapped. Tom slowly opened his eyes and saw Nailz watching him. The cat was lying on him, breathing heavily into his face as if he was trying to see if he was still alive.

'I'm here, I'm here,' Tom coughed. Nailz jumped off and disappeared over his shoulder with his tail high in the air. He turned to Tom and sniffed again. 'I'm alive but still crazy and hallucinating.' Tom stared at the cat as he leapt into the air and disappeared over one of the big tubes.

Tom levered himself up by one elbow. As he pulled himself onto his feet, Nailz rushed back into the space and up to the top of the tent. Tom followed him and as his blurred vision cleared, he saw the strangest creature he'd seen in a long time. It looked like a cat; black as night but twisted and bent. It jumped into the air and landed heavily on the ground. Tom realised then that he had been mesmerised by the strange shadow projected onto the wall by the bright lights of the medical tent.

The creature was Craw. She must have recovered enough to move. She turned to Nailz. 'Thank you for looking after the boy,' Tom thought he heard her say. 'We still need him to help us. Things are bad, and we may need to use him to talk to the Providers or do things that we can't. Can he stand?'

For some reason, Tom felt the need to respond to them. They were watching him with something nearing a quizzical stare. 'I can stand,' he heard himself say defensively. 'You're an eerie sight.' Half of Craw's head had been shaved and both her sides had lost all their hair.

Before they could move any further, Tom heard the tell-tale *click-click-click* of guns being readied. They sounded close; a group of soldiers must be standing just inches from him. When their leader spoke, Tom recognised the voice of Sergeant Wilkes.

'This is what we've been expecting,' the sergeant said.

'The vet boys have found something funny about the cats—
a brain thing. From now on, do not touch them. Shoot first.
Not official yet, but bad news, at least for the cats. The
people are still undergoing tests. If they've got this thing,
they'll be moved by secure vehicles to the Headquarters of
the Surgeon General, Lichfield, and under the tightest
controls.'

'What are our orders, Sarge?'

'All units in the zone are being called up. All the
bigwigs are being informed. Then they'll finally tell us what
the plan is. We're always the last to know, even though
we've got to clear up their mess over and over again.'

Craw and Nailz both were flat to the ground. Tom
watched them mutter to each other. He now felt he knew
what they were saying to each other.

Craw croaked to Nailz 'If you're ready, we have to raise
the alarm. We need all the spirits to be with us, not just
those that have escaped, but all spirits everywhere—all the
thinking spirits. The message of the threat to cats
everywhere must be told. We must sound the alarm. It is the
time for the Caterwaul.'

Nailz put his hands over his ears waiting for the din.
Tom felt he had to follow the sign and did the same.

Craw stood and raised her tail slowly, moving towards
the big pipes. Nailz ran up to her and they both turned
slowly to confront Tom. He knew they wanted something.

'Come on,' Craw said. You've come this far with us.
We need your help.' Craw drew on all the strength in her
body and leapt upwards as Tom crawled beneath the fattest
pipe just behind her. He saw her distorted shape and her
awkward movements. With a gentle lift he pushed her
towards a gap in the tenting and into the outside world.

Craw stretched her neck towards the outside world and
cried a fearsome cry. 'The Caterwaul begins!'

Chapter Nineteen: The Caterwaul

At first, the sound was like a slow whine. Other spirits close by, those who had escaped captivity, picked up the sound and its volume grew. The warning of danger was getting to the nearest and then would be passed on to the furthest. It could travel from coast to coast if all thinking cats heard the message, and this was just the beginning.

As the sound turned into a hiss, Craw called out, 'We are different!' Then she changed the tone. 'We have evolved!'

Craw was in the open and saw a policeman close by who put his fingers in his ears to block out the piercing sound.

'We are better!' Craw sang. 'We will win!'

Another passer-by fell to his knees, his mouth wide open in shock. He looked in Craw's direction and placed his hands over his ears.

Craw's tune was echoed by cats in the close streets, in the parallel alleyways and in the nearby fields. 'The Catskill is willing!'

She paused to try and hear the echoes. 'Trust only those you really trust. Pass on the Caterwaul. This is the warning of the Great Catskill!'

Craw lifted her head. Tom was watching her, his face pale. She knew she must be frightening him, with her loud, powerful voice, weakened, damaged frame and shaved head. She could almost see the hairs on the back of his neck prickle, and he shook as if taken by a sudden chill

Nailz appeared and ran to Craw. 'It isn't enough!' he said. 'It hasn't the power. Catskill's warning needs to be bigger, louder, stronger! It must travel much further beyond the streets that imprison us!' He appealed to Tom with his big eyes.

'If I knew exactly what you want,' Tom said, 'I'd help.'

'I must send out the warning!' Craw yelled. 'I must make the alarm ring out like the sound of bells!'

'Like bells?' said Tom. 'Was that what you said?

'Bells, bells you must understand me!' Craw begged. She knew how the tiniest bells worn by some spirits warned of their arrival from a distance away. Birds flew away, mice froze to the spot and fellow spirits awaited the arrival of their friend with the necklace and its bell.

Craw stared at the Cathedral and saw Tom follow her gaze towards the tall spires. The three spires that had been a banner for pilgrims across the centuries.

Three spires... Tom saw them silhouetted against the sky. 'Do you want your cry to carry further?' he asked the cats. 'Get up higher and it will!'

'Higher,' said Nailz, nodding. 'Up there! Catskill can shout the Caterwaul and it will be heard by those beyond our boundaries. The story can be passed on over the fields and until we have all Catkind behind us. This is a fight to the death—all our deaths!'

Craw was hypnotised by the spires. Without another sound, she ran away from the shelter of the tents towards the three spikes in the sky. The full moon made them stand out against the sparkling, starlit firmament. She turned again to Tom who was transfixed by a small grey cat.

'Piner!' he said. 'You did get away.' Tom held out his arms and Piner leapt straight into them.

Cats were appearing from every doorstep, alleyway and culvert on Dam Street and along Quonians Lane. They had all heard the Caterwaul.

Craw looked back to the Spires. She wondered whether she could get that high, high enough maybe to send the Caterwaul further around the catworld. She rushed along the street and as she hurried towards the large body of water more and more cats joined her. Twitcher came up from behind and the stream of small bodies became a flood as they filled the narrow street. Craw could see Toot and Skoot, Tel, and all her closest friends and allies.

Seeing a gate barring the way, she jumped onto the bar and faced her followers. 'You are the strongest, the bravest and the brightest!' she said. 'We are here to send out the Caterwaul together, to warn the whole of Catdom of the dangers they face. This building of three towers is a great place; a place of peace, safety and truth. This great hope comes from the spirit of Catskill.'

The chant began. 'Catskill... Catskill... Catskill...'

'Time for the real Caterwaul,' Craw said. She needed Tom to understand. 'Let's make some noise and show this boy and the rest of the world!'

Tom stared and put one hand to his ear.

Piner leapt out of Tom's grasp. 'Come on,' he said, nodding, 'we'll need you boy. We trust you.'

Tom picked up his pace and ran with the cat-crowd towards the lower edge of the Cathedral. The multi-hued mob followed Craw and stopped at the weather-worn, pock marked statue of some fancy dressed provider. Craw looked at Tom, pleading. *We need to get in*, she thought.

'I've only ever been through the main door,' the boy said. 'I'll find another way in for you.' He rushed to the main door, glancing up at the carvings of the gathered kings, queens, saints, prophets and bishops as they stared down at him. There was no way past them. They were the silent, motionless guardians of this place.

Tom looked towards the Cathedral School. Some of the cats set out like scouts, running in lines around the walls. Craw ran under some white plastic sheets hanging from great poles. She stopped. There was an opening in the wall. It looked like a window, like those the Providers had in their homes, but much larger. The top curved upwards into a point. However, there was no glass. *No glass means this could be our way in*, Craw thought. *If we're lucky.* She crawled from under the sheet, touched Tom on the foot and then rushed back into her new hiding place.

'Is there a way in?' the boy asked. As he pulled up the sheeting, he saw it. 'A window, under repair smashed in the recent strong winds! This is the way inside!' He stood up and leaned towards the space, gripping the ledge with his hands. Craw clung onto his back. 'That tickles,' he said.

Craw led the way up and over Tom's head. 'Don't move,' she said. Cats ran up his legs and over his head. 'Come on!' Craw hoped Tom was beginning to understand their cat ways with or without speech.

Nailz looked Tom in the eyes and said, 'Understand—I am the last one!'

'But how am I supposed to get in?'

Nailz jumped onto the ledge and dislodged the sheeting. 'There, climb in.'

Craw saw their helper tumble inside and stagger forward. She watched more cats come into the cathedral through other unseen ways. They were clever.

Craw knew she needed to be high up. She stared upwards.

'You want to be high up?' Tom asked. 'The tallest Tower. I think it's this way!' He rushed off in the direction of the stairwell. Before he reached it there was a noise of scratches on steps, and Craw knew they had found their own way.

She strained up stair after stair after stair until she could go no higher. She was above the city, above the lights; as high as she could be. She could see the sky, and the way to the rest of the world. She wondered if the Caterwaul would carry across the city if it would travel across the empty fields and countryside to the other towns beyond. If it reached the place the Providers called Birmingham then London, many thousands of cats could be raised from their slumber!

Then the old nagging doubt gnawed at her. What if her band, these few brave spirits, were the only cats that had changed since the *shudder*? If they were destroyed no one would ever know their story. All the cats in the world might be destroyed too or condemned to a life of ignorance of their potential.

'Cry, Catskill,' Tel called from his position on the stairs. 'Cry!'

It was time to make the sound, the final cry for help. The greatest of all Caterwauls! As she began the cry, every cat in the Cathedral repeated the call to action after her. It reverberated as if a huge loudspeaker system had burst into life, coming out of every corner of the Cathedral and ringing out across the city. Craw hoped that cats in the farms in the countryside would hear the message. Cats in town after town would pass it on. Cats in the wild on riverbanks, cats in cages and cats in zoos would hear the message and do likewise.

The wrap-around sound dropped to a hum and then tailed off to eerie silence. The cats who had managed to sit on the stone stairs to the tower were now trooping back towards the nave. Craw moved through them awkwardly as they stepped aside to let her pass them. There was a large open space in front of the pulpit, and it was there that the cats were gathering. The moonlight was still bright, and it seemed as if one window was lit up by a great light. Craw stood at the nave looking towards the pulpit. Craw heaved her tired body across the nave and to the top of the great pulpit, getting as high as she could so that all could see her. She pointed to the window. 'There.'

All eyes followed her paw which she moved to shelter her eyes from the brightness.

'Why is that so bright?' A cat voice called out. 'Is it giving us some light? I've heard the Providers' tale. The huge man is called Goliath.'

'I knew that cat, squealed out a voice. 'He was a brute.'

'Not that one!' said another. 'Goliath was a man, a Provider from the past.'

'He was still a brute, that Goliath,' added a third.

'Wish he was here now!' said a tiny Siamese.

'I am!' said another. 'Over here.' A huge ginger heaved himself up—he was the tomcat to beat all tomcats. A space appeared around him as he stood; everyone seemed to understand his size. His face was wide and strong, his head broad like a tiger. He was a male cat in every way.

'Thank you, Goliath,' Craw said. 'Your Providers gave you a good name. This Goliath was strong like the Providers, like the ones who are trying to kill us. But David was his enemy. He was tiny and had to fight Goliath.'

'I'm here,' came a smaller voice. The tiniest cat of all had spoken. He was less than a hand's length from floor to the tip of his ears. 'David, that's what they call me!'

'He's a pussy,' said Goliath.

'No,' David said, 'I'm munchkin. I'm as big as I get and I'm one of the very clever ones. My brothers and sisters all went with the *shudder*.'

The glowering Goliath then dropped his head and said quietly, 'They call me Golly.'

David swelled up and raised his tail. Cats turned and smiled and nodded.

David may be small, Craw thought, *but his heart is as big as Goliath's.* 'Yes, spirits, that's it. The story is in the window glass. How the tiny David defeated the huge Goliath by being clever.'

David lifted his head and raised his nose at Goliath.

'Not you two!' Craw said. 'Look at the glass.' The moonlight illuminated the figures on the window. 'You must see that we are *all* David! We must take on the dreadful Goliath outside. We are the chosen ones. We *can* think, so let us do so!'

Craw stood tall on the wooden pulpit. Her words had

forced all the cats to sit and bow their heads as if in prayer. None of them moved and there was total silence. The light drifted slowly across the coloured window and the colours reflected on the gathered cats. Sometimes they were all red and then green and then blue. The cats lifted their eyes and gazed at the glass as if hypnotised by the changes. They waited and waited as if expecting some kind of magic.

The magic was happening in the streets. Craw's Catskill cry had worked and every cat spirit in immediate caterwaul distance was making to the source of the great sound, a sound the like of which they had never heard but knew it was a call to action. Even the dim spirits knew it was something they should do.

Craw waited as cats came from every corner—hidden cats, home cats, hospital cats, office cats, cats of every colour and every size. They appeared onto the streets of Lichfield—squatters from the Dimbles, the aristo-cats of Gaia Lane, others from Netherstowe, Rotten Row, Cherry Orchard and the Cathedral Close. It was the first gathering since the beginning of cat memory; a massive joining of all the cats in the city, united in their aim to protect Catkind everywhere.

Dam Street was full to bursting. Mothers and fathers were reunited with sons and daughters for the first time in years. There was recognition and excitement as well as fear. Fathers nosed their daughters and mothers nosed their sons. Creaking grandads nodded wisely. All they knew was that the Catskill had returned to help them and was the leader of the new bright cats. The Catskill would see them all to safety and show them the way to salvation.

'They are here!' Craw cried out. 'The spirits who have heard the Caterwaul are here!'

They were still coming. More and more cats appeared from every hole, every window; even every drain. They came from all directions, finding ways into the Cathedral that had been secret for over a thousand years, ever since it had been a wooden building founded in the memory of St. Chad. The nave filled up and then the north and south transepts and they perched as far as the eye could see. The choir stalls were full as if a great hymn was about to be sung.

Craw turned on top of the pulpit as the chant began.

'Catskill... Catskill... Catskill...'

No longer did she deny the title. She lifted her shaved head high. Many spirits were shocked at what they saw—she knew she must look less a cat and more a sad creature, scarred and cropped. 'Now is the time,' she said. 'We must make the choice to stand. Some of our heroes are gone, but we must survive. For the sake of the whole of Catkind! Are you with me?'

The cats let loose a low-pitched whine of agreement, which grew into a full-throated roar.

'You are with me!' Craw said. 'We are Davids and they are Goliaths, but we have to win. Our thinkers are here!' She turned to her little band on the steps of the pulpit. 'They have been brave and bright. Trust them and trust others.'

She looked at Tom. 'You know who you trust amongst the Providers,' she said, 'and we may have to go to them. The end is near. Many of us have been killed. Many of your sons and daughters have died. Remember, we are not inbred like dogs. We have strength in our bodies and our souls. We are cats; we are quiet spirits in a busy world. But now it is time to make a great rumble and show we have real power!'

Tails began hitting stone floor, slowly at first, building gradually until all the cats were doing it. The noise reached earth-throbbing proportions, forcing young Tom to put his hands over his ears.

Suddenly, there was a massive explosion. Swathes of light hit all of the stained-glass windows. That evil noise came again, as did the lighting up of the glass.

'The attack has begun. Be prepared!' Craw shouted. 'We are all in danger! Use every part of this great building.

Show cat cleverness and speed! Evade capture and hide everywhere! Victory will be ours!'

As she finished, a weird whistling came from outside. It was followed by a second of silence and then another loud bang. As the sound swept over them like a wave, the cats shrunk back as one, bending and bowing like a huge carpet of fur being stroked. The whistling started once more, and a lightning strike accompanied it, blinding all of them.

In the distance, a thudding began, pounding and chopping its way closer and closer to the Cathedral until it was directly overhead. The thud was awful and filled Craw's head with a remorseless pressure. The cats milled around the pulpit, trying to find somewhere to hide.

Then, an even more brilliant light hit every window at once. It caught their colours, making them sparkle outwards over the Cat-kind. Fear gripped them; the pounding grew louder, announcing itself as a terrifying, ultimate danger to them all.

Though she felt the same fear, Craw forced herself to stand against the maelstrom that raged around her. She saw the others cower, afraid of the invisible invasion that was taking place. Even Tom looked certain the worst was now happening. *The sound and the light may signify the death of all cats*, she thought. *But I cannot let them see my own fear.*

The sound swelled ever louder; the light shone ever brighter. Yet just when Craw believed she could take no more, the blinding whiteness disappeared and took the horrible thudding sound with it. Silence fell across the Cathedral, punctured only by the sound of shuffling cats.

Is it over? Craw asked herself. *Is that it?*

Chapter Twenty: Operation Tom Cat

The moon was hidden by cloud. A dull thud broke the silence and with a gentle whistle, a flare shot up into the sky. The first group of soldiers fanned across the street of the Dam, in full battle garb with blackened faces. The bright, sharp illuminating light would show them the enemy. One had a sniper's rifle and wore night-vision goggles that enabled him to see everything that lay in the darkness. Night was the best time to attack, with the enemy lulled into a false sense of security and feeling tired and ready for sleep.

In front of them, a few cats rushed in all directions, frightened by the intense light. 'Leave those!' one of the soldiers ordered. 'Make for the gate!'

They moved onto the Cathedral Close and went left. A second group appeared silently and moved past the gate to the right. Others followed, some went for the front of the Cathedral, whilst the rest set up gun positions by the Deanery and the Cathedral School.

The thudding sound seemed muffled by the clouds but gradually grew louder and louder until it was like an explosion in the sky. The soldiers on the ground never looked up at the helicopter, instead keeping their eyes focussed on the Cathedral. Seconds later it was lit up by a bright light coming from above. No cats could be seen. The coloured windows of the Cathedral were brighter than a thousand suns and more magnificent than ever. The whole building was alive. Anyone who dared to go to their front door was barked at through a bank of loudspeakers and told to listen to the radio.

As the light shone from the sky, a truck wheeled into the

Close followed by soldiers on foot. Every twenty yards a tall spiked post was hammered into the ground. A second vehicle had a huge roll balanced on its nose like an earth mover. As the poles were secured, the roll was unwound and linked from post to post, revealing a huge net that was fixed in seconds. From the great door to the transept and beyond, the posts were sunk deep into the centuries-old graveyard, disturbing the buried bones of a hundred generations. There was a screeching sound as each pole was driven into the ground, as if the silent beings in the graves were echoing their pain as they were shaken out of their sleep. The net was a tight metal mesh topped with tiny razor wire, meaning death by a thousand cuts for any cat that tried to climb over.

The light from above circled around the great Cathedral—now not a place of sanctuary but of imprisonment. A place watched by the spirits of cats who had been hunted with hounds by Roundhead soldiers in 1643.

***

The atmosphere in the medical centre was tense. The command and control centre was set up at the rear of the hospital unit, with banks of radios and other equipment at the ready, all linked to the operational units, the army HQ and the Ministry of Defence in London. Haskins, Dorothy, Major-General Summers and Sergeant Wilkes were jammed in the cramped space, waiting for the soldiers at the cathedral to report in.

'Operation Tomcat—Phase One complete,' one of the radios crackled. 'Trap set. Over.'

Haskins watched the attack commander, and hoped he was aware of the position of his men and the need to prepare for the final phase. 'We are ready,' the commander told him. 'Operation Tom Cat was intended to drive the cats into an open space such as a field and trap them in the

236

netting. They are trapped, but in the Cathedral instead. It's worked out better for us—this way we can catch more of them than we ever imagined. That'll end the problem once and for all.'

Major-General Summers' face was grim.

'You're in charge, sir,' said Haskins.

Summers shrugged. 'I may be the senior officer, but I'm here to manage this medical situation and the investigation process, not order a kill. Your team—the invisibles—seem to be calling the shots.'

'We are simply here to provide intelligence for this operation,' Haskins said. 'It is and always has been the job of people like us to get the information for you to do the necessary dirty work. For the greater good, as they say. Without us you wouldn't have got this far.'

'We have been involved at the last minute,' Dorothy added. 'From a silly little localised incident, this is now a national, even *international* crisis. We've got the leaders of the West turning up in less than seven hours and we need a solution by then, or at least some answers and a strategy! Otherwise we'll all be out on our ears.'

The radio spat out another brief communication. 'Still on standby for Phase Two.'

The attack commander turned to Sergeant Wilkes. 'Tell HQ the first phase of operation Tom Cat is achieved, and we are ready to go. Confirm to HQ that the cats escaped the police and the cat catchers. Local residents have reported a mass movement of cats towards the Cathedral. The units here had already devised a capture plan to deal with what may become a siege situation.'

'That's the British army sir,' Wilkes replied with a touch of sarcasm. 'Supremely adaptable.'

'I'm still awaiting the final results on the testing of animals and humans,' Major-General Summers said. 'I can confirm there is evidence of disease in the dead cats we've now examined. Tell that to HQ as well. Get on with it, sergeant. You're the operational soldier!'

Wilkes saluted and moved to the radio operator. As he dropped his head to talk to the soldier, Haskins was pulled aside by Dorothy. 'This situation is horrific,' she said. 'The medical results are frightening enough, but can there really be murder in a Cathedral? If nothing else, think of the politics of the situation!'

'That has, certainly, caused problems for Kings in the past,' mumbled Haskins.

'H, I don't want a history lesson. Once the cats had escaped there was no option but to exterminate them, but why have they gone to the Cathedral? The military has thought quickly and say they have the means to contain them. They've done it before.'

'Yes, but with people!'

'The cats are a threat,' Dorothy insisted. 'We know that. They are going to have to die. But we can't have shooting in there.'

'There's the gas and smoke option.'

Dorothy laughed. 'Do you know how many priceless treasures there are in that building?'

'More than you might think. There's the Angel of Lichfield, the Chad Gospels and—'

'Okay!' Dorothy interrupted. 'Just because you live here! They will never have had soldiers trying to smash it down before.'

'Wrong again,' Haskins said. 'The Roundheads smashed parts of the Cathedral in 1643 during the English Civil War. It was bombarded by a new 'engine' brought from Coventry called a mortar that rained burning shells onto the Cathedral. It's just history repeating itself.'

Dorothy looked troubled. 'So, devastation has returned to the Cathedral? Poor Sheba.'

***

The lights went out from the helicopter above the

Cathedral. It began to drift away, taking the thud of its rotors with it, and there was relief even for the soldiers holding the siege. They were gathered in several groups. Some covered the main doors, whilst others were placed to ensure that no part of the building went unobserved.

Once more, the radios crackled into life. 'Phase Two—GO!'

A third of the troops moved towards the Cathedral, quickly taking up positions at each of the doors. The soldiers stood shoulder to shoulder and then began to move together.

The thumping sound began quietly at first but increased in volume and tempo. It was rhythmical, regular and intimidating. The men had small shields in each hand with small grips that allowed them to create the harsh sound. It lasted for minutes before losing all form and regularity becoming a disjointed, ragged, crashing sound. A sound that echoed harshly off the tall Cathedral walls. Anyone who could hear it wanted it to stop.

The clouds dispersed suddenly, and the moon's brilliance shone down, if it had been a pre-arranged signal for silence; the awful racket stopped, and the soldiers fell totally still. Then, they pulled back and a different set of soldiers took their place.

Again, they took positions at the entrance. Large black pads were placed on the ancient wood of the great door. There was an odd sucking as the pads seemed to take on a life of their own. The whole machine was like a mechanical spider of enormous proportions. The fat black body settled eventually on the centre of the door and seemed to begin to tremble of its own accord. Each of the doors had its own throbbing, wood-eating spider locked onto it.

The fat, black door-eating tarantula began to speak. It was a low hum that grew into a throaty moan. Gradually, the pitch of the weird sound became higher and higher until it was a piercing, penetrating, unbearable squeal.

The sound echoed inside the Cathedral, and the cats moved away from the great door in one movement like a wave of fur.

Craw was swept into the frightened throng, frantically thinking how she could stop them, and wondering if she had led them into a trap. She shook herself free, crawled onto the pulpit again and caterwauled as loud as she could. Tom heard her. Nailz heard her. Some of the cats at the edge of the cat wave heard her too but were carried along by the fearsome momentum.

A combined hum grew and grew until it seemed as if the doors were trembling. Craw looked from door to door to door. Why had she come to this place? *I should have led them away to the country, into open fields. But even there they might have been easily trapped.*

Now the throbbing was unified it was greater than ever before. The cat wave had nowhere to go. Every cat in the Cathedral sank to the floor, as it was the only place to avoid this horror.

Craw felt nothing but pain.

***

The operator took off his headset and turned to Sergeant Wilkes. 'They've started the Krakatoa,' he said, putting on massive ear protectors. 'Even with these on, and at this distance, it's a vile sound.'

'Krakatoa?' asked Haskins. 'That was a volcano.'

'And the loudest noise ever in the history of the world when it exploded,' the operator said. 'This new engine is intended for terrorists—anyone barricaded in a building holding hostages. It's a new weapon, powerful and top secret until now. They tried it on us during the experimental phase. It's worse than gas—unbearable, even. We operators don't get the direct sound, but we still have to wear special headsets.'

'I was at the tests on monkeys,' Major-General

Summers said, 'supposed to be taking care of their health and welfare. Apart from the intense pain, it causes perforation of the ear drums and then impacts on the brain with quite frightening consequences. It's never been used like this. It's been approved here because of the proximity to the local population. The aim is to create submission from those in the siege area and it is an extremely focused system. It's never been tested to extermination level.'

Perhaps now it will be, Haskins thought.

'Not lucky for the cats.' Dorothy muttered. She turned away from the group and walked to the rear of the tent. 'Are our own cats with them? Roots and Sheba?'

Dorothy placed her hands over her face. Haskins thought she was going to cry. He'd never seen her cry, even when their colleagues had been killed on duty.

***

As the sound died away the Cathedral floor was like a living cat mat, covered with whimpering figures. Many of the cats were rubbing their ears on the floor, trying to soothe them. Some were licking each other's ears in an attempt to ease the discomfort. There was no fight left.

Craw remained in the pulpit, lost in her thoughts, staring at the massive roof and then the statues and the tombs, and the flags that had flown over ancient battles. 'Can you hear me now?' she cried out. 'We have to act! I brought you in here. I asked you to come and help. Something told me it would protect us but now I need to ensure that whatever happens to us our story must be spread. It must be told to the rest of Catkind.'

Slowly, the familiar chant began again. 'Catskill... Catskill... Catskill...'

Craw waved her left paw in the air and the chant died away. 'I need some of you to leave this place and find anywhere that Catkind is living or hiding. I need you to tell them all our stories of bravery, of wisdom and strength; to talk of Twitcher, Nailz, Bootsie, Purrl and the others. To inspire cats to believe in us, believe in themselves, their future and the spirit of the Great Catskill.'

Craw dropped her eyes towards the crowd. Again, she grew. Slowly, her head lifted, and she unleashed a terrifying cry from deep within. Her tail rose, reaching for the sky. 'I want not the bravest or the strongest! Those must stay and fight. I want as many different spirits as are here. I want one with short hair, one with long hair, one with a long tail, one with a short tail. A spirit with a long body, another with a short body.'

As she listed the different types she wanted, one by one they stepped forward. The sea of cats parted to let them through. There were twelve, with Nailz at the front.

'Nailz,' Craw said, 'I will need you here—I rely on you.'

Nailz turned slowly and surveyed the small band. 'They need me,' he countered, 'and they can rely on me. I must go. It is my duty to Catkind.'

Craw leaned towards him. 'Tell your story and the legend of Catskill. You know the story from the start.' She looked at the others. 'You are my messengers and you will spread the word.'

Craw turned to Tom. Sounds came from her and she somehow forced him to understand that it was his job to help them escape as he had helped them get into the Cathedral.

Craw faced the little band. 'Take care, chosen ones, whatever happens. Whoever falls, you must keep going. Now, go before the noise starts again or even worse things happen.'

***

Tom went back to the window that had enabled them to enter. A light from the helicopter was circling the Cathedral grounds. It would be impossible for them to leave. They'd be seen and finished off. Suddenly, it went dark and the light moved away from the window. Tom realised there was a chance that as the searchlight passed by the small group could escape. It would be even more possible with a decoy.

That decoy must be him.

Tom stepped up to the space and looked at the little group. Their eyes were so keen, and they watched him with expectation. 'I'm going out first. I will take away the light and then you must run.' His hands gestured at them trying to demonstrate darkness and running. He was sure the small Burmese was laughing at him.

Tom was sure the cat had understood his words. 'Go on give me four swishes of a tail to show you know what I said!'

Four swishes later Tom knew the cat understood.

Tom dangled his legs through the window and then lowered himself to the ground. He was still hidden by the massive white plastic sheeting. 'Here goes.' He took a deep breath and walked briskly away from the Cathedral wall. Maybe twenty seconds later, a bright light blinded him. A voice from a loudspeaker barked something at him but it was almost unintelligible. He kept walking, but with the light in his face he was not sure of his footing. All he knew was that he had to keep going as long as possible to give the group any chance of getting away. As he held his hands in front of him, he felt the wire mesh of a barrier.

A voice blasted in his ear. 'It's that kid again!'

He was thrown violently to the ground. He knew he needed to play for as much time as possible. 'What's the matter?!' he shouted as loud as he could. 'I haven't done anything!'

He was hoisted up by his collar and pushed towards the fence. 'Open up and take him out!'

A soldier from behind the fence ripped open a gap, allowing Tom through.

'Take him to the command truck—and *don't lose him*

again!'

A shot rang out from the far side of the Cathedral. Tom was pushed to the ground again, a knee in the small of his back, his arms held behind tightly behind him.

'Cats on the run!' someone shouted.

The fence was sealed, and the soldiers fanned out, guns ready to fire, aiming towards the Cathedral. Tom lifted his head from the soil and could see Nailz leading from the front. A sharp crack rang out and Tom saw Nailz twisting in the air and skidding across the grass. The remaining eleven cats were still running along the side of the solid fence.

Tom blinked as a massive searchlight lit up poor Nailz. He twitched on the ground and the light showed up every tiny movement.

The attack commander was shouting into his radio. 'Pick up the rest! There might be more out there. I want them all down! Now!'

Tom was deafened as guns sparked, their automatic fire rattling across the gravestones before silence fell and nothing stirred.

Chapter Twenty-One: An Unearthly Noise

In a moment of darkness, a voice shouted, 'Light here!'
The spotlight picked out Nailz as he used every ounce of strength left in his damaged frame to reach the edge of the fence in a series of spasmodic lunges.

'It's all right.' A soldier leaned down towards the stricken body. He shrugged his shoulders then bent down and picked up the limp cat.

'Put it down, fool. It's infected!' screamed a voice through a loudhailer. 'What the hell are you doing?'

The soldier turned and walked towards the light. 'Taking it to the medics.'

'Put it down and get back to your position!'

The soldier slowly placed the still body of Nailz on top of a flat gravestone and stared back at the disembodied electronic voice of his officer.

A voice barked out through the stillness. 'Stop! Lights, lights! South side, now, now! I have sight of three people—south side!'

The light operator took her eye off the tragic scene and moved her spotlight towards the voice. There, enveloped in an intense light, were three figures—one tall, one medium and one small. 'What the hell is that?'

The officer shouted out another order. 'Hold fire, hold fire!' Under his breath, he muttered to his sergeant. 'Get over there—who are they? How did they get here? I thought this area was supposed to be a sterile zone! And where are the dead cats?'

Sergeant Wilkes took off towards the light and the statuesque, ghostly figures. 'Who are you? Stand still! Who are you?' he repeated.

As he approached, Wilkes saw the young girl he had previously encountered. Victoria expected Mrs Constance to answer but it came from another direction.

'We were left all alone,' Samsy Beaman said, 'and we tried to find somebody to look after us. Where's my Mummy?'

The little girl had given the perfect answer. Esme Constance dropped her head and smiled, vacantly. Victoria was bemused and avoided the sergeant's glare.

'Who lifted the fence?' the sergeant asked angrily. 'Who lifted the fence?'

No-one answered him. He ran to the fence in time to catch a glimpse of the ginger outline of a huge cat staring back at him before turning, raising his tail, and scooting off after his fellow escapees. 'Who lifted the fence?'

'Nobody did,' said Samsy. 'I'm frightened.'

'Alright!' the sergeant barked. 'Alright.' Wilkes knew this wasn't proper army work.

Large tears rolled down Samsy's cheeks. 'Where's my mummy?' she sniffled.

The sergeant spoke deliberately and slowly into his microphone. 'No cats within the perimeter. Repeat: no cats. Three people are outside the perimeter—they may have been responsible for helping them out.'

'Confirm?' said an exasperated voice. 'No cats, just three people. Confirmation, sir—no cats, one adult, two children.'

'Children?'

'Yes, sir, and the smallest one is crying.'

'How can you cope with civilians on a battlefield?' asked the voice.

'With difficulty, sir?' The sergeant pulled apart the fencing by stripping off the fastenings and waved his gun at the three to come into the contained area.

He held Victoria back for a moment. 'And I thought, young lady, you would be keeping out of trouble for now?'

Victoria smiled. 'We've just come from the hospital tent,' she said innocently. 'We were just following everybody else.'

***

Inside the Cathedral there was hardly a sound. Craw stared at the ceiling but could barely make it out. 'Skoot, you are my eyes, Toot you are my ears. What's happening?' Skoot and Toot ran up to Craw as if one was the shadow of the other. 'Skoot, what did you see?'

'Very little, Great Catskill. This coloured glass is so hard to see through, although in the bright light I did see one thing.'

'What was that?' Craw stooped down. 'Tell me, but quietly.'

'I saw Nailz leading the group, but something stopped him running—an invisible barrier of some sort. A sharp crack rang out and he fell.'

Craw listened intently as Toots took up the story. 'I heard a man say Nailz was infected, whatever that means.'

'There were lots of flashes,' Skoot said. 'I'm not sure if anyone got away to tell the story of our siege.'

'More lost spirits! Will this never end?' Craw slumped as pain swelled in her body. The clips and catches that had imprisoned her on that awful torture table suddenly seemed very sharp. But so was her mind, and she had become the Great Catskill. 'They have to come to us.' she said. 'They have to come to us.'

The group around her listened, seeking the wisdom of the Great Catskill. She hoped she could provide it. There was a breathless hush as she closed her eyes and thought deeply. 'Perhaps some of our number have escaped the trap and will be able to spread the news of our story,' she said. 'We sense that they heard the first Caterwaul. But if the men really wish to stop our story, they have to come and get us. They created that fearful row. They can do it again, but still they have to come in and take us out one by one. This is a big place with many doors, many rooms, many chairs, many screens, many statues and many more hiding places. If they come in, we can be nowhere and everywhere. No one can herd cats. We shall run and hide. When one of us is caught ten of us will help the spirit escape, and then run and hide again. They will need a thousand soldiers to catch us.'

Craw's mind was running at such a speed she could hardly keep pace with her thoughts. 'Bootsie was a great soldier cat who lived with and learned from the soldiers. He taught me to think as they do and that it would help us win. Some of you know Bootsie. Tell others his story if you can—he was the first of the brave. Remember Bootsie! Without him the Catskill would not be here now.'

The spirits that were left from her special band draw close and nuzzled her in agreement and memory of Bootsie.

'As they enter, we shall hide and fight!' she said. 'Stand firm and wait. If the noise begins again, go to the furthest part of this building and bury your ears in your paws. Then be ready for the final fight.'

All the spirits nodded and made ready to find their own corners.

***

Sergeant Wilkes pulled Esme Constance firmly by the elbow. 'You should not be here! You need to leave. This is an operational area! You're all ill; I know you've just come out of the hospital tent.'

'I am not ill,' insisted Mrs Constance.

'I'm not neither,' agreed Samsy.

'I feel all right too,' said Victoria, 'and I was scratched and bitten.' She showed the sergeant her scratched neck. I was only obeying orders.'

Wilkes was getting frustrated. 'All right! Let's not debate this now! Control, can you get these people away from me? We have to find the missing cats, but most of the others are trapped in the Cathedral.'

'Sergeant,' Control responded, 'get the civilians to the control unit. We have orders to finish off the cat activity in the Cathedral.'

As he began to usher them away, a soldier approached dragging another civilian in his wake. Wilkes sighed heavily. *The boy, Tom.* 'Not you as well,' he said as he recognised troublesome Tom.

Tom was held by his collar. The soldier raised his gun, releasing Tom's jacket, and shouted, 'Identify!'

'Tom Cat One,' Wilkes shouted back. 'Come forward and get these civilians out of here!'

One soldier moved forward as instructed and signalled to Tom to follow.

'Come on lad,' Wilkes said.

But Tom saw Nailz lying still on the slab. He moved away from the soldier and ran to Nailz. There was a small trickle of blood running from the corner of the cat's mouth. 'No, Nailz,' the boy said. 'Don't die.' He touched the cat very gently, smoothing down his fur. There was no movement, no sign of life.

'Don't touch it!' Wilkes shouted. He couldn't stop Tom picking up the little limp creature, its legs drooping towards the ground.

Tom held him tightly to his chest and squeezed the soft frame. 'Come on, wake up.' He turned Nailz onto his back and cradled him.

'Come on son, put it down.' Wilkes spoke firmly but Tom gripped the cat's ribcage.

'I feel something,' the boy said. 'I'm not sure... it's almost like the fluttering movement of a trapped tiny bird!' He squeezed his hands a little more. 'A heart!' he exclaimed. 'It's the fast beating of a little heart! Nailz isn't dead!'

'Put it down!' said Wilkes 'That's diseased!' He spoke into the microphone at his lips. 'The boy has picked up the dead cat.'

'He's not dead!' Tom shouted. 'His heart's beating!'
'Mine!' screamed a little voice. Samsy Beaman pointed at the creature in his arms. 'Mine!' she repeated.

Wilkes wasn't happy. *This isn't real, this certainly isn't warfare.* He waved his hand for the soldier to pass through the fence. Tom followed holding Nailz protectively.

'Mine,' Samsy said again, and before Wilkes knew what was happening, she had grabbed the little creature and was holding him under his front legs. She kissed Nailz several times on his face. 'Is he poorly?'

'This is too much!' Wilkes said exasperatedly. The little girl was squeezing the cat and he saw a small smudge of blood drop onto her white top. He would have to take the cat from her. *At least I'm protected by my uniform.* He held out his hand slowly so as not to frighten the girl, and then the cat turned its head and licked her face.

'Let me have him,' said Wilkes. 'Your baby's poorly, and we must get him to the cat doctor.'

Samsy was most definitely unwilling. Her bottom lip jutted out as if she was about to cry. 'Mine,' she said again.

'Yes, he is, but let's make him better.' The sergeant raised his hand. 'Stand there, all of you, and don't move.' He touched his microphone. 'Control, I have four civilians and one dead or dying cat. Please advise.'

'Do not touch,' Control replied. 'Bring all to the holding area at Control Point One. Body bags and sterilisation materials are all there. The attack on the Cathedral is about to begin.'

Wilkes turned to the group. 'I have to take all of you to a place where you can be safe.'

'I'm not going,' said Tom.

'I'm not going!' said Samsy, stamping her feet.

'You can't make me go,' asserted Mrs Constance.

'You cannot, said a new voice.

More civilians! Wilkes turned and saw Mr and Mrs Biggins along with Mr and Mrs Beaman. *It's practically a family party.* He held up his hands in despair. Mr Beaman went up to Victoria and put his arms around her. 'We had a visit from your Aunt Julia who said she'd seen you in the Close,' he said. 'You know where she lives. All the phones have been dead for hours and she couldn't reach us. Something very funny is going on. So, we've all come.'

'You all must leave now!' Wilkes pleaded.

Mrs Biggins stepped forward. Wilkes remembered what she was like. *She will have her say, and no soldier is going to stop her.* 'We decided we'd all come down to find out what the hell is going on,' she said firmly, 'and find out what Tom is up to. There is no news coming out. Nobody is saying anything, not even the Police. So, we decided to find our way in here. Just as well my husband knows his way round the back alleys—and his 'so-called' secret route alongside Netherstowe Pool—and you soldiers don't. What on earth is going on?'

'Not allowed to say,' the sergeant replied, waving his gun, 'but you'll all have to leave *now.*'

Mrs Biggins was wearing her anti-authority hat and her tone was decidedly frosty. 'Not until we have an explanation.'

'The commanding officer can provide that,' Wilkes replied smartly, 'once you've left this place. We'll have to get you out of here because it is dangerous. Follow these soldiers now.'

'Why should we?'

Mr Biggins put his arm on his wife's shoulder. 'We have to listen to what they have to say,' he said gently.

Mrs Beaman walked over to Samsy and gently lifted Nailz out of her arms.

'Mine,' said Samsy.

'Yes darling, but let your mummy take him.' She held the poor creature tightly and winced as she saw the wound in his fur. 'How and why did this happen?'

'Come on—we'll get a full explanation, I'm sure,' said

Mr Beaman.

'You will,' said Wilkes. 'I have to emphasise this is a difficult and dangerous place. You must follow the soldier, or we'll have to force you.'

Mr Biggins at least understood the insistence in his tone. 'You won't have to do that. Come on everyone, let's go and find out the truth.'

Wilkes stared at the group as they walked away. Soon enough the sun would rise, the surprise of the night attack would disappear and the whole town would wake up. When killing was on the agenda, this was his worst nightmare.

***

In the Cathedral, the spirits followed Craw's instructions and sought some tiny bolt hole or covering to protect themselves against the vile sound that was to come. One ingenious little group had found the shredded flags of various army regiments presented to the Cathedral over the years. They had drawn them together into a shroud that they wrapped around themselves. Others ran up stone steps; yet more squeezed under ancient doors.

Some returned to the towers and scurried their way into every nook and cranny. They sought out any type of cover, pulling at hangings or drapes and even pieces of rope lying on the floor.

These are the most ingenious cats that have ever lived, Craw mused. Her mind was still alert, but the possibility of their deaths preyed upon her. *Will they live much longer?* The final push would come soon. 'Away from the doors, as far as possible!' she shouted.

From beyond the fenced perimeter of the Cathedral, a voice barked out. 'Stand by!' it ordered. 'All points secured. Secondary netting is now in place. Attack to commence. Five minutes of Krakatoa followed by entry into the building. As the animals come out, they are to be shot.'

'What can you see, Skoot?' Craw called out.

'They're coming,' she said as she waved her paw. Her signal passed from spirit to spirit.

When the men came in Craw would be the first sight they would see—the Great Catskill standing proud. She looked up at the vast ceiling—a ceiling built by men, soon to cover a graveyard for cats.

The throbbing began as it had before. Craw waited. The pain grew in her head and water welled in her eyes. In the vast space, she saw tiny eyes shining like stars in the darkness. These were her spirits in every corner, their eyes illuminating their souls. Had she led them to the deaths? *Surely some have got away, some will have heard the caterwaul and understood the message.* But was it a symphony for cat survival or an elegy?

The noise grew and grew, covering every inch of the Cathedral. Craw's body began to shake. The insistent sound was drilling into her head and her paws trembled with the impact. She fell into a crumpled heap on the floor of the pulpit. Everything had gone dark.

Those nearest to the door who had found no hiding place were the next to drop to the floor—some lay completely still with their paws clasped to their ears.

The dreadful sound had won.

***

'Cut!' The order rang out and the soldiers nearest to the great doors took off their ear guards, breathing deeply with relief and standing aside to allow the attack groups to enter the building.

Every door opened with searchlights illuminating the interior of the Cathedral. Soldiers ran into the huge space, immediately spotting some cats still on the floor. A few here and there, some scattered around the pulpit.

'Where are they all?' a soldier called out. His words echoed and filled the building.

'Keep searching! Drive any live ones to the doors. Keep

shouting at top volume—they'll hate that. Leave the ones on the floor alone. Get those lights higher up.'

One soldier had a large light on his shoulder. He targeted the pulpit, which would give him a great vantage point over the whole Cathedral. As he got to the top, he touched something soft with the cap of his boot. It was a cat, but one that had been shaved strangely. He kicked it roughly across the floor. 'One here!' he called.

'More down here!' said another voice.

'Not many though,' added a third. 'Where are they all? We were told there were scores of them.'

'I've got some wrapped in flags over here. It's like they were trying to get away from Krakatoa.'

The attack commander came into the Cathedral, his eyes following the path of the light that showed some of the great treasures of the place as well as its impressive size. Another bright torch showed up the outline of a massive stone tomb. There was something on the face of the impassive stone figure. He walked over to it and saw a motionless cat. 'This one picked the perfect place to go!' he said. 'There's something wrong. If any of these cats have got out, I'll put you all on a charge.'

'Yes sir,' said a soldier. 'There is only a handful here. They must be hiding or something.'

'Clever cats, really. Locate the power source and let's get some full light on the matter.

A strange echoing then resounded above their heads, growing louder by the second.

'What's that?' one asked. 'I think...'

The astonishing dissonant booming drowned out his voice. It grew and grew; disorganised, chaotic, but ever greater. There was some other presence here; someone or something else making this powerful noise. It was not a sound that cats could make—somebody or something inhuman was helping them.

Chapter Twenty-Two: Cats Shall Swing

Dreamer had managed to go all the way up the tallest tower in the Cathedral. But he was sure that from somewhere in his deepest dreams he had seen three spires of this building rising into the sky. Just as the Great Catskill had started up the Caterwaul from here, this was a place of stories, of hope for the Providers. Dreamer had seen this all around them—in the pictures, the statues. This was not some ordinary building. Each spire had its own entrance and only one had the special quality of the great sound. He scurried and bustled away from the throng outside to find the way into the tower of sound. There in front of him was another solid door almost hidden but with a tiny space at the bottom just allowing him to squeeze through and confront another steep staircase.

Rushing up the steps he opened his cat eyes wide and making the most of the light filtering into the space, he could see hanging leads, ropes there to pull - somehow that might make a great noise. But he had to go higher and as he did and went through another door, he saw great circular shapes - the biggest bells in the world.

Dreamer sat and stared. He thought about the little bell his Provider had once strapped around his neck. He hated that bell. Whenever he wanted to be silent during an attack, the slightest movement would make it tinkle. It served as a warning for little birds and fills. He had shared his dislike of the bell with Craw and they'd laughed at how a tiny ring could warn everyone within listening distance.

The Providers loved bells. Bells were a big deal for people. The sound was a warning, an alert, a call to action.

Craw always said that where dogs will jump at a whistle, people will jump at the tinkle of a bell.

Piner had been following closely behind Dreamer who shook his head and went down to the floor below with the ropes that went nowhere – what a puzzle! In the dark Piner felt something softly touch his leg and then move away. He leapt a foot in the air, pushing his tail up to frighten whoever or whatever it was. The thing hit him on the back of his head and brushed his face. Piner opened his mouth and tried to bite it with his sharpest teeth.

He could not catch it, and as they fought it swung around his face. Piner remembered some of the fighting taught by Twitcher, and so, resting briefly on both his back paws, he leapt at the creature above biting and gripping on as hard and as tightly as he could. His paws lifted off the ground and he was pulled from left to right and back again. He looked frantically for Dreamer, for he would know how to fight off this hairy creature. However, his friend was nowhere to be seen.

'It's a bell!' screamed Dreamer from behind him. 'The biggest bell in the whole of Catdom!'

Piner was now swinging in the air and a low dull sound rang out. 'It's attacking me!' he shouted over the growing boom. With each swing the boom became like the harmonic of his little bell, but much, much louder and more terrible.

He had always hated heights. Now, he was being swung through the air at increasing speed. Every time he fought with the living rope, he spun out wider and wider and faster and faster.

'Jump, you fool!' Dreamer commanded.

'And cats might fly,' said Piner under his breath as he loosened the grip, and, as the rope reached its lowest point of the swing, let his claws withdraw. He flew majestically through the air, twisting and turning his body ready for the landing. *Cats always land on their paws.* Piner did not land with paws together, but one leg at a time. He skidded ten feet across the floor, sure that he saw sparks flying off his claws, before stopping dead. As he hit the wall his head swung backwards and slammed into the brick with a crunch. Dimly, he saw Dreamer wince in sympathy.

His friend watched him for a moment, and then approached slowly. 'All right?' He pushed Piner with his paw.

'All right? What do you think?' Piner moved to his left and felt a shooting pain. He placed his front paw on the floor. 'Ooh.' It hurt, badly. Dreamer gently put out his right paw. With effort, Piner pushed it aside. 'Don't you dare push me again!' He stretched and stood on all four paws. 'I'm all right... I think.'

The bell was attached to his attacker, which was a big rope with a fluffy end. Piner moved cautiously towards it.

'Don't touch it!' yelped the stricken Piner. 'It kills!'

'Don't be silly,' answered Dreamer, as he watched the circling rope gradually come to a stop. 'Pull the rope, ring the bell,' he said. 'Send a message.'

'What are you talking about?' Piner asked. He began licking his wounds.

'Pull the rope. Ring the bell. Send a message.'

'Piner, I don't get it! I've been attacked by a living rope!'

'It's the rope that rings the bell!' Dreamer said. 'Once again, you've been a genius. You've shown the way.'

'I have?'

'Yes. Remember, the Great Catskill tells us we must learn from everything. This bell is another louder signal to the whole world to wake up and help us.

A scraping of claws on stone announced the arrival of Skoot, followed closely behind by Toot as always.

Dreamer smiled. 'Where did you two come from?'

'Same place as you!' smirked Skoot. 'We've been watching everything that goes on as well as following our noses.'

'And we know who has broken out from this place!' asserted Toot.

'Nailz didn't,' Dreamer said. 'He didn't get away.'

'Nailz is gone?' Piner asked.

Piner gingerly tested his paws and managed to stand a little higher than he expected. 'Nailz is one of the reasons we're here. If he's gone then we must do this for him. Follow your noses up there.'

The four looked up.

'These are the biggest bells in the world,' Dreamer said. 'A bell that can be our warning to the people in this Close who have cats. To the people who make this building live every day. To the people of the city. To every spirit who has heard the Caterwaul and to every other that's heard our story from those who escaped.'

'So, what do we do?'

'We ring the bells.' Dreamer turned. 'We can't have much longer before we hear that terrible sickening noise from the soldiers.'

As if it had been a prediction, the low throbbing from outside began again. Piner put his hands on his ears. As the vile sound built up, Dreamer had only one aim in mind. *Hold the rope.* He pushed himself forwards, jumped up and gripped the rope with his claws. 'Come on, all of you— whoever is near! Grab the rope—it is our only chance for a future!'

Piner dragged himself from the floor, gripped the end of the rope and held on as tight as he could. Toot uttered her special warning, sounding like a snarling duck. It usually had the effect of alerting everyone near that she was on her way.

More claws came up the tower. Twitcher was the first to stick his nose around the wall. 'That awful squeak means you need some help,' he grunted.

Purrl and Tel followed behind. 'We can hear you way down there!' Purrl said. 'What's up?

'Grab a rope, all of you!' Dreamer ordered. 'Find a space, grip on, and put all your weight behind your claws.'

Wherever there was a rope a cat attached itself. Very soon it seemed as if a cat Christmas tree had sprung into existence around it, with every decoration being a different cat, of a different colour and a different size.

'Close your eyes and hold on!' shouted Dreamer.

Every one of the spirits clinging onto the ropes felt their bodies begin to beat with the power. It was like a slow, physical throb beating into the brain. Claws began to lose their grip and one or two of the weaker spirits slipped down the ropes. Purrl was the first to fall to the stone floor. As she dropped, she tried to hide her ears from the enveloping sound.

'Hold on as long as you can,' said Dreamer, 'and let your body give with the movement of the rope.' His shoulders moved from left to right and he felt the rope begin to drop then jerk up his tiny frame. A dull booming sound rang out.

With each pull, the hammers struck the bells with greater impact. The ringing began to grow louder. Dreamer's eyes watered, and his brain shook, but they had to keep going. 'Hold on!' he shouted as loudly as he could. 'Keep pulling! Think of the Great Catskill!'

While their bells sang out its chaotic tune, the pressure in the air gradually ebbed away and the evil sound from outside ceased altogether.

'Keep swinging!' Dreamer said. 'Now it has stopped, we must *keep swinging*!' Far below, human steps clattered through the cathedral.

Piner heard him. 'I'm here. What should we do?'

'Pull. Make the bells ring. Pull all of you. Don't let go!'

The cats held fast to the ropes, knowing their lives depended on it. They were almost there but needed more noise.

Purrl and Tel had fallen from their rope and were sitting

dazed on the floor. 'Come on!' Dreamer shouted. 'We need all of us to do it!'

Purrl pulled Tel to his feet. 'Grab a rope!' She half held Tel, pulling him towards her. Together they leapt for the ragged end and just managed to catch it.

Together, the cats swung with all their might. 'More!' shouted Dreamer. 'It's working. More!'

At last, the hammers struck home. The hums became a boom, and the great bells began to ring. One booming bell followed another. Dreamer wanted to let go. His front legs were tiring but he knew he had to hold on and keep pulling the rope.

The hammers hit the bells over and over, swinging to smash each side. 'Hold on for your lives! Dreamer shouted. 'This message will go out to everyone!' As he screamed his eyes felt a stinging pain—they stung as they were hit by an intense golden light. The bell seemed to light up and shine. His eyes filled with water and he blinked. 'What is this? Another weapon of cat destruction?' *If noise couldn't destroy us, then a searing light might be the next attack.*

They kept pulling and the bells rang out to anyone who could hear them. As the booming of the bells grew so did the intensity of the light.

Dreamer knew they couldn't hold on much longer.

Chapter Twenty-Three: The Catmist

Haskins and Dorothy stood close to the cat cages, all empty apart from their own Sheba and Roots. They had been placed in there at Dorothy's request. 'Sad that I've been responsible for the imprisonment of our two cats,' she said.

'It was your call, Dorothy,' Haskins replied. A loud bell drowned out the sound of her name. 'Just a second! That's a Cathedral Bell not the little Tantony bell but the great bells' He pulled open one of the tent flaps. That sun was bright and red, colouring the whole cathedral.

'There's no-one in the Cathedral,' Dorothy said in confusion. 'The bells can't be ringing.' She knelt and reached through the cage to stroke Sheba, who raised her tail and gazed wistfully into her eyes. She nodded very slowly, and Dorothy pulled her hand quickly away from the black fur.

Dorothy furrowed her brow. 'What do you know?'

'This and that,' the cat spoke. 'I can guess who is ringing the bells.'

'H, she's talking to me.'

'Translate then.' Dorothy was silent. 'You've got it as well,' he grunted. 'The madness spreads but I can hear the sound of the bells and it is ringing in my ears.'

***

Dreamer kept pulling and the bell kept ringing. Gradually, the momentum slowed, and the ringing was replaced by a humming. His front legs were so tired. He knew he'd have to stop. Almost before he knew it, he felt himself slip. Claws out, he slowed his downward flow only to bump into other bodies on his way down. He landed on something soft.

'You're heavy,' panted Purrl.

Dreamer stood, gently, on her neck and jumped onto the floor. 'I did it. I rang a bell.' He punched the air with his paw.

'Do you mind?' Purrl asked, affronted. '*We* did it.'

'And don't forget us,' Skoot said as she pulled herself up and dragged Toot with her.

The final humming of the bells caused Dreamer to wonder if their efforts had been enough to wake the world to their plight. A bright, beautiful shining day had started, causing the colours to twinkle inside the cathedral. *Perhaps it is a sign*, Dreamer thought. *A new day, a new life. A tenth life if cats are supposed to have nine lives one more will help. We play for three, stray for three and stay for three and one more for luck?*

When the soldier waved a printout in his face, Haskins had both hands to his ears trying to rid them of the dull hum. 'Sir?' the soldier said. 'I have the report from Porton Down—it's the result of the medical tests.'

'Tell your Commanding Officer, not me. Not my call.' Haskins looked at the miserable Roots in his cage. 'I hope not, anyway.'

Dorothy couldn't stop staring at Sheba in her little prison. 'It has to be the C.O.'s call.'

'But he's gone up to the Cathedral,' the soldier said. 'Everyone's gone up there. You're the most senior people here.'

'Just tell him. Radio him!'

'This is top security – it's "eyes only" stuff.'

'For goodness sake!' Haskins snapped. 'These aren't terrorists. Cats aren't listening in on your communications. They're not intercepting your transmissions, decrypting your top-secret codes, watching your Skype calls or logging your e-mails! That's *our* job. Just tell him!'

The soldier was uncertain. 'I need your kind of high-level clearance,' he said. 'All the important people are arriving. We're trying to ensure that everything is ready. We've cleared a helicopter landing site by Netherstowe Pool. The area is totally secure. Several hundred extra men have arrived and are sealing the perimeter of the city. There's all this going on at the Cathedral and it is daylight and the bells are ringing.' He was completely exasperated. 'Anyway, it's bad news for the cats. The tests are positive.'

Haskins avoided Dorothy's narrowed eyes. 'Positive. So, we must do what we have to. Soldier pass on the report details. Whatever clearance you need, you have it. On my authority.'

Visibly relieved, the solder saluted and left the tented area preparing to communicate the deadly report.

'I suppose we did what was required in the end,' Haskins said with resignation. 'I got involved in the problem by accident and provided the information required from the other side.'

'And we will lose our cats.'

'Yes, and we will lose our cats.'

'And we cheated some kids.'

'And we cheated a couple of kids.'

'Stop repeating what I'm saying!' Dorothy said, genuinely annoyed. 'This is the worst job I've ever done!'

'And you've done some rough jobs in your time,' Haskins sniffed.

'Thank you for that. But this isn't over yet. And we have one thing to do. Get Roots and Sheba and try to ensure that they don't suffer. There was always the fear that this disease wasn't just located in this area but might spring up anywhere. Perhaps my Roots has infected Sheba.'

Haskins walked the few yards back towards the hospital tent and the cat cages. He pulled back the tent flap to allow Dorothy to go back inside. She stopped while Haskins was still holding the flap.

'They've gone,' she said.

'Who have gone?'

'Our two cats!'

'Don't be silly. They were in the cages.' Haskins rushed into the caged area and saw they were empty. 'They've escaped!'

'How can they?'

'There was the breakout. Perhaps they learned how to unlock the cages.'

Dorothy pulled at the cage door and it swung open. 'Somebody let them out, more like.'

'They should have used proper locks.'

'Then the cats would find the keys and use them.'

'And ring the Cathedral bells to wake the world up, I suppose.'

'Well, do you not find it odd that the might of the British army can't sort out a bunch of cats? It's almost as if they don't *want* to be rounded up.'

'You can't herd cats,' Haskins retorted. 'They've always been like that. What do we do now? Our job is over.'

'We must try and find Sheba,' Dorothy said.' I don't want her dying alone. I think she knows what's going on. She'll have gone to the Cathedral and taken your Roots with her.

Haskins gently put his arm on her shoulder. 'All right. Come on, let's find our cats. I don't want to see them die a horrible death. We need to get up to the Cathedral.'

***

'Why the hell were the bells ringing?' Major-General Summers barked.

Sergeant Wilkes rubbed his temple. 'I don't know sir. We don't believe there are any people in the Cathedral—just cats.'

'What about the ones that got away?'

'One down. I don't suppose the others will get far.'

'Can this get any worse? We've got to get this sorted before the whole world turns up.'

There was a burst of static in Sergeant Wilkes' ear. 'Radio contact for you sir,' he said. 'Urgent and apparently for you only.' He passed the radio over.

'Summers here. What is it?'

'Porton Down say positive.'

'Positive?' What's that mean?'

'Positive—the cats are positive.'

'For what?'

'It says "positive for species to species transmission", sir.'

'You mean cat to human?'

The voice sounded faint and hesitant. 'Yes.'

'This is a human killer?'

'They said positive, sir!'

'Thank you, perfectly understood.' Major-General Summers turned slowly towards the men around the command centre. 'The results don't lie. These cats must die, all of them. They've all got to go, including those who've escaped. And I want whoever is ringing that bell and waking up the whole world.' He faced Sergeant Wilkes. 'All of these animals must be killed. Your Cathedral group must not let any of these cats go.'

He was interrupted by an angry voice shouting very loudly. 'You! You!' A man in a dressing gown was waving. 'What's going on? This is totally unacceptable!'

'Wilkes find out who he is and get rid of him,' Summers ordered. 'We don't want spectators for this shooting match. Encourage him to return to his house and to stay indoors. Preferably quietly.'

'Yes, sir.' Wilkes trudged across the grass towards the dishevelled figure. The angry man waved his arm. 'What is all this?'

'I'm afraid this is a top-secret exercise,' the sergeant said tiredly, 'and I am unable to let you have any further information. I must ask you to go back from where you came.'

'I live here!' said the angry man. 'This is my Cathedral. I'm the Dean. You can't do any exercises or ring the bells without my permission or the Canon Precentor!'

'Sorry sir, but it doesn't matter who you are. This is a matter of national security— *international* security, even. I must ask you to return to your house and keep away from this location. We aren't the ones ringing the bells.'

'I shall speak to the Bishop,' the Dean said. 'And the police! And anyone else who is awake at this unearthly hour which, given this cacophonous peel of bells, is probably everybody in Lichfield!' He pulled his gown around himself, suddenly aware that perhaps this wasn't the kind of uniform that impresses people and stalked off towards the Deanery.

Wilkes returned to the General. 'It was the Dean, sir,' he reported. 'Says he's going to speak to the Bishop; reckon that'll stir up more trouble. Krakatoa may have damaged the cats with its focused sound, but these bell noises will surely have shaken the city out of bed.

Summers checked his paperwork. 'I think, sergeant, we have to assume that Krakatoa may not have worked as we wished. We dare not try Krakatoa now, not with everybody waking up. There may be injured cats—perhaps they are unconscious, and we can clear them quickly. We've hundreds of medical disposal bags for the bodies and we've brought in the Lachrymatory Agent in large canisters. It's a new type of tear gas. We can pump some into the building to start with and then use the explosive canisters as we break in.'

'Tear gas? Untested on cats, I guess?'

'Yes, it's intended for people, but it will hurt cats. Their eyes will run, their mouths will sting, and their breathing will become laboured. It might kill some of them, especially those close to the exploding canisters. It's pretty horrible.'

Wilkes was not happy. 'Surely, the problem is that this is a huge space and the gas will disperse. It'll find any gap to escape.'

'When exploded, this gas disperses at ground level before rising. It's perfect for affecting the cats at their height. After it's been set off, we'll enter and pick the moggies off.' Major-General Summers shrugged. 'We can deal with the immobilised ones easy enough—we'll have to shoot the rest. Brief your men, and let's do it.'

***

Craw's body ached but she needed to find a moment of inspiration and hope. Then it came. A great, great grandmother and her tiny great, great grand kitten walked up to her and the baby smiled. It helped, and Craw knew she had to draw from the Catmemory, the Catstory and the legend of Catskill to give them a chance. She dropped her head and thought again. *Perhaps this is the end for this generation of the best and brightest. Even the nicest Providers won't allow us to be a part of their thinking world.*

Cats had managed people since the day the first cat realised it didn't need to hunt. *Just be nice to the Providers; lie on your back, purr and cuddle them when they feel low.* It was survival that was important.

Craw ascended the pulpit for what might be the last time. 'Hear me, bravest of the brave! Hear me, ringers of the bells! Hear me, saviours of Catdom! You are bright, you are wise. We have sent out our tale. The Caterwaul warned of our plight. We don't know how many are clever like us. They will come to our aid if they can. Some of our Providers will have heard the bell and will wonder what it means. They will come here and witness what is going on. We know some of our friends have broken through the trap and will be hiding in the darkest wood, creeping through the narrowest gutter, be on their bellies in the dampest swamp. They will live and will tell the story of our last stand. The day we died but took on the men. The day when we succeeded in getting our tale to Catdom and the world.'

Her paw slipped, and she dropped momentarily from the top of the wooden pulpit. There was an intake of breath that sounded like a gentle wind as all the spirits feared for Craw. She felt she might fall. Everything that had happened to her had weakened her, but she must be strong.

She stood up once more. 'The men will come again, and again we must be cleverer than them. We must hide and wait for those who will relieve our siege, those who will come to our salvation. This place has become our refuge and our home. You have seen and heard the images of this place, the great light, the great sound, the great stories. We shall survive. Hide and be ready. The end is near and then we can all sleep for days.'

Craw felt an intense pain and tried not to cry out. Every spirit who was watching her felt uplifted by the power of her words, by her noble head and her shining eyes. She stared up at the great ceiling

As she did, every spirit in the building looked up. They were following her every movement. Her pain was somehow inspiring them. 'Hide again, great spirits. Remember—think, always think.' A pain was stabbing her side in time with her beating heart. 'Hide the pain, hide the fear and we shall win.'

Every tail in the building thudded on the stone floor.

'Lie silent if all around are taken. We can be invisible in busy streets, in noisy gardens, in great mansions. Use this skill and we shall survive. We shall tell the story and it will be our story.'

The pain was close to unbearable, but Craw had no choice but to go on. Strength left her neck, and her head dropped, but every spirit thought it was a moment of great strength, great power.

Twitcher saw her slump. In a bound he had reached the top of the pulpit and shouted, 'Catskill, Catskill, Catskill!'

Every spirit responded. The chant grew and grew and filled the huge building.

Twitcher heaved her up, and she nodded her thanks at him. On her other side, Dreamer appeared to support her. She smiled at them both. They were her spirits.

'Be ready, as the Great Catskill says,' Twitcher said. 'Be ready, and everything that the Catskill has said will come true. Learn from her words and we shall win.'

The tail pounding rang around the building.

'Go now!' shouted Twitcher. 'Be ready.'

The spirits rushed away with their tails held high, their hopes as bright as their minds.

Twitcher lay Craw gently on the ground. 'Thank you,' she said. 'You must hide too. We need you.'

'But we must help you, Craw. Tel, Toot, Skoot—take her to the deepest part of the building you can find. She needs to heal.'

'Twitcher,' Craw sighed, 'I am tired. I am hurt. Remember, the Catskill never dies.' She put her paw on his head and then slowly scratched his ear.

They heard a strange hissing sound. It was not a cat hiss. 'It's starting,' Twitcher said grimly. 'Take her and get all the help you can.'

A mist was seeping under the massive door. Its smokiness drifted further and further into the Cathedral like an unrolling carpet. Some of the older spirits slipped and fell, and the slower spirits were swallowed up by it. Inside the rolling greyness, Craw heard violent coughs, not like the ones caused by fur balls, but horrible, hacking sounds instead.

Craw blinked her eyes. 'What's happening to me?'

Twitcher had taken her position in the pulpit and stared grimly at the smoke. 'What is it?' he asked.

Toot put out his front paw. 'I can't see.' His eyes were

weeping like a tiny stream.

'Blink!' Twitcher said. 'Come up here.' With difficulty, he pulled Toot onto the pulpit with him. 'Blink, blink!'

Toot tried but his eyes were flooded by the stinging cloud. He couldn't see. He was blind. Soon, they were all blind.

***

Roots and Sheba had found a hiding place within the tented prison.

'That was a very clever trick with the catch on the cage, Sheba.' Roots was impressed. 'We are clever cats.'

'Does it matter if we're going to kill people just by breathing?'

Tail down, Sheba stalked off and Roots followed. They wandered through the almost totally deserted medical centre. Cages were thrown open. There were bins full of medical refuse. But still there were people around, some medical assistants.

'Silent as a cat,' ordered Sheba as she heard a voice.

A man and a woman rounded the corner. He wore a white coat, whilst she was dressed in green and had matching gloves. 'Everybody's gone up to the Cathedral or are manning the city perimeter,' the man said. 'We're supposed to make this boy scout camp seem like a state-of-the-art animal clinic.'

He bumped up against the statue of the great Dr Johnson. 'And do you know what? They want us to clear a space for this stone character and his mate down there, so they can impress the President of the USA. She's a bookworm, apparently and the former US ambassador to the UK had told her she should visit Lichfield. The statues have to be lit up tastefully from underneath. We haven't got rid of the cats yet and there's only hours to go till this international circus arrives.'

The young woman nodded. 'The soldiers will kill the

remaining cats within the exclusion zone in the city,' she said. A moment later, she gasped. 'A cat!' she exclaimed.

Roots had been listening so hard to what they were saying and trying to understand that he had forgotten they were supposed to be hiding.

The man stared at Roots. 'I'm sure it's listening to what we're saying.'

Roots turned his bottom and waggled like a real tom cat through the tented tunnel.

'Catch that cat if you really think it's spying!' the woman said. 'Mad cat, mad soldiers, now mad medics. It's not our job to catch them. I'm keeping well away. Shoo! Shoo! Go and find your friends.'

Roots did not need to be told twice. Sheba slid under the first tent flap in her skittish way and he followed behind her. 'I told you I'm a killer with the ladies,' he said. 'They'll do anything for me.'

'Yes,' agreed Sheba. 'Ignore you and shoo you off. Now, let's find the report that proves we're killing people.'

'And what do we do then?' Roots said sullenly.

'I don't know. Let's find it first! Where are the machines that send messages? My Provider would spend hours on the letters on the board.'

'So would mine,' agreed Roots. 'He even used to turn to me and tell me that the office had been nagging at him all day. I never heard him speak to a soul. He hated the telephones.'

'Follow me.' Sheba raised her tail, pausing only to check Roots had fallen in behind her. 'It's this way. My Provider, the difficult Dorothy, took me in here while she checked things and printed things. She only printed things she would need later. She used to say to me "I should eat this," but I think that was a Provider joke.'

Once inside the deserted office, Sheba jumped on to the desk and began to scratch at a pile of papers.

'What are you doing?' said Roots.

271

'Here, find the red top.'

'The red top? Red top what?'

'The red top. Top Secret, top.' She continued to scratch and scratch. Papers flew off her paws.

'Hold on, there are red tops.' Roots held some under his paws and was biting one sheet to stop it flying around.

'What's the matter with you? Your nose is crinkled.' Roots spluttered and spit out the smelly paper. 'It's vile.' He stared down at the paper which had an impression of his teeth marks in the corner.

Cat/Human Testing: The Results

Roots had discovered he could read the words of people, but it still wasn't easy. He stared at the sentences. He tried hard to understand the strange combination of letters.

'What does this mean?' Roots hadn't been reading long and he was a bit slow with some words. '*Pos... positive for specs to specings transmissing—the tails follow.*'

Sheba snatched the paper from Roots. 'Silly man, it can't be *tails*. Let me read it. *"Positive for species to species transmission—details follow".*' She paused and stared hard at Roots. 'Where are the details? Come on, where are they? This is a matter of life and death!'

'Details? I don't know. You just threw the papers at me!'

'Well, come on! Check it!'

Sheba read the first lines of the red-topped document. 'Detail of results from the Porton Down experiments on cat brain tissue, scans and the examination of all humans suspected of being receptors of the disease and the likelihood of positive transmission.'

Roots was confused. 'So, what does it mean?'

'I think it means that the words the soldier read were the same words you read, but not the rest.'

'So, what does it mean?' he repeated.

'Let me read,' Sheba screwed up her eyes. '"There is positive transmission from cat to cat and possibly all related cat species. There is no evidence to suggest that this condition has been or can be transmitted from cats to humans. There is no evidence of the jump across species. It seems not only unlikely but impossible on the evidence of our research. There has been some change in cat brain tissue structure. People have nothing to fear from cats apart from their unwanted attention. All laboratories have agreed with this summary."'

'But that wasn't what the soldier said, was it?'

Sheba turned in circles. 'No, he just read the first page with the highlighted line - the first fourteen words. We're mad, but not mad and we don't kill people. Oh dear! Oh dear!'

'Right,' Roots said decisively. He stood up, his large body throwing a shadow across the table. 'We take it to them.'

'Take it to them?' Sheba repeated. 'Yes, we just say "Hello, we're a couple of mad cats—please read this!"' She turned on her tail again.

'No, we take it to them and *make* them read it because of what we do.'

'Meaning what?'

'Meaning they can't ignore us. We'll choose our moment. I'll be the decoy and you have the paper. When you are in close, drop it in front of them.'

'And they'll ignore it.'

'Not if our Providers are there! Didn't you hear that? Your Provider, Dorothy, she won't ignore you!'

'I don't know,' Sheba whined.

'We have to do it, this *minute*. If we fail, everyone in the Cathedral will be gone.'

Sheba stuck out her tongue with distaste. 'I'm not a dog. I don't carry things in my mouth.'

Roots dragged the sides of the sheet together and bit a

corner. 'I'll carry it, I don't mind.' The taste was dry and disgusting, but he was ready.

Sheba pushed her cheek against her hero. 'This is for every spirit in that place, for every spirit everywhere. For Catskill's sake—and for the life of Catdom—you must get that message to the world!'

Chapter Twenty-Four: Weapons of Cat Destruction

The great Cathedral doors were slowly pushed open to allow the soldiers to see in the growing brightness. Slowly, the light seeped in and there was a scene of carnage before them. Cats were lying still—some on their backs, some curled up tightly in a ball, some lying flat their paws splayed out. The soldiers moved in, confident in the knowledge that no-one would fire on them but still aware that these animals were a danger to them. Gas masks obscured their vision, but they appeared more threatening and monster-like. Some of the sick cats were dragging themselves along the stone floor, gasping for air. Others were coughing and choking, with their eyes covered by a dull glaze.

'Get the leaders! The leaders!' a voice shrieked out.

'Not you?!' a soldier said, pushing the man aside.

Even under the mask Cairns was easily recognised. 'I'm here officially,' he said. 'It has been agreed. I'm the civilian observer and I know these filthy animals.' He rushed past the soldier who casually tried to stop him with a wayward foot. 'Get the ring leaders!' he shouted waving a wooden cudgel.

'Get that man out of here!' Sergeant Wilkes ordered.

All the soldiers were occupied dragging away bodies of cats, so to Wilkes' consternation, Cairns was able to rush from group to group seeking out those he knew were the cleverest of all cats.

'I must find the shaven one!' he said. 'Take that one and the rest will give in. I want the ugly one.' He picked up a large tabby and shook her until a sound of expelling air burst out of her limp body. 'A live one—somebody do for it!'

The soldiers were busy piling up lifeless creatures.

***

Twitcher blinked his eyes and from his vantage point surveyed the scene. It was horrifying—so many spirits were scattered across the floor. As the smoke rose and the breeze came in through the door, he saw the fallen figure of Craw. She was pulling herself along gasping for breath. Dreamer was still trying to hold up Craw's head as every movement seemed to be a huge effort.

Twitcher looked back to the soldiers and realised they couldn't see perfectly. They were bumping into each other and sometimes tripping over those cats who were crawling towards the smell of the fresh air. *They think we are all done,* he thought. *They're just dropping us in piles.* He crawled flat on his belly over to Dreamer. 'Still,' he said. 'Lie still. Don't move. Play dead and we may just survive.'

Next to him, Craw could do nothing but nod. Her breathing became slower and slower. Dreamer took her in his paws and slowly lay on top of her. Twitcher gently joined Dreamer, just leaving enough space for her to breathe. His ears moved back and forth as he thought about what they could do next. *Craw will never be able to run from this place.*

***

Dorothy turned towards Haskins. 'I am going mad,' she said. 'I swear I saw that dustbin move, or something inside it wobbled.'

'We haven't got time to stop,' Haskins said. 'Let's get to the Cathedral and see what's happening. I imagine everything will be over by now.' He was practically running, pulling Dorothy by the arm.

She pulled herself away. 'I'm not the fitness queen I once was, H. Let me get my breath.' She blinked several times and looked at the gardens as if she could hardly believe her eyes. 'I am mad.' The gardens seemed to swarm with movement as if there was a shimmering heat rising. 'They're moving,' she turned to Haskins. 'The gardens are moving.'

'My dear, you *are* mad.'

'But what is that?'

She pointed to where the rear gardens of the flats in the Close dropped down to the water. Haskins stopped several yards in front of her. His eyes followed the line of her pointed finger. He saw strange patterns moving from place to place as if a drunken cartoonist was sketching in front of him.

'Is it cats?' Dorothy tried to focus on the changing shades. 'Is it the light?'

'Or is it aliens?' Haskins smiled. 'I think we are in alien territory here.' At that moment a long, lithe Siamese dashed across their paths, stopped to bow imperiously at Haskins, raised her tail and was gone in a second. 'Did that one disappear?'

'No,' Dorothy said, 'but it moved very quickly. Something dramatic is happening! Remember the report. Cats are killers and they have to be stopped!'

'Including the missing Sheba and Roots.'

'Come on!' she shouted. 'I've got my breath back—let's hurry!'

***

Cairns was rushing from pile to pile of the prostrate bodies. 'You need to find the ring leaders! They're the killers.' He knelt and put his thick wooden stave on the ground and pushed his black rubber gloved hands into a small group of piled up cat bodies and pushed them away, first with his right hand and then with his left. 'Not here, try the next one.' He moved on to another pile and performed his vile ritual again.

***

Twitcher opened one eye very slowly. A soldier pushed him with his boot before speaking into his microphone. 'Not much movement here. The only activity is from that barmy Catcatcher. Can't we kick him out?'

'Focus!' a voice crackled. 'We need to ensure there's no life in there, then regroup and be ready for the VIPs and the summit this afternoon. It's time to clear up.'

As he held her close under his body, Twitcher could hear Craw breathing very heavily. She wasn't well. What could he do now? He saw the dreaded Pawman move in his direction. Cairns was wiping his goggles. The atmosphere in the Cathedral was still thick with the smell of the smoke.

Twitcher could see the sweat on Cat Catcher's forehead as he put his gloved hand out to brush him away. Twitcher silently drew his claws and, just as the Pawman tried to lay his hand on him, darted forward and implanted them deeply into his arm.

'Argh—a live one!' screeched Cairns, trying to hit Twitcher with the stick that he had in his hand.

Boots came running towards them. Twitcher knew he had to get them away from Craw. Pulling his claws out of the pudgy arm, he sank his teeth into the fingers that gripped the bat. Cairns dropped the wood and screamed. Twitcher twisted his body and his teeth pulled away from the hand. He landed on the floor and sensed that there was something wet in his mouth. He realised a small piece of the man's finger had been wedged in his teeth.

Cairns jumped and extravagantly shot his hand in the air. 'I'm dead! Get me a medic! Get this monster. It's one of the leaders!'

Twitcher ran without having any idea where he was going. He rushed into the legs of one soldier and then smacked into the feet of another. He dodged and twisted and turned until he hit a small cupboard and a door that helpfully sprung open as he collided with it. Twitcher leapt through and the door slowly closed after him. It stopped a few inches from the catch, the slight gap allowing him to see into the Cathedral. His trick had worked.

Twitcher saw Cairns trying to spot where he had gone as well as trying to stop the bleeding from his finger. The Pawman had left the still bodies of Dreamer and Craw alone. Twitcher had drawn them away. He closed his eyes. What could he do now? How could he help Craw, who had become the Catskill? All he'd done was to distract the men for a moment. He wanted to think, to use the new skills that he still only half-understood. Sometimes they frightened him.

Twitcher squeezed his burning eyes closed. After several moments he lifted his brows, but nothing happened. He pushed his eyebrow whiskers against the door. He felt something hard but couldn't see it. He took a deep intake of breath and his chest stung as if he had swallowed a thousand bees. He tried again to open his eyes and failed once again then he heard the voice of a soldier close by.

'That one was probably on its last legs,' the voice said. 'There's no sign of it now. Clear the area. Remove the civilians who rang the bell. There must be sympathisers in here who will be in some physical difficulty and we need to be careful with them. The bleeding hearts will come out in sympathy when we start pulling bodies out—cats *and* humans.'

Twitcher heard a soldier's voice. 'Cats—weapons of mass destruction? I'm being stupid. This isn't a real war! Let's get on. This area is quiet. Let's do it, clean up and clear out. This is sickening.'

Twitcher tried again to open his lids. He licked his paw and wiped his face several times. It was comforting but after the fifth or sixth wipe he felt one of his lids pull slightly apart. Of course! Licking and wiping would heal his eyes. Licking was the best thing for cuts and bites and perhaps this disgusting muck that seemed to cling to his face could be wiped away.

After a few moments of furious wiping and blinking, Twitcher was able to peer through his sticky eyes. The worst possible sight greeted his cloudy vision. Dreamer and Craw had gone. At first, he thought he was looking in the wrong place, so he cleared his eyes again. However, they were definitely gone. His trick had failed—they'd been taken. It was all over. He blinked and blinked and blinked and each time he saw more and more.

Twitcher was surveying a scene of devastation—cat bodies everywhere. Cairns and the soldiers were pulling cat carcasses into piles. Was he the only one left? Was it all over?

Then a catcall rang out reverberating off the pillars and walls. It was high and proud. It was the call a mother makes when one of her kittens has died. It was the call a cat makes when its Provider is ill or lonely. It was the call of cats before they leave Catdom forever.

***

'They are cats on the move, aren't they?' Dorothy asked.

'Like Wildebeest in the Serengeti, tracking hundreds of miles, driven by instinct and the call of the wild,' Haskins said.

'Why do you have to be so pompous and... and clever?'

'Isn't something like that happening?'

In the silence they could just hear a painful high-pitched cry. It echoed repeatedly until it became an intense sensation in Haskins' head.

'Haskins, they've stopped.'

He turned to the gardens. He could clearly see that the strange patterns were indeed cats. They had stopped moving and were joining in this hair-raising, ear-splitting, tear-inducing, painful song.

'One of those sounds familiar,' Dorothy said. She turned around. 'Sheba!'

Haskins looked behind and saw the black-haired, green-eyed Sheba followed closely by Roots, who was holding something in his mouth.

Dorothy touched Haskins and pointed at the cats. 'Contact has been made.'

Sheba and Roots had stopped behind them.

Dorothy stared straight at Sheba. 'What is it now? Please tell me or show me.'

Sheba ran up to Dorothy, raised her tail and cried in the same tone that was ringing around the Cathedral precincts. Her voice sung out and she swayed her head with the sound, tipping it from side to side while keeping her eyes on Dorothy's eyes.

Dorothy felt exasperated. 'Right, what do you want?'

'Here,' said Haskins.

Roots was still gripping the paper in his mouth.

'What's this, Roots?'

Roots dropped the secret note onto the road.

Haskins bent down and picked up the wet-edged paper. 'What on earth are you doing?' He straightened out the document and once he saw the writing on the top, he recognised it immediately. 'It's the report.'

Dorothy looked quizzical. 'What report?'

'The medical report about the experiments—the Porton Down Report. The complete summary. Also known as "the Cats Killing People Report.".' Haskins read on gradually increasing the furrows in his brow.

'H, you are being particularly obscure. What is it?'

'The order was wrong.'

Dorothy was troubled as she heard a shot ring out. 'Wrong?'

'Wrong,' Haskins repeated. '*Something* has happened to

the cats. That's positive, but it doesn't transfer to people. It isn't infectious. It has killed some cats and done something to the brains of others, but it cannot kill people.' Haskins waved the paper in the air. 'It's all here! Roots, you are a star!'

He bent over, picked up Roots and threw him in the air. Sheba dropped to the floor and gazed up at him.

'Something's going on here between these two,' Dorothy said. 'It's almost unseemly. But this is great news.'

Another shot rang out. 'We must get there quickly before there are more killings!' Dorothy said. She started to run again but found she nearly tripped as twenty cats overtook her. Sheba jumped into her arms.

'What are you trying to say to me? I know—if I'm holding you, *my* cat, the *other* cats won't go for me. Makes sense, H?'

'Can't see why not!' Haskins dodged the cats coming from every direction and then scooped up Roots and put him on his neck. 'Hold on—this is going to get wild! I think you're right; having these with us will help. Come, on D! Let's get to the Cathedral. They have misinterpreted the report. Cats have been killed, and it shouldn't have happened!'

In seconds, they had arrived at the ancient gate to the Cathedral Close. It was covered by razor wire and manned by two soldiers; a corporal and a private.

Haskins strode forwards confidently. 'H and D,' he said to the guards. 'We have top security clearance and we need to get into the Cathedral.'

The corporal pointed at Roots and Sheba. 'Not with those you won't.'

'These are control cats that have been tested.'

'And pigs can fly,' said the corporal. 'I'm sorry, not you and certainly not them.'

Dorothy regarded him with cool superiority. 'My clearance is of the highest order. Stop me, and you stop the

Government of the United Kingdom and His Majesty the King from the pursuance of legitimate activity.'

Sheba was gazing at her bossy Provider.

Haskins leaned towards the corporal and spoke very quietly. 'We are representatives of the international security community. When the world leaders arrive in a few hours and I mention that you, corporal, have been obstructive, I fear for your future. These animals are cleared but still are an important part of the clinical trials. We are... managing them, so to speak.''

'It's all gone gaga,' the corporal said. A slight crackle came from his headset and he turned, placing his hand over it. 'This area is controlled and quiet,' he said after a few moments. 'Let's clear out and clear up.' Turning back to Haskins and Dorothy, he said, 'This has been the worst thing I've ever been involved in—my wife hated me being in Afghanistan, but if I have to kill cats, she'll go bananas. Show me your clearance.' He spoke into his microphone. 'Gate to Control, Gate to Control. Two top level clearances at my gate. Can I let them in? Repeat: two top level clearances at my gate. Control, can I let them in?'

'Control, come in!' There was more wave crashing sounds in his earphones. 'I don't know!' he said. 'It all seems mad!' Eventually, he looked at Haskins. 'You two have the authorisation you need. You've no weapons, so in you go. But I'm warning you, those cats will be killed!' He pulled back the edge of the fencing and waved them on with his gun.

Neither Dorothy nor Haskins were prepared for the scene they saw before them. Smoke was rising from the doors and floating towards the spires of the Cathedral. It appeared as if the building had been hit by explosive shells.

Roots nodded at Sheba, jumped from Haskins' shoulder and ran towards the gate opening beside the pock-marked statue of King Charles.

Sheba pushed herself from Dorothy's arms took four

steps turned and stared her straight in the eyes.

'She wants us to follow her. Come on, H.'

***

A soldier raised his gun but then sensed some movement around him. He was trained to be alert at all times and he sensed something was moving to his left and to his right and behind him. He turned and turned, but when he thought he saw something it was gone just as quickly.

'Special guests coming into the sterile area,' he spoke without confidence into his lip microphone.

'Who?' rapped another voice.

'Secret Service, bringing dangerous one and two.'

'Cats?!' shouted a voice.

'Yes, dangerous one and two, moving to the centre of Cathedral. One man, one woman—dangerous one and two.'

'As if we didn't have enough problems. Okay—all units prepare for final clearance and watch for intruders.'

Another voice answered immediately. 'Control, we have intruders east and west.'

Another said, 'Control—we have intruders at south.'

'Control—intruders at north,' rang out another voice.

'This is Control. Describe intruders,' demanded the operator.

'This is north—intruders are cats,' another voice rapped out.

'This is south—intruders are cats.'

'This is east—intruders are cats.'

'West here—cats appearing and disappearing. Cats are everywhere, rushing from spot to spot. What do we do?'

'Open fire on sight! Repeat, open fire on sight!'

'Control—this is Centre. I have people coming out of buildings and others at the secure perimeter. I cannot open fire without endangering civilians.'

'Sir, what can we do? The perimeter is in disarray. There are cats appearing from all directions. People have been woken up by the bells and are approaching the fences at the sterile area.'

'Kill is the order. Kill it must be.' The order was clear. 'All units—kill, kill, kill.'

Random shots rang out around the edge of the fenced area. It was like trying to shoot flies. As one cat fell several others ran around drawing the fire and confusing the soldiers.

**

Twitcher heard the shots from his hiding place in the Cathedral and feared the worst. However, the sound of wheezing cats was growing as those affected by the dreadful cloud were beginning to draw breath again. He pushed his head out of the door. His eyesight was still blurred, and he had to keep blinking to try and clear his eyes. He could see that the soldiers seemed be in a dreadful rush to ensure there were no living spirits in the Cathedral. Craw and Dreamer had gone or been dragged away.

Outside shots seemed to multiply second by second. Soldiers were crouching into the shooting position around the Cathedral. At every sighting, a shot rang out and a spirit fell. The sound of gunfire became more and more intense.

Twitcher crawled from his hiding place onto the Cathedral floor and stared around at the devastation. Only then did he see Craw. Next to her, Dreamer lay on the floor. Craw was trying to stand on all fours, but she slipped. Her legs splayed out in all directions and then she uttered a heart-rending cry before falling on the stone floor. In one movement Twitcher leapt towards her. *Craw, the Great Catskill, must be saved.*

A brick wall hit him in the face as he rushed towards Craw. Something had smashed his head but there was no real pain; just darkness, and the echoing of an exultant voice that cried out in victory.

Chapter Twenty-Five: The Cat Will Have Its Day

Sucked up by the wind, bitter smoke billowed from the dark interior of the Cathedral, swirling into smaller and smaller spirals. The evil mist flew in front of the faces of all the Kings, Saints and the Great Prophets carved on the Cathedral front. It seemed as if some of the great figures of history moved or turned in disgust at the noxious fumes. William the Conqueror tilted his head, Moses nodded in agreement, their stone hearts softened after a thousand years. The great St. Chad, the first Bishop of Lichfield, seemed to have tears in his eyes as the mist touched his cheeks and formed into liquid droplets.

From their hiding places appeared a thousand cats, maybe more. They stared up at an amazing illusion that was developing before their eyes. It was the dream of all Catdom. They knew they were special. Stone had moved for them.

The ordinary citizens of Lichfield were gathering behind wire fences. They were Providers and friends of Catdom and had ignored the broadcast warnings of dangerous viruses abroad. Soldiers surrounded the fences, pinning back the people, but as they stared at the strange sight, they lowered their guns. It was like a mass hallucination. The great figures of thousands of years swayed beneath the bright sun and the intense shadows of this spectacular dawn.

A yelling voice commanded attention. From the small opening within the Great Door a figure appeared. The smoke clung to his body like a dark cloak. It was something monstrous, something fearful. Its face was grey. Its hands were black. It had no eyes, no ears, and no mouth. Its arms were held aloft. Its coat flapped behind like a pair of black wings. 'I am the victor!' the figure said. 'I told you I would win!' Its breathless voice crackled through a mask. 'This is the evil in your midst!'

The mist blew away, the light shone, the stone Kings and Queens and Prophets were still.

'These are the killers!' Cairns shouted. 'These are the ones that will kill everybody! These are the leaders and *I've got them!*'

In his smoke suit, he held Craw around the neck in one hand. In the other he held Dreamer. He squeezed their shattered bodies at the same time and held them higher in the air, thrusting forwards at first with the right hand and then the left. Each time he held one up Cairns would utter a triumphant sound. The limp creatures swayed and slowly stopped, incapable of movement or reaction. They were defeated. 'Yes!' he shouted and shook both bodies in unison.

Then the strangest thing occurred. A cat like Twitcher appeared, running at first and then leaping into the air with its paws stretched out. It hit Cairns' shoulder and sunk its teeth into his face as hard as it could, finding a small piece of cheek uncovered by the mask and goggles.

Cairns screamed, dropped Dreamer and raised his stick high in the air. This would be the killer blow.

A voice rang out through the smoke. 'Hit him, and you're a dead man!'

The stick stopped mere inches away from Twitcher's head.

'What do you mean?' Cairns yelled. 'These are killers. It's official!'

One soldier with gun raised dropped to his knees and aimed at Cairns. 'Sarge?'

'Hold fire, boy.'

Cairns walked forward; hands outstretched. He raised one arm up, his palm facing Sergeant Wilkes. With his other hand, he threw Craw to the ground with a dismissive sneer. Craw bounced an inch off the hard ground and lay motionless.

An angry voice rang out from the crowd. 'Don't do that!'

The cry was echoed by others. 'No, no, no, no!' All those gathered chanted in unison.

Cairns kept coming forward. 'I've been telling you for weeks. These are killers and you useless fools don't get it! I've seen them operating—they know what they're doing, and you don't have a clue. They know what's going on and their fever or flu or whatever it is will kill you all!'

Cairns gazed in astonishment at Craw as she drew herself to her feet and uttered a really harrowing sound. Every spirit in the Cathedral precinct stopped completely still.

'You can't kill our cats!' shouted a voice from the crowd.

Cairns had ignited the anger of the people. The instinct of the military men was to take up defensive positions. Strained voices asked for orders. The fence rattled as people vented their anger on this annoying barrier.

'The cats—they're gathering together!' one soldier rapped into his microphone. 'They're all around. They've taken up attack positions!'

Major-General Summers turned to his left and then right. 'What do you mean, "attack"? These aren't soldiers— they aren't the enemy. These are cats!'

Where moments before there had been fleeting images in the dawn light, suddenly there were many cats walking slowly around the Cathedral grounds. They raised their noses high, drawing in the scents in the area and listening to all sounds. They turned their heads in unison towards a cat high on a wall. He dropped his head and waved his paw three times, once towards the Cathedral and then to the east and then the west.

They moved in three blocks and then stopped crouching low to the ground. In the centre were the heaviest and the biggest spirits and to either flank the lightest, the fastest cats in Catdom. The cat on the wall nodded as he accepted, they had obeyed his order.

'It's like the Roman army,' said Summers. 'Remembering your military history! They're in cohorts. The big strong cats are in the centre and the smaller lighter more mobile cats are on the two flanks. It's classic.'

Everything stopped. The spirits were completely still, all staring at the soldiers who were ready to fire. The field of battle fell silent. It was the moment at the beginning of all great battles, a deep breath before the fighting began.

As if on cue, a gentle thunder began. The cat sitting on the high wall was swishing his tail more and more aggressively. It was a signal, and every cat began to bang its tail. In the space before and behind each spirit, tails hit the ground in unison and the pounding sound grew and grew. It was like a marching rhythm. Then there was a massive exhaling of cat breath, nasty and sharp. At the same time, they all dropped on their bellies. There was no movement at all, not a twitch, not a blink—just complete stillness.

The crouched army was menacing and ready to pounce on its prey.

Sergeant Wilkes observed the stillness. 'Sir, they've stopped. The ball is in our court?'

'Yes,' Summers said. 'They're waiting for us to move. It's our call.'

The sergeant thought of Bootsie, the soldiers' cat who would sit with intense concentration in the corner of military history lessons for the young soldiers. He knew they called him the soldier cat.

As the last of the smoke drifted across towards the Cathedral School, Wilkes was sure he saw Bootsie with his distinctive white patches standing high on the school wall, looking east and west and waving to someone. Was he directing matters? He couldn't be. *The cat's leg had been shot to pieces. He couldn't be on that wall.*

'Sergeant! It's a wedge!' Major General Summers pointed at a group of a dozen cats. 'That's another classic Roman army move. They're going to make some kind of cat attack on us. Prepare to fire! Avoid the people. Aim for the cats.'

Wilkes waved his arm, signalling for the soldiers to be ready to fire. 'This is the attack, sir.'

'Yes,' Summers agreed, 'this must be the effect of this cat madness. We need to direct fire into the centre of the big group. That surely will frighten them off until they can be mopped up one by one.'

They watched the climbing sun flood over the area as the catwedge seemingly took its signal from Bootsie, the army's friend, and moved as fast as they could. They swept across the battle ground, hit the hole in the fence and within seconds had surrounded the still figure of the shaven cat. It was a total protective shield and their bodies were the shield.

'They're protecting the big one, the scarred one. Aren't they, sir?'

'Just animal instincts,' Summers said. 'It must be. Let's get on with it.'

Cairns was waving frantically at the wedge, his gas mask now hanging around his neck, his face covered with blood from the cat bite-sized hole in his cheek. 'Take this lot out. These will be more of the smart ones.'

General Summers turned towards his men. As he did there was a sudden rush like quiet wind. The three blocks of cats had moved twenty yards, stopped and dropped to the ground again.

Sergeant Wilkes caught sight of Bootsie. He had moved to the right flank of his army and held his head high. 'It's another order,' he said.

'Prepare your men to fire.'

The nod and the order went out just as Bootsie dropped his head towards the ground. It was the final command. The sea of cats seemed to have grown. All the warnings had been received and they knew they had to defend their right to life.

There was a surge of cat bodies. The central block ran hard and strong at the soldiers who began to fire directly at their first line. Many fell but they kept going and the soldiers were having to fight them off at close quarters. Each soldier was swamped by cats, fighting for their lives. They could shoot no more. They had to use their hands to protect their faces from the sharp tiny teeth and claws that were lashing at every part of them.

The Major-General watched as the attack continued. 'Sergeant Wilkes! I think we are under pressure.'

'Sir, we'll have to use the gas in the open.'

'We thought we were dealing with a bunch of cats hiding in a church, not an outdoor army of cats. Get every soldier here, not at the perimeter. I want every gun immediately. Force those civilians away by gunpoint and get this area covered with gunfire before we lose men. Get those armoured vehicles up here.'

***

At the Control Unit Tom, Victoria and everyone else had been pushed to the floor of the vehicle by the remaining soldier, the radio operator. Samsy alone still stood, clutching Nailz to her chest.

'It must be the end!' shouted Tom, daring not to stand and look.

'The cats are drowning men,' said Samsy. She was on tiptoe, peering through the small gap in the door of their temporary prison.

'What do you mean?' said Tom. 'Get down!'

Tom reached out and tried to grab her, but Samsy darted away and pointed through the gap in the door. 'I said

291

they're drowning men.'

'Tom,' his mother said as she pulled him back, 'keep away! All of you, keep away!' As she looked out, she saw the disastrous scene of soldiers being overwhelmed by cats, but then coming from the back of the cathedral was a military vehicle aiming for cats' bodies.

'Let the gas go,' said a voice.

A bitter mist began to swirl again around the Cathedral. Shafts of bright sunlight shone onto the battle scene through the wispy smoke.

The door of the Control Unit was pushed open and a cat dropped in.

'Roots,' said Tom. 'It's Roots! He can hardly breathe. There—the black one!'

Sheba rushed through the gap and fell on Roots' back. She stared at Tom her green eyes wide.

'She's trying to tell me something.'

Sheba turned her back on Tom and went to re-enter the swirling mist.

'Nobody's leaving,' said the radio operator. 'I've got to keep you in here till this is over!'

A radio crackled into life. 'All units to the Cathedral Grounds! We are under attack. We have insufficient numbers on the ground! We need armour and air support.'

'What now?' the operator grumbled. He pulled on his gas mask. 'Stay here. Do not move.'

Tom's father protested. 'You can't leave us here.'

'I've got to go.' The operator picked up his gun and rushed away.

Tom followed him and slipped out to find Sheba. He held his face and dropped to his knees seeing Sheba's black tail in front of him. She turned to see him following. As Tom breathed deeply so the bitterness hit his lungs, his eyes were full of tears. He saw a figure crawling towards him. Another soldier?

The masked man confronted Tom, but he recognised the

eyes immediately. 'Haskins?!' he said.

'Tom, can you get me to Control? I followed Roots, but I must get to Control. Here's another wet mask. Put it on, we thought we might need more than one.'

Tom put the shirt on his head allowing himself enough vision to retrace his steps and see the bottom of the door of the Control Point.

'Go!' shouted Haskins. 'This is life or death.'

Tom scrabbled along the ground, his knees scraping on something hard. After a few yards he saw the door and dragged himself as quickly as he could to the control vehicle, dragging Haskins with him. Once inside, Haskins wiped his face and stared at the strange group in the control van.

Tom's mum was furious and ready to have a go at anyone. 'Mr Haskins!'

'Madam, not now. This is a matter of national and international security! Your son has courageously helped the Security Services of the Western World. Please... Shut up!'

Tom saw his dad stand up to speak, but then was aware of the intense fury on Haskin's face. He sniffed, coughed and put his arm firmly around his wife.

Tom thought that Haskins was talking to himself as he looked around the mobile unit. 'Okay—no soldiers. Where is comms?' Haskins grabbed a microphone. 'H here. Low Threat. He repeated himself 'Low Threat, this is H. Desist firing. Desist firing. Low Threat.'

The radio operator turned from the microphone. 'Low Threat?' he said. 'I know it's a non-call - Response Normal - but do we back off?' He paused. 'Sir?'

'Cease fire!' Summers ordered. 'Haskins has top level clearance and authority. If he says Low Threat, it means listen up and back off.'

The order rang around the killing field and echoed in the soldiers' headsets. They stood up where they could and stopped firing. As all the soldiers stopped struggling so did the cats. It was as if they understood the order too; they stood on all fours, keeping very still and staring at their enemies but ceased fighting, clawing, scratching and biting.

Wilkes saw Bootsie raising his white paw from his command position.

***

Tears poured down Haskins face. 'We've done it. We've definitely done it.'

Tom's mum was totally bemused. 'Done what?'

'The Helicopter attack,' Haskins said. 'Apaches were ready to go. Anyone in that area would have died, it was that serious. It didn't matter who died or how many. It would have been to save the rest of mankind.'

'And Catkind,' Haskins saw Sheba scowl.

Haskins surveyed the scene. If the tear gas had caused his eyes to water, then this vision made him cry. Before him was a scene of devastation—many cats lying still, some soldiers struggling to their feet, some not moving. 'This should not have happened!' he shouted.

Smoke covered the battlefield. Haskins knew that the same feeling of despair hits everyone at the silence that ends a harrowing battle and a frightful waste of life—be it Gettysburg, Balaclava, the Somme, Fallujah. Tears flooded his eyes and he felt an overwhelming sense of loss. Roots was no longer with him, and his cat had found the report that had halted the slaughter. Haskins looked at Sheba who had been the final messenger of victory. Dorothy would be delighted, and she had done her job by getting the truth from the medical centre to the attack helicopters and the others.

Haskins felt something rubbing his leg. It was Roots, the ginger monster. He was still alive! Haskins picked him up, turned him over and stared into his ridiculously wide face.

Roots put out his paw and gently touched Haskins on the cheek. He was purring for the first time in a long time.

The job was nearly done. He wondered if he should he have done more to stop the carnage. 'Come on!' he shouted, quickly gathering himself. 'It's over.' He turned to the group. 'Please stay here.' Haskins saw the Major-General to his right. He waved and walked over.

'You stopped it?'

Haskins nodded. 'The order you got was wrong. Here is the full version.'

The Major-General read the document twice for good measure. 'I should be glad, but I don't believe it,' he said. 'We saw these creatures take us on. They lined up in a battle formation not seen since the Romans were in Britain. They took our men in a way that was inconceivable. This report must be wrong!'

'It isn't, it comes from the highest medical authority. Their brains are affected in some way. Some die, but it doesn't affect people. It won't even give you a little cold, let alone cat flu.'

The Major-General was totally drained. 'All this devastation, for nothing.'

'Do you want to tell my men that?!' Sergeant Wilkes shouted.

'It's over, sergeant. Check the men. We'll need the medics; the human and animal kind.'

Haskins stood back and stared out at the Cathedral. The stone figures were completely still. The mist was rising into the sky. Beams of light shone through the gaps and the morning sun became brighter and brighter. Soldiers were slowly getting up from the ground or helping other colleagues. Some were bleeding from multiple scratches and bites while others were lying motionless.

Cats were scattered across the grass and paving slabs. Some were staggering, some frozen where they lay. In patches the grass was red. The speed of their attack had gone; the withdrawal was so slow as many paused to lick their comrades. A mother was hunched over one of her sons, her rough tongue tugging at his closed eyes. A large tabby was limping away from the Cathedral when she stopped suddenly, recognising a fallen friend. She stumbled and collapsed onto her front paw, gently laying her head on the still figure.

The sorry shape of Craw lay motionless where she had been dropped. Her little group of cat guards had pulled away from her. She no longer needed their protection. They sensed she was beyond their help. Her strange, shaved body was covered in deep lurid incisions; there were bright red burns on her flesh where the clips had gripped her so tightly. Her tiny tongue pointed from one corner of her mouth, a small trail of blood lingering on her fur.

She didn't move. The people gathered to watch as those who had tried to save her stood near. One at a time they moved forward each one gently touching her with a paw. Twitcher was the last. He licked the blood from her face and gently turned her head to the warming light of the morning sun.

Chapter Twenty-Six: Memorial

In front of the small yet distinguished international group, the President of the United States and the Prime Minister of the United Kingdom pulled away the small sheet covering the statue. They nodded at each other. It was raining, and this was going to be a short ceremony.

'Madam President,' the Prime Minister began, 'when you last visited this area, we felt we might be facing a disaster of immense proportions. Fortunately, humanity was not threatened by another dreadful pandemic. The creatures that have become one of man's favourite companions are still at our firesides. There was a tragic error that resulted in loss of life for some of those attempting to protect the human race and for some of the cats. Today, we unveil this monument to their memory.'

The President turned to the Prime Minister. 'Mr Prime Minister, thank you for inviting me back. Millions of cat lovers across the world will be delighted with this memorial to all those humans and animals involved in this harrowing affair. Our meeting that day was shorter than we anticipated but achieved a positive outcome.' She looked at the statue of the bronze cat sitting with its head held high, gazing towards the sky. 'I would just like to read out loud the inscription on the plinth.' Bowing her head slightly she read aloud very slowly. 'It was said cats have nine lives. Now they have found the Tenth. This cat will live forever. Never forget the Great Catskill—neither heard nor seen!'

Haskins squeezed Tom's shoulder.

'You should feel very privileged to be here,' Dorothy said. She was standing very straight.

Everyone was on their best behaviour. Even Mrs Constance was wearing her best hat. Little Samsy was bored but at least she had her babies back.

Tom looked back at the statue. It was so familiar like the poor cat strapped down at the medical tent.

Sergeant Wilkes was glad to be on normal duties. No more cat killing for him. He couldn't forget what had happened to a handful of his men. Their names were inscribed on the plinth. It had been very painful. Amazingly, Bootsie had recovered and was back at his military home. He'd been picked up by one of the soldiers during the clean-up at the Cathedral. They'd no idea how he managed to get around with his shattered leg, but the lads had built a little trolley for him and he scooted around just like before, although steps defeated him.

Within a day of the battle, people everywhere found their cats crying on their doorsteps, squealing at windows and knocking at cat flaps. Cats went back home to wherever they were most comfortable and safe.

Piner had appeared back at Tom's door. Purrl followed the injured Nailz and had gone back to Samsy. Toot and Skoot rediscovered their home, much to the shock and delight of the new owners. Blackie watched her babies grow up. Roots relaxed into country life and Sheba found herself a mother for the first time, with kittens of many colours—and one the spitting ginger image of Roots.

Some never got home. Some couldn't get home. Some didn't want to go home. Their lives were changed, and they desired to be free. Their Providers were sad but sought out other cats and gave them warm sanctuary.

Suspicion prevailed amongst the cat haters, like Cairns, who were convinced all was not well. His website *Cat Haters of the World Unite*, was the last resort of cat and animal haters, although many of his keenest fans were those who were the most sceptical of his claims that cats could think, read and communicate. Often, he could be found on the streets of Lichfield searching for strays that he never found. He couldn't understand it. Little did he know that as soon as he left his house, at any time of the day or night, the word was passed from cat to cat to beware that the last of the Pawmen was on the prowl! Cairns was one of the few people in the world who would never ever see a living cat again.

The Prime Minister led the small party to have drinks and refreshments at the café on Heroes Square. The President took his arm. 'It was such an excellent idea to put this statue at the National Memorial Arboretum, devoted to the concept of remembrance, fashioned on our Arlington National Cemetery in Washington.' She turned towards the Armed Forces Memorial high on its mound in the background. As she stared for a moment at the shining white stone topped in gold, there was a rustle in the undergrowth. She spun her head but saw nothing.

Twitcher had safely avoided being seen having dropped to the grass until the group had passed. He raised his head and sensed another spirit near.

Dreamer saw Twitcher's tail rise in the air and stumbled after him. His body was never the same after the day that was known as 'The Last Great Cat Battle' amongst all the thinking spirits. Bits of him still ached, and he'd developed a limp. At least it eased the pain in his hip as he walked.

Twitcher was staring at the statue. 'I know you're there, Dreamer.'

Dreamer drew up beside him and bumped his head on Twitcher's. 'Had to come—read about it in the *Lichfield Mercury, The Times of London* even the *New York Times.*'

'Still a big reader, eh Dreamer?'

'Has to be done. Keep up with the news and alert the thinking spirits.'

Twitcher looked up at the proud cat statue again. 'It's her isn't it? She was the Catskill. She'll live forever. No-one who was at the Last Great Cat Battle and saw what happened to her will forget. She was there and then she was gone. Craw is still the Catskill.'

Dreamer turned to Twitcher. 'And if Catdom is ever under threat again, one day we may need the Great Catskill.'

'But now we've got ten lives—it says so up there.' Twitcher turned and was slowly walking away, only waiting for Dreamer to catch up. 'Come on, slow coach.'

You will never see a cat at the Tenth Life Memorial, but they are always there, coming and going. Some travel for days to pay their respects, to recognise that cats are different. Some travel for years over great distances and then go back to their Providers who thought they were lost forever. They have all made their personal pilgrimage to the statue of the Great Catskill, Craw—the cat who lost all her ten lives but will never ever be forgotten.

And still when mob or monarch lays

Too rude a hand on English ways

The whisper wakes, the shudder plays

Across the reeds at Runnymede

Epilogue

Cats come, and cats go.

Piner was here and back in Tom's life. He pushed his head hard against Tom's knee. It all seemed a dream, the Pawmen, the shooting, the attack on the Cathedral. These cats had changed forever but they were still the same, living with people, following their own noses and keeping to themselves. The nightmare was over and the town and the country and the world could relax. No one was going to die because of the cats.

Piner pushed hard once more against Tom's leg and looked him straight in the eye. He moved a few paces away, returned and pushed Tom again. 'No, Piner. Stop it. It is all over.'

Piner moved towards the open door, raised his tail, turned his head to Tom and tilted it, 'What do you mean? It isn't all over?'

Printed in Great Britain
by Amazon

43652041R00172